SWALLOW
HARD

SWALLOW HARD

o o o

Sarah Gaddis

ATHENEUM

New York   1990

Collier Macmillan Canada   Toronto

Maxwell Macmillan International
New York   Oxford   Singapore   Sydney

This book is for my father.

The author wishes to thank Sylvie Barrens, Thibault Guinard, Anne-Shelton, Gianne Harper, Bertrand de la Haye Jousselin, Carol Mukhalian and Dr. Oren Ellis.

Atheneum
Macmillan Publishing Company
866 Third Avenue, New York, N.Y. 10022

Collier Macmillan Canada, Inc.
1200 Eglinton Avenue East
Suite 200
Don Mills Ontario M3C 3N1

Library of Congress Cataloging-in-Publication Data
Gaddis, Sarah.
  Swallow hard / Sarah Gaddis.
    p.   cm.
  ISBN 0-689-12106-7
  I. Title.
PS3557.A27S9   1991
813'.54—dc20   90-46833   CIP

This is a work of fiction. Names, characters, places, and incidents either are the product of the author's imagination or are used fictitiously. Any resemblance to events or persons, living or dead, is entirely coincidental.

10 9 8 7 6 5 4 3 2 1

PRINTED IN THE UNITED STATES OF AMERICA

PART ONE

...

Chapter 1

○ ○ ○

When Rollin Thompkins was born on the third of December 1955 in New York City, her father tapped on the viewing window with a quarter and waved wildly until the nurse hurried out and told him to please put out the cigarette. Nodding towards the baby, Thompkins said he wanted to know if this was his daughter, because she had something in her eye. He hadn't seen his daughter yet and this baby had a mole, caught like a grain of sand in her dark lashes. Yes, this was Rollin Thompkins. Now would he put the cigarette out please?

He threw it on the floor and stepped on it.

Then: The mole wasn't dangerous?

No?

Now he smiled. He wiped his mouth, wiped his whole face from nights without sleep, and then he looked at Rollin again. "Well," he said. "Well well."

The nurse stood there, her hand on her hip as though waiting for him to buy something. "I ought to make you sweep this up," she said.

Lad Thompkins didn't hear her. "Because really it sort of distinguishes her, doesn't it?" he said. There was relief and pride in his voice, and he raised his chin in discovery and continued, "I think it does. Look in there. When I look in there I see her and apart from her all I see are little Eisenhowers," he said, and he laughed. Then quick as a gangster's gun another cigarette appeared and shaking the match he asked for his wife's room, where he was told he wasn't allowed to smoke either. Why not, he wanted to know, it was a private room and he was paying for it and he'd goddam well smoke in there if he wanted to.

Actually Lad Thompkins wasn't paying for the room, a woman who probably shared his opinion of babies and Eisenhower was paying for it, the woman who had just sent the giraffe from Schwarz's. Her name was Pauline Dampierre and she wore mended cashmere sweaters. She wasn't in love with Lad Thompkins, but she believed in him. Although the giraffe would have been equally appropriate for someone in love: tall and gangly, expensive and stupid, those limpid eyes. It had just been delivered when Thompkins appeared on the fifth floor of St. Vincent's. He laughed when he saw it, and the nurses pulled away as he approached, as though they'd dressed his bride. Sun was coming in through the long windows at the end of the hall. He arranged his tie. One nurse giggled.

"I don't know anything about France or anything that goes along with it," Sally Ann had said after she met Pauline. Sally Ann had grown up in a small Southern town, and when Winifred Kipps had remarked that actually, Pauline hadn't been happy since she'd lived in France, Sally Ann had asked why didn't she go back there then. "A woman who grew up with a twenty-foot-high dollhouse with Chippendale furniture copies in it, I guess she can choose the country she wants to live in."

Sally Ann had never seen the dollhouse. "I'll bet she's got copies of oriental rugs and Persian rugs on the floors," she would say. "And paintings. There's anything in the world people will pay for. What about a tiny Renoir in the drawing room? Twenty feet high? I wonder how high the walls are."

"Why don't you just ask her if you can see it?" Thompkins had said. She had grown obsessed with the dollhouse and had a faraway look on her face whenever she spoke of it.

4

"Oh no, Lad. I couldn't. You know, Winifred told me about it when she told me about the kidnapping."

He thought about the dollhouse when he read the card, which was in French, and he thought about it when he saw Sally Ann standing in the blue distance of the hospital room.

He thought about the dollhouse when he had been there some minutes and she said, "You saw her?" and looked away quickly and said, "I guess somebody figured she wasn't a boy so she didn't have to be perfect either."

"What?" he said. There was a sick feeling in his stomach. Who was she talking about, God? "What?" he repeated.

She was fooling with the blanket. The giraffe smiled down at them from a heaven of fluorescence.

He said, "Pauline sent the giraffe," and watched all hope go out of her eyes. He gave her the card.

"It's in French!" Sally Ann cried. "I don't believe it, French, for a giraffe!"

"You mean if it were a silver cup the French would be right," he said.

"She knows I don't understand French," Sally Ann said. "She knows that. And yes," she said, patting the bedcovers around her, "it would be different if there were a silver cup. There would be, I don't know." She was frowning. She was moving under the blankets. "An atmosphere of invitation in the air," she said.

"An atmosphere of invitation in the air," he repeated.

"You're not supposed to smoke in here," Sally Ann said.

The nurse came in then, clipboard down in front of her like a gangplank, full of talk about "our dinner." "Oh, that giraffe was for you," she said, plumping pillows. She was an older woman. When Thompkins said he was leaving she said cheerfully, "It's raining, and they say it's going to change to snow."

The giraffe stared glassily ahead at the elevator numbers and stood stiffly in front of Thompkins as he put on his coat. He disagreed with Sally Ann, who said she couldn't have the giraffe in here, its eyes followed her. The giraffe seemed to look everywhere except at him; for instance now it seemed to be looking past him at the nurse at the desk.

Tying his scarf, Thompkins gave her a curt nod.

"Never fit that in a cab," she said.

He supposed she was used to opening doors for wheelchairs and stretchers, which was why she saw no reason to help him as he struggled through the two sets of doors with the giraffe.

He stood on the curb, feeling ridiculous. Surely he could have left the giraffe in a broom closet, a supply room, and instead here he was, standing on a corner in the rain with it. He had forgot to call people from the hospital and he felt even more ridiculous when the distant white figure in the lobby dissuaded him from going back. He walked to the next corner, where there was a phone booth, and he had the giraffe in at an angle before he realized the phone was broken and then it was another minute before he could extract himself because he'd lit a cigarette.

"Goddammit," he said. "Goddammit," he said, kicking the door.

Thompkins went into the next bar he saw, where a group of doctors watched as he ordered a beer. They had been talking about malpractice and were obviously drinking ginger ale except for one who was off duty and held up a beer in a toast when Thompkins received his.

"A daughter," Thompkins said.

"Yeah," the drinking doctor said, "you can't walk around with *that* and be incognito, especially in this neighborhood." He shook his head. "What people will buy for babies."

Thompkins took a long sip of beer. It had just occurred to him to ask about the mole and something had stopped him, pride or shame, he didn't know which. He glanced over at the phone booth, still crowded with noise and color.

The drinking doctor asked him if he had far to go. "I guess you live in the city," he said.

"No no," Thompkins said. "Long Island. Drove in here the wrong way on a bridge to get my wife here, you know, police stopping all the traffic for the nervous fool with the pregnant wife."

The doctor laughed. "It'll be easier next time, promise you. First time's always like that."

And what would he have asked? Not whether it was dangerous, although they would have assured him. He would have asked about taking it out. How delicate the operation would be, how much it would cost. About insurance. They might have argued with him on a moral ground, saying he had no right to make the decision. Look at Marilyn Monroe, they would have said. That's what makes her who she is.

He tried the numbers, but his mother's line was busy and Kipps wasn't home. Thompkins left the bar, the doctors behind him. Now they were talking about the Knicks game.

He went from bar to bar, sometimes to call, sometimes to get warm. He took a bus partway, the giraffe reverberating with the vibrations, jumping with the potholes. Already there was a black smudge on its hindquarters.

In every bar the Knicks game was on, and Thompkins looked at the screen every once in a while. But he couldn't get excited like all the uncontrolled voices and elbows around him; a whistle had never meant anything in his life. In college Kipps used to get red in the face trying to explain:

"Come on!" Shaking him. "We're at Harvard, what's the matter with you? For Christ's sake! You can't keep your blood running sitting in English 101, huh?"

He could pound in the rules, but not the enthusiasm.

"No no no," Douglas had said as if he were in pain, the last time they'd talked about football. "That you would miss the beauty of it. Don't look at the pile of guys, watch the passes."

Thompkins had said the only way he knew where the ball had gone was to look for the pile of guys.

"Baseball I like, though," Thompkins had conceded. "Strike one two three you're out, it's all very clear. There's a tension. In football

I don't feel the tension, and in basketball—well. Basketball's like a circus. Something going on everywhere. Someone running with a ball, someone standing somewhere too long and then someone else has the ball. The constantly interrupted journey of the ball, there. Like football. It frustrates me," he said. "Like I'm not getting my money's worth."

Kipps had broken out laughing. "The constantly interrupted journey of the ball, Jesus. You want to tell one of those guys that? Six-seven two-seventy?"

Kipps could have played pro baseball but he'd married a wealthy girl instead. Last year he'd put a cigarette out on an ebony table watching Harvard and Dartmouth, and to Thompkins it was all connected in some way they'd never talk about.

He tried Kipps again from a bar on Fifty-fourth and First but there was still no answer. He listened to the ringing. He thought of the view from the living room. At the bar, someone was trying to steal the giraffe.

"I saved him," a blonde said when Thompkins came back. "The bartender wouldn't have done anything. Just look at him," she said. "Like a big warm puzzle."

"Did you want, could I buy you a drink?" Thompkins said.

"That's not what I meant at all," she said.

There was something of Amelia in her, or maybe it was the giraffe between them, its ribbon trailing for a few inches on her bare arm. The bear he'd won for Amelia had been nothing compared to the giraffe, of course, but she had loved it so. The girl had taken out her compact and set to work, and Thompkins ordered himself a scotch and tried to order her a daiquiri but she said no thank you, not even looking away from her little compact to say it. He was too drunk to call his mother. He could never be too drunk to call Kipps, and bracing himself on the giraffe's back he turned and with the help of someone's elbow caught the rounded edge of the bar before he fell. Something was wrong now. The girl's lips were red and she was angry and the bartender was waving his rag. Thompkins tried to offer her a daiquiri but she was pointing to her smashed compact, angles of it everywhere like facets of a huge diamond.

"Move it out!" the bartender called.

"Last call?"

"For you, buddy, sure is! No, no phone. You're not the president, what you've got to say can wait. Move it out."

By the time he made it to the next bar he was quite drunk and the giraffe was almost auctioned off by the piano player. Still no answer at the Kippses'—they must be out in the country. The last time he'd used the key the maid had popped out of the master bedroom balancing two half-finished bowls of chili. "You won't say anything," she'd pleaded. "He's my handyman."

Tonight Thompkins wouldn't care, he'd just fall down in the room papered with elephants and never wake up. How could he face the doorman? He couldn't. How did Kipps do it? That long hall, measured with mirrors and flowers. Well, Kipps was funny as hell when he was drunk—he spoke Spanish to anyone who'd listen: *"El reloj es de oro,"* he usually said—"The watch is made of gold." He'd learned it (they both had) trying to pawn a watch in Madrid.

In the park when Thompkins was questioned by a policeman the giraffe was missing an eye, but it had started to snow and Thompkins hadn't noticed, he didn't notice until after he'd left the astrologer's.

Of course he didn't believe in astrology. It was just that, crossing the street in the light snow, he saw an orange light in a window and what he thought was a bar wasn't. And once in past the beads and sweet smell it was too late, a woman's hard eyes were on him through the smoke and Thompkins was hustled to the round table in back where he could see someone standing behind a paisley curtain. In the corner of the room was a mynah bird, and so part of what he was told he might have confused with what the bird said. What he was told was that his daughter would always be taken care of. Something to do with Jupiter and Leo, Sagittarius; she would fight with those in authority and begin life late, but she would be watched over through bad marriages and foreign countries, through choices often made for her by others. Thompkins would remember this, but never as he did that morning in an alley when he came to looking at the giraffe, which he noticed was missing an eye. Lad Thompkins was then thirty-two. He had published a few stories in *The New Yorker*, and he was going to Yaddo in the spring.

They were living out on Long Island when Rollin was born, in a town with an Indian name where in summer you could sit outside and hear a cigarette burn. This was before the school and the shopping centers and the car wash with its neon arrows. Before the banks. As the agent put it to Lad Thompkins's aunt, the only selling point was the manageable distance into New York. That was why, with the road being paved to the bank on the corner and out into the world, the property would be worth more.

Thompkins stood out in the yard and considered all this. The cigarette fell from his fingers, and he cleared his throat. It had happened so fast.

A year and a half ago he had laughed about a manageable distance into New York because he wanted to get out. He had started a book in Europe, and staying out all night at the Cedar wasn't helping any. He needed to get away from the people and buildings, what Dowling called the mean level of noise. There was the honking and yelling and the bell at the dry cleaner's, but Dowling was from the Midwest and he was talking about the noise which was there constantly, like the fine grit falling from the sky. "You've got the mean noise and the mean level of noise," he was fond of saying.

Out here, even straining you couldn't hear anything. Even the house seemed to be fading from his sight.

"And on top of everything it's fucking pink!" Kipps said when he saw the house. Actually it was a very pale pink, as pale as magnolias or a sunset in January. But the city had stayed fresh in Thompkins's mind, even after he'd been out there awhile some part of him clung to its abrasiveness, remembering that last day edging the box spring around a corner, metal pinching his fingers as an argument came at him from down the hall.

Dowling and Kipps had stayed a few days and they'd gotten drunk trying to think of a jingle for Dowling's diarrhea medicine campaign.

"An ailment characterized by abnormally frequent evacuation of the intestines," Dowling read from the dictionary.

"Christ, that's revolting," Kipps said.

"Think singing," Dowling said, and by the early hours of the morning they were all drunk and singing.

They left Thompkins with a hangover, sitting in the yard in a broken nylon-and-aluminum yard chair. The blue sky, his papers in boxes, dry and sealed and numbered for when he was ready. It was midafternoon. It was as though if he stayed quiet, no time would pass.

"That Southern girl, she'll follow you," Kipps said. "Home from the dance."

He looked around, wondering what night and winter would be like here. Neither seemed possible, he thought as he lit a cigarette.

He jumped for the phone, but there was no phone. There was no car. An hour passed, then two. He might be hungry, he thought, rising from the lopsided chair.

But instead of going inside, Thompkins walked around the house. He had never known his aunt. She had been on the stage, it made sense that the house was pink. He looked over at the barn, and decided what he really wanted was to live in the barn and rent out the house.

Maybe he wouldn't mind, after a while, if Sally Ann followed him.

He walked around the yard throwing cigarette butts with the regularity of a dog claiming territory. A friendly, singing voice: "Admit it, you've got it so admit it, you need it—" It was so goddam quiet here he couldn't get the goddam jingle out of his head.

o o o

He remembered: Amelia in her thin cotton dress, the light of whatever kind of day searching its folds. He remembered walking, the spring air warm around him and Amelia farther and farther behind him as the six-pack chilled his underarm. She would only walk towards Hardy Road as far as the loop, because she didn't like the dirt road and she didn't like to wear shoes either.

"We could go to the movies, maybe," she said to him. "But then you don't have a car." She pushed her hair back but it fell in her face again.

"I've been living in the city," Thompkins said. "It's crazy to have a car in New York."

"It's crazy to live in a place where it's crazy to have a car," Amelia said, smiling across the bar. "But then maybe that's why you're here." Her voice was a thin cord stretched cool and straight, and her smile was thin and real.

The bar was greenish, blackish, reddish in the back where there were lamps. In the front enough light came in so that when he first saw her he saw that the flowers on her dress were pale yellow with gray stems.

The afternoons passed.

Thompkins didn't have a car, but he didn't need to go anywhere he couldn't walk. Once or twice he went into the city, but the train station was walking distance. Otherwise he went for cigarettes, groceries, to the package store for beer. The package store was called Elmo's and was connected on the inside to the bar, where there was music on Tuesday nights, and he called Sally Ann from there on Thursday nights.

Of course he was working, he told her.

But mornings Thompkins pulled on his pants and walked outside as dutifully as if he were being paid to do yardwork. He had come out in May, now it was June. It was a Sunday, and he remembered

Perry Street and smiled. There had been Sundays when he could've sworn he'd heard the bell at the dry cleaner's.

Amelia said, "Did you decide? About the paper?"

Her brother, Bobby, delivered the local paper and was paid according to how many subscribers he got. The paper was a town weekly, and Thompkins didn't want it.

Amelia stirred her daiquiri and looked at him.

"It has a good wanted section," she said. "Swaps, bicycles. Used refrigerators—that kind of thing."

"Well," he said, hesitating.

"News too," she said. "It's good to know things. Town meetings, all that. You'd want to know if a road was going through." She raised her eyebrows, then her eyes traveled down his body. "Why don't you ever sit down?" she said. She said softly, "It's not because of a war injury, is it? I saw that in a movie once."

He laughed. "No," he said, "I just like to stand up."

"Lots of men lean on bars," Amelia said. "Men who drink tequila lean on bars, I guess because they drink it so fast like that. It's better going down if you're standing up." She smiled suddenly. "Is that true?"

He looked at her. He looked at her daiquiri, which at seven o'clock on a summer evening was the color of the light coming in from the parking lot.

"Dance with me," she said, and she swooned a little. "If you won't sit down, dance with me." She took his hand and danced three steps alone. "Are you writing many, many pages?" she said.

More than anything, she wanted to work at the post office, and something about this broke his heart.

It turned out he found the Ford through the wanted section, later. He had only taken her out in it twice—when they had gone to the carnival, they had walked.

And what a night that had been: the carnival was cheap and bright, scraps of paper quickly littering the grass and wearing it down to dirt, a fine glittering dust which drifted around the ankles of the men, women, and children. Thompkins won Amelia a small bear, and Bobby laughed and picked at the ribbon around its neck.

"Go with me on that," he said, pointing to something which dipped and turned.

"All right," Thompkins said. "But then Amelia wants to go on the Ferris wheel, and we're going alone."

"Then the Rocket," Bobby said.

"You go on it," he said. "I don't have to and Amelia doesn't have to if she doesn't want to."

"Amelia wants to," Bobby said.

What happened was that while Thompkins went to buy more tickets Bobby sent his sister up in the Rocket alone, and it got stuck. Bobby told Thompkins he had watched the Rocket go up and turn upside down and come down, and then halfway up the track the second time, everything had stopped.

"Well, which side is she on?" Thompkins asked. "Goddammit, which side is she on?" The Rocket, poised up in the sky, looked old and heavy on its track.

"How should I know," Bobby said. "Leave me alone. You don't know what she does, you don't know anything."

Thompkins grabbed him by the shoulder. There were colored lights everywhere, laughter, and he had this kid by the shoulder. "What do you mean?" he said. "What are you talking about?"

"Ha. Want me to tell you?"

Thompkins let go of him in a push. He looked up at the Rocket and watched the men work at the gears.

"You want to know or what?"

Thompkins didn't answer.

"You know that guy that comes in with the tattoos—"

"Shut up," Thompkins said.

"You're dumb, mister. Just real dumb."

She had told him that sometimes she had to wash her hair twice a day if she had been in Elmo's with all that smoke. "And put lemon in it," she said, watching the smoke from his cigarette curl. "I'd never tell you to stop," she had whispered, and she had swallowed, a shadow bulging on her pretty neck.

He saw her only twice after the carnival, and then for a time he sat alone in the evenings, waiting for it to get dark. In the west, the straw grass turned pink gold and the dots of wildflowers scattered like blood from a hunted animal and even the sounds were wild— a kind of a stunned hushed buzzing. To the east the yard clung to the house and its arena of light, spreading in the gathering darkness but excluding the barn, which slept like some huge protective animal beside it.

Then Sally Ann came. He remembered how sudden it was—how quickly she stayed. Three days after she had unpacked she sat in the driveway planting. She had bought a hat at the five-and-dime, and the ribbons were already fraying, bits of color in the breeze.

"Are you laughing at my hat?" she said.

"Is that summer squash? If you knew me better you'd know I don't like summer squash."

"I don't know what you all call it up here," Sally Ann said, "but if you knew me better you'd know I'd plant it anyway. And if you're not nice I'll plant okra." She looked up at him and laughed, and said she supposed she might as well have raised the Confederate flag—was that was he was thinking? "Did Douglas tell you about that song that friend of his is writing about me? 'Confederate Eyes,' he's calling it." A breeze came and seeds blew. "And could you at least put all your ashes where they'll do some good?" she said impatiently.

"Why yes ma'am," Thompkins said.

She asked about Amelia, but there was nothing but curiosity in her voice, she wanted to know who the strange girl was who walked around the parking lot barefoot.

"You know who I mean, she walks around like it's holy ground or something."

They were having a picnic with a couple named Ken and Joanne

Burford, and Thompkins worried Joanne would say something. But she only said, "They live on the edge of town, don't they? Ken, you'd know."

Ken Burford taught at the junior high school. "Her brother's no good. I know that," he said. "And his friends are worse."

"Oh, probably just a bunch of boys," Sally Ann said, pouring her hair into the sun. "A little stupid maybe."

"I'll say," Ken said. "Firecracker in a bottle—nearly blew his hand off."

Thompkins didn't care much for the Burfords but at the time they didn't know anyone else. And it was Joanne who remembered Sally Ann's birthday, lost, late that summer in the tangle of bad news and new friends, in his complete submersion at the news that she was pregnant, news he found neither good nor bad but just plain stunning. The Burfords were trying to have a child, and Sally Ann's condition was Joanne's idea. "Maybe she's pregnant!" she said when Sally Ann complained of being tired, not feeling well.

Sally Ann had run upstairs and tried on her green backless dress, which usually fit perfectly. Joanne had gone after her, and Thompkins had been left alone with Ken Burford's jokes about fatherhood.

Thompkins wondered later if Sally Ann had scared him into working. Her secret smiles, her sudden calm. It seemed the more his fear of a child grew, the more Sally Ann grew—but there was something else. The responsibility which was steadily easing its way into his life also earned him a certain insulation from the world which afforded him the isolation he needed to work.

But she was lonely, and he knew she was upset about her mother—she'd said a few things, and he had a feeling the South was complicated.

So when she suggested having his mother out, Thompkins said yes, even though he didn't like the man who often came with her, a man whose business he didn't know and whose after-shave he couldn't stand. The scent was so strong it remained in the house between his visits, as though to welcome him back on his return.

"Rafe's just too cheerful for you," Sally Ann said.

"He wears lifts," Thompkins said.

"Lad, talk to me," she said. She meant the book. She said this at odd times, as she brushed her hair before bed, or as she stood at the sink, looking out the window.

He couldn't talk about it; the pages were coming apart in his head and he'd ruined a section by giving it to Kipps.

Instead he gave Sally Ann some books to read. All she read was the trashy magazines Joanne brought over, and of course Joanne saw nothing wrong with that:

"Why can't you let her decide for herself?" she said to him one day on the path. "It's not like she pays for them."

"That's not the point," Thompkins said.

"And those books you gave her," she said, groaning. "T. S. Eliot? D. H. Lawrence? Don't they have first names? Or I guess they're just so important," she said, her face suddenly close as they reached the door. "Don't you see? She doesn't care what Mr. T. S. Eliot writes—she could care less. She cares what you write. She loves you."

Thompkins cringed, his embarrassment for her outweighing his dislike. She left, but the next day she joined them for lunch, and something would have to be done about that, she talked constantly, as though breathing were a waste of time. And lunch! Lunch was a delicate time for him. Hearing the first cautious sounds of preparation, the plates, the forks and knives being placed on the metal table, the cranking up of the parasol, his skin prickled. There was something about the almost feminine sound of the silverware which annoyed him, reaching out to him like a plea. He would almost rather hear the sudden roar of the lawn mower, a merciless invasion of noise familiar to him from boyhood. Of course, there were days when his work wasn't going well and he listened for the silverware and often what he heard on those days was the wind chimes.

Sally Ann called to him, or his mother did, if she was there; and as he moved across the lawn towards the table he could feel what was in his mind being overrun by Sally Ann's accent leaning out of a breeze or by his mother's laughter, their talk about the weather or curtains. Pitching his cigarette and wiping a hand over his face, he felt unprepared for the perfection they had created. Flowers from the garden, cloth napkins (no ashtray), the plain white shiny plates where perhaps a seed or leaf or berry had fallen like an exquisite rare first course. His mind was as full as his stomach was empty; he wanted to look at it all, at Sally Ann's lovely face; but he didn't want to know about the baby or the world. He didn't even want to eat—he wanted to have eaten.

On afternoons when Joanne Burford joined them, Thompkins smuggled a sandwich and a beer inside. It was late one afternoon, some days after their literary conversation, that he walked in and found Joanne in the living room, where she had made herself comfortable with some bad news. She was sitting on the sofa and had lit a cigarette and the thought suddenly seemed to occur to her. She clicked her lighter shut and said, "Oh. You know that boy we were talking about—he drowned."

Lad and Sally Ann had argued about it—she had wanted to go to the funeral—but as tears came to her eyes he knew that was not why she was crying. Finally, a few days after the party at Pauline Dampierre's, Sally Ann flew to Mexico for her divorce from Paul Tucker. She wore the same hat, the ribbons cut off, but whenever Thompkins thought of that day (she had never flown before, she was frightened) he thought of the ribbons flitting as she waved and bravely boarded the plane.

They were married in October, in Connecticut, in a town called Ridgefield; it had amazed and then alarmed them (and then struck him funny) that this was one of the few places where a Mexican divorce was good. They had a choice of getting married in a bank or the dime store, where for some reason the justice of the peace had an office. Of course, it was the bank they chose—Sally Ann's grave face, years in a Baptist town—but Thompkins had to admit there was a part of him which would have relished the dime store, standing solemnly in the aisle (wooden floors) with the party hats and favors and confetti, a world where nothing cost more than a dollar, and promising things.

But it had been the bank, an atmosphere which made the dime-store ring seem quite real, or it might have been the way Sally Ann kept looking at it, spreading her fingers and looking at it, smiling, then shyly hiding it away. She wore it until it turned her finger green, and that she had not been wearing it in the hospital upset him before the irony struck him: he had wanted to assure the nurse, so protective with her clipboard and dinner menu, that he was really the father, the husband. Why had Sally Ann said that, about a daughter? The thought of a daughter charmed him, where the prospect of a son had been alarming.

"Face it, Lad," Kipps had said, "you just aren't the type. Bet you've got no idea who won the Series last year!"

They had been walking down Third Avenue, collars up against the cold, and when Thompkins had muttered that it was probably more complicated than that, Kipps turned and grabbed him by the shoulders and shouted, "What? What do you mean? Are you saying you'll need help? Is that it? You're asking me to be godfather, is that it? Tell me yes. Tell me no." He stopped Lad Thompkins right there, shaking him as he had in college trying to explain football. "You tell me yes, goddammit!"

And what if it was a girl?

"A girl? Are you kidding? If it's a girl you'll need five godfathers!" Kipps cried.

An icy wind blew. In the first days of Rollin's life her father waited out at the pink house, his walks confined to a step out into the yard. Three days, two, then they were coming home. He walked out to the car, grass crunching under his feet. He thought of the word "father" and the word "writer," and how in Europe he had been simply an American. Around him the grass was dead, pale as the desert, but the winter sky was a bright blue.

Chapter 2

...

"And this is my wife," he would say. "Miss Cotton Queen 1935."

Sometimes he introduced her that way, but he didn't like her to say it. Her to tell people.

An angle of sun widened towards the cradle, and Sally Ann looked at the photograph again. When she had been pregnant she had looked at it wondering what the baby would look like and now there were times the picture caught her eye and told her who she looked like.

Sally Ann had been seven when the picture was taken and what she'd always liked best about it wasn't the MISS COTTON QUEEN banner which jumped across her little chest but that she was all alone in the picture. Her sister, Ruth, wasn't in it; nor her brother or cousins; Sally Ann's fluted organdy dress took up the whole picture, which wasn't taken in front of the First Baptist Church but in a studio, with lights and a man who brought her mother coffee.

"Smile!" the man taking the picture had said.

"Now? Right now?" Sally Ann had said.

The man had smiled and turned to her mother and said, "She don't waste them, your little girl. No ma'am."

A garden mural had been borrowed from the high school drama department, and in the photograph Sally Ann did appear to be sitting in a real garden, lit up in sepia tones which had no edges, like a dream. Recalling the bright colors in the mural, Sally Ann had been disappointed. There were two copies of the photograph, and she got hold of one and feverishly colored in the background. Her mother had been furious.

"Look there," she had said. "I'd be ashamed."

Sally Ann wasn't ashamed, she was worried about how much the switching would hurt and she was worried that her mother would tear up the picture into tiny pieces. When it sailed into the wastebasket, whole, she ran to retrieve it, to hide to give her father when he came home.

Had she ever given him the picture? She remembered keeping it in a drawer for a long time, hidden as though it were something he'd given her. He did come back—returned, it seemed, to give his reasons for leaving.

Step on the crack, Daddy won't come back, they'd played.

Step on the line, he'll leave you behind.

Behind in that big house, dark rooms cool in summer, where Sally Ann's mother and four aunts and Uncle Cyrus had grown up and where her grandmother, a strong cord of a woman at seventy-five, still lived. The house was on the main street, one of those houses with a swing on the porch and holders for American flags. Somewhere Sally Ann had a picture of the house, set back in shadow behind huge trees in bloom. She had not been able to find the picture when her mother was here and they had argued about whether or not there was a window to the left side of the front door.

"I reckon my opinion should count for something," her mother had said, touching buttons on her sweater. "I reckon living there all my life should count for a memory," she had said, sitting right there beside the cradle.

What upset Sally Ann was that she couldn't convince her mother it didn't matter. "Don't mean to go rummaging through your things," her mother had said, searching in drawers for the picture.

"Well, Mother, then let's just call," Sally Ann said.

"Who do you want to call?" her mother said. Her glasses caught the light. "Mama? You're not going to call down there for that, Sally Ann, don't be ridiculous." And the argument was over.

When her mother had been here, Sally Ann had had to take Lad aside before every meal and whisper, reminding him about grace.

Looking towards the cradle, the picture caught her. Her father's mouth . . .

The typing picked up again. When Lad had typed down the hall, Rollin had cried when he stopped, and so he had moved downstairs. It was cold downstairs, but it was warm up here. Before she had left, Sally Ann's mother had sewn a navy velvet curtain which hung next to the sky in the doorway. Other curtains hung heavily against the tiny paned windows.

"Just get you a ticket and come on," her mother had pleaded, but Christmas was coming. If they left, Lad's mother would spend the holiday alone, opening rum fruit cakes from her clients. "In the spring we'll come," Sally Ann said, even though she knew they wouldn't.

Her mother had cried when Lad loaded her suitcases in the trunk, but Sally Ann hadn't cried until they'd gone. She had climbed the stairs and checked on Rollin and looked at the picture, at the shiny ringlets and the one leg dangling down, the other crossed under it, the organdy exposing just the tip of a white shoe, and she'd cried.

She had not cried when she left home. She was seventeen and her father had come back around that time, bringing with him new coats and a Monopoly game and a baseball mitt for her brother, David. Her mother had been angry about the presents, and her father had said well he reckoned he could just bring nothing the next time around, if there was one. Ruth had cried, and David, too shy to tell his father he was left-handed, worked his hand awkwardly in the right-handed mitt. The Monopoly game had wooden pieces. North Carolina Avenue was one of the most expensive properties. The coats had fake fur collars.

Nothing made sense.

"Problem with that boy," Uncle Forster said about David, "he thinks it's all up to his daddy. His daddy comes back, we'll all be wearing new hats."

How long had her father stayed that last time? He had told David go run get his mitt and they'd oil it good, but David had already thought of that. He knew the mitt would be useless to trade all dark and stained, and so he lied and said he'd lost it.

Their father had suddenly become a father then, carrying on about the value of a thing, about making your way in the world. He had paced back and forth on the rug in the living room where usually the children weren't allowed, and he had reeled off all the states he'd been to or been through. New York, California, you should see those orange groves, he said; and Sally Ann had thought why, really, should he care about any of them? He had seen the world. Why should he care about this awful town? Whether Uncle Forster's typewriter business worked or not—why should he care? The last time it had been cars, and her father had even bought one. It was a used car. Sally Ann didn't remember the car, but she remembered being in it, going for a drive. It was just as though he lived with them all the time, and they were going to the drugstore for something. But it wasn't. Sally Ann had looked at him at every stoplight, wondering if he'd turn around. Sally Ann had wanted to keep going, over any border into any state. Under his mustache he smiled and told her she was brave; but he was driving and didn't see her crying.

Her grandmother tolerated her father's presence, but this was her house, and she had ways of not letting him forget it, one of which was talking about how she was going to leave it to the church. Uncle Forster would grunt and Aunt Jane, who played the organ, would nod. Uncle Cyrus would tell her she really didn't mean that—"Sadie, now, don't go saying things you don't mean"—but Sally Ann's father, his mustache twitching like an animal in danger, could never leave it alone. With all respect, he accused Sally Ann's grandmother of being selfish and keeping control over her children with the house.

Sally Ann watched her mother look away and her grandmother's profile sharpen with satisfaction, and she knew her father was right.

But it was not until later that she understood that her mother had refused when her father asked her to come away—to leave with him—and she swore to herself that if he ever came back she would go with him. But he never did.

"You won't either," her mother said when Sally Ann announced she was quitting her job at Collins's. "That's a good job you've got there, you hear?"

"Well, I hate it," Sally Ann said. "Collins boys spinning the day away, ordering whatever they please—you can't tell me Mr. Twitty stopped leaving me tips just like that—no ma'am."

Sally Ann looked back on that in a dramatic way, as the reason she left. "Well, not the reason, I guess I'd had it in my mind forever to go," she said later. "But seeing my daddy and hearing about his 'deals,' seeing that boy stealing from his daddy, made me wonder about us. About the South. Whether we'd become mean."

She wanted to study theater, but mentioning any big city to her mother was like mentioning rheumatic fever or the girls on Ash Street—her mother simply turned away towards any corner of the familiar room. "What do you want to go around stretching your face like that for?" she would say, coming up behind Sally Ann with clean laundry. "Someday your face'll freeze like that and then what'll folks say? 'I declare,' they'll say, 'there goes that crazy girl.' "

"I don't care," Sally Ann said, and within a year she was living in Charlotte with her Aunt Virginia, and acting in the Little Theater. In the daytime she had the apartment to herself while her aunt kept books at the offices of the Bodie brothers and at night she rehearsed. Or did what Mr. Shelton called "traveling."

"Imagine you're in New York City and you've just had your purse stolen. Imagine you're in Paris, France, and you want to find the Eiffel Tower but you don't speak French. Imagine you thought you were going to Paris and suddenly you're not."

"Mr. Shelton was the one who told me I should come to New York," Sally Ann said to Lad Thompkins when she met him in fall

1954. Having left a short harmless marriage, she was living with a friend from home, Betty Jane Pearly, who was not the one who knew about the party on Barrow Street.

Lad Thompkins: she watched people come to him, and yet he hardly spoke. After she had talked with him Sally Ann watched him talk with two women, who were replaced by a blonde, then a redhead. Then a stocky man slapped Lad on the back and took over, but Lad didn't seem to mind; he watched his friend's antics with an amused tolerance which suggested he'd seen more. Sally Ann wondered if she'd talked too much. But he seemed to want to know things. He had lived in Europe, but he'd been curious about her maiden aunts. He asked what trees grew down there.

"We had a fig tree in the back," she said.

"A fig tree?" he said.

"You've never seen one?" Sally Ann said.

"To tell you the truth I thought they grew on vines," Lad Thompkins said.

"Vines?" She smiled. "Why it's a tree as big as—well, a tree. You know." She blushed. She wished he'd leave but come back tomorrow and never leave. She said, "We still call you Yankees and I guess I see why."

"Why?" he said.

She shrugged, unable to stop smiling. He asked how long she had lived in Charlotte, and Sally Ann had a flash of the tiny apartment, the unopened wedding presents in the dark hall. "Oh, not long," she said. "You see, I'd heard about New York my whole life. It was like a fever, and it got to be where I couldn't stand even hearing about it. It was far away but it was under my skin and—" She looked at him and away. "And one day someone else's word just wouldn't do." She paused, but he waited. She kept talking, telling him about Betty Jane and her contract with Revillon not working out. "But she stayed. She wrote me that New York was full of people doing any old thing so they could be here. Well, I'd felt that way about a person, but a place?"

"Why didn't you go to Hollywood?" he said, lighting her cigarette.

"Hollywood?" Sally Ann said, and she laughed and told him about Paul. "He was kind of short and he thought he'd stand a better chance there where you can stand on a soapbox." Thompkins laughed. "I can't think of one question to ask you about Paris," she said. "How would—"

"Magic," he said. "But I didn't see it like other people did," he said. "The war, you know. We were there afterwards."

She mentioned the Eiffel Tower and he said it looked like a child's toy which had landed right side up; that the military building at Invalides where Napoleon was buried looked like a child's bank.

Profiles came between them, and Sally Ann watched from an increasing distance, losing his voice. She saw him incline his head to one side, she saw a girl laugh. She recalled Paul's short angry gestures as she watched Lad Thompkins, watched the cigarette travel its measured distance. Apart from that movement there was nothing extra about him, no flesh or gestures, he was so contained that his reserve fell short of grace. But there was something else. He was saving his strength for something, and he was weighted to the ground. He was not tall or imposing, but he was like statues she'd seen where all the weight of a man was in his hands and feet.

Someone said he was writing a book, someone else said a play. When she saw him next and asked him, he scratched the bridge of his nose and nodded and said, "Yankees, was that it? Enemies?"

Sally Ann shook her head. "You didn't answer my question."

How did he turn it around again? In another moment she was telling him about Uncle Forster. "You see, he blamed everything on the North. The Depression, the war—he had us thinking the North was this other country. This better country which put up with us because we made it look bigger. For other countries. And Granny said she remembered her daddy talking the same way about the Civil War and it all got so old, old like the wallpaper. I got to where I was feeling old. What—why are you laughing?" she said. "Are you making fun of me?"

"I'm certainly not making fun of you," he said.

"Hey, Lad," a voice said behind them. It was the stocky man Sally Ann had seen talking with Lad earlier. He was wearing a suit like paper and a shirt like candy. His hair was tousled, even a little dirty, but it added to his face as the wrinkles added to his expensive clothing. "Winifred says I look like I've been to Tangiers and back," he said winningly.

Lad Thompkins introduced them. "Douglas Kipps," he said to her. "Talking about wars," he said to his friend.

"Only losers talk about a war," Kipps said, animation in his voice, his boyish face.

"I'll be back," Lad Thompkins said, and she thought he touched her elbow. She watched after him briefly, Kipps taking up the rear, laughing. "You might as well know, there's a redhead here and everybody's got to talk to her, so relax." She didn't know what to say to him. He'd been carrying on about the pitcher Billy Loes and the '52 World Series, "losing a grounder," putting spit on a baseball. But she didn't need to talk. Douglas went on, "You know what they said about the book that lady writer wrote, some Jew from Hollywood said, 'Who wants to see a movie about the Civil War when you know who lost before you walk in?' "

"What are you talking about?" Sally Ann said, smiling.

"Come on," Kipps said, leaning charmingly towards her. "That Civil War movie. Refresh my memory," he said. Then he stood up straight and flicked back the shock of hair, hanging lank. "Tell me how you like it up here in the 'free' North," he said, jiggling his ice. "Tell me how you escaped the South with all sorts of dreams or prayers, or which was it, anyway?"

"Excuse me?" Sally Ann said.

"Something got you up here," he said.

"You'd never think of ambition, would you?" she said.

"Depends," Douglas said. "Depends on if you left to come here or to leave behind." His smile was dim, but for a moment he seemed to see right through her.

"Well, I didn't rob a bank or anything, if that's what you mean," Sally Ann said.

Douglas Kipps roared with laughter, and what he said next smelled like whiskey. "Lad tell you about me? No? We were at Harvard together. I'm the one who got him to go to Texas. He didn't tell you? About our *Lampoon* days?"

"And what's that?" Sally Ann said, raising an eyebrow. "A drinking club?" She was looking over his shoulder for Lad, lost in the sea of heads, but Douglas was in the South now, taking her back there, not the way Lad Thompkins had (in a tentative, interested voice, "What trees grow down there?"), but on a crusade. He proceeded, in drunken run-on sentences, to talk about freedom.

"You think you're free, because of all that shit you left behind, the family, jealous boyfriend bullshit—you—"

"Excuse me—"

". . . only free in a certain context. Context is the key here, you got it? Because then meanwhile you're on your way to the next hellhole where maybe you won't have the jealous guy but some asshole who never calls and then you're the prisoner of the goddam phone, an inanimate object for Christ's sake. Winifred! Hey, baby," he said, catching a tall cool blonde around the waist. Then he started in again. The fact was, he proclaimed, that Sally Ann had only been free during her hours of travel ("You came by bus? Train?"), and even then she hadn't really been free because she had already bought her ticket. "Chosen destination, key words," Douglas said, and in a rare moment when he wasn't talking the blonde stepped forward and introduced herself.

"I'm Winifred Kipps," she said.

"She sure is!" Douglas said, beaming and turning to look at her. "Isn't she something? She used to have these eyes. Dark blue when I met her, but they've faded. I make her cry so much they faded."

"I'm sorry," Winifred said to Sally Ann, "what was your name?"

A voice behind her, familiar but not one she was quite comfortable

with, said, "Miss Cotton Queen of the South, wasn't it? Isn't that
who they're talking to?"

"Oh," Sally Ann said, smiling. She shook her head. "That was a
long time ago, nothing to do with my legs or talent or anything
or—I mean, I was seven."

Winifred Kipps smiled and said wasn't that quaint. "Miss Cotton
Queen. A contest with Negroes, I would've thought."

"And why not!" Douglas said. "They've been free a long time."
He looked at Sally Ann, then at Lad Thompkins. "Confederate eyes,"
he said. "Watch out, Lad. Listen to what I'm telling you."

Sometimes she saw him. Parties, or they met at the corner place
with the booths and specials.

"You like grease, don't you?" Sally Ann said. "That's why you
like it here."

The waitress wasn't pretty, just in a hurry; licking back receipts,
pencils behind her ears like spears. But she took time to pour his
coffee, leaning on a hip, and Sally Ann could see Lad liked that. He
watched her and always found something to make her laugh.
"Yeah? Is that so?" she said, pouring, laughing. Her name was
Sherry, and once Sally Ann caught Lad staring at the single pearl
which swung nervously from her neck as she reached for the empty
napkin holder. Sally Ann didn't blame him, but when Sherry poured
the coffee she was compelled to fix her eyes on the filling cup while
he could stare at the pearl or anywhere he pleased. It reminded her
of Mr. Twitty, who never drank his ice cream sodas, he just liked
to watch the girls bend for scoops. "Which one's the lowest?" he'd
say, talking about the ice cream. "I'll just finish that flavor up, shall
I?" He took up two stools, one for his hat.

They went to parties in the Village mostly, but Lad was funny
about parties. He didn't talk about his work and he wasn't interested
in what other writers were doing. "It starts to get late and then

29

you're smoking someone else's cigarettes and you know it's time to leave," he said, and Sally Ann knew he was talking about the other night when someone named Phil kept saying, "Who cares about a first look first reading? Give me the money every time!" And then he'd take another of Lad's cigarettes. There was spaghetti, and there were children wandering around and cats. Douglas was there, annoying Lad by asking him about the book in front of other people, in front of this man Phil who announced that he wasn't hiding anything, he was writing a best-seller. "Yup, going to dedicate it to Pete White. You know Pete White? Of course you don't. He was my idol, and where's he now? Wouldn't I like to know, and that's what it's all about!" Then he went on about a magazine, its cost-of-living allowance not even amounting to a cost-of-drinking allowance. He gestured, almost knocking a drink off the mantel, and when Sally Ann asked what he meant by "long fact" he burst into deep-voiced laughter. "Hey, we know, don't we, Lad? Huh? Long fact? What's long fact, it's gotta be a lie! Yup, give me the money every time."

Lad had no idea who he was. "A jolly, party type," he said, shrugging. The following week when they went to dinner at the Kippses' Sally Ann decided Lad fit in better on the Upper East Side, where people behaved. They listened and spoke clearly, and went home early. Douglas fit in better at the parties with the urchin children and bongo drums, although he also fit in supremely well here, where there were bookshelves filled with books which seemed measured to fit. ("Yeah, Winifred loves biographies," Douglas said. "But when whoever it is starts getting old, bang. That's it. She closes the book.") Sally Ann was aware of dinner being prepared by someone else as Winifred regarded her guests coolly from a corner chair. They were waiting for Johnny Semard and his wife and another couple, and looking at Winifred, her long legs drawn up underneath her, Sally Ann thought, We're as opposite as black and white. Considering what Winifred had said about the contest, there was something funny about that. There would be no prized Cotton Queen photograph in Winifred Kipps's collection; instead there would be pictures taken on horseback or ship deck, or like those in the hallway. "Where's that? That's beautiful," Sally Ann had remarked, and of course it was a sand spit off Spain. A picture she had understood was taken in Morocco was taken in a restaurant.

"El Morocco, the restaurant," Winifred had said. "Right here in New York. The restaurant."

Douglas had hurried them on down the hall past two odd cutout figures, saying, "Don't show off, Winifred. Winifred's a little older than us so sometimes she's got to show off. Come on, let's go, through the ass darkly let's go."

The evening continued in stops and starts until coffee, when Winifred decided she wanted to be friends. In Sally Ann's experience you either took to someone or you didn't, but by then she didn't care. The other guests had been late—a sick child—and they had eaten at an impossible hour (Winifred's way of putting it), and Sally Ann just wanted to go home. She had a fitting in the morning and she was exhausted.

"Let me show you these cups," Winifred said, and she led the way into the hallway, where she bent in the half-dark to open a small gilded door. "See?" she said, as though it were a cage and there was something live to see. "Douglas hates them so we never use them but I think they're sweet," Winifred said. And that was that. Winifred closed the cabinet and turned the useless key, and they stood up friends. But Sally Ann did not understand that it was to be a friendship shown off in the company of certain others, like a complexion shown off in a particular light. Like the blue-gray Chinese screen which separated them from their husbands now, the friendship would stand off by itself; used when needed, it would not suffer time or distance because it was based on husbands.

"You could learn things from Winifred," Lad said, but by that time Sally Ann had begun to see.

"Like what?" she said hotly. "Like why Morocco 'amused' her more than Spain? Or why it was better after all that that friend's child was kidnapped because she got a European education? No," she said, "it's too late for me to learn things like that."

Lad answered quietly that it had been the child's father who had taken her. "And there are trade-offs," he said. "There are always trade-offs."

"It all works out, though, doesn't it?" Sally Ann said. "In that world. Douglas is afraid of bridges, so he has a plane." They were walking in the dark wet streets of the Village, closer and farther apart as though drunker than they were, and she hardly heard him when he said something about children. She stopped. "You mean Winifred Kipps can't have children and you've been going on about your friend's missed sports career as if it's the biggest tragedy—"

"Something you can help is always the biggest tragedy," Lad Thompkins said, stopping and facing her.

Sally Ann said nothing, but looked at him in disbelief. She already knew the story, how Douglas Kipps, who was from Greenwich, Connecticut, had gone home weekends from college to play for the Elks in the Colonial League, and then for the Stamford Giants. He pitched. "The twilight league," Thompkins said, amusement in his voice. "I always thought it sounded like a retired men's bowling team." In a low voice she moved closer to hear, Thompkins told her about how it had all come to nothing one day in White Plains, New York, when Kipps had tried out for the Giants. "*The* Giants," he said.

She knew what he meant, but she confused it with football.

"The New York Giants?" Sally Ann said. "How awful. A bad day—well, it's like an audition. You're up there for ten minutes and if—"

Thompkins shook his head. "He was hungover. I know what you're saying, I know how lucky I am with my anonymous brown envelopes, but he'd been out the night before. . . ." He muttered the rest, how Douglas had met Winifred that night at the Greenwich

Country Club, which she was visiting as the guest of her fiancé's family.

"But now wait a minute, Lad," Sally Ann said. "You're not saying it was *her* fault."

Thompkins said nothing. Sally Ann was ill at ease around Winifred, not even sure she liked her, but there was something about her Sally Ann admired. Winifred knew what she liked and did what she pleased. At a party a few weeks later in Stamford, men arm-wrestled and a couple threatened to kill each other in the kitchen, and Winifred walked right over to the local phone book and dialed a taxi. She had given the evening its chance, she said. Earlier, Sally Ann had walked up to her as she was talking to a sculptor. He was younger than most of the people there, a kid really.

". . . and I almost married her! Could you believe *that*?" he was saying, laughing. "Because her neck was very dirty, really. If I had married her, we would have had children with dirty necks—horrible!" He turned to Sally Ann and looked at her with warm brown eyes. He had an accent she couldn't place, but she thought he might be South American—that tan skin. The hole in his sweater as he turned to the hostess was somehow endearing.

"Does he manage to make ends meet?" Sally Ann said to Winifred when he was out of earshot.

"He grew up with eight maids," Winifred said. She shook her head. "Well, you know his brother—Johnny Semard. Half brother actually—George is half Mexican, half French. Half crazy. We have a friend in common, but Nolan's crazy too. A good painter, though," she said, folding her arms. She leaned up against the wall, her head tilted. She was watching Douglas referee a wrestling match. "Do you know where I went to school?" she said.

Sally Ann was watching Lad talk to someone she knew he didn't like.

"I went to a school where once a week they'd ask you what you were—imperfect, nearly perfect, or perfect." She looked at Sally Ann. "Some nights I couldn't sleep, wondering how I'd answer. It sounds crazy now," she said. "Crazy," she said wearily, as if her pearls were heavy.

Later when she had called the taxi Douglas came and stood behind her and kissed her neck. "You know what Winifred does on rainy days? She sits there staring out the window, feeling her pearls and feeding the dog vitamins." He was drunk, and she was too, enough to rest her head on his shoulder and say nothing. It occurred to Sally Ann that they had something, and perhaps he understood her, and that it was hard.

The next time Sally Ann heard from Thompkins after that party he was on the phone, drunk in New Jersey, asking which bridges connected New York and New Jersey. He said she had given him the idea—didn't she remember?

"Lad, where are you?" she said. "It's after midnight."

He started talking about textbook publishers. "New Jersey's full of 'em," he said. "Kipps passed out," he said. "We did it all for him and he—"

"Deposit—"

"Wait!"

". . . come out and learn to drive," he said.

"Pull off and sleep somewhere," she said. "Lad?"

But the line had gone dead.

Sally Ann had been afraid, when she had first come north, of the bridges—she didn't see why such big places had to be connected at all. She thought if she left the city she'd never find her way back. Tunnels weren't so bad: you went blindly, there wasn't that arch of metal distancing the land behind you, measuring how far you'd gone. Lad thought her fear would be cured by learning how to drive, and he had promised that in the spring he'd teach her.

She thought of that when he didn't call. She thought of it a week later when she stood awkwardly in the doorway of Winifred and

Douglas's bedroom and Winifred put clothes into a shopping bag. She tried not to notice all the clothes, price tags still hanging, all the shoes, belts, hats on the upper shelf. The wall of mirrors. She tried not to understand what Winifred was telling her.

"Anyway, as I was saying, his aunt left his mother a house on Long Island, and he's going to try it out there. It's pink," she said. "We'll go and see him." She handed the shopping bags to Sally Ann.

"You act like he's sick," Sally Ann said.

"Oh no," Winifred said, and she frowned and pressed her temples. "You see, he's not just sitting around and imagining things. Sometimes that's what people think writing is. But Lad—*c'est un génie*," she said.

"I don't speak that language," Sally Ann said, looking out at the far-flung bridges and roofs. She looked back at Winifred, and maybe it was the way she crossed her arms, or the way her weight shifted into a position of authority, that made Sally Ann wonder if she'd played this role before. She'd said something about Europe—how it had been the same, Lad ruining all the fun. Sally Ann took the shopping bag. Winifred was saying that there was no phone at the pink house, but that Lad would call. "Actually, I might go home for a while," Sally Ann heard herself say. The handles of the shopping bag were cutting into her fingers. The suit Winifred had given her was pale green, from Saks. Sally Ann had never owned anything like that—her sister's eyes were brown.

"Let us know where you are go—" Winifred said as Sally Ann stepped into the elevator. She seemed the least bit worried, and Sally Ann made sure she was still smiling when the elevator doors closed.

"You wouldn't even heat up a can of beans?" Lad had said once or twice, when she'd been angry. He said her voice absorbed anger. "Even if the warmth in your voice isn't for me, even if you can't help it, if it's just your accent."

He wrote her about an empty house, so empty when he listened to tango music and she was not there. Tango? Or was it banjo? She couldn't read his writing.

She couldn't stay angry.

"Tango," he said over the phone when he asked her to come. "Tango, of course."

Chapter 3

o o o

When Sally Ann moved out to the pink house that spring they did get a phone, they had to have a phone, what would her mother think?

"Lad, I can't have her worrying like that, you know that." And she was lonely sometimes.

"How do you do it, anyway?" Joanne said. "You're so patient. Aren't you curious? What if Lad's writing something pornographic?"

Sally Ann laughed.

"Well, I guess not," Joanne said. "But are you sure it's going to be published and everything? Does he have a contract and, you know, whatever they have?"

Sally Ann picked at the ribbons on her hat.

"That doesn't matter, I guess," Joanne said. "You said he knows the right people."

Lad was working in the room off the kitchen. He had said the white pages hurt his eyes when the sun came in like that and Sally Ann had made curtains, but they hung ragged because he wouldn't clear away his papers so she could hem them. One afternoon she had found herself near his window. She had watered the garden, and she was near enough to see the paint peeling on the windowsill and hear him clear his throat. She took a step, and there he was in the open window. He was muttering and he looked up and they both jumped. Sally Ann turned away quickly, but not before his expression froze in her mind. His lack of expression—he hadn't recognized her.

She avoided the window after that; after that she watched safely from the hayloft as Lad walked towards the froth of honeysuckle. He looked distracted, but she knew it was the opposite. He was reaching. It reminded her of the theater, trying to get in character.

But as she looked out over the property she also noticed the uncut grass, the wild hedge, and a pile of metal and glass which had never been hauled away. Lad always nodded when she mentioned it, but it was still there now in December. A child could cut himself, a dog. The last time she had brought it up, Douglas and Winifred had been here and Douglas had warned them that the leaves growing around it, through it, were poison ivy—they'd have to get rid of that first.

"Well, you'd need gloves anyway, darling," Winifred had said. "For the glass."

The glass and metal looked pretty down there, like something decorative, as though Christmas were over and someone had thrown away decorations. Sally Ann looked away from it, but like a magnet it drew her eye back. That boy had drowned last summer, and standing there she often looked out towards the pond, which was on the town line a short distance away. The towns had been awful about the incident, treating it in a political way, arguing in their respective weeklies which town should assume responsibility for the boy's death. There had even been editorials questioning the use of taxpayers' money for the investigation.

"He wasn't some animal who wandered off!" Sally Ann cried. "If he'd been from a big family in town, it'd never be treated like this."

No one cared that he'd been twelve years old and had had a paper route. Yes: actually the paper route had been mentioned because it linked the boy with Wantaugh.

Lad wanted no part of it, no part of even talking about it. He was strange and nervous. His work wasn't going well, and Sally Ann felt like everything was falling apart as her stomach only grew. She had wanted to go to the boy's funeral, and Lad had looked as though she was speaking an unknown language. When a classmate of hers had drowned in the fourth grade, even people from Rutherfordton where the boy's mother had had cousins had come. Even strangers.

"But it's not like that up here," she said. "We call people kin, but I guess you all don't understand second cousins and all that. You have fathers and sons who run big companies and make money. You have brothers and shares."

"Not me," Lad said, smiling like a brave child. "I've got just me, no one to compete with, and I don't have to share, either. Come here."

Later that day, she watched him walking in the hot dusk. Cousinless, brotherless, and there she could imagine nothing—not a copied nose or gesture for a larger younger brother; and any image of a son stumbled towards caricature. She did not understand him. Beside their bed was a stack of books he'd given her to read, but he hadn't given her any of his manuscript to read, and there had come a point when she had stopped asking. He had given a hundred pages to Douglas, who had passed on the pages—that was what he called the manuscript—to someone else. Lad was furious, and Sally Ann shared his anger even though she was still hurt.

"Well, I'm sure he didn't give it to just anybody," she said. "You always said I wouldn't be objective—well, maybe Douglas thought he couldn't be."

Lad looked like he might laugh, but that was anger. They had finished lunch, and yellow jackets descended on the melon rinds. His plate was decorated with burned matches. He got up. She said his name, but he kept walking, his shoulders hunched. He disappeared into the barn, and emerged with the lawn mower. Sally Ann had never seen him mow the grass, which had gotten long since the boy drowned, and now he came towards her, the motor getting at her heart as the sweat built on his shoulders. He turned abruptly at each corner, turning and turning in smaller squares until he had finished and the quiet and fresh smell was everywhere.

Sally Ann left him alone for the next few days. She started one of the books he'd given her. She answered the phone, canceling things, whispering.

"This is bullshit," Douglas said on the phone. "There's a party tomorrow night and he should be there. I told him a long time ago. Sally Ann?"

"Yes."

"We'll be by at eight."

Sally Ann remembered the sunset the following evening because it seemed the two men were arguing about it. When the car drove up, she had been sitting in the hayloft listening to the radio. Douglas led Lad out into the field and started talking and gesturing wildly, and when she turned down the radio, bits of his voice shot back like glass. Lad listened, his head down, as the sky took color from what she saw below: Winifred, her lighter in her hand, sitting at the white metal table lighting a cigarette. The sky was a tirade of pinks, oranges, changing gradually to a violet mist. The light was gray and then silver on the white table, and her diamond was blue.

She looked up, and if she had blinked she would have missed it: Douglas slapped Lad on the back and brought him back like a prize. The party was far out on Long Island, at a house trapped lazily between the ocean and a pond and a swimming pool, where the day before under a hot sun, one of a pair of Scotties had drowned chasing a ball thrown by a child. Douglas said he'd always wondered about the sexes of those dogs—weren't the females always white?

"Why?" Winifred said. "Was it the white who drowned?"

Sally Ann looked at the back of Lad's head and thought about the boy, who she had learned had been the brother of the girl Lad had been seeing. They turned off the road and drove through woods now, and lights appeared through the dense pines and she forgot everything.

"It's like a hotel," she said breathlessly, looking at the spread of shingles and lights.

"Probably what this queer'll do with it if he gets his hands on it. Lad, you'll like this one," Douglas said, slamming the car door. "Tell me you don't need more than a grain of sense to know covering walls with cloth isn't such a great idea in a place where bug spray outsells suntan lotion."

Sally Ann pulled her shawl about her, conscious of her largeness; but once they entered the house, a huge white room with high ceilings ("You ought to do this with the barn," Douglas called back), she did not feel so awkward. Winifred broke away and went over to talk to people she knew—nearly perfect? Sally Ann had never come to terms with Winifred after that day with the shopping bags full of clothes, and she did not know if she ever would. She was looking at the high ceilings and beams and tiny windows and dresses when suddenly she heard Douglas's voice, louder than usual.

"Wait a goddam minute—off limits? Pool's off limits because some little shit dog thought he was a retriever? Hey, Johnny," he addressed the bartender, "what is this? I've got my trunks on and if that pool isn't *drained* no one's going to stop me. It's fucking August, for Christ's sake. What?" He turned around. "Wreaths?"

". . . these artists out there claiming the value of . . ."

"*Four dozen*?" someone said.

"With black ribbons," a man said, laughing.

Sally Ann followed Douglas and Lad through the crowd.

". . . and even if he'd been here he can't swim, poor dear, and that would have been so much worse," she heard a woman say.

". . . some pictures. Actually we could use . . ."

"Where's Pauline?" Douglas shouted. "Where's Pauline and where's the bar?"

"What an amazing party," Sally Ann said to Lad, who didn't hear. "What lovely—"

"Will you look at that?" Douglas commanded.

From the back steps they stared out at the moonlit pool, filled with so many wreaths Sally Ann couldn't see the water, except when a breeze came and she could see ripples of blackish silver.

"It's beautiful," Sally Ann said.

"It's fucking ridiculous," Douglas said. "Let's have a drink, Lad. Let's have six drinks and maybe they'll go away."

He pushed through the crowd and Sally Ann followed, but then a film crew got in the way and she was left behind. She didn't mind, though—the atmosphere of the wreaths and the summer night changed everything, and the dresses she would have envied lost out to the magic. She found Douglas again and he got her another glass of champagne, and then he disappeared again. The party grew louder and denser. Voices tangled. Sally Ann saw Lad across the pool; he was talking to a rather pale woman wearing a shawl. Between them, the wreaths bobbed in the moonlight, a vast oval like a rug in a dream, keeping them apart. If the pool had been in its normal state she would have thought nothing of it, but now it seemed strange that she couldn't get to him. She would remember that there had been music but there wasn't. There were floodlights now and flashes from somewhere and in the sky there was heat lightning and still people looked up as though expecting more, fireworks perhaps. Sally Ann took more champagne from a passing tray and looked dreamily at the wreaths.

Douglas yelled in Sally Ann's ear, "Pauline Dampierre!"

Kidnapping, Sally Ann thought, and a light flashed in her eyes, which after blinking focused on a pale presence as subtly critical as the moon-buffed matte. The woman who had been talking to Lad.

She said, "And Nolan Perry," gesturing to a heavy-set bearded man who growled hello. "Shall we go over here? In the shade," Pauline Dampierre purred, taking Nolan Perry's arm.

Sally Ann's first impression of Pauline Dampierre was that five minutes ago, she had been robbed of everything. Winifred had highlighted a life of cruises (crossings, Winifred had said) and fur hats left on taxi seats, and yet Pauline Dampierre wore no jewelry; absolutely nothing about her glittered even on a night like this. She had been married to a Frenchman, had lived on the Riviera, had had lovers. (And had given someone a "string" of polo ponies, whatever that meant.) And then the kidnapping—it had been a daughter, Sally Ann remembered. She tried to fit the face with the history, but the face and the shawl, the darkish dress, seemed to crave camouflage.

"Little scotch," Nolan Perry said. "No water," he said, nodding thanks.

Douglas left, saying over his shoulder, "Go on, Sally Ann, tell them how you live in a barn."

Sally Ann looked after him, furious.

Pauline Dampierre smiled. "A barn," she said, "Well, Nolan, there you are. Nolan is a painter," she said to Sally Ann. "Although I must say," she continued in her lazy yet deliberate way, "that if Nolan does a barn it will be his barn. His version, his vision of a barn, of 'the barn.' "

"Oh, go to hell," Nolan Perry said.

Pauline Dampierre laughed like a bad child. She continued to talk about barns and annoy Nolan Perry, trying to enlist Sally Ann's help.

Finally he interrupted her. "They're making this place into a dump," he said. "Pauline. Or don't you give a shit."

They glanced over at the pool, where plastic cups poked out of the wreaths. Pauline Dampierre looked at Sally Ann, perhaps for the first time. "Are you having a good time? Do you find all this," she swept a hand across heads, "amusing?"

Sally Ann hadn't realized the house belonged to her. "I—yes," she said.

"There," Pauline said wearily. She gestured emptily. "Anyway, it's Harry Long," she said. "He's paying for it, he—"

"Little shit's over talking to the newspapers," Nolan Perry said, laughing shortly. "I wouldn't be surprised if he had the idea before the dog drowned," he said dryly.

Pauline Dampierre burst out laughing and launched into a jumble of words. "Oh, go have your own movement, Nolan Perry," she said.

"I just want to know who's going to get them out," Perry said. "That's all," he added darkly.

"Get what out?" Douglas said fiercely. "Where's Lad?"

"Oh, Douglas. Good," Pauline said.

Douglas blinked at a flash and pushed back a photographer. "What the hell's going on here? Can't you get rid of them?"

"They're having their movement," Pauline said, still amused.

"The needles are going to be a bitch, I'm telling you."

"We'll have the neighborhood children come," Pauline said. "We'll give them each a net and they can fish out the needles. It's a grand idea. We'll give each of them a net they can take home afterwards, Harry will love that. Winifred," she said, "there you are. Wait, Nolan—Winifred, I want you to tell Nolan about the island, and I want you to stay here, Nolan, and speak to Lad Thompkins. About Yaddo. Where is he? Nolan went, oh there he is. Here he is."

"Yaddo?" Sally Ann said.

"Oh?" Lad said, dropping a cigarette at their feet.

Sally Ann watched their eyes connect as Pauline spoke. Douglas sang in her ear like a mosquito, "Yaddo Yaddo you're standing in my shadow," and she felt the baby kick.

". . . spring," Pauline was saying.

"True story," Douglas said. "A child couldn't pronounce shadow, he said Yaddo. So that's what they named it."

"Named what?" Sally Ann asked.

"I don't know," Lad said in Pauline's direction.

But Sally Ann watched as he let them pass names back and forth, his head lowered. She understood that it was some sort of writers' colony, not only writers but all kinds of artists. Nolan Perry had been there last year. Pauline Dampierre continued to talk in that measured commanding way, her buoyant white gestures by now harnessed by the night air as she drew her shawl around her. She didn't look like the kind of woman things happened to, but perhaps that was why she continued to look the way she did: older, but not as spent. "Pauline was cool even in Morocco," Winifred had said. "She simply doesn't sweat." There was the calm distance, the pale weariness summoned not by life but by the remembering and planning of it. And this was the woman who had read Lad's work. Sally Ann had waited all evening for her husband, and all this woman had to do was wait in the "shade."

"Yaddo. What a strange-sounding place," Sally Ann said the next day. "Do you think, do you want to go there?" She turned to Lad. "It won't be because you can't work here," she said softly. He didn't answer, and she went on, "That grand staircase, I can just see that Nolan Perry at the bottom, dead drunk, lucky not to be dead period. Fifty people getting their lunches in black boxes, I'd drink too." She turned off the faucet. "Lad, you wouldn't stop working if you had lunch brought to you like that, I know you. And you say yourself that sometimes you should stop but you don't and it starts going badly. And all those people. No normal people, all artists and mu—"

"Sally Ann," Lad said, laughing. "You act like it's a cross between the army and an orgy. Come here."

"Well, it is," she said. "That's what it sounds like."

"It probably won't work," he said. "You heard what they said. And if I go it will be because we both think it's right. All right?"

She nodded, but the next day they argued about it. "Actually it's been nice for you," she said to him. "You were angry, so angry at Douglas, but really he's sort of your agent. The only difference is you don't have to pay him, and the nicest difference there could be, I guess. The best kind of friend you could have, kind of like a brother," she said. She seemed unable to stop herself. "A brother wouldn't take money, so—"

Lad stood up and threw the paper down on the table and walked that walk, one hand in his pocket. Pauline Dampierre called a few

days later, and even though Lad said it was nothing, Sally Ann
didn't believe him. She walked slowly over to the clothesline and
unclipped the sheets. It was September, summer was over; the
fading garden was at its best at sunset, when any brown looked
pink. She rubbed her arms. She was afraid of winter.

"You never taught me to drive," she said that day after lunch.
"You'll have to, you know, before you go."

They'd argued minutes before and he'd attached it to that and
Sally Ann couldn't blame him, that was how she had meant it
probably, somewhere. She never meant it to but the conversations
always went this way lately, always; there was something in her
she couldn't stop, and anyway she didn't want to. Since she was a
child people had told her she was stubborn like her daddy, and she
was glad, glad, because if you weren't stubborn you weren't brave.
She would rather have had a father like hers than Paul's, old early,
afraid of cars because things came too fast; on buses at sixty he'd
ridden facing backwards. Afraid of his wife, "She'd poison me if she
could, boy, you be sure of that," he'd said to Paul, but no one grew
surer than Harry Brown Tucker, Brownie his friends called him.
When her Aunt Virginia had written that he had died Sally Ann
had pictured his face and the chair he used to sit in, but more strongly
she remembered the smell of broccoli which filled the house on
June Street every Thursday night. She remembered the smell of the
hair product Paul's mother had used, a nasty vinegar smell for which
her sons were grateful because it reminded them to compliment her,
moving around her as though she were a Christmas tree.

Sally Ann shook the South out of her head, but she couldn't quite.
When she had told Lad about being married it hadn't bothered him,
in fact he made fun of Paul as though he were an awful younger
brother Sally Ann couldn't help. She started back towards the house
and she was midway there when Lad ran across her path to the
ringing phone. That night, there were no stars and the moon hid.
Sally Ann pulled a hair from the soap as Lad waited in bed. She
looked in the mirror. She had never felt so beautiful, and so alone.

o o o

Sally Ann shivered. A door was open somewhere. Yet outside it looked warm, almost inviting, not like winter at all. She stared down at the yard and couldn't take her eyes from the pile of metal and glass, which flashed back at her in strips and points of sunlight, blinding her. When she looked back at the cradle she couldn't see anything and she panicked. There were brown spots, burns where the cradle had been. Her blood quickened and her hands went numb and there was typing and then Rollin cried out, everything ran together and Sally Ann felt for a moment that she didn't exist. The summer, the parties, the colors of rooms and dresses, the boy drowning; last winter this summer this winter, being pregnant—everything ran together but nothing connected so nothing made sense. Sally Ann gasped. The crying stopped and she breathed. She swallowed. When had her mother been here? Her past and the cold strange present, which she couldn't quite find for the moment, changed places as Sally Ann reached like a blind person in unfamiliar territory. Then she came to the knob at the corner of the cradle. There. She heard Lad's voice. Telling her about the bottles she'd been sterilizing. They were ready, he thought.

There. Good. "Good," she said. "I'll be down," she said breathlessly.

That June, when Lad really did leave for Yaddo, just vanished wearing a hat Sally Ann had never seen before, she was almost relieved. There was a day she could visit, he had told her cautiously, he would write her about it. But Sally Ann had said no—she didn't think she would want to do that. She had said it politely, because that was how they behaved towards each other in the days before he left. He had been getting his papers together and she had been planting, although every once in a while she looked towards the blue Ford, shining in the sun in the turnaround. Finally, Lad had taught her to drive, and in a way she couldn't wait for him to go, to leave her there. Walking into the house she sometimes touched the car as if it were something new she owned.

He left on a Thursday. He would have to change trains in the city, and as she held Rollin up to wave, Sally Ann couldn't imagine that this little train with its fans and wheezes would get him very far. But then, it had brought her here, all the way from North Carolina it seemed sometimes.

Back at the house while Rollin took her nap, Sally Ann contemplated the garden. Seed packets lay at her feet, and in a minute she was on her knees with the trowel, moving sideways in the sun. There had been a flurry of parties before Lad had left, they must have gone into the city six times in the last two weeks. They always took Rollin and she usually slept, but still it was exhausting. It felt good to be in the sun. Joanne Burford came over and invited her to dinner, but she said no, thanking her for the open invitation which followed.

Two days passed, then four. She had been ready for him to go, and now there was a restlessness within her, and she packed the ground hard imagining that grand stairway. And she didn't sleep well. There were sounds. "I don't know, just sounds," she said to Joanne. By now over a week had passed. "He's in the same state and I just don't understand," she said impatiently.

"The same state . . ."

"New York!" Sally Ann said. "Why should it take so long? I've already sent him two."

She waited angrily, impatiently, hating the mailbox and its rotten little victory flag the color of dried blood. She had seen pictures of Yaddo—the huge trees, rolling lawns, the big terrace—and she imagined him there, eating and talking and meeting people. The stained glass in the Main Hall had been made especially, according to Nolan Perry. Foreigners—Germans, Sally Ann had understood —had been brought over to do the work. There was a sad history to the place, which had been owned by a man who owned railroads, but Sally Ann hadn't really been listening when Lad talked about it. To her, stained glass had always meant church, the church at home; those thick glass colors which refused to tell the time or weather, an hour had seemed like days. But at Yaddo there would be a clock—she had imagined a grandfather clock ticking politely on a landing. Everyone, in fact, polite; opening their doors for their mail or lunches. In afternoons, walks; curt hellos behind which an intensity suffered and boiled until it was absorbed into the thin spring air, like when Lad exhaled cigarette smoke. But then there was the other side to it, the drinking Nolan Perry had mentioned and the antics, the musician who'd been asked to leave, she couldn't remember why, something to do with a radio. When Sally Ann's thought traveled helplessly in this vein, she balanced her checkbook, tried to ignore the night noises, and thought of going home.

The summer Paul had done summer stock in the mountains had been the same. Sally Ann had understood what hard work it was, what long hours and exhaustion, but she also knew the kind of intimacy that pressure breeded. The celebration and exclusion. When she had gone to visit she had been forced to join the cast at the birthday party of the girl Paul was obviously involved with, a girl named Cindy who like Sally Ann was taller than Paul. For a brief drunk moment Sally Ann had thought this quite funny because it recalled to her how they had met. Halfway through telling the story she decided it was wrong, which only made her tell it more energetically, how it had been at a restaurant, somebody knew somebody, that kind of thing, and they had joined his table.

"Just like now," Sally Ann had said, looking around her at the table of strangers. "Well, I knew I was crazy about him right away when we got up and it didn't even matter that he was half a head shorter than me!"

Recently her mother had enclosed a clipping of Paul in a play called *Highway* which had gotten quite a good review. It wasn't fair. The last time Sally Ann had gone home people had behaved as though it had been a lifetime, as though she should either have children or be a star. "Well hey, Sally Ann, how you been? Hear you been up in Charlotte, doing real well. Your mama showed us the program from that play, what was it? Something by someone pretty famous if I do recall." As if *Little Foxes* would be performed once in a lifetime, and Sally Ann had been chosen. Her mother had looked at the theater as an "interest" which ended when school ended, something which when that part of your life was over you watched other people do. Professionals. And yet when she had sent the clipping she'd written, ". . . it does seem a shame that you couldn't make a go of it here." How could her mother say that? Sally Ann had reread the letter with the concentration one devotes to a road map, but she might as well have been looking for back roads. (Her mother had also sent the recipe for sour-cream coffee cake, and it was a long time before Sally Ann realized that she could copy it onto another piece of paper instead of saving it, keeping it folded in *The Joy of Cooking*, which each week for months she opened to follow the recipe in her mother's hand, and read, at the top of the blue stationery, ". . . of it here.")

Her mother had had the same reservations about Lad. "Nice to be married to someone creative, I'm sure," she said, looking up at the cold staring beams. "Now, you want me to stitch up those curtains? That's right pretty, that material, you get that in town?" She always looked at Sally Ann in a certain way when she said that—or maybe it was the way the light hit her glasses. Sally Ann couldn't drive then, and her mother could not understand that Lad could not just be called upon when there was a stray errand to do. The reasons her mother found to go into town always started an argument. Postcards, a certain color thread, hair nets. They argued because Sally Ann knew how to argue with her mother—with Lad she was less sure.

They had talked about her learning to drive in terms of an emergency while Lad was gone, and after he'd been gone ten days she suddenly had the nerve: She piled Rollin in the Ford, and with one last angry look at the mailbox and quick glances to either side, she drove out of Hardy Road leaving dust behind. Once out on the road, however, she recoiled a bit, and felt extremely lucky to be sitting at the drugstore counter five minutes and fifteen hundred yards down the road.

The next day she felt braver, and after stopping at the drugstore for a Coke, she set out again. She went far enough so that she had to stop again and get gas. Each time she cut the motor Rollin clapped, and each time Sally Ann got out of the car she stood back amazed and a little frightened: A large pale blue hunk of lazy shiny metal standing so still when she had just been driving it? Rollin was looking at her trustingly, and suddenly it all seemed so dangerous. The attendant reminded her to start checking the radiator now that summer was approaching. Sally Ann nodded and smiled. She paid him. The car looked so still in the sun, as if it would never start again.

Her fourth day out, Sally Ann was looking for a place to turn around when she saw that it was lunchtime, but simultaneously—in midturn—she realized she wasn't hungry, that Lad wasn't there, and that she had brought something for Rollin. Quickly she made a circle of the turn, and then kept going on the dead gray never-ending road. The magnolias were out, and over the wall near the estate they'd glimpsed in winter, fruit trees were in bloom. She had no map, but the roads she found had nothing to do with any map she could imagine. Dirt roads through fields measured by fences went on forever, handpainted signs turned at indifferent angles meant nothing. Rollin pointed ahead and said unintelligible things. They were discovering a new world. It felt good to lose track of time this way. When she thought of Lad, she thought of him in an abstract loving way, but she didn't wonder what he ate, didn't worry about his drinking or his hard-won chapters. She just drove. She worried about the road.

Of course they got lost, but only in small ways, until one day when they were really, totally lost. Sally Ann had packed a lunch and brought a book and a blanket, as usual. She had carried Rollin some distance from the car, and first they got lost trying to find the car again, Sally Ann had walked in circles, Rollin grabbing at her hair and cheek. Then on the way home they had tried to find that river again. That was how they got lost. The river had reminded Sally Ann of home, and that day she couldn't find it. The light was going, and they'd driven miles in a circle when finally they approached the same dead animal in the road she'd seen before. When they stumbled into the house the phone was ringing and Sally Ann was pulling burrs from her hair. It was Winifred, furious that she hadn't been able to get Sally Ann on the phone.

"You shouldn't have worried," Sally Ann said. A part of her registered that she hadn't talked to anyone in days. She massaged her foot as Rollin grabbed at the burrs on the table. The sun was going down in a hurry. Yes, she said, picking at her matted hair, she'd love to come in for lunch one day soon.

It was much later, when Rollin was in bed and it was good and dark, that Sally Ann realized she hadn't checked the mail. It was black as pitch out there. Somehow she knew, standing in the kitchen looking out, that there was a letter from him out there in that dark tin box.

The next day she got a dog. By the time Lad had written her once, Sally Ann had written him three times and had driven two hundred and forty miles.

There was the sun on the Ford, the milk truck and the noon whistle and Rollin's nap, the sun pulling away each day more reluctantly. The school bus and the mail truck, by which time the sun was only a matter of light. After she got the dog (no particular breed; it slept on the end of her bed) they stayed home a good deal, and although she might not know the day or date, Sally Ann could tell what time it was within ten minutes up until sunset. The afternoon they saw the naked man she had decided they stayed home too much, and they had gone for a drive.

A naked man.

They had taken the same roads as before, and Sally Ann knew they had been to those woods before. She didn't hear anything, that was what frightened her, if he had wanted to he could have killed them both.

"No, the naked man? Kill anyone? Mrs. Thompkins," Mr. Keller at the drugstore said scoldingly. "You haven't seen him before? I can't believe that. That's just something I can't believe. Now, what can I do for you?"

She had sat completely still at the sight of him and held Rollin tight, resisting a reflex to cover her mouth. She'd been so shocked she'd looked away quickly, then looked back to make sure she'd seen what she thought she saw. She had thought Mr. Keller would laugh at her and say she'd imagined it, not laugh at her because he believed her and thought it was the most normal thing in the world to see on a Friday in springtime.

By the time Lad's mother and Rafe arrived that evening, Sally Ann had calmed down to a case of punchy laughter, because even Joanne said he was all right. "He's just always been around. He never does anything. I'm only sorry I wasn't with you."

Mary's and Rafe's question only made her laugh. "Well, how old was he?" Mary said.

"Oh," giggles, "forty?"

"I've heard about ways to capture a girl's fancy," Rafe said, shaking his head.

"Well, he must not have done anything, Sally Ann seems all right," Mary Thompkins said. "Was he—"

"Pale," Sally Ann said, laughing. "And looking back it was so funny, we sat there watching him, so quiet, like he was some strange graceful animal."

"You're not just trying to convince us you're not bored out here in the country," Rafe said.

Sally Ann turned and smiled. She liked Rafe. Lad didn't trust him, but there was something to do with his charm which reminded her of her father. She was aware that there were difficulties in his life —he was married but there was also a sickness, she wasn't sure. Was it a sadness in a man's life which made him cheerful like Rafe? He wore his hair slicked back and he smelled good, and he made her laugh.

"He travels and he wears lifts," Lad always said.

"And some women dye their hair," Sally Ann always said.

"We're awfully fond of each other" was all Lad's mother would say. A striking woman with gray hair, almost white hair, which blew back like beach grass, she stood tall. As the first woman employee "of consequence" at Con Ed, her picture had been in the *New York Times*. She adored Rollin, singing her to sleep in a lazy gravelly voice, reaching towards the top notes of "Aunt Rhody" or "Bill Bailey." When the train pulled out Sunday evenings, she struggled with the window and then waved and waved, not like Sally Ann's fragile soft mother, clutching a handkerchief, thinking anything might happen.

Like the naked man—she wouldn't dare tell her mother about the naked man. When she told Winifred, Douglas grabbed the phone, but not before Winifred said something like didn't they have that kind of thing where Sally Ann came from, and Sally Ann had immediately thought of her mother and how horrified she would have been.

"Did you call the police?" Douglas said. "You can't fuck around with this kind of thing, Sally Ann, come on. Fucking maniac, come on." Sally Ann said it was all right, the pharmacist said it was all right. "Probably who it is," Douglas muttered.

It occurred to her that perhaps Douglas didn't believe her.

"For Christ's sake, of course I believe you, I just told you to call the police, didn't I? Of course I believe you. And Winifred believes you, I'll probably never get her out of the goddam apartment. She's always sure she's going to find the dead body of a hitchhiker if she goes more than five hundred feet from the—what's so funny?"

"I was thinking," Sally Ann said. "I was thinking that I guess that's the first naked man Rollin's ever seen."

"Look, hold on," Douglas said. "We're coming out, okay? Yeah, let's make a day of it, okay?"

Douglas arrived the next day, crisp and clean, dressed for the country by New York stores. Sally Ann introduced him to Joanne and explained about Douglas's worry over the naked man. Joanne laughed, Sally Ann thought a little too long, too loud.

"I think he actually has a degree," Joanne said. She turned to her husband, who had just joined the group. "Ken, didn't someone tell us that?" Her smile was quick, and she looked back at Douglas, her eyes wandering up and down the stripes of his shirt. They talked about Lad for a few minutes, Joanne laughing loudly again and saying they were counting on him learning to ride a horse up there. Douglas grunted. "Ha," he said. "He didn't learn in Texas, he'll never learn." He fiddled with his keys. "Ready?" he said to Sally Ann. "I had a bumpy ride out and I'd—"

"Bumpy ride in that?" Ken Burford said, nodding at the shiny car. It was the first thing he had said.

"No. I mean, I flew out," Douglas said.

Sally Ann went in and got Rollin and when she came back the men were talking about a man in such familiar terms it seemed they had a friend in common, but Ted Williams turned out to be a baseball player. Their talk wound down and Douglas tossed his keys in the air and leaned over to Rollin, who took them from him. "Okay?" he said. "Come on, we really—I've got this photographer out there, and—"

"A photographer? This gets more ritzy by the minute," Joanne said. "Are you sure about this guy, Sally Ann? How do we know he's a friend of Lad's? He could be whisking you off and we could be here watching and not knowing."

Douglas slammed Sally Ann's door, and waving to the Burfords he got in the other side.

"And look at that, Ken, he even opens the door for her," Joanne Burford said.

"These are the people you're palling around with?" Douglas said, glancing at Sally Ann as they pulled out. "Them and a naked guy and a theater group? Great," he said.

She shook her head no to his offer of a stick of gum, and looked at the road coming at her. Last night she had gotten the news that her Uncle Forster had died. Her first instinct had been to pack, get down there; but then her grandmother had gotten on the phone and told her this call was getting expensive, which somehow made taking a plane down there out of the question.

"Excuse me?" she said. Douglas went on with his theories about theater people, but Sally Ann wasn't listening; she was proud of the fact that one day she'd followed the sign off Route 86 to the Gary Players' theater. From the outside, the building did indeed resemble the hunting lodge Ken Burford said it once had been, and when Sally Ann commented upon this, Mr. Torrs, the director, said, "I know it's a great building—everybody wants this building." He wasn't even looking at her. "The alcoholics want it, the Boy Scouts want it, who sent you?" He looked at Sally Ann and then back at the stage. "I told you, that won't do," he said.

One place Sally Ann could not be intimidated was a theater. Mr. Torrs told her they weren't casting yet for the fall, but that she could help with set ideas. She wasn't sure she was interested in trying out anyway—they were doing a children's series starting with *Peter Pan*—and set design intrigued her much more at the moment.

Douglas took the exit with a swerve, almost as though to get her attention. "Sorry," he said. "So have you seen it?"

"What, seen what?" she said.

"Dowling, the new ad campaign. 'Cashmere mere cash,' you haven't seen it?"

"That's Bill's? I've seen that," Sally said, smiling.

"Yup, Mr. Madison Avenue Dowling they call him," Douglas said. "Says they'll probably use it again at Christmas. Jesus, I remember when he was doing one-column ads for fifty bucks. One of those chic Fifth Avenue stores, Bonwit Teller I think it was. Wiley Church was making the same thing, fifty bucks a picture, and I mean he was in it good—*Fortune, Life.* You know what it is now?" They were on a country road and he slowed down. Sally Ann hadn't been here in a long time—maybe twice since the wreath party. "Talking to someone the other day and it's up to five hundred bucks. Single-page black-and-white photo—shit! But you know Wiley, probably keeps it under a mattress." He looked over at Rollin, who was asleep in Sally Ann's lap. "Jesus, I can't believe it," he said, "how fast she grows!" And he stepped harder on the gas, as though trying to get to the photographer before she grew up.

It was as though they had descended on a hotel out of season expecting accommodations: the photographer had not arrived, and Pauline and Winifred were out by the pool but neither rose to greet them. Douglas didn't care, he immediately stripped to his trunks and dove in the pool.

Pauline finally looked around. "Now tell us about this naked man," she said, as though he had been some new archaeological find. "He had nothing on? Here, sit. He was wearing a watch, perhaps?" Pauline was wearing a dark skirt of no particular length and an Indian wrap which wasn't tied properly. "Douglas said you said he ran by, just like that? I don't understand."

"Apparently he even has a degree," Sally Ann said. Pauline had been to visiting day at Yaddo, and yet all she wanted to talk about was the naked man. Sally Ann looked over at Winifred, whose expression was hidden behind dark glasses.

"So he's an educated man," Pauline said. She was taking this very seriously. "An educated man, who has had enough of what has been offered him in the—"

Suddenly Winifred's chair scraped cement and she went inside. She had been watching Douglas swim, back and forth, back and forth, and now they heard a door slam.

"Winifred's been here for a few days," Pauline said. "She seems better."

"Better? Why, we had lunch the other day and she seemed—"

"There he is!" Douglas called out.

The photographer had arrived, a pale thin man who shook hands too long. Pauline offered him bathing trunks and chicken and a drive around later. ". . . insist you take a swim first," she said, also gallantly pale. "Photographs? Who wants to take photographs? Take them tomorrow," she said, waving the thought away. "Take a swim now. The chicken's here—"

"Well, we have to get back," Sally Ann said. "Before too long, I mean."

"You're the parents?" the man, whose name was Terry, asked, looking from Douglas to Sally Ann.

"No, I—"

"You do what suits you then," Pauline interrupted. "The chicken is mine but the camera and time are yours, and I won't make any claims to the sun, which is out now but may not be out tomorrow." She made a sort of bow and retreated.

Terry (what was his last name? One syllable, and Douglas had mumbled it and she'd missed it) looked after Pauline and then turned to them and said a trifle nervously, "The mother and god-father. I see. Okay, well, let's start then. Did you have a place in mind?"

They started towards the pond, Douglas keeping up a banter with Terry about photography. Sally Ann knelt down and arranged the blanket, holding Rollin and pulling at each corner. Terry was saying he wanted to get into textbooks. He said his friend had an uncle who did that and every time they used his photograph he got a royalty.

"Sort of like newspaper file photos," Douglas said.

"What was your friend's picture?" she said.

"His uncle," Terry corrected. "Oh, he got a picture of a baby masturbating. They say it's common enough, but I guess actually getting a shot of it took some luck. It's in all the psych books," he said.

Douglas was laughing, and Sally Ann just stared at him. Remembering it all later, the whole afternoon seemed like a dream. Her thoughts kept going south, where at that moment a procession of birdlike widows carrying casseroles was filing through the dark house, mourning the last suitor, outlived by his mother and sisters. Later Johnny Semard's brother George came by and they had gone out for ice cream, which made no sense because it was dinnertime, but she had been glad because it was the only nice part of the day. George had made her laugh. Also he had been at Yaddo, and talking to him made her feel close to Lad. Douglas was in a bad mood on the way home, and she found herself wishing she'd accepted George's offer of a ride. They pulled into the driveway after dark. She missed the ringing phone. Joanne calling to tell her the puppy had run into the road.

Chapter 4

. . .

Rollin, at five, was afraid of the big bearded man who made her stand still in the dark hallway. When he stared at her for too long she dropped her eyes down to her patent-leather shoes and stared at them until her eyes glazed over, or until he called her name. He looked like the captain of a ship. His name was Perry, but she didn't think that was his first name. He did other pictures of shapes and lines, and she didn't understand why he was doing a picture of a little girl. And anyway if he wanted to paint a person her mother looked much more like she should be in a painting, sitting perfectly still on the velvet bed in the corner, reading a magazine. Every once in a while she closed her eyes or smiled at Rollin like when they went to the doctor's and they were waiting for him to give her a shot.

She moved a little on the box when Perry wasn't looking. She had slipped over to look at the painting but all she saw was blue and brown everywhere. It looked like someone standing in the mud in the middle of the night. No wonder her father wasn't going to pay for it. She knew that, she had heard the grown-ups talking. Pauline was paying for it. And at least the dot in her eye didn't show—in the pictures she'd seen of other people in olden times, you could see their eyelashes sometimes.

There was never anything to eat or drink at Perry's, he was always drinking something gold which wasn't for little girls. It looked like ginger ale. It didn't smell like what her father drank even though it was the same color. She was thirsty. Her legs were burning because the heater was too close. She was tired. "Is it almost time?" she whined.

They took the bus to her grandmother's, where they had Welsh rarebit, which her grandmother said had nothing to do with rabbits. After lunch, maybe her grandmother would take down the Chinese dolls which were on the top shelf of the closet. They were very delicate, like the things at Pauline's she wasn't allowed to touch. At Pauline's she especially wanted to touch the small Buddha, but it was too high up. It looked smooth and cold. Pauline said it came from somewhere far away. It looked more like a real person than paintings, and that was why Rollin thought she'd like a statue of herself.

"But look up there," her grandmother said. She nodded towards the drawing of her father's face near the mantelpiece.

"But mine doesn't look like that," Rollin said. She looked like she might cry. "Mine is all messy like finger painting."

"Because this one is done with pencil," her grandmother said. "That painting of you is big, isn't it?"

"It doesn't look like me," Rollin said. "Except for my braids."

"But we all know it's you," her grandmother said in a grand way, "and that's what makes it more special. That's like a secret."

Rollin smiled and shrugged one shoulder. She wished her mother weren't here, because now she was going to say it was time to go home. She was going to say they couldn't see the dolls now because there wasn't time, they had to go shopping before dinner.

"Come on, honey, time to go now. We've got shopping to do before dinner. We'll see the dolls another time."

Rollin was always afraid the bus would fall apart it made so much noise, but it never did.

o o o

Sally Ann touched Rollin's head, telling her to stand right there, then she tied her scarf and they waited for the bus. She would write out the recipe when they got home, and give it to Winifred tomorrow. They were meeting at the Plaza, where she knew Lad went with Pauline. She always worried that they'd run into each other; that they'd see each other across a sea of tablecloths, that Lad would be a little drunk. Winifred said it had happened with her and Douglas at "21," where he was sitting with a table of men from *Time*. "Of course they weren't drunk," Winifred said, "but they were together and with men that's the same thing." Sally Ann never felt quite at ease with Winifred anyway. Winifred, who took her to lunch, who gave her clothes, who had proposed this recipe idea. Actually that might work out, Sally Ann thought—and fifty dollars! The rent on the apartment was forty-five. She tried to recall the ingredients for hush puppies, but she wasn't sure that would be right for a magazine like *The Ladies' Home Journal*. Maybe they wanted tea cakes. The bus came, and staring out at winter in the city, Sally Ann thought about the island again. Another of Winifred's suggestions, Fire Island, it was called. "The piece that got away, Douglas says," Winifred said, referring to the sand spit off Long Island.

"It sounds great," Sally Ann had said, not unenthusiastically. She didn't hear whether Winifred said "So Southern" or "So stubborn."

"There's even a sleeping porch," Winifred said. "There's lots of room, Sally Ann."

Not for two men writing books, Sally Ann thought. She looked out at the snow, dirty against the curbs, the people in their dull colors. An island. No cars, only bicycles and wagons; the sun, hats, the beach . . .

"Mom, how come Pauline never comes to see me getting painted?" Rollin asked, breaking in on her thoughts. "How come?"

"She's allergic," Sally Ann said. "Like you with beestings. Pauline is allergic to paint."

Rollin was silent and then she said, "We don't have paint at our house."

Sally Ann said nothing. Pauline always had excuses, and Sally Ann had stopped inviting her. They got off the bus. Sally Ann knew that when they got home Rollin would go straight to her room and draw. She was a quiet child, which didn't worry Sally Ann except when sometimes Rollin would stand in a certain place in the apartment, half waiting for her father to emerge, not understanding that often he came out simply to come out, to stand, to pace or stare at a lamp or table. He stared hard, as if he couldn't make out objects through the cigarette smoke, and often he muttered to himself. There was always that moment when he emerged from the alcove and it became apparent whether or not he would bring into focus the world around him. Rollin watched him, waiting for some signal, some glance; but often he didn't see her and turned back towards his work without a word.

Rollin took out her crayons and lined them up like the rainbow. She was very quiet in the apartment, because her mother said there was a taxi driver who lived downstairs who slept during the day because he drove his taxi at night. That was why her father typed in the bedroom sometimes. His typing made lots of noise because he typed fast, but that wasn't his real work. His real work was thinking. It was better to interrupt him when he was typing, her mother said. Sometimes he even talked to himself, but it wasn't the same as when the men lying in doorways talked to themselves. They spit afterwards.

She didn't sit in her father's lap as she did with Douglas but she leaned on his chair and he let her taste his scotch, which wasn't very good. Her mother opened all the windows all the time because of the cigarette smoke, but Rollin didn't mind the smoke, because it smelled better than the way Rafe smelled. Rafe was her grandmother's friend, who smelled like a lady's perfume and had eyebrows which looked like daddy longlegs. He laughed a lot, and even though he wasn't her real grandfather it was almost just the same.

Thompkins had his bad and his good days, when he even marveled at the way the light hit the mottled-green hallway of the walkup at a certain time on a sunny day. He saw Dowling, George Semard sometimes, and Kipps, but Kipps was trying to write a book too and the discipline he lacked made him focused in a smoldering, trapped way. In the months he'd spent at the foundation out in California he'd scrapped one book—his words—and started another. Thompkins disliked his own words coming back at him with Kipps's frustration, but there it was. "You told me you're supposed to write what you know but it can't come out that way. What the hell does that mean? Whatever it is I'm not getting a handle on it. The element of discovery and all that bullshit."

Thompkins didn't know what had gone wrong in L.A., Kipps had written enthusiastically about a community of scattered houses in a canyon and refrigerators stocked with pâtés and cheeses and canned hams. Dowling said the trouble had had to do with a woman, of course.

Today they met at the grill on Forty-sixth Street. Long and dark, the bar to the left and red booths to the right. "Grill's closed," the waitress informed them at the door, as though to dissuade them altogether.

"Closed?" Kipps said loudly. "What if I told you I was from out of town and I heard that in New York you can get a ham sandwich at two a.m.?"

"You want a ham sandwich? You didn't say anything about a ham sandwich, is that what you want?"

They slid into a booth and ordered roast beef. "And beers," Kipps said over his shoulder. "What have you got on tap?"

She came back around and recited beers. "You see that?" Kipps said when she'd gone. When she came back with the beers Thompkins saw that her uniform was made to look like a jumper; false straps jumped over her shoulders, hinging to useless buttons on her chest. "What do you think, they hold her up or she holds them up?" Kipps laughed, leaning forward in the booth. "Saw Charlie Fontenals last week. He's at Morgan. Looks pretty good."

"He was the one—"

"Always trying to get at the waitresses," Kipps said, laughing. "Right, Pearl Harbor's happening and all Fontenals can think about is the waitresses being pulled from underneath him, Jesus. Pretty goddam funny when you think about it, all these Harvard boys thinking they're going to change the world and then there's a war on and what do they do but race around changing fucking majors." He got at his beer and then set the glass down and made a laborious task of spreading mustard and mayonnaise between the layers of roast beef. He bit into it, and without his voice and laughter the place was quiet except for the sounds of silverware and the ring of the cash register down at the end of the bar.

". . . that Crocker's at Chase?" he said, his mouth full. "Got a promotion too, fuck. Well, hell, he was always a switch hitter, I remember—"

Thompkins had a sudden flash of Sally Ann and Rollin, then walking in the Yard one bright fall. Then Kipps's face now, close up and real. Older. Chase Manhattan, Ogilvie Mather, mentioned like classmates who had succeeded, which wasn't far off the mark. Opportunities supplied by fathers and grandfathers, but what about the rest of it? Getting up in the morning with enough interest in something to get you to a desk across town? What about Elliot Fine, calm unambitious Elliot Fine, who had been through the Tufts dental school and was "excited about gums"? And Dowling, excited about frozen peas or suntan lotion. "Now he's gunning for bathroom tiles," Kipps said. "Yup, big account he says, some company based out in New Jersey." He laughed shortly. "Says every time he goes out there all they want to do is go out and have a big lunch and get plowed."

And where was he now? Struggling around page seven hundred?

"You know what the French would say, *gonflé*," Kipps had said at some point. "*Il est gonflé, lui*. He's fucking conceited, him." Sally Ann said she thought Kipps was jealous. "Well, I know you haven't published it yet, but it's the discipline I'm talking about. And Yaddo—just accepting you meant they believed in you. They were sort of announcing to the world that it was only a matter of time, which they were willing to give you."

Kipps had lacked the discipline to stay with the thing he had loved; but on the other hand there had been times Thompkins had envied him. The houses and travel, the unlimited time which like the good whiskey he drank anesthetized him, put him to sleep after a big lunch. He played tennis, he swam—walking in the street he might gesture in someone's path, but he skied beautifully. The discipline he lacked in sitting still, in concentration, was heartily invested in movement, in harnessing energy into the grace of a pitcher's windup. Sitting in the booth he was like a trapped animal, and Thompkins could tell he'd missed squash this week.

"Hey, you listening? You're going to tell me to jump in a lake, but hear me out okay? I've gone through all the pros and cons— you listening?"

"Listening," Thompkins said.

"It's this. That business out in L.A. really shook me." He played with the pepper. "How do you do it? Tell me how you do it." He shook his head, laughed. "I just couldn't stay shut up in a room working, I don't know if I'm a writer, who knows? But that situation wasn't fair to tell me yes or no. Wasn't healthy." He leaned forward. "I got to thinking. Sitting in my little house with my refrigerator full of hams, what did I have to do but think? These places, all of them, Yaddo and MacDowell, you know that weird friend of Perry's was up there and what I've heard's all the same. It's all so internalized. Long-suffering and brooding. Yeah. I know you like that, thrive on it, huh? But—"

"Dessert for you boys?" A rag came at them across simulated

wood. "Apple pie blueberry pie cherry pie ice cream? Vanilla straw—"

"No, you? No. Two coffees, one light one black. Thanks," Kipps said, elbows spread like wings as he leaned in. "Point is that the writer's always been this model of abstention. Except for drinking. But sports, sex, right? Even eating, for Christ's sake. Keep the energy so it'll explode on paper, just like in boxing don't have sex so it'll, you know, anyway, right? Wrong. In L.A. you could sit around in your cabin getting blasted, sit around with the canned hams for company pouring down the scotch, and who's to know or think it's anything but normal? You're brilliant when you're drunk, right? Exercise," he said, tapping the simulated wood, pulling his coffee towards him.

Thompkins ground out his cigarette and stirred his coffee.

"Okay, okay, so if you want something done right, I always thought that was funny because what it means is if you want something done your way, do it yourself," Kipps said. "So I'm going to. I've bought a place. It's in Bucks County and it's fucking gorgeous." He fell back in the booth and burped. "It's not for a while yet, because there's this guy living on the property and we've got to get him off. He's got his mother there, senile, both nuts, but once they're out we'll go ahead. Shouldn't be hard, they live in a trailer near the river, hey, did I tell you there's a river?"

Thompkins laughed as they rose. "No," he said, "I don't think you did."

He said it in the tone of one indulging a child, and Kipps laughed and shot back, "You asshole, you'll see!"

Thompkins fumbled with money and Kipps told him to put it away and led the way through the ramps of dust-filled light, the cash register awaiting them like a treasure at afternoon's end. Kipps was joking, "You should've seen Winifred's face when I suggested we keep the old guy. Give the place a little atmosphere."

He clapped Thompkins on the back and peeled off bills and a

moment later Thompkins released him into the crowd and bright light towards Madison Avenue and stood looking to his right and left like an old man. For Kipps there would always be a river, and if there wasn't he could afford for there not to be.

Thompkins started to his right, glancing at shop windows, women, the weight of pages darkening what remained of the afternoon. Page seven hundred, who did he think he was? Taxis and people had their plans, his friends were in their offices on scattered floors of different buildings in this great city, learning languages he'd never know. Cities were for people like Dowling and Kipps and Fine—what the hell was he doing here? Why had they moved back here? All he wanted was to sit, in spring, in that broken chair on the green, green grass. Not in the Oak Room.

Pauline had urged them back here, helping them financially, making up what the rent from the pink house missed, but they were still constantly looking for things to do which were free. "Lad, you remember. In Paris the best apartments don't have elevators," Pauline had said at some point. *"C'est comme ça à Paris, Monique, non? C'est vrai, non?"* she had asked the French woman who had been with her for many years, and to whom, each time she flew somewhere, she left her flight insurance. Of course it was true, but the expression on Sally Ann's face when he repeated that to her made him turn away. Of course: Then take me to Paris, the expression said. His daughter was having her portrait painted but there wasn't a wall big enough to hang it on, and pointing out that often Paris apartments had no elevators or toilets (the concept of a Turkish toilet would have horrified Sally Ann) would have done no good because Paris was Paris. Thompkins hated it when Sally Ann didn't have new clothes, or wore the clothes Winifred had given her, which were inevitably some ghastly shade of green, or a dead gray. Sometimes he hated it all.

o o o

It rained during the sittings. February, March; Perry's studio was
cold and damp and smelled like turpentine, and Sally Ann was afraid
the child would catch cold. She looked at her watch and drew the
blanket around her. The sittings lasted an hour, Rollin couldn't stand
it any longer than that, and Nolan Perry was beginning to learn that
he didn't like children. Holding her place in a magazine, Sally Ann
leaned back and closed her eyes.

"Mama, what if Pauline doesn't like it?" Rollin asked after they
left the studio one day. She let her mother take her hand and asked
again. "The painting, Mama. What if—"

"Sweetie, of course she'll like it. Why are you saying that? Of
course she will. And anyway, it's coming to our house."

Rollin nodded and looked at the dirty street. "I want to go away
from here. Men spit in the streets here and I want to go somewhere
else," she announced.

"We're going to the beach in the summertime," her mother said.

"In France Pauline says you can bring dogs in restaurants," Rollin
said.

"Honey, we don't have a dog."

"I want a dog," Rollin said.

Perry said the painting was almost finished, but he always said that.
Rollin climbed on the box, but today Perry had put a bucket over
her chalked footprints. There was a leak, he explained. He was in
a bad mood, and his glass was full of the gold drink. He was talking
about per-, persp-, she didn't understand.

"Move to the left," he said. "No, your left," he said, and his voice
wasn't very nice. He told her to go get something to eat. When she
came back he had hung an ugly green curtain behind the box.

"There's nothing there except stuff that looks like dog food,"
Rollin said. "Isn't there any peanut butter?"

"Rollin," her mother said.

"Ready? Let's go," Perry said.

"We'll stop on the way home, honey," her mother said.

There was a knock at the door and the man with the spread-out ears came in. Last time a woman with a fur coat had come and kept it on the whole time she was so cold. She had been here before, and Rollin knew her mother didn't like her. The man with the ears played music, her mother said. Rollin didn't understand why he came to visit—he only seemed to go to the bathroom and leave.

Rollin climbed back on the box and took the pose, but water dripped on her arm and she jumped. "It's not my fault!" she cried. Frowning, she took the pose again, but then she saw the cracks in the walls which looked like countries and her eyes wandered, and she scratched her neck. She started to tell her mother something funny which had happened at Jack and Jill, and Perry told her to be quiet. When he wasn't looking, Rollin stuck out her tongue at him. Her mother made a face at her, raising just one eyebrow. She had learned to do that in plays. Something tickled, and Rollin reached around quickly and scratched.

"Look, will you—" Perry began. He sighed a big long sigh and scratched his nose. "Look, I know this is long—"

"You just scratched!" Rollin said. "You can scratch whenever you want to."

"Honey, he's almost finished," Sally Ann said. "Then we can take it home and show it to your father. Okay, love?"

Perry said, "Just this one last sitting, and—"

"They're not sittings!" Rollin said fiercely. "I stand and I stand. You don't know when it'll be finished, probably never."

"Rollin," her mother said. She said to Perry, "And you can't get them to sit still when they're sitting." She laughed nervously.

There was a moment of silence, and then Rollin asked Perry, "Pauline has to pay you each time, right?"

There was a sharp sound and Perry cleared his throat. Sally Ann's mind went madly in search of what they'd said in front of her. Perry said nothing. He reached for his cloth. He dried his brush. Rollin was watching him, but he didn't look at her or her mother and he didn't talk. Her mother tried to fix it, her voice turning Southern as it always did when she was sorry or angry. "Nolan," she was calling him now, but he paid no attention. Rollin moved slightly, waiting to see if he'd tell her to stand still. She shifted her weight then, taking one step and then another, toward the edge of the box, as quietly as if he were blind. With a grunt Perry hoisted the canvas over and leaned it up against the others in the corner. Then he went out to the kitchen.

They walked in the ash-colored daylight, not talking, not stopping at the park, but then they never stopped on Thursdays, because Rollin was wearing her sailor dress and her party shoes. Her mother explained that they weren't taking the painting home because it was still wet, but Rollin wasn't sure.

"Anyway, it's too heavy," she said. Her mother didn't answer, and Rollin said, "Anyway, Pauline's paying for it so he has to give it to us."

Sally Ann said nothing. She was glad the sittings were over, she didn't like the smell of turpentine or Nolan Perry's friends. Winifred had come by once and they'd gone to lunch afterwards, but then there was a girl named Pamela who was trying to model, and the musician from upstairs. (Perry drank Hanky Bannister, and offered it around when people came, and for a long time Rollin thought it was a friend of his. "Where's old Hanky?" he'd say, looking around. "I think it's sad that Hanky Bannister never comes," Rollin said one afternoon. "Perry's always waiting for him.") The photographer was all right, but Sally Ann never told Thompkins about the man named Igor who slept it off on the daybed at her feet, nor had she mentioned the day in the kitchen when a sculptress, a woman named Jan, had made a pass at her.

One of those gray, dingy afternoons, Sally Ann had had a headache. The kitchen was also dingy, and greasy; but it was warmer than the studio, and Sally Ann had been glad to have someone to talk to. The redheaded girl and her mother had not been in the park yesterday and Sally Ann had been almost as disappointed as Rollin. Lad was always saying he wished she'd make some friends, be more outgoing and not be content with park talks with nameless women, and this Jan, tall with no chest and dressed in black even around her eyes, talked about a banker father and land in Vermont where she wanted to build someday. Sally Ann had been intrigued. Where she came from women didn't think of building someday, they had what they'd been left.

"What do you work in?" Sally Ann asked her. Jan had thrown her fur coat around Sally Ann's shoulders when she said she was cold—it felt good, heavy.

"Black marble," Jan said, and offered her some gin. "No? A colorless drink for a colorless day? No?"

Sally Ann peered into the other room, where for once Rollin and Perry seemed to be getting along. "My godfather says I can't cut my hair till I'm twelve," Rollin was saying. She was even posing slightly, like a dancer, her mother saw. Her head was raised in the air, and her braids hung down her back like something she'd forgotten.

"Cute little girl," Jan said, coming up behind Sally Ann. She moved and there was a draft. "I guess it's bourbon Southerners like, isn't it? Or absinthe. In New Orleans I tried absinthe and milk and absolutely hated it." Her voice had the faint sound of Winifred's schooling. Jan smiled, and Sally Ann smiled, feeling awkward in her longish skirt, her loafers, and this magnificent coat.

"No, I love the way you dress," Jan said then.

"A Southerner's interpretation of the North, I suppose," Sally Ann said.

Jan smiled again, rattling her glass. She turned back towards the sink and in a series of angular movements reached for the bottle, removed ice cubes, shut the refrigerator door. "What I've always wondered about is mezcal," she said. "I guess your husband would know about that, being from Texas." She looked directly at Sally Ann when she said this, convincing Sally Ann for a wrong moment that that was where her interest lay. "He is, isn't he? From Texas?"

"Not at all. He spent a little time there—how do you know Lad?"
she asked.

Jan shrugged one of the black-swathed shoulders. "Mezcal is
made from the juice of a cactus, doesn't that sound absolutely awful?
Imagine how many cacti that would take. Like a mink and mink
coats," she said, moving closer, replacing a bottle. "Pauline's
writer," she purred; and her arm brushing against Sally Ann's fore-
arm didn't register until it reached into the crevice there, but then
it was too late, a bottle tipped, fell; and Sally Ann's own clumsiness
was all that was real to her, not the close face and pores, the laughed-
out apology.

Sally Ann didn't mention it to Lad then because she hadn't put
it all together. It wasn't until a few weeks later that Sally Ann had
understood what Jan had done that afternoon. They had been talking at a party, and the subject of Pauline had come up. Jan, leaning
up against a wall, still in black, said, "No, I've got my own resources,
thanks. Pauline had to think of something else to offer me."

Bookshelves covered one wall in the walkup, and the other wall
displayed the only window. The portrait leaned up against the narrow partition which separated the kitchen from the living room. As
yet unframed, it resembled a mural. A little girl watching from a
dark hallway which in those rain-reflected colors promised more
elegant rooms beyond. When they moved to the apartment on
Twelfth Street, the painting was given its rightful place on a big
white wall. The morning it was sent out to be framed, Rollin was
impossible, and when it came back she acted as if it had been on
loan to a museum. She asked her father, one day when he was
staring blankly at it, if he wouldn't mind facing the other way, his
cigarette might be bad for it.

At that Twelfth Street apartment Rollin played hide-and-seek with
Henry the elevator man, a black man so dark she couldn't see him
standing in her path when she came in from the bright pavement,

except for his teeth. The book grew, strips of paper taped to the wall, pages and pages in numbered cartons and whispers in the alcove.

Thompkins decided he might even have been looking out the window when it happened. Not that he would have seen anything, so high up, and what could he have done?

Sally Ann was crying and he was glad Rollin wasn't there. "There were people everywhere and no one did a damn thing," Sally Ann said. "A man caught my eye, Lad. Wearing a suit and carrying a briefcase, and you would have thought—" She sniffed, tried to calm down.

Thompkins was looking out the window.

"I want to leave here," she said. "You wanted to come back and we did. We tried. But it's not human here. Lad? Couldn't we? Go somewhere, I don't know where, it doesn't matter." She crumpled the Kleenex in her hands. "If we started looking in the pa— What are you doing? I can't believe it. Some man just grabbed me from behind and you're writing something down? Right outside where I was because you were working and we needed milk and all you can say is are you sure he had a knife? And then you're writing something down?"

"Sally Ann, you're—" he began.

"You should be calling the police!" she said. "But you turn your back and you're writing. Is it interesting enough to use somewhere but not to talk about?" Her voice had reached a feverish pitch. "Is that it? Tell me. Or is there something more interesting that bears writing down?" She shook her head and let him bury it in his shoulder, half-pushing him, crying. She pulled away and went for another Kleenex. Across the room he cleared his throat. She swallowed. "You know what Rollin said the other day, we were at the laundromat and some fool man, some bum was going on and on, and you know what she asked me? She said, 'Mommy, if he had all his teeth would he say all the words?' " She sniffed again, following Lad's gaze out the window. Silently they watched the same window, the same woman undressing until she drew the curtains, forcing them together, back to the perimeters of a slanted square of light which during their embrace moved and shrank to include neither of them.

They moved to a college town on the Hudson an hour from the city, but Rollin wasn't used to it and she was afraid. Even after they got a dog (Sacha, a Labrador) the witch and the woodpecker still came. They were shadows, country sounds, her mother explained. Didn't she remember the pink house and the barn?

Didn't she remember? And the hayloft?

Rollin remembered the hayloft. She remembered the hayloft and the pink trees and the bees which stung her father. She remembered the blue car. Her mother went on talking, but Rollin wasn't listening. She was going to Diane's after school. Everyone wanted to go to Diane's because she lived near town and her sister went to the college high up on the hill. But there were colleges all over the United States, her mother said.

"Even in California?" she asked.

Her mother nodded. Sometimes her mother answered her questions and sometimes she just looked at a chair and didn't say anything. When Rollin asked her mother about her father, she had looked at a chair and said he was far away. Rollin picked at a button on her mother's dress. "Did he ever send you postcards like Douglas sends me?" she asked.

"Oh, not very often," Sally Ann said. "But he brought us presents sometimes."

"Like Diane's father," Rollin said. "And he goes to Chicago and Texas on planes for just one day."

"My, my," her mother said. She had finished ironing the dress and held it out to Rollin and told her to go and put it in her closet until just before Pauline came. Rollin took the dress and went upstairs. She had never told her mother that the witch was Pauline. Her mother said it was a dream because of *The Wizard of Oz*, but how could Rollin explain that it wasn't a dream, there was a real witch that flew around her room at dawn before the woodpecker came? If the witch didn't come by the time the woodpecker started, Rollin knew she wasn't coming that morning. The witch wasn't bad, she was no more than the shadow of a profile which wore Pauline's cape and whispered in her voice.

"Here she is," Pauline always said when Rollin came into the room in her crisp dress. Then she kissed Rollin on both cheeks—she kissed everyone that way—and Rollin stood beside her for a moment. Just close enough so that their clothes touched, not like when her grandmother came or Granny T. or Olive, the cleaning lady they'd had in the city, who used to squeeze Rollin so hard she could smell the salty heat which made her black skin so shiny. Rollin missed Olive. She didn't come anymore, because New York was too far away. And instead of her grandmother coming to baby-sit, a girl named Penny came, a girl who talked on the phone all the time and brushed her hair.

Pauline always brought someone with her like the man with the mustache or the tall lady and sometimes the Kippses came or other people and Rollin could hear them laughing and then arguing late into the night until her father said it was the last train. Her mother would cook all day and make the house look pretty and last of all she would put on a pretty dress and lipstick and put on perfume she kept in the top drawer still in its box. Sometimes Rollin was allowed to brush her hair, but usually there wasn't time. Rollin liked it better when her grandmother and Rafe came and her mother wore just one pretty thing and laughed. When her grandmother and Rafe came they all ate together and everyone acted the same the whole time.

With the others grown-ups there was always a problem. Mrs.

Kipps cried in the kitchen once, and once Rollin saw Douglas, her best, wonderful godfather, break a glass in the fireplace. No one was angry—they all laughed at him. But one time he hit somebody and no one laughed. She didn't see that because they were in the other part of the living room, and she had to be careful. The stairs didn't have backs on them and once her mother saw her.

Mostly though it was just arguing and she mostly heard men. Her father didn't argue loudly. He talked in a very hard voice like last week when he talked to the policeman.

"Why are they arguing?" Rollin asked her mother late one night when she had gone downstairs and her mother had taken her back up to bed.

"Oh," her mother said, "ideas."

"Ideas?" Her mother was leaning over her and she didn't smell like the perfume anymore and her hair wasn't so pretty. "But ideas don't make people mad. Ideas aren't even real," Rollin said.

Her mother laughed. "I'll tell them that," she said. "That will give them something to argue about. Okay? Okay, love?"

She wanted her mother to go away now.

The next morning there was a cigarette burn in the sofa and a stain on her mother's dress and candle wax stuck on the table. There were cigarette butts in all the ashtrays and even in some of the glasses. Someone had forgotten a scarf. In the kitchen, her mother stood at the sink with dishes all around her and the radio going and a far-off look on her face. Her bathrobe was dirty at the bottom. If her father came down for more coffee before she left for the bus Rollin would see him, but usually he didn't. So early in the morning, her mother and father already seemed so separate. Her father upstairs talking to himself behind a closed door, her mother at the sink, listening to people on the radio who made her laugh.

But in the afternoons she was different. After school Rollin walked past Corner Gifts and then into what used to be the Hobby Shop, and there was her mother sitting behind a desk talking on the phone.

She was wearing a dark blue suit and her polka dot scarf and the round gold pin Rollin's father had given her for Christmas, and behind her was a huge picture of Mr. John F. Kennedy's face.

"People come in off the street and often they're the most important," her mother had said to her father last night. "Because they haven't made up their minds. And the phones—well, voter information is—"

Her father had tucked his hair behind his ear, which meant he didn't want to listen anymore. Her mother was laughing. "I believe you're jealous of JFK," she said, pinning a pin on him. "Well, you're not alone. So is every other democratic husband."

"What's democratic?" Rollin asked.

"Mr. Kennedy is a Democrat," her mother said.

"I thought he was a Catholic," Rollin said.

Her father laughed.

Today her mother was talking on the phone about Mr. Kennedy's record. Rollin sat and played with paper clips. She hadn't known he was a singer too.

They went home, but her father was still upstairs. He had promised he would stop smoking when he finished his book, but Rollin had been told not to ask anymore. He kept saying he was almost finished, but Perry had said that. Diane had been very impressed when Rollin told her about the painting. "Well, it doesn't really look like me but it is, it's me wearing my sailor dress and party shoes and everything."

But Diane was disappointed. "On my television we have pictures of everybody," she said. "My big sister's graduation pictures and her wedding and everything."

"Well, a painter paints a painting before he paints a portrait," Rollin recited, remembering what Pauline had said, but Diane didn't care.

One cool morning in May, Rollin stood with her mother while Thompkins loaded cartons into the station wagon and drove away. "Now let's throw away all his cigarettes," Rollin said.

Her mother laughed and said that it would still be a long time before they saw the book in stores. They were walking around the yard, where the roses were coming out. Her mother was explaining but Rollin interrupted, impatient.

"How old will I be?" she asked, looking at the little pink house her father had built her at the edge of the yard. "As old as you?"

Chapter 5

. . .

When Rollin's grandmother bought the house on Fire Island, walked here and there on every boardwalk between the ferry and no-man's-land, there were no numbers on the houses. Mary Thompkins had come out to the house the Kippses had rented on Bay Prom and she had come out last fall looking to buy and if she had seen the house on Surf Walk at any of those times she would have remembered it. One of the houses built in the twenties, it marked Surf Walk's dead end; legend was that it had washed to the bay and back in the hurricane of '38. The dead end was marked by their bicycle rack, and as Rollin's grandmother said when the walk went through and it was taken away, "It was that bicycle rack. That was what really made me feel like I owned a piece of something."

The house was nearer to the ocean than the bay by one boardwalk and sprawled in a study of gables and huge windows made up of small panes that wrapped around the house, which like most houses out there sat on stilts. They had sold the pink house to get this, not an even trade, as the house out here was unheated—people rarely stayed out past September. Few people had telephones, and there were no televisions; Sally Ann's remark that "we're trading magnolias for poison ivy" seemed to say it all. No doubt she was remembering the summer before, when Rollin had played in the poison ivy for an entire afternoon. Her face afterwards resembled a pig's face, especially when she smiled and her eyes swelled shut. Sally Ann did not have good memories of the house on Bay Prom, where the children slept on the sleeping porch with the mosquitoes and Douglas, trying to write a book, stayed drunk most of the time. Winifred hardly came out at all, but the Dowlings did; Sally Ann would never forget the night she'd found the Dowling kids, who were older than Rollin, melting crayons on a lamp. The lamp was metal and she had smelled burning and panicked, and was only slightly relieved when she found the three children crowded around a table, the light of the downcast lamp lighting their faces eerily.

"What are you doing?" she'd cried. It was a weekday, Lad had gone into the city and Douglas was at the club and Bill and Kay Dowling had gone to Ocean Beach for dinner.

"Aw, there's nothing to do here," Mike Dowling said.

Anna Dowling looked guilty.

"Do you know how dangerous fire is here?" Sally Ann said. "Haven't you seen all the signs and the fire extinguishers everywhere? What do you think that bucket of sand outside is for?"

Just then Douglas came in from the yacht club, drunk, singing. The club was nothing by his and Winifred's standards; it was the size of a largish house, and its bar faced the bay and a smattering of windows on the other side looked out on a few tennis courts. But Douglas loved it.

"You make me happy . . . when skies are gray. Sunny boy—" He stopped singing and smiled, and the children laughed. Then he came over and put his arm around Sally Ann. Douglas was a physical person, he was always putting his arm around her, around women in general; and Sally Ann knew that he was in a bad way. Still, she was struck by how the situation must have looked. They were the only adults in the house, and two of the children she had just put to bed belonged to neither of them. What if there had been a fire? What if she had gone to bed, leaving the children melting the crayons, and Douglas had come home ("You'll never know, sunny boy—") to a rented house on fire? What would people have said?

This was a family community; what were people saying now? Douglas told them at the yacht club that he was going home to his best friend's wife and three strange children? Rollin was his goddaughter, but still. And Sally Ann smiled to herself—she realized that she was thinking as her mother had all those years. She took on Douglas's weight, the children on their heels like elves until he plunged into the safety of the daybed and pillows. The children hoisted his feet up and pulled off his shoes and Douglas pulled off his watch. *"El reloj es de oro,"* he mumbled. He pushed it onto the night table, and slept.

The next day the children screamed when he swallowed a raw egg, and then followed him out to where he'd been working, where he quickly read over what he'd written the day before, ripped the page out, and sent the typewriter flying out into the poison ivy. There was a chorus of "What did you do that for?" and Douglas turned to Sally Ann and shook his head. "Can't do it, Sally Ann," he said. "I start over and over and I either think I've already read it somewhere or someone has." He crossed his arms. "Maybe I'll be a sportswriter," he said.

"Be a sportswriter!" Mike said.

"No," he said. "Not a sportswriter."

"Well then what do you want to be when you grow up?" Rollin said so seriously that Douglas broke out laughing and pulled her towards him. "Oh, Rollin. Rollin, Rollin."

Sally Ann's first reaction to Douglas's literally throwing it all out the window had been an amused astonishment—it was only a typewriter, after all. But then she wondered, what if Lad, seven hundred, eight hundred, pages into his book, abandoned it? With Douglas nothing was lost, not even time it seemed, because there was money. She was folding towels, stiff and faded from the sun. Was she crazy to think this way?

A year later, standing on the dock, it all seemed a long time ago. Here they were again in a town laid out like a vast gameboard under the sun, boardwalks turning left and right and dead-ending at a dirt road or a field of poison ivy. A game where one would lose one's turn picking blueberries or catching poison ivy or impetigo, or confusing the tiny firehouses the color of whipped butter marking corners here and there; a game where the American flag flying at the ocean meant good swimming and a white flag meant swim with caution and a red flag—she had not seen one of those yet—meant danger.

Here they were to stay: Rollin had sat in her mother's rocking chair watching as the boys unloaded furniture from the *Isle of Fire*. Some of it looked familiar and some of it didn't, and Rollin hummed and rocked, hummed and rocked as her mother and father talked to the lady with the red hair and flowing scarves who had sold them their house. It was lucky that Johnny Farrell was looking at the sailboats in the Great South Bay instead of doing his job, for at that moment Rollin rocked way back and her eyes registered terror just as the boy grabbed the arm of the chair and pulled it upright.

"What do you think you're doing?" he said. "You know how to swim?"

"Don't let me fall!" Rollin cried, gripping his arm.

"Wait, you've got something in your eye," he said.

"No it's—" Rollin said, swallowing, unable to talk.

"I won't hurt you. Come on. I just saved your life." He took her chin and she looked into his brown eyes. "Oh, it's a mole," he said, letting go of her with a near push. He sounded almost disappointed.

"Hey, Johnny, a little young for you, huh?" one of his friends called. "You gonna help us with this piano or what?"

Rollin looked after him, frowning slightly, the same frown which would appear on her face when he was a lifeguard, then went away and came back and sold drugs for a while, and went out with Nancy Pughe.

That day though she wanted to ride with the furniture, loaded on a huge cart with giant wheels which rolled heavily over the boardwalks, pulled by Johnny Farrell. It looked like some sort of stage. She would look like a queen, sitting on that chair which looked like a queen's chair. But Johnny said that wasn't allowed. The cart was so big, so heavy, how did they get to the house first? Her mother and father had done shopping, but that didn't take long and yet when they reached the house the furniture had been unloaded already.

"Well, where the hell are they?" her father asked, lighting a cigarette. He was furious because they had delivered someone's piano by mistake. "Don't they want the tip they're not going to get?"

Rollin ran her fingers along the wood, which because of the way the light hit looked like the chest of drawers made of all kinds of wood at Pauline's.

"Don't touch it," her father said.

"Lad," her mother said, frowning.

"Well, who knows? I could be liable for the damn thing."

"What's liable?" Rollin asked, but he didn't answer.

"Do you see an ashtray anywhere?" he said.

Rollin ran from the piano and brought him an empty clam shell. "Only promise you won't get them in trouble about the piano," she said, holding the shell away. "Promise?"

The long ash fell on the floor.

"Goddammit, Rollin," her father said.

"Goddammit, Papa," Rollin said.

They all came out to claim their bedrooms that summer; Rollin would always think of Douglas and Winifred in the Goddard bedroom and she would always think of Pauline or Rafe in the harbor bedroom upstairs across from her grandmother's room. The Dowlings in the middle room and other guests scattered here and there, on the daybeds on the porch, on the porch swing. Her grandmother had the room at the top of the stairs, the room which got the ocean breeze. A large white room, it was just right, Mary Thompkins said as she grew older, for someone old and still who liked to watch the light change. The double beds were repainted rusted iron, those beds from the pink house which with their white bedspreads with the pastel pompoms looked like two great forgotten cakes. The tight wind of stairs made a hollow sound as Rollin ran up to see her grandmother and Rafe, who when he visited had the harbor room across the hall. They left their doors open, and approaching, Rollin could hear them talking back and forth. Or else her grandmother's transistor going. If both doors were open (they were both always closed when Pauline Dampierre had the harbor room) one could feel the breeze fighting at the top step. When Rafe was there the harbor room smelled like him, a sweet hard smell. Her grandmother's room, if it hadn't been for the breeze, would have smelled like cigarettes. Rollin liked it up there. While Rafe read his detective stories, she played cards with her grandmother or sometimes they just listened to the radio, half waiting for Thompkins to call her name—because he always did. He came halfway up the stairs and stopped, and called her name. When it was only her grandmother up there he let her stay, he even seemed to forget she was up there.

Rollin explored the house that first summer because it was new, as she explored it summers afterward because it was familiar. The harbor room was at its most distant and private when Pauline Dampierre came and standing before the closed door Rollin remembered her apartment in the city. She had not understood why her mother told her not to touch things which looked old and useless; but maybe it was the high ceilings and polished floors, not the paintings themselves but the little lights under each one, which had made her obey. Certainly she had understood why she was not to touch the telescope. And so that day when she stood on the landing before Pauline's door, hardly breathing, the sound of her grandmother's radio faint behind her closed door, Rollin felt a sense of anticipation. She pushed open the door slowly, nervously, they were at the beach but they could come back, and what did she feel, looking around that room? There were a few cosmetics on the dressing table, but nothing like the creams Winifred had and nothing like all the suntan lotions Mr. and Mrs. Dowling had. There was a shawl over the chair and a book on the neatly made bed. The corner of the shawl fluttered in the breeze, as though that were all that remained of Pauline. In the closet hung three blouses of no particular color. Usually the rooms took on the characters of the people who stayed in them, but here Rollin found nothing. Smelled nothing.

Her godfather's room, Winifred's room, that was where the interest lay, where there was the smell of cream and perfume and the liniment Douglas used, the tangle of sheets at four o'clock. They stayed in the Goddard room, which was a dark room named after a headboard Rollin's grandmother had found in the Goddards' spring cleaning. The room was downstairs, just inside the porch, and with a window on either side it was like its own little house. The windows stayed shut deep into the day when Douglas and Winifred came. Douglas might appear in his trunks early and go for a swim, but it wasn't until noon that Rollin, returning from camp, would see him taking coffee to Winifred. Balancing the cup, his trunks still damp as he disappeared into that dark cave of robes and sheets, and the jars Rollin had glimpsed on the monstrous dresser. Once, way in the back of that dresser, Rollin found French sleeping pills, another time French soap.

Most people had a preference for the bay or the ocean, but Douglas liked them equally, the bay to swim laps in and the ocean to "crash around," as he put it. Often Rollin tagged along, bringing the stopwatch for when he swam laps. For her father hardly ever came with them to the bay or the ocean, not unless her mother pleaded, and he never went in the water. He didn't own any bathing trunks, he simply rolled up his pants and his sleeves and sat looking at the waves through his dark glasses as he smoked a cigarette, which he then put out in the sand. Then he went home.

Neither Douglas nor her father was there the day Rollin almost drowned at the ocean. The year before, she had been content to stay at the edge of the water, building sand castles, but this year she had waded bravely out into the surf, glad for the slap of the waves, the taste of the salty spray. She had been warned about the undertow, but the undertow was what revealed all the treasures, the shells and stones which gleamed for an instant before they disappeared forever; and she was reaching for a conch when she had seen another wave come. The sand gave way underneath her and for an instant she thought of cartoons and quicksand but then she fell, still grabbing for the form of the conch as the water changed directions and fought for her sideways. Suddenly her body wouldn't work for her anymore, the ocean was using it like a pipe, rushing through. Nor did her arms help her. The green-and-white water was thick as mucus, touching her eyes, rushing by. She heard the hasty sound of the sea taking her, entering her brain and slipping consciousness as voices called from another, drowning world.

Then suddenly the strong able hands of a weekend guest, hoisting her up onto his shoulders as though she were the hero, not he. Rollin felt the abrupt pull up to weightlessness, saw the blur of his head as she hung on and searched in her tipped vision of the beach for her mother or father. Her father had left, but her mother came running towards them, her arms out, hair flying. A minute later Rollin was lying on her towel in the sun, her mother stroking her hair. She had stopped crying, and it was comforting to listen to the grown-ups talk. The man who had saved her was saying that was how he liked to go in anyway: "Just plunge!" he said. His name was Rick, and he was a friend of the Dowlings. Raising her right elbow, Rollin peeked over at his laughing profile and felt shy about him. Then she was drowsy. Her body was very light, as though moving in the air, and there was a breeze and the voices faded and seemed, as she fell asleep, as far away as they had when she was underwater, drowning.

Those summers on the island, evenings went on forever, people didn't go home, they just closed their doors. From her bed at the end of the curl of porch Rollin could hear the voices and laughter growing louder; Douglas telling a joke, Mrs. Dowling laughing; her mother's end of a sentence. The sounds of silverware and eating, chairs scraping the floor as some voices traveled to the kitchen and others to the porch. Sometimes there was a voice she wasn't used to, and often a familiar voice didn't sound familiar. Then, as the lighthouse light continued to swing tirelessly across her room, the voices died as one by one the guests went to bed. Two voices? Three? Someone got up, and now she could even hear the wicker give. Once after she thought everyone had gone to bed she heard the piano. Slow and heavy, beautiful! Sad. Who here could play the piano like that? In her mind she went over the guests who were there that weekend, but she couldn't imagine any of them playing a piano like that. She thought of going to see who it was, but whoever it was wouldn't let her up, and she slept, wondering the next morning if it had been a dream.

"A dream? Come on, credit where credit's due. That was Winifred," Douglas said.

"Well, Chopin," Winifred said.

The piano had been hard to resist, and there was plenty of time, in the three weeks it sat there, for accidents to happen. For instance, Douglas sat on the bench on a wet towel. Cigarette burns appeared on the top of the piano, and then there were the various-size rings on top from whatever whoever was playing was drinking. They'd had it about two weeks when it was finally discovered that it belonged to the mayor, who didn't seem to give a damn about it, and what could Thompkins do? He'd had enough of it, it had driven him out of the house.

"I tell you if I have to listen to that infernal ragtime once more—" he said, referring to Rafe. So he worked on the back deck that summer, carrying his typewriter and papers out in the morning and back inside in the afternoon. Part of his bad humor came from not being used to this—to having people, guests, sleeping all around him, hanging around, a thirst for entertainment in their eyes. Of course some of them deserved it, a "vacation"; Dowling worked damn hard; but hearing Kipps talk about Peninghen constantly was a bore, on and on about what he was doing for the artistic community when he hadn't even been in the country for more than a month at a stretch—anyone could do without that. And Rafe. Thompkins was so quiet in the mornings he ached; making coffee, stealing out to the back deck. Then walking to the store, hoping, on his way back, that no one (Rafe) had wakened, but Rafe always had. There he was on the back deck waiting, eager to have someone to talk to, he seemed incapable of pulling himself together in the mornings without making cheerful comments about a day which hadn't even started yet.

"Oh but Lad, he's so fond of you," Sally Ann said. She never failed to remind him of the paella episode. Clearly she was oblivious to how the incident had annoyed him. When Thompkins had prepared the paella, Rafe had insisted on being responsible for the clams, and he had spent all day clamming and getting sunburned. Then when they all sat down (the yellow fringed lamp hanging crookedly, Douglas crying out "¡Una paella! ¡Qué bien!"), Rafe announced that he was allergic to seafood.

"Well you poor thing," Kay Dowling said, and there was a chorus of sympathy around Rafe's apologetic sunburned face.

Finally the piano was taken away. Wheeled down the boardwalk with a blanket thrown over it, it resembled an odd animal.

"Hell, it's not your fault the mayor of a summer town takes his vacation the first two weeks in July," Dowling said.

Thompkins laughed shortly. "And if my house burns down I'll be standing out here alone with a hose," he said.

After the near-drowning at the ocean, it had been decided that Rollin should take swimming lessons, but even those were a disaster. The lessons were held at the bay, and one damp gray day Thompkins and Douglas had gone to the ferry to pick up medicine for Winifred. Walking out onto the dock, they spotted Rollin's group in the water, a circle of blue-lipped children looking up at a towering white-haired man calling through a megaphone. Rollin had often complained about "Uncle Pete," the swimming instructor—this must be he. His voice boomed: "*Kick!* Chin, cheek, to the side." He blew his whistle and the children stopped splashing. He blew it twice and shins on their kickboards (Rollin had made a scene about having the proper one, available at the overpriced candy store for $6.99, and Thompkins could see why) ten children kicked tirelessly as the shrill whistle blew intermittently as if in an army drill.

"Guy's a fucking maniac," Douglas said. "In good shape, though." They had picked up the medicine and were on their way back. "Wait, is that Rollin?" He hadn't known this was her group. "Have you got Rollin in there?"

It was beginning to drizzle now, which did nothing for the humor of the instructor. "*You!*" he cried.

Several children pointed to themselves in frightened response, but he was after a dark-haired girl who shook her head, shivering. Her board had floated a distance away. She said something inaudible and a boy shouted: "She says she's cold!"

"You bet your fanny you're cold!" Uncle Pete yelled. "Standing there like that—look at you! Look at her!" he cried to the group.

Rollin looked over, not knowing what to do. Tory was her friend.

"And there goes the board out past first!" Uncle Pete yelled, as if it were a race. "She's going to lose it because she can't swim!"

Rollin moved and was about to duck under the ropes but she heard, "I said don't!" Uncle Pete's face was red and the veins in his neck bulged. He laughed. "Ha! What was that? You mean you think I'm going to get it?" There was a new brand of poison in his voice now. "Is that what you're waiting for?"

"No, goddammit, who's expecting you to move anything but your goddam mouth!" Douglas Kipps cried.

There was a splash. Rollin, grasping her board, stared. She looked up at her father, and then watched as Douglas came up in deep water, waving the board.

"I thought godfathers were responsible for the religious upbringing of a child," Pauline said back at the house.

Douglas took a beer. "Damn right," he said. "I was trying to keep

these kids out of the hands of this fucking evangelist who was trying
to convince them they'd go to hell if they didn't know how to swim.
He should pack up that face and voice of his and be a missionary."

Later, when her father joined them at the ocean for his fifteen
minutes and asked her if she'd like to walk back with him, Rollin
expected him to say something. She had said she wouldn't go back
to the camp again. The sun was hot and his pace was strange. "Well,
here we are," he said, opening the screen door.

Rollin watched her father disappear into the shadowy depths of
the house, and then she went over to the corner cupboard and chose
five of the games. A client had given the games to her grandmother,
and more than playing them Rollin loved how they looked: small,
about six inches square with colored paper around the sides. Bright
yellow, green, red. The object was to get all the balls in a cogwheel
by gently tapping the side of the box, making the cogwheel turn,
tapping six colored dots into corresponding colored squares. Each
one was like a whole little world. "The *Queen Mary*" was a ship
carrying cargo, making its way through a narrow port; and in "*Alice
in Wonderland*" the table had to be set, silver balls at each place.
Douglas said the best way would be to have two of each game so
that you could race with someone. Rollin sat on the metal swing,
gently tapping, trying to match the dots to the squares. She had the
red and blue in and the green on the other side, but then the yellow
fell out. It was always like that. She always lost her patience and
wanted to break into the game and arrange everything and glue it
down so none of the dots would ever move again. When her father
played, he was very patient and almost succeeded in getting things
where they belonged, and then he wouldn't finish. He would put
the game in a safe place for someone else to finish.

Pauline jiggled the boxes and the balls went everywhere. Rollin
had shown her the gentle tapping motion that Thompkins used.
"But they never work," Rollin said. "They would only work if you
cheated like Douglas says."

9 1

Pauline said that told a lot about a person, how he played a game.

"Douglas says in baseball they cheat all the time, though," Rollin said. "He says it isn't cheating because everybody does it."

"But that doesn't help them play better, does it?" Pauline said.

"Yes it does," Rollin said. "Douglas!" she cried.

"Can I shake you something?" Douglas said, rounding the bend of the porch. (Only *some* men shook the porch.) "Rollin, a Shirley Temple?"

They all drank something: Douglas drank beer in the daytime and at night, he drank something fast with a lemon and salt and everyone watching; Winifred's drink had no color, and her father and Rafe and her grandmother drank bourbon. Pauline brought wine. "Very nice wine," her father always said, looking at the label. All the liquor was kept in the pantry but at cocktail time there were so many bottles on the yellow tin table in the kitchen you couldn't see it.

Summer was almost over. In a way, Rollin missed camp. She had had one friend, Tory, who lived in a grand house by island standards; her father was a director. Rollin had been there once after camp, for lunch, but the grandmother had scared her and she hadn't gone back again. The house was dark with heavy furniture, except for a solarium, where Rollin was surprised to see the queen's chair. There it was in the corner of the room, except that she couldn't sit in it because Tory's grandmother was sitting there. She was old, and Rollin was afraid of her, of the great moles which indicated her face. Rollin wondered, did moles spread? Did little ones grow? Could you catch them? When Tory had invited her again she had said no, although she hadn't noticed, looking in the mirror every day, any change in the mole in her eye.

But that wasn't what she was thinking about that night as she lay in bed—what she was thinking about was that soon Tory and all the other kids would know how to swim and she wouldn't. It would be like magic: suddenly they would know and she wouldn't.

There was such a giant difference between knowing and not knowing.

Her door was open, the lighthouse briskly striping her body in a rhythm like breathing. At first that summer she had been afraid of the shadows of the reeds moving, but it was worse when she shut her door because then she was cut off from the rest of the house. The grown-ups made so much noise they wouldn't even hear a robber. At home she wasn't afraid, because her room was upstairs, but here the boardwalk was right against her window. Robbers never came in doors, and anyway her father always locked the doors, so wasn't her window perfect?

But that night the moon was full and it wasn't a robber Rollin saw but Douglas, standing just outside her door, as if he were guarding it. She pretended to be asleep because she could tell he was looking at her. Her eyelids fluttered. Now he hung his head, shook it back and forth. He had had too much to drink. Winifred said it last night when he was talking about Peninghen, his club which looked like a castle, and her father had said it earlier when she looked through the crack in the door. She saw Douglas shake her father and make him promise not to send her back to the camp, and her father said he'd had too much to drink.

And now he was outside her door. His arms were crossed and his face was shiny from the moon and the lighthouse and the liquor, and his eyes were closing and she worried that he would fall.

But when she woke the next morning he was gone, off for a last swim while Winifred packed, and it wasn't until they were on the dock saying goodbye that he even seemed to notice her presence. He knelt before her and said, "Oh, Rollin, shit! I'm your godfather and I never bring you anything, do I? Anything but trouble. Oh, baby," he said, hugging her.

The next thing she knew the warning whistle sounded and Douglas was yelling at her father over the motor from the top deck. They waved and waved until the people on the ferry stopped waving and all was quiet, the boat a speck in the distance. Her father locked the wagon with all the others and he put his hand on her shoulder for an instant as if to steady him rising, and then they walked home. He let her choose: towards the ocean or along the bay.

Rollin didn't go back to the camp again, and when a few years later she took sailing lessons, she rode over to no-man's-land where the son of friends had access to a cove. Every year Douglas went to bat for the town; he was not a member of the yacht club (yacht club: it was hardly bigger than their own house. Rollin went there for the Tuesday-night movies, the only time its ratty screen doors were open to nonmembers), but as usual, with his charm and a friend or two Kipps managed to spend a good deal of time there, in fact he had a large part in talking the commodore (he knew Tom Hallowell from the Racquet and Tennis Club, not far from the apartment on Park Avenue) into adding another tennis court.

Pictures taken that year by Douglas show them standing in front of the newly painted door, Thompkins's hair cut short and it was early in the season, the brush still down in front of the house. Sally Ann is wearing a white cotton dress, quite full, cinched at the waist with a red patent-leather belt, and Rollin is wearing what looks like an Easter hat. Mary Thompkins is a good-looking woman, hand-some; a proud-looking woman with good legs, who looks as if she would have liked to have had more than one child.

"Come on, you want to win you play the game," Kipps said, and Thompkins had laughed shortly, shaking his head.

"All that laughter—just don't have that much laughter in me, Douglas," he said. "Don't have the clothes."

"Bullshit!" Kipps said, and Thompkins said, Well, exactly.

"That's exactly what I'm telling you," he said.

Over the years the town and the club became one in the same for Thompkins, and he resisted their insidious natures, the rules and the fines, once for garbage cans protruding onto the main walk and "obstructing traffic" and once for a guest opening a can of beer in front of the house, and finally, years later when he returned, a fine imposed for riding his bicycle after dusk. By then, when Margaret saw it, the house showed neglect, a weathered crate of tiny windows thrown in among a shivering collage of green. Finally one couldn't pick out the shingles through the quaking aspens, couldn't see the dozens of windows through the tangle of green; but by then Thompkins liked it that way, a refuge. Hadn't he felt exposed, working on the porch in June and July when the windows were clean and the brush was down? Especially as he grew older he looked forward to August, September (during the court case he stayed out there one year until November), when the camouflage of green thickened like a tapestry hung to keep the world out. In August the mosquitoes descended and the poison ivy turned red and mean at the edges of the boardwalks. A child wearing a white sock meant he'd cut it on a shard of glass, or a splinter had become infected or he'd caught impetigo in the bay. As Thompkins said in one of those early seasons, in August Nature had had enough. The freshness of June had ripened to a point of poisoning itself, until that one day in September when you could walk past the field at midday and see no one.

Chapter 6

o o o

Rollin's point of view reasoned that books made money according to pages, and that should mean a lot of money for her father— seven hundred and nineteen pages' worth. But sitting in the blue-green velvet dress that Douglas and Winifred had given her that Christmas and watching the inauguration on television, she took timid sips of New York State champagne and had the odd sensation that Kennedy had won and her father had lost.

The book stood on a shelf beside the radio next to the leather chair, just at eye level when Rollin listened to story hour on Saturday mornings. In red and gold and black, her father's name looked like a row of buildings, not like his name at all.

PART TWO

...

Chapter 7

° ° °

"Are you going to get drunk tonight?" Rollin asked Douglas. She could ask him things she could never ask her father.

"Hah. You've never seen me drunk, have you?" But Douglas was smiling. He reached for a glass in the corner cupboard, which rattled because it was an antique. All the glasses were, too. Her grandmother had promised that someday she could have the tiny colored ones, so Rollin was watching now, making sure he didn't use one of those. She was sure he wouldn't, though—you didn't drink scotch from those, she knew.

Douglas had come from the magazine (Rollin said "his magazine," although he was merely an investor) and he was wearing one of the shirts with all the colors, white with bands of orange and green and black, all moving as he moved, stripes fine and close like a hundred highways which never touched. "Even when Douglas is behaving his shirt is not," Pauline Dampierre had said once. They were monogrammed or they were not ("redundant for someone with a seventeen neck," he said) and they were expensive—women in Texas waited for his shirttails for their quilts, there was a part of him on every bed in Texas, he liked to say. All Rollin understood was that they were different from the close smell of her father's blue oxford-cloth shirts, because Douglas smelled like traveling, like nothing at all, like a suit dry-cleaned overnight and delivered to a hotel room.

Now he paused between the two rooms of her grandmother's apartment, which were separated by glass doors. He rattled the ice in his glass and grinned at her, and Rollin grinned back. Douglas was the fun one, he was stocky and funny; his pockets were always bulging with keys and money and he was either looking at his watch or waiting for a phone call. He was the fun one.

Her father she had to grow into. Each time he did the dime trick, Rollin watched as he sat in front of her, rubbing the dime into his elbow and making it disappear, and even though he told her to watch, watch now, she could never grasp the exact moment when the trick happened. The dime was gone, she looked at his empty hand and at his elbow and she looked at the floor; she made him move his foot.

Years hence, she would watch Thompkins reading to a child and she would realize that it had been his voice which had distracted her. She would listen to him make his way through a particular passage, his gravelly voice at a pitch which was almost hypnotic, which drew the child closer as they stole looks at each other, the child's expression somber and afraid.

Douglas didn't have time to read to her.

"You should be president!" she cried, and he laughed and spun her around her grandmother's apartment until she screamed. For her seventh birthday he gave her a painting, a lady in a comic strip so big you could see the dots. She was crying—there was a big tear which ran down her cheek. "That's love, baby," he said when they hung it. ("That's an investment," he told Thompkins. "I paid a thousand bucks for it, and you just watch.")

"So, are we on this week or are we off?" Douglas would say to Rollin, for now and then she was angry with him, hated him, always promising other things when he failed to keep the first promise. He had promised to take her up in the plane over Peninghen, for instance, and then he didn't. Her father said no and she didn't know who she was madder at—of course it was harder to stay mad at her father because he was in the same house. (It didn't do any good anyway; Rollin had watched her mother storm in and out of rooms without her father even noticing.) And she didn't see her godfather very often, and sometimes she forgot she'd been mad, and Douglas sent her postcards and how could you stay mad at a postcard? Once she refused to look at the picture, but that only made her more curious, which made her madder.

Now he was having a maze planted at Peninghen, and he could always win her back with that, telling her about mazes in Italy and one in Munich which belonged to the Duke of Bavaria and one with fountains and a hexagon which belonged to an emperor in Spain. (Her father said there were no emperors in Spain but Douglas said he'd read about it.) Douglas gave her Xeroxes of various maze designs and she followed the pathways with crayons—it reminded her of her grandmother's games. He showed her pictures of real mazes, some of which he'd actually visited: Glendurgan and So- merleyton Hall in England, and one in France; beautiful thick green hedges as perfect and sharp against the sky as walls, with vases and statues and pagodas.

"Do you want to hear the story behind mazes?" her father asked her, and he had told her about a place called Crocodilopolis in Egypt, and a Minotaur in Crete. The Minotaur was half man half bull, and the maze was a construction to imprison him. The part of the story Rollin liked best was about Ariadne, daughter of Minos, who fell in love with Theseus, who then killed (her father used the word "slayed") the Minotaur and took her away on a ship to Athens. "And then he left her behind on the island of Naxos," her father always said, and Rollin put her hands on her ears. "No," she said, "that's not true."

What was true was Douglas flying to England because he had friends who knew a duke and duchess who were planting a maze, Derbyshire, Chatsworth House, or maybe it was the other way around; but Rollin was consumed with such information. That the

SARAH GADDIS

queen of Scotland lived there and Douglas was going there seemed
out of a fairy tale, and that was better than a myth.

But when they went to Peninghen, Douglas had done nothing.
He claimed he was still looking for a "site." Of course, the buildings
were beautiful, but Rollin didn't care about the buildings or the
tower room or any of it. Douglas had told her a maze took twenty
years to reach its full height and she wanted to see it here now.

"What do you say, Rol? They say mine should be holly because
I cheat and it'll prickle me if I try to get through."

"What grows fastest?" Rollin demanded. "Not the slow one you
were talking about, that would be stupid, that—"

But Douglas burst out laughing. "No!" he said. "That's s-l-o-e.
It's a plant. They make gin out of it."

Rollin didn't laugh.

When he came to the island that summer he didn't bring any
pictures with him and she worried. First Douglas said Gilling Bore
and Mizmaze (she loved that, Mizmaze) were huge—forty to eighty
feet in diameter—but then he said they were only six inches high.
They were in England, and boys in the towns would bet beers on
who would get out. Rollin thought that was ridiculous. She didn't
know what diameter was but she was afraid that was what they
would end up with: after twenty years, there she would be, looking
at something six inches high.

Her memory would serve her: she would forget who had been to
the island house and who had met there and as she grew older
there were events around which and between which she tried to
put people to remember. (Anyway she didn't care about the people,
she cared about the house. She drew pictures over the winters because she wanted to remember how the rooms were. She dreamed,
once, that they forgot how to get to the house from the ferry, and
so she drew it. Her mother said it was wrong. "But that's how it is
to me!" Rollin cried. Of course her mother was right—that summer

she saw that the baseball field was not that near to the ocean because it was beside the church, which was near the store.)

Death figured largely on her small horizon, on the remote but grand scale of suicide, last summer a writer—she remembered Douglas crying out, shaking her father and running out of the house—and this summer a movie star, and so the news of Tory's grandmother's dying didn't seem like anything really—an old woman dying in her sleep. Rollin was surprised to discover that the chair, huge and round, all that crisscross straw, had a seat which was actually quite small. How had the old woman fit in it?

Rollin sat in the chair each time she went to Tory's. They saved Bazooka comics and ordered diamond rings, they looked under the boardwalks with flashlights for money, and near the post office they even found some.

"Isn't there a way to work those fans?" she asked Tory. "Your grandmother always turned them on and I never knew how," Rollin said. "Show me and then I'll come to lunch, I promise."

Tory's father was never there, he was always off making a movie, and this room looked like a movie—the wood floors and fans, the strange bright flowers. It was an odd household. There was a big Negro lady who carried out baskets of laundry to the clothesline, but Rollin didn't see where so much laundry came from, or what Tory's mother did all day. She was cheerful and dressed as if she were going hunting or riding, except she never went anywhere.

"Where's that?" Rollin said when Tory said her father was in Peru. Douglas had never mentioned a place called Peru. Peru didn't sound like a place to make a movie. Tory explained that it was in South America. She said that each time her father went away, her mother would get out the globe and show her where it was he had gone. It was their secret.

"On the globe each country is a different color, so when someone says to my mother, 'Where's John these days?' we laugh and say 'Green!' 'Pink!' "

"He doesn't ever send you postcards?" Rollin asked.

"Oh no. Never postcards," Tory said.

Rollin never saw her friend again after that summer. Early the following season, she cycled by and saw the woman with the flowing scarves on their deck, which meant the house was being sold. Still, it would always be their house. Years of strangers on the front walk or on the deck would not erase Tory's voice crying, "Green! Pink!"

Rollin would never forget Douglas's birthday that particular summer. As Douglas said, "Now no one has an excuse to forget my birthday—it'll make the headlines every year."

She waited anxiously when the seaplane landed, hoping Winifred had not come. (Of course she had—it was Douglas's birthday.) Rollin had brought the stopwatch just in case, and her heart leaped at the sight of Douglas alone. She waited for him to strip down and run across the dock to the bay, where she would follow and time his laps. But sure enough, Winifred was with him, and as usual his pants got wet and he swore and then they were fighting, not as her parents argued about money, but about something little. Rollin had not yet understood what Douglas had meant about love and the lady crying in the painting, but gradually she saw that people weren't happy sometimes so meanwhile they talked about baseball or politics, or something else which annoyed them, like bad hotel service, because that was someone else's fault. For instance, when Winifred complained that they didn't have ice abroad, she was really mad at Douglas. ("Angry, Rollin, not mad," her father corrected her. "Mad is for mad people, crazy people," he said, and Rollin nodded eagerly. "That's just how I feel when I'm mad," she said.)

The news about the movie star came over the radio after they had cut the cake.

"No!" Kay Dowling cried.

"Oh, shit," Douglas said. "Can we still open the champagne?"

Rollin looked at her mother, who looked as if she were going to slap him. Then Mrs. Dowling was crying and they were all listening to the radio. "Who is it?" Rollin kept asking. And then they were telling her, trying to explain as though each of them had known her in a different way.

"Married a baseball player," Douglas said. "Played for the Yankees and in '48 led the—"

"For God's sake, Douglas!" Mrs. Dowling cried. "Who cares about that?" She turned to Rollin and told her that the movie star had been beautiful; that men had liked her but women had too. "Because she was innocent. She—"

"—had a beauty mark," Mr. Dowling said, raising his eyebrows. "Just like you."

"Don't you remember, honey?" her mother said. Sally Ann knelt in front of Rollin, and she had tears in her eyes. "She sang happy birthday to our president."

Rollin looked over at her father, who said nothing.

". . . called him 'slugger.' "

"Downright sexy." Mr. Dowling set his glass down.

They all seemed to agree about where she had come from and that she had had dyed hair. Rollin wished there were televisions out here—it was as though they were all telling her the same story in different languages. Douglas and Mr. Dowling were disagreeing now, Douglas was saying she was too big *here*. He said, "I like—"

"Stop!"

Everyone looked at Sally Ann. "That's exactly what did her in!" she cried. "Men like you! People, everyone saying what she was and wasn't and should be."

"For Christ's sake, Sally Ann, she was a movie star," Douglas said.

"She was a *woman*," Mr. Dowling said, smiling as if he were remembering a joke. "Hard to think of what IQ was behind—"

"She *was* a woman," Sally Ann interrupted, "who wanted something! She didn't know you couldn't find it in a man!"

"Hey, I'll drink to that!" Douglas cried.

"Oh, you'd drink to anything," Sally Ann said angrily.

Poor Douglas: his half-eaten birthday cake sat on the table, and Winifred had gone.

Later, in bed, Rollin asked her mother what the movie star had looked like. They would see her picture in the paper tomorrow, her mother said. "What do you think she looked like?" Sally Ann asked, sitting on the edge of the bed.

Rollin wasn't sure. "Maybe very long hair," she said. And mean eyes like Winifred's, she thought. That would be the kind of lady who would sing to the president.

It had been the writer the summer before, and now a movie star, and by the time, that Christmas, that it happened in the context of her own life Rollin just wanted to know how to spell it. "Suicide: how do you spell that word anyway?" she said. Her father had encouraged her to start looking up words in the dictionary, but her mother had looked at him, horrified, and said, "You're not going to tell her to look that up, are you?"

Rollin said quietly, "Well, it's not as if I don't already know what it means."

That morning she had sneaked downstairs, where she had seen the silhouette of the tree against the dawn-tinged window. Tinsel glistened over the mass of presents, packages wrapped in silver and fuchsia and green; but she didn't see anything she'd asked for—it was a day which started with disappointment (even the weather; no sunset and no snow, the rain, in a feeble effort at decoration, freezing on the trees) and ended in tragedy, her father's sharpness over the phone and hollow cries in the hallway. Later, after her grandmother was given the sleeping pills, Rollin lay awake listening.

". . . cheerful," her father said. "It isn't the same thing."

Then there were dishes and the sound of her mother's voice and then the water stopped and they were talking about her father's guns, stored in his closet in his workroom.

"Promise me!" her mother cried.

Rafe had come for Thanksgiving, and the table had looked as it had tonight: the blue-and-white flowered china, the cloth napkins and candles. But they'd had turkey, not pig, and Rollin could hardly finish because she had her eye on the chocolate Santas Rafe had brought her. It was a tall thin box of chocolate Santas wrapped in tinfoil, five to a row like soldiers. Rollin remembered him saying they were in the stores so early, they probably weren't fresh anymore by Christmas, but now she wondered if he had bought them knowing he wouldn't be around.

"White meat, dark meat, it's all the same to me," he had said. Rollin remembered his face, but not his last name.

After that Rollin was afraid of her grandmother's apartment, which seemed sad and dark like her grandmother, who dressed in dark colors; that tiny maroon diamond print, black and green roses across her ample bosom—she had always worn those dresses but now they were old. Once Rollin said something about Rafe and she thought her grandmother was going to say that she had loved him very much. But she just stood there, shaking her head sadly. No one would talk about it; after the first outburst it was as though Rafe had been put up in the closet, high up in the dark with the Chinese dolls.

Over the years, she would cast back to a night when she had stood on the darkening sand and watched as a beach taxi—a jeep actually—carrying her grandmother and Rafe disappeared. In the daytime you could see the Ocean Beach water tower far down the coast; surrounded by a purple haze, it resembled a spaceship perched on a network of steel. But at night, the water tower and the waves and the Sea Turtle Restaurant were just somewhere out there in the black. It was one of the last nights of summer when they went, and her grandmother had dressed up for the occasion. The strong headlights of the jeep had lit the waves in sections like a searchlight and Rollin had stood there until the taillights, points of red defining the night, were gone. Years hence, she would walk into the Sea Turtle and she would be disappointed at the bright lights and noise. But by then, twenty years down the road, enough time would have passed that she could reassure herself that it had been like that, once; that somewhere along the way the owners had changed.

Home changed, too. Around that time her father started writing speeches for companies. He was away for a day or two at a time, and brought back vitamins and perfume and film. The vitamins turned green and even though her father said it didn't matter her mother threw them down the toilet. Her mother wasn't happy. She sent the perfume away, down south to Aunt Ruth and the black people, and that was what started the argument with Douglas.

"So they can smell so sweet while picking all that cotton-pickin' cotton," he said about the perfume, but her mother didn't think that was funny. Then he told a story about when he was on a plane and her mother didn't think that was funny either. Then Douglas got mad.

"For Christ's sake, Sally Ann, I'm offering my seat! Do you see blacks traveling on planes all the time? Of course I thought they were together—Jesus!" He muttered, "Next thing she'll be saying I gave up my seat so I wouldn't have to sit next to one of them."

Sally Ann raised her eyebrows. "You said it, I didn't," she said.

"Armstrong, Gillespie—why do you think I don't learn the trumpet?" He went over and looked at her close in the face. "Because I don't have the time?"

"Yes!" Sally Ann said. "Yes! Isn't that—"

"Just listen!" Douglas said, but Sally Ann flew at him.

"Some men are more equal than others! Isn't that what Harvard taught you? And where do you get that right?" she said. "Thinking you can keep them happy by telling them they're keeping you happy!"

"Hold it just one fucking minute!" Douglas said. "I didn't grow up with that history behind me, baby, you did. And it's true: if there hadn't been the Civil War there wouldn't have been any jazz. There wouldn't have been the bands, the instruments wouldn't have fallen into the right hands—''

"You rhymed!" Rollin said. She looked at them, at Douglas, who had caught her mother's hands in the air and was standing so close to her he could have kissed her. He was was holding her arm, his face tilted down towards hers. He relaxed his grip and then her mother broke away as if she'd been trying all along, and his arm fell at his side.

Chapter 8

...

When Rollin was born, people commented on what a perfect combination this child would be: Southern sentimentality and Yankee cynicism. But Sally Ann saw nothing of herself in her daughter. Lad corrected her grammar and Rollin corrected guests; there was something of Douglas in her, his brashness and sense of dare. Sally Ann wasn't sure how this would balance out in a woman. Also, Rollin had a false sense of her godfather's finances. Douglas was merely an investor in the magazine he bragged about, and Winifred had put up most of the money for Peninghen, but of course Rollin didn't see it that way. When they had gone to the Easter show at Radio City and Douglas had carried on about the Rockettes, Rollin had looked back and forth between her godfather and the pairs of flashing legs and said, "Why don't you buy them then? They're much prettier than a baseball team." When Sally Ann had overheard Douglas telling Rollin about mazes constructed for the entertainment of dukes and popes, she had realized the whole idea was perfect for Douglas. The way he referred to the "Grand Hall" (Lad had told her they'd had a Grand Hall at Harvard, at the Lampoon) and "The Great Lawn" was not far from his own self-image. All Rollin heard about was Douglas's plane, Douglas's magazine—what did they expect? Of course she was precocious. Sally Ann was sick to death of hearing about the magazine, which professed to be a magazine about the performing arts even though it was filled with ads for jewels and cruises.

"Sure, we advertise stuff like that, you've got to," Douglas said in defense. "You put the Eagle shirt ads in with the Nike Hercules and reach everybody, right, Dowling?"

"It's a marketing thing, Sally Ann," Dowling said.

"Well, I'm not stupid," Sally Ann said. "But I think it's in bad taste."

"I love it!" Douglas said. "Capitalism is bad taste—great!"

Sally Ann shot him a look. "Advertising real planes with Monopoly money—who do you think you're talking to?" They were at Pete's Tavern and the booth was hardly large enough for them and the Dowlings and Douglas, and then just as the food arrived someone else showed up. Sally Ann went on, "I'll tell you who you're talking to, you're talking to people who play with money. Who think real money is play money. *You* do," she said, looking at Douglas, who had swept the magazine away, unmindful of the tomato sauce which dotted his tie as he did so. "That French money you gave Rollin? She doesn't think it's real. You and Winifred call it funny money and—" There was laughter from Dowling and the editor who had shown up, a man with thinning hair who wore a bow tie. "Fine, laugh. When Rollin asks you to send her to Europe as a graduation present I hope you don't disappoint her," Sally Ann said.

"Sally Ann," Lad said.

"I'm finished," Sally Ann said.

The rest of the dinner was spent with Douglas and the editor trying to convince Lad to write for the magazine. Douglas said he didn't even have to come into town, he could just send in the articles and reviews, and the revisions could be done over the phone. "What could be so hard about that?" Douglas said. "Or give us your ideas. What about that space thing—did you ever finish that?"

1 1 1

"That's not exactly per—" Thompkins began.

"Hell it isn't," Kipps said. He turned to Snyder, the editor. "Great idea. Piece about testing voices—how they transmit. This guy Van Riper came up with a passage containing all the speech sounds in the English language. You should hear it!" He looked at Thompkins. "Just do it."

Thompkins shook his head quietly. "The pay isn't—"

"But that's it," Douglas said, "You get in on the ground floor. Then there's plenty of it. Point is he—"

"Who is *he*, anyway?" Sally Ann interrupted. "Lad said—"

"Sally Ann," Lad said.

Kipps looked back and forth between them. "Who gives a shit who he is? Maybe he makes baby food and maybe he makes tear gas. Maybe he makes typewriter ribbons! Who cares where the money comes from, it's there." He took great bites of his veal and went on, "We've had this conversation a hundred times. Art needs business. Hell, it is business. You're dealing in a world where a gallery owner was a shirt manufacturer in another life. Made his money putting shirts on execs' backs and then ran over to the gallery side because that's where the money was. So what? Maybe he does get into tear gas. You think a painter's going to say no? His first show and he finds out the money comes from strange places—" He shook his head, wiped his mouth. "The pay's not what's bugging you, Lad, I know you. But this isn't selling out—nobody sells out at our age. Hell."

Dowling cleared his throat. He nodded at the editor and said, "Now Snyder seems to feel that the four-color—"

"And business needs art, don't think that business doesn't need art," Douglas said. "Because it's all about image, right Dowling?"

Dowling closed his eyes and nodded. "Yes, Douglas, it's all about image."

"No, but really," Douglas said. "You think the Container Corporation of America cares about painting? Or what about that fruit company—help me out, Dowling. That lady painter from Georgia they sent to—"

"From Texas," Dowling said. "She was from Texas. Her name was Georgia, Geor—"

"Yeah, yeah, and they sent her to the islands," Douglas said. "Dole, that was it. Right. And you can't tell me—"

In the smoky ladies' room Sally Ann looked at herself in the mirror. Her ears were ringing. Lady painter: who did he think he was? Throwing around the word "capitalism"—who did he think he was? When she returned to the table they were talking about a painter they had known in Paris, then they were talking about the *Paris Review* and the Olympia Press. It was always like this, evenings which went on and on and ended with nothing settled. Now they were talking about *Lolita,* the book which had been published the year Rollin was born (Douglas liked to point this out) and had caused such a scandal.

"No, it was part of that Traveller's Companion series," Douglas was saying. "Sort of an offshoot of Olympia. That guy Girodias used to pay what, a thousand bucks? You were gone by then, Lad." He laughed. "Or weren't you?"

Apparently other books in the series, which were written by authors who often used pen names, had been pornographic, and as now, Douglas liked to wonder out loud if Lad had done this on the side. Lad never thought it was very funny, which made Douglas push harder.

"Someday we'll know!" he said. "Someone will find a letter in your papers and everyone will know—"

"Except we'll all be dead," Dowling said.

"Another round!" Douglas said, and he went on about the thin line dividing pornography and literature, parading his ideas and sleeves across the table. "Fuck the English!" he said. "That guy from the *Sunday Express* didn't even read the goddam thing—Humbert Humbert wasn't French, he was Swiss. He just didn't like it that the mother was English." His eyes had the glassy look which signaled he'd had too much to drink; he was getting loud and was rude to the waiter.

No wonder Winifred had her Miltowns.

"She goes and goes but always comes back to Miltown, don't you, baby?" Douglas had said, and Winifred had thrown an ashtray. Miltown was a tranquilizer, and fortunately the ashtray had had rounded corners.

"He makes me mad like my brother makes me mad," Winifred had said about her husband, and there was something to that. They were like an odd pair of twins. Winifred's winter eyes, his summer ones, only twins could breed a hate so safe. At the island house they would fight and then Douglas would go and get drunk, go out over the dirt road to the Kismet Inn, where he would start a fight or break a phone, at best pass out and be carried home. That was how they were. Winifred threw things, he caught them. That was how they were.

"Well, what did you think a Miltown was, Winifred's home-town?" Douglas had laughed. He sang, "Goin' home to Miltown, baby . . ."

Why would Sally Ann know what a Miltown was? Her life was calm. Lad wouldn't argue, he spoke less and less until you realized you were talking to yourself. Douglas didn't stand for it: "For Christ's sake, Lad, stop standing there like you're about to burp, Jesus, you look like you just killed a man!" No, tranquilizers had no place in her life, in a house which was alternately too big and too small, where once recently she and Lad had bumped into each other in the hallway. Sally Ann had jumped back, surprised, and then Lad had stepped out of her way, sweeping his arm in front of her as though asking her to dance. But it had been a curt gesture, and he had continued on down the hall. Sally Ann was overcome with an urge to throw something and he walked as though he thought she might, his shoulders hunched in a little. But there were only books within reach, and while she appreciated the irony of that she also realized that giving any thought undercut it as the reflex it should have been. Egged on by Douglas's comments—"Come on, baby, let's see that jug handle!" or "You've got nails, give me a knuckleball!"—Winifred would have reached and thrown.

Going home that night they took the West Side Highway and as usual Sally Ann looked eagerly at the ships. Each slip was either black or filled with a haughty prow, and she remembered the first time they'd driven by and the *France* had been in port. Douglas had been drunk on it, Pauline had been pregnant on it, but it was enough that Lad had said, "She's beautiful, isn't she," as though he were talking about their future.

Now he was angry with her, she knew that. But she couldn't stand the way Douglas talked to him. He didn't seem to care. Maybe he didn't listen. She looked at his darkened profile. The other day she had come across a letter he'd written her from the pink house. The tango music. Sally Ann didn't remember ever having heard it; but she remembered how imagining Lad responding to it had made her feel. That was where her passion for him, shy at first, had begun—in imagining his. Douglas had been right—if Lad had written for that series of books no one would ever know. If Douglas had, everyone would know because he would have wanted it that way. He would have announced it and been proud of it. Not Lad. And if she had been Douglas's wife, it wouldn't bother her to learn that about Douglas, whose personality guaranteed that anything like that would come off the top, skimmed off from a harmless part of his fantasies. (When the Playboy Club in Chicago had opened a few years before, Douglas had pocketed ashtrays for the mothers— he specified that—of his friends.) With Lad there would be something deeper, darker, and wherever that part of him was, his temper was.

Sally Ann had not wanted to be impressed with Peninghen, but her first glimpse of the estate through bare trees made her catch her breath—this must be what England was like. Even the stone wall, crumbling in places and flooded with dead leaves, added to it. A cold sun flashed through the trees. Neither of them had talked much on the way down, as they were caught up in listening to the radio, a constant report from Dallas, Texas, and Washington—in fact, Sally Ann remembered that Douglas's first words of greeting were indirectly related to the assassination; Harvard and Yale had canceled.

"First time since 1875," he shouted. "Shit! First time in fucking history!" As though Harvard's history were the definitive history of the world. Behind him was the darkening skyline of the main building, and as Rollin ran to him he recited, "Built in the eighteen hundreds. Thirty rooms, all told, including a ballroom and a music room. Imported molding, mantels, balustrades, some *grâce à moi.*" He smiled and as they walked together he went on, "A fountain— Italian marble—and a lawn that goes to Indiana! *Entrez!*"

They walked to the end of a corridor, Douglas gesturing this way and that, until they came to a vast room which looked out onto the back of the property. High ceiling, tall windows trembling with the last sun. "I can see my breath!" Rollin cried, and her shoes clattered on the wood floors as she ran to the far end of the room, where there was a walk-in fireplace. "I'm in the fireplace!" she called, her voice scattering brightly across emptiness. Dust, peeling wallpaper, a chandelier dropped in the corner—but of course Douglas had made the most of it; *Vogue* had used it in a fashion shoot.

". . . afraid if I take action the town will go against me," he was saying now. He was talking about his "tenant," the man who lived on the edge of the property and kept a goat, which had gotten loose. "I had a contractor here and the damn goat wrecked his car," Douglas said. "Jumped up on the hood—can you imagine? Jesus Christ, hundreds of little dents! 'Eloise likes to dance,' the owner says." Douglas laughed and said the contractor didn't bat an eye. "Grew up around here. We settled on two hundred bucks."

"Why Douglas, don't you like the country life?" Sally Ann said, smiling. "Where's Winifred?"

"Her mother broke a hip," Douglas said. "Up at the place in Bedford. The tavern's not so bad—"

"A tavern? For Thanksgiving?" Sally Ann said.

"I want to go to the tavern!" Rollin cried.

They stayed in the section of the place Douglas supposedly kept heated. In the morning, Sally Ann leaned out into the weak November sunshine and looked out past the gazebo and tennis courts and her sleeplessness—she had never gotten warm—came back in a dazed wash of sun across her face. The mystery of the long halls at night, the chill, and the wind were all erased with that sun. Douglas had a girl named Janet who came in from town during the day. She was showing Rollin how to make animal pancakes when Sally Ann appeared downstairs. Douglas was going on about a restaurant-capacity stainless-steel refrigerator he had ordered.

"Because they're not getting refrigerators with little hams, I'll tell you that," he said. "And I'm thinking about a pay phone in the entry hall, you know, Getty-style. Now his place, he paid thirty million for it and then it cost a couple of thousand a day to run it —I'm nowhere on that scale of operation, but shit—the laundry service alone! So I'm doing the bathrooms the French way—give them a sink and the toilet's down the hall. Long as everybody's got his own towel, right?" He tried a light switch. "Whoops, no electricity here. This way then," he said, nodding. "Some things are straightforward," he went on, "like that painters get good light and no drugs, excuse me *rugs*," he corrected, laughing.

They followed him outside, around the back of the property towards the gym. "This is my favorite," he said. "Wait till you see this." They were standing in front of a grim brick building covered with ivy. Douglas fiddled with keys and pushed hard, revealing a greenish-blue room lit yellow. It was like being underwater, Rollin observed. Douglas grabbed a basketball hoop. "Can't you see the girls in their uniforms, dribbling up and down?" he said. "Maroon with white shirts—I've seen the class pictures."

"What's that?" Sally Ann said, pointing upwards.

"Looks like a punishment," Thompkins said.

"Come on, it's the track," Kipps said. "Yeah, well, punishment, as you say." He laughed.

"Why don't you make a gallery out of it?" Sally Ann suggested when he mentioned tearing the track out. "You said you wanted a gallery, and it would be perfect. You could have paintings up there and sculptures down here." She looked at Douglas, then Lad, then back at Douglas, who nodded.

"Not bad, Sally Ann," he said. "Change the lighting—not bad."

They walked out towards the tennis courts, where Douglas pointed at the gazebo. "And of course that's got to go," he said.

"No!" Sally Ann said.

"Got to," Douglas said. "It splits the property. You know, for the maze."

Rollin had been disappointed—that wasn't even the word—she didn't believe him about the maze anymore, even though he tried to explain that the plants were being raised in a nursery until they were big enough to transplant. "You don't want them to die, do you?" he said. He said he had decided on yew. He explained that yew and cypress were expensive but worth it—with box you got slugs, and hornbeam and lime lost their leaves in winter. "And they say I can get up to eighteen inches of growth a year if I do it right. I've got to feed them blood and fish and bone—how do you like that?" he said. "Some diet, huh?"

"But couldn't you move the gazebo?" Sally Ann said stubbornly. "It would be so wonderful. Poetry readings and bands, even weddings."

"People get married on the beach these days, Sally Ann," Douglas said. "At sunrise with the sand blowing in their eyes. Foundation's rotten anyway. No, it's coming down."

It was the strangest Thanksgiving Sally Ann had ever spent. Sitting around in a tavern with the locals, hunters and their wives drinking beer before going back and having their Thanksgiving dinner. There was even singing at some point. Looking back on it, Sally Ann did not remember seeing Douglas so happy—or maybe the word was "content." He was king of the mountain here (they were invited to have dinner by one of the hunters) and he knew it. Of course, the story about Winifred's mother was true; but Sally Ann knew she hadn't taken much interest in the place—she'd only been there a few times, once to sign the check. When they left two days later, she was just arriving. It had started to snow—scattered flakes—and wasn't it just like Winifred to arrive without snow tires, a rare and beautiful rug (neither big enough nor warm enough to be of any use) in the trunk. Sally Ann had come upon her kneeling, straightening the zebra rug, her fur coat trailing behind her on the dusty floor.

Peninghen opened its doors on schedule the following summer with three days of teas and cocktails and lectures, box lunches and a charity dinner, and, for those who wished, tennis and softball. The program which circulated organized the days 1, 2, and 3, and all in all about a hundred and twenty guests roamed the grounds. There were the fellows and their families, speakers and board members and gallery people from New York—even a group of women from a local garden club. They had come to see the maze. Dressed in bright pink, orange, and green, they could be spotted here and there; from a distance they resembled bright flowers.

Rollin watched the festivities from the bay window in the alcove opposite her godfather's office. Except for a boy named Tim Dayton, who was just enough older than Rollin to be uninteresting to her, she was the only child there. Although she did not have an especially good time, she was not given to understanding what she saw as her father's privilege in remaining behind. For they were not going to the island house that summer—there had been a storm and the house had been damaged. They were going down south—that is, Rollin and her mother were going—and Rollin was not looking forward to it. Her great-grandmother had died a few months ago, and there was furniture. "We don't need any more furniture," Rollin had said, and her mother had looked hurt. She looked down, dangling a leg out the window. Her father said he was going to work, but what she saw was people laughing and drinking. One writer she followed through the crowd by watching the parrot on his shoulder, another by a crazy hat he wore.

Nell Dayton, Tim's mother, was the only one who seemed serious. Her hair in a kerchief, she spent the better part of two days inspecting the site proposed for her sculpture, the sketches and prototype of which were on display in the gallery. She had given a short talk, for which she had not removed her kerchief—in fact, she looked as though she had slept in her clothes. Chain-smoking, she spoke in a coarse voice about the violation of space (there was muted laughter at the chance entrance of the largest and mostly brightly dressed of the members of the garden club); then, instead of joining the others for lunch, she had taken her son, Tim, into town, where after eating at a place Douglas called "that dive" she went over and zealously started a tab at Vero's Liquors.

Thompkins's quarters consisted of two adjoining rooms, which after seeing the artists' studios, Rollin thought were quite small. Over the bed hung an etching of a street in a foreign city, but that was all. "There's nothing to look at in here," Rollin said. Her mother talked about the view, but Rollin looked at her father's typewriter and stack of books and she felt a confinement. When they had arrived, she had wandered over to the other building, already alive with hints of its first occupants, and she had sensed excitement. A glimpse into the various studios revealed piles of belongings, supplies, she supposed, although some of it looked like it should be thrown away. There were rolls of canvas and paper, there were boxes and crates and bags of every size and description, taped or tied and bulging with metal or wood or plastic objects protruding in every direction. From school she recognized glue and shellac, paint; but cans marked FLAMMABLE, a jar marked GESSO—she had no idea as to their uses. She went into one studio and then another, noticing the same sorts of things, materials which had as their common denominator a certain careworn appearance familiar to her from Nolan Perry's studio, possessions which although intensely personal shared the generic air of use.

The last event on day 3 was a round-table discussion on the future of the American novel, held in the theater. Seeing her father on the stage was exciting for Rollin, although she was disappointed when, claiming his microphone didn't work, he stopped participating. (At the end, he was heard to mutter through a perfectly functioning sound system, ". . . can get down to work now.") He had turned the microphone away from him when he was interrupted, and Sally Ann thought it was not a coincidence that the writer was a woman. She knew Lad was annoyed with Douglas, who had not mentioned the round table until they arrived. "You didn't have to prepare anything," Douglas had said, "and I knew if I told you you'd just prepare the answer no."

Rollin didn't want to leave. Her mother and father were talking to Douglas, and then they said goodbye and Rollin was walking with her mother. It was still light out, and quiet. On some stone steps, a sculptor and a writer were disagreeing about whether a spiral went up or down. The writer, whom Rollin recognized from the round table (he kept pouring water), was insisting down. "Spiraling down," he said. "Not spiraling up, spiraling down." The sculptor, who was sitting down, shook his head. He had a long strand of grass in his mouth and he said no, a spiral was simply a shape. His name was George, and when her mother said goodbye to him he jumped up and kissed her on both cheeks. He had a funny way of talking.

They got in the car. "Well, I hope your father gets some work done," she said, but there was an edge to her voice which spoke not of hope but of consequences. Sally Ann was remembering when they had gotten the news about her grandmother.

"I can't do it, Sally Ann, can't do it," Lad had said about going to the funeral, as if it would have been a luxury. For him perhaps that was true—Sally Ann had seen long ago that any time away from his work was a luxury, one which he never felt he deserved.

Taking him to Peninghen that summer, Sally Ann had felt a surface envy—it was so beautiful there—but she also had the impression that this was a big hospital, where he could get something he needed that she couldn't give him.

Rollin said nothing. She was thinking about their trip. She was thinking about spirals, what the men had said.

It was the kind of conversation she had always heard late at night. In her childhood men argued about ideas, and when she thought about women arguing about furniture she had the vague notion she was losing something.

The mirror and chest her mother had shipped north arrived some weeks after they got home, betraying nothing of what they had left behind. Her mother and her Aunt Ruth had started arguing the second night and didn't stop for two weeks. Mostly it was about the house, which the church was going to tear down. As Mary Thompkins fought to rebuild the island house, Sadie Forster Birchett had quietly willed this house to the Baptist Church. Rollin hadn't believed that could be true, but now she did. The language made her believe it, the heat and smells of the food. She couldn't believe her father had never been here. It was the past, but it was right here, described more sharply than any life Rollin had ever seen.

"They called me a Yankee," she said to her father when he came home from Peninghen.

Thompkins laughed and squeezed her shoulder and said, "And so you are. So you are."

Chapter 9

○ ○ ○

It had been a shock, that spring, to see the extent of damage done to the island house in storms no harsher than those of previous winters. Sally Ann had imagined fire there, people evacuating the island in droves, the boardwalks burning behind them—but never a house of cards ready to fall. Sally Ann's high heels had caught in the cracks of the boardwalk as they stood in front of the lopsided house, trying to remember the building inspector's name. From the air, the house appeared just slightly out of line, but on the ground one could see the violence: the house torn from its frame (Queen Anne's lace growing up inside the locked front door), beams ripped from the walls, furniture mid-journey across the porch in the downward slide of the house towards the bay.

It was the houses. It was the houses which charted their courses and the houses she blamed: when the island house had fallen, it had sent Sally Ann and Lad in different directions, which had done something to them; and when Lad returned from Peninghen, Sally Ann found herself staying away. She took Rollin to the lake, where the sand was cool and white and damp, so fine, nothing like the coarse gold grains near the ocean. Sharing a beer with Kay Dowling, the waves a distant crash in the strong salty breeze, now seemed only a part of her life's education. Here there was a limp breeze, and the mothers stood in threes at the edge of the gently lapping water, which was yellow at the edges. Rollin said she bet every boy there had peed in it, and they sat there like foreigners who would know better next time.

Sally Ann had vaguely recognized one of the mothers standing in the group, but sitting there she realized she had no real friends here. When they had moved out of the city she had made a feeble attempt at entertaining, but mixing New York people with their new friends had not worked out. She remembered one evening in particular, when she invited a local painter to dinner with "the crowd." It had not worked out because Pauline Dampierre especially had not wanted it to work out. She'd insulted John Stribling by expressing more interest in his regular job—he worked at a denture factory—than in his painting. It was obvious that in part at least she was trying to deflect Douglas's temper as everyone watched Winifred's embarrassing flirtation with the man (even though Douglas and Joan Sugarman were seen disappearing behind Rollin's playhouse). But Pauline was also saying that Sally Ann could not pick a Nolan Perry (or a Lad Thompkins) so she'd best not try, just as John Stribling should stick to teeth. (Pauline's velvet voice uttering, "I would have thought a *sculptor* would have been the man for a job like yours.")

"You get his card?" Douglas said to Winifred when Stribling had gone. "Huh? Fucking pansy if I ever saw one. Jesus—couldn't give a shit if it's the wife who gives him a hand or the husband who gives him a hand." Douglas's laugh, when he was drunk, was piggish. "Wherever the wind blows the money blows, right, the—"

"You're talking about a man's career!" Sally Ann cried, totally missing Douglas's intended brand of humor.

". . . *talking* about a man's sex life," Douglas said and with sudden energy turned and hurled his glass into the fireplace. A quick pitcher's windup, following through to the sound of shattered glass.

Sally Ann was recalling that particular evening because she had run into John Stribling at the framer's in town; but there had been plenty of other nights like that, nights followed up (Joan Sugarman calling Douglas) or not (John Stribling not calling Douglas, as Douglas had dared him to do).

But whatever those nights had been separately, together they had formed a pattern over the years, relieved by the summers, a pattern she now saw jeopardized by a summer which had come to pieces. Women talked about the first child's being easier, and Sally Ann felt that about the first book. There had been a sort of complicity between Lad and her then, which had allowed her to think of herself as part of the creative process or at least important to it. Fitting in chores haphazardly according to how he was working, keeping Rollin quiet and loved, their social life in order—that had been a life which had made her happy. It had been her contribution to priorities they shared. She saw when the book came out and she had nothing that she had mistaken complicity for involvement.

"If it had made a couple of dollars," Thompkins said, shaking his head. Last year at tax time he had tried to make a joke: "Now what was that on royalties? We can't cheat the government out of that. Thirty-six cents? We can't forget that."

Lad had never wanted her to work, though, even for reasons of her own. "I don't blame you," he said about a job at the gallery in town, as if it were just an excuse to get out of the house and had no value of its own.

"You don't blame me? What do you mean, you don't blame me? It's not as if it's a job at the Woolworth's counter, Lad!"

Thompkins wiped a hand over his face and looked out the window. What he had meant was he knew he was hard to live with; how could she be so angry with him when he was so disgusted with himself.

Sally Ann turned away as he reached just short of her, then when she turned back and he saw she was crying, he touched her chin, a shank of hair. "You want so much to be taken seriously, don't you," he said softly.

He was—last week he had gotten a letter from a grad student who was doing his thesis on Thompkins's work. Sally Ann watched as Lad read it, smiled, and put it back in the envelope. He said the boy had read it four times. "I think it's sold about seventy-six copies and then there are thirty-five people who are passing it around," he said. "That makes a total of seventy-seven copies, not including libraries." He said it with a certain self-satisfaction.

She said, "Is that supposed to be funny?"

It was one of those fall afternoons which had gone gray around them until they were sitting in the near-dark, and then he lit a cigarette and the smoke thickened until she could hardly see him at all. When he went out for his walk, she vacuumed. She always waited until now, when other wives were turning on lights to powder their faces to meet the trains. She thought they were lucky and they thought she was, as though Lad were there during the day to fix a faucet or wait for a delivery. They wouldn't imagine that she would never ask him.

The following summer, Rollin remembered her mother that summer as just showered, her hair up as though she'd made her mind up about something. She remembered her father in the suit he had worn the day he left. He had shown Rollin the tape recorder he was going to use to interview German generals, then, with his hair slicked back and darker, he came into focus for one perfect moment before he was gone. She watched as her mother took the good radio from its niche beside the leather chair and put it in the kitchen, and then flowers replaced her father's typewriter on the highly polished table, a huge summer bouquet which magnified the outdoors framed by the picture window.

In the mailbox were postcards of castles high above rivers, crinkly blue airmail envelopes with "USA" underlined twice. Rollin was used to Douglas's erratic postcards, his childish scrawl, but her father's handwriting looked like sticks. The German stamps were heavy on the envelopes, and his return address looked like a frightening place. Her mother read her father's letters in the leather chair, where she never looked quite comfortable. The onionskin made noise as she went on to another page, and when she moved, her skin made a sound as it unstuck from the chair. Often in the confusion of pages she lost one, but instead of picking it up she looked as if she might crumple up the whole thing and throw it in the fireplace.

All this had nothing to do with Jim Dover, but the truth was strange when it didn't matter, and Rollin found it easy to put together later what at the time had been quite innocent, a train ride on a hazy summer morning soon after Thompkins's departure when Sally Ann had taken Rollin into the city to see her grandmother. Jim Dover was simply the father of someone at school, and Rollin had not paid particular attention to her mother's talking to him about Europe and Vermont. The three of them had walked into Grand Central together, where Jim Dover disappeared into the crowd. He walked deliberately, almost mechanically, his newspaper under his arm, his seersucker suit bright in the dim yellow echo of the station.

"He was nice, wasn't he," her mother had said.

"If you like bald men," said Rollin, and she had already forgotten him.

The blowup occurred on a hot day in July. Sally Ann had suggested a picnic, but instead of turning towards the lake she said she had another idea. They were still driving after forty-five minutes and Rollin was hungry.

"Why couldn't we have just gone to the pond?" she whined. "It's too hot to drive around. I'm hungry."

"We'll be there soon," Sally Ann said.

Soon stretched into another twenty minutes, when it was obvious to Rollin that her mother was lost.

"Would you just let me do the driving, please?" she said. "It's not far."

"Great," Rollin said. "That's what you said last summer with Aunt Ruth when we were trying to find that lake." She trailed an arm out the window. "We're probably going in circles, or else we're getting really lost. Do we at least have enough gas to get lost? Couldn't we ask direc—"

"Will you stop nagging me!" Sally Ann cried. "I got you this far, didn't I? You're almost eleven years old and you've never been lost a day in your life, have you? When you were a baby and your father left us out in the middle of nowhere that summer you weren't even a year old, and we came through that, didn't we? I didn't even know how to drive, and who was keeping us from getting lost then?"

"All I said was why can't we stop and get directions!" Rollin cried. "But I guess you can't ask directions when you don't know where you're going, can you!" She threw herself back in the seat and crossed her arms. "If we were at the the island house none of this would be happening!"

"And stop talking to me about the island house!" Sally Ann said. "There's not a damn thing I can do about it, so stop talking about it!"

"Your father says Pauline has joined them," she said a few days later from the leather chair. "Where are they exactly? Do you know? You got a letter from Douglas—he must have said something about their plans."

"He didn't," Rollin said from the doorway.

"Well, honey, I'm sure he did, you just must have forgotten. Let me see the letter."

"No," Rollin said.

Sally Ann looked up, and they looked at each other across the space of light which separated them.

"Rollin, honey."

Rollin stood there. The light shimmered between them, making it impossible for Sally Ann to see the expression on her face. Last night they had gone to the Sugarmans' for dinner, even though Rollin had not wanted to go. The Dovers were there. Mrs. Dover was tall and shrill, and Mr. Dover laughed loudly and wore a wedding ring and had been in World War II, and Rollin had seen him put his hand on her mother's as she reached for a cigarette. She remembered that they had run into Jim Dover on the train earlier in the summer, and she began putting it together as easily as if it had been true all along.

Any of the boys Sally Ann had dated in high school could have grown up to be Jim Dover, a friend of Jim Dover's—not that he was Southern, not at all. It was just that there was something vital and simple about Jim Dover. He was what he was. He had gone to a state school and he worked for the state; he had fought overseas and he smelled like soap, he was a good dancer.

"Get the map out of the dash, would you, Sally Ann? Great. Now let's see where we're headed."

That seemed to be his attitude towards life.

"What do you mean, you've never been camping?" he'd said to her on the train that day, and the scenery behind him had changed through dirty windows from lush green to chopped gray city hardness and glitter, as though to make his point.

Sally Ann remembered how the idea had appealed to her, a tent you put up and took down and folded up at will. None of the problems one had with houses. He said they were trying a new place this year. He had shown her on a map. He loved maps, and there was something animal about the way he held his keys in his mouth while he searched for the river. It had what sounded like an Indian name, and Nancy Dover had giggled last night trying to remember what it was.

It was the houses.

Before Lad had left, they had gotten the official report of the investigation of the island house, which stated what had previously been suspected—that the pilings had rotted and it had only been a matter of time.

"Look like Tara?" Douglas had joked about Peninghen, and then he'd made a comment about how Rollin would make one hell of a

Scarlett O'Hara. "That is, if I've still got it," he said, laughing. "Instead of Yankees camping out there it'll be the IRS!"

Or the church, Sally Ann had thought angrily, resentful of her past and, suddenly, of Rollin's future. These men would always take care of her. Douglas's offer to pay Rollin's way to Europe had been voiced delicately, predicated on the condition of Sally Ann's going, but that in the end had only pointed out that she was keeping Rollin from going. Sally Ann had been furious when Lad had refused to handle the situation and explain it to Rollin, who never should have been told of Douglas's offer.

And now Rollin was holding back the letter, perhaps instinctively, a gesture of protecting her father and Douglas while also showing her mother how it would be. Us against you, she seemed to be saying. Sally Ann knew that. She had known that since Rollin was born.

Shadows patterned the living room as Sally Ann stared at Rollin's portrait, at once more judgmental than the figure which had stood in the doorway moments before. Sally Ann did not know what Jim Dover meant to her. All she knew was that the day she had received the newspaper clipping about the church's intended use of the vacant lot where her grandmother's house had once stood, she had accepted Jim Dover's invitation to lunch and it had led to more even though (perhaps because) she had cried practically the whole time they were together. She had opened her mother's letter in the parking lot of the Grand Union and she did not get to the clipping or the letter (blue stationery, her mother's familiar hand) because the photograph had drawn her attention first: a photograph emptied of the house which had once stood there. Only the low hedge trimming the sidewalk, separated by those three steps where she'd skinned her knee and sat with countless beaux, remained.

"What was the house like?" John Stribling asked her later that afternoon. He leaned on his elbows on the table in the back of the gallery. Tall and sandy-haired, thin, he was easily camouflaged in a room of blond wood and moldings. "Do you remember it very well?"

He was trying to calm her down. She supposed that one had someone one told about something like this, and she had told him.

"Of course I remember it," she said. She was putting on lipstick, and as he pointed out, if she had been lighting a cigarette she would have burned herself. "I was there a year ago," she said. "And of course I sat on that porch hundreds of times, watched parades from the—"

"Then draw it," Stribling said. He slid the clipping across to her. "Go ahead, draw it in. It'll make you feel better."

Sally Ann looked away. Already Jim Dover seemed to exist for her in the memory of one summer day, the shimmering streets and blinding sun, the streaks and points of silver on the Hudson under the Tappan Zee.

The reason they gave themselves and each other for meeting again was a hair clip Lad's mother had given her, and anyway it was too late; Sally Ann had already noticed that the town looked different with him in her life, her own house looked different.

"I don't know Lad's work," he said heartily, and Sally Ann almost shivered in the isolation of their private afternoons. It was partly for this reason—wanting to distance herself—that she was tempted to give up any explanation of her own in favor of what critics had said. She meant to be objective. But parroting their views only made her attitude more reflective of an intellectual snobbism she did not claim and distanced her from whomever she was speaking to.

However, Jim Dover noticed none of the trouble she was having, he cheerily said he really didn't read novels at all. He spoke as if no amount of brilliance could disguise the fact that to sit down and read any novel was a luxury—that after all no novel should be taken seriously. Sally Ann smiled, remembering Pauline talking about Flaubert's desire to write a book about nothing, where style was the content.

1 3 1

When Jim took Nancy and the children to the mountains, she thought she knew the moment—there was a cool breeze through town. She recalled feeling the same way the times her father left— missing him immediately, desperately, blaming herself for something she had said (or Ruth or David) which had precipitated his departure. Then collecting herself, deciding that good or bad, emotions were emotional and there was something good about nothing, the cool breeze through town.

Nothing like the coolness of Lad's return, when he walked in the door and she tried to trace his foreignness to something he wore. But he wore that suit, that same suit; the distance was in his eyes. (There was a foreignness, but it was the money in his pockets, strangely helpful to Thompkins as he looked at Sally Ann.) They stood at the edge of the yard.

Rollin watched from her father's workroom, which was the only room upstairs with a view of the backyard. First they were talking. Then suddenly, her mother slapped her father. Then she was crying and he was just standing there. Her mother started walking away, and her father turned towards where the yard dropped down a steep hill thick with trees. You could see a long way from there, and he looked like he was facing the world. Her mother was walking towards the house.

As the sky turned rose, the room around Rollin grew darker. In front of her hung a picture she had never liked because it had always frightened her. Now it didn't. It was a black and white woodcarving of a boy and an angel. All the carved shapes were like little daggers. Now there was a layer of dust on it from the month which had passed.

Chapter 10

o o o

Perhaps it was the first impulsive thing Thompkins had ever done; and within five minutes the navy-blue Pontiac LeMans convertible was filling with cigarette smoke as he drove up the hill to get Rollin and take her out to Long Island. He had found the house through Douglas, who had kept in touch with a man they'd known in Paris, Harry Carnahan. Rollin looked from her mother to the car, which was used, but this only made it more mysterious as it sat in the driveway reflecting everything so cruelly and grandly. Sally Ann stood out of its way, rubbing the sides of her arms.

It was only that night in unfamiliar surroundings that Rollin thought about what was happening. Her father sat in the only lit corner of the room, smoking and watching her unpack. Her grandmother was asleep in the next room. Rollin was quiet, opening the drawers. Whispering, she asked about the woman who lived in the other half of the house.

"Nice enough," Thompkins said. "I guess there was a family at some point."

She made a comment about the drawer paper and that was all, except that for a moment when Thompkins stood in the doorway it was as though he were saying something else. She didn't know what.

The next night they went to the Carnahans' and Rollin jumped when Harry Carnahan yelled, "Get out!" He pointed to the back of the house, big and old with rambling rooms. "Everywhere I look there are girls, so go make friends!"

Yelling at her father, pointing at Thompkins as he headed for the bookshelf. "You've said it all, so you shut up! You can't fool me! He can't fool me—I was there! Can't tell me you didn't expect to sell it by the pound!" Passing Thompkins a whiskey as he cringed in a couch corner, bringing him his book as he sat trapped in a wing chair. "Remember? Page four fifty-one? Ha! Ha ha!"

Obediently Rollin had followed Misty Carnahan upstairs to her room, where the television went all the time, apparently. A year or so older than Rollin, Misty was blond, and in a low voice she recited the recipe for vodka martinis as they went through the kitchen.

Rollin would remember the Carnahans' living room, the Rileys' living room, better than the one on Highland Street. The bright rugs at the Carnahans', the pictures which hung crookedly, as though Harry Carnahan (his daughters called him Harry) had gestured once too grandly. At the Rileys' every surface rested on delicate legs, like Mrs. Riley, who was nervous and had money, and called her daughter Darling Ann.

"But where did they all come from?" Rollin asked.

"Indeed," Thompkins said, laughing.

Rollin made her bed every night on the porch. Her father had the alcove at the back of the house, Only her grandmother, in the side room off the living room, had a real bedroom with a door that closed. But it didn't matter, for Rollin was never there in the daytime. That was the summer she played telephone jokes with Misty and Ann, and Monopoly when it rained; the summer her father read aloud to her from the *Iliad*. She did learn to swim, finally; Misty's mother taught her. Mrs. Carnahan was a square sturdy woman from Chicago who hadn't seen the ocean until she was seventeen. "After those lakes I had a horrible time," she said to Rollin. "The ocean had a mind of its own and I wasn't going to get out alive."

The island house seemed very far away. She remembered shells in that ocean, and here they collected stones, more round or more oblong in shades of gray and sunset. After tumbling in the rock polisher they were perfect, except for one, a smoky stone with a red vein running through it. She had seen it wet on the beach, and when it dried it was dull. Now, polished, the vein stood out. The stone was more beautiful because of the imperfection.

"Sort of like that thing in your eye," John Riley said.

John was Anne's older brother, and Rollin blushed and didn't know why.

"No, no, you go ahead," the woman across the hall had said about the rock polisher. "It was my son's years ago and now it just sits in the closet. Please." According to Misty, her son had been killed in Vietnam. She handed Thompkins the rock polisher. "I warn you, though, Mr. Thompkins, it does make a racket!"

"Awfully kind of you," Thompkins said.

August, then. Light and airy dashes in from the beach for an apple, back and forth between the Carnahans' and the Rileys' and the house on Highland Street. Her father working in the room where Rollin slept; all day, his typewriter going and the sound of the rock polisher turning, the constant sound of something spilling. All August, the dim light in the side room where her grandmother stayed, slept even with the noise of the typewriter and the rock polisher and her transistor. August. The word sounded to Rollin like dust, dust falling in a yellow room. August sounded like her father.

Never before or again would Rollin see him as she did that summer, because it was a new way of seeing him which concerned her especially, herself and her father and the world. He was alone suddenly, unprotected and protective; and neither had she ever watched him so closely. She watched him with men and women, children and waitresses and gas station attendants. For the first time she wondered at his being a writer; she knew he'd been called brilliant but she could not connect his seriousness with writing, with characters, imaginary people.

He didn't say much about her mother.

"Your mother thinks I didn't want her in Europe. I wanted you both there, but it wasn't possible. I had a room. I ate with the tape recorder going." He talked in short sentences, and she believed him.

"You never visit anymore," her grandmother said from her bed. Near night, as the side room grew dark, she seemed to fill it. Even during the day the room was in shadow, nothing like on the island where the sun streamed in all day. "You love it here, I can tell," she said to Rollin accusingly. The room was filled with smoke, and she was propped up against her pillows. In a frustrated search for something on the night table, crowded with a lamp, her transistor, postcards, her pillbox, an ashtray, a lighter, and glasses, she knocked the transistor off onto the floor. "Damn."

"What are you looking for?" Rollin said. She bent to retrieve the radio and was replacing a battery which had fallen out and rolled under the dusty bed.

"You don't have to visit if it's just to pick up after me," her grandmother said, and for the next few days Rollin stayed away. But she could hear the false cheer of the radio as she walked by, and one day as she passed she could see her grandmother through the crack in the door. She was centered in the stale air, her wild white hair frozen on the pillow, an ashtray balanced on her chest.

Rollin knocked, and the blue eyes came alive, and quickly and furtively the ashtray found a place on the night table.

"We could go for a walk," Rollin said.

Her grandmother looked at the door.

Instead, Rollin wrote letters for her grandmother.

"I'll be back here like the grand duchess, and you're my social secretary," her grandmother said.

It was her grandmother who said Rollin must write to her mother, and after the day at Shelter Island, she tried. But when she reread the letter it wasn't quite right. Something was missing. That day had been the only day she'd seen her godfather all summer; and even though while it was happening the day was alive, each incident distinct, it fell apart when she tried to describe it. The sailboat, a ketch, had belonged to Mr. Riley, and they had sailed it to an island called Shelter Island, where they had been invited for lunch. Douglas had been there, and Rollin wondered if perhaps the strangeness came from being used to seeing him on the island. There had been a baseball game on and the house had many windows, and Douglas kept checking to see if the beers were cold. The weather wasn't so nice—the air was soft and light gray. Rollin didn't remember the island, just the house. The windows. She remembered the house better than the people.

She figured. it out later, years later. Winifred hadn't been there, and Douglas had been different, and it wasn't just that his hair was lighter or thinner or that he'd gained weight or that they weren't at the island house. It was a house of strangers—an older woman dressed too brightly, her two daughters, all people who knew each other from somewhere else. Douglas sat watching the game. All afternoon Rollin had hovered in his peripheral vision, watching him reach for the sweating cans of beer. His watch was familiar and his glasses and the way he laughed, but he was distracted. He joked with the two girls, but otherwise his attention was on the game.

What it was was that she had changed. She had grown to an awkward age where she had to compete for his attention, which she had never had to do before.

"Douglas? I learned to swim," she said.

"Hey! Go, go, go!" he cried to the television.

"Don't you believe me? Come tomorrow and I'll show you."

"Yeah? Great," he said.

That was the closest to a conversation they had the whole day. Douglas didn't sail back with them, and looking at the island from the stern of the boat Rollin imagined never seeing him again. He had made a big production of saying goodbye until someone had shouted that it was the bottom of the eighth and then he ran back inside. Something of that afternoon hardened in her. When she got braces that fall she didn't even want to see Douglas, she was acutely aware of catching herself between those girls as she had once or twice in the mirror that day, their long hair, their tan knees touching his as he played with the beer cans.

"Douglas Kipps wishes he was a great writer," Misty said one day when they were walking to the beach. "And I *know* he has affairs because my mother thinks he's an asshole. Harry thinks it's funny, but that's only because he's an asshole and he wishes he was doing it."

"That's awful, to talk about your father like that," Ann Riley said.

Rollin said nothing. That summer her father was demystified, but Douglas, turning away from her in a strange house, became more oblique. He had always presented his life so that she could ask questions: "And where do you go after that? Did you get breakfast trays all the time?" They were questions which knew no bounds, but now she was growing up and watching those bounds change.

When she and her father arrived home, her mother had moved out, and her father led the way through the half-empty house out to the yard. It was early fall, late afternoon, and the sun was warm. She looked up at him. He had taught her that the world was large but small. That they could leave the island house and find their world somewhere else.

He said, "It was a good little house, wasn't it?" He was talking about her playhouse. A shutter had come loose and the roof had warped so that it held berries and twigs. "The only thing I've ever built," he said, and he was talking about the shutters when he said, "The stars were easy—all angles. But I had the damnedest time cutting out those hearts."

It was John Stribling who hauled Rollin's portrait out from behind a bureau in the cottage.

"There," he said, stepping back.

Rollin couldn't help smiling. She started to explain why the portrait hadn't been finished, but he shrugged. "It's a lovely picture," he said.

"Did you know him?" Rollin asked.

"Met him," John said, and they both looked back at the painting.

"It doesn't really look like me," Rollin said.

"Sure it does," he said. "And anyway that isn't the point." He asked her if he could try a sketch. "Just while you're helping your mother there?" he said. He was still looking at the painting, his head tilted.

Rollin looked down at her dirty sweatshirt.

"It doesn't matter what you're wearing," he said.

The "sketches" John Stribling did were like cartoons, He used a thick black Magic Marker and he drew quickly, looking up and down. There were hardly any lines in the drawings at all, but they looked like her. Within fifteen minutes he had produced no less than thirty-five drawings. Even the mole in her eye didn't bother Rollin—it was like a punctuation. It made her look like somebody.

"I love them!" she said.

John laughed. He stacked them by the phone, weighing them down with a tile ashtray she had made in second grade. "If you don't like them just pitch them," he said when he left. He kissed her mother on the forehead and she blinked, and he said, "And do me a favor and find a place for that painting. On a wall."

But the walls of the cottage were not strong enough to hang a painting like that, not to mention the fact that between the low ceilings and amount of furniture there was no room for a life-size portrait. In fact the cottage Sally Ann had rented looked more like a trailer with a porch attached to the front. It shared the back wall of the Fishers' garage on Briar Lane, but the land was terraced so that the long graveled steps curved gently down around forsythia bushes to the front door, which looked out on a meadow of wild strawberries. Inside, it was damp. The linoleum which spread from the kitchen up into Rollin's room was black with bright spots, like jewels stuck in a sea of tar, and was no help. Sally Ann slept in the living room, crowded with the piano, a couch, a dresser, and lamps and tables of various sizes and heights which spilled out onto the screened-in porch. Rollin's old giraffe stood between the piano and the dresser and the cat slept on top of the refrigerator. The dog had insomnia at night, and walked the length of the rooms. It was like a zoo, or a storage warehouse. That was how Rollin felt sometimes: as if she were being stored until they decided what to do with her.

Neglect buried things at the cottage, but at her father's there was always a fine layer of dust on the slate coffee table. Rollin saw her father on Wednesdays and part of each weekend. Once when she arrived he wasn't there, and she walked around the house aimlessly until she realized she had come on the wrong day. She stood for a moment in the hall in a shaft of light and looked up into the twist of stairs, and it was then that she had a vague sense of not belonging—a feeling that the atmosphere was no longer one of waiting, but of an empty house. A Tuesday in her father's life was not her business. He could come home with a woman in the car. This had occurred to her in town, that when she was not with him he was a stranger. Once she had gone into Freeman's and he had just left. Mr. Freeman had smiled at Rollin and said, "Oh, he decided to take them after all?" At Rollin's confused expression he realized his error and recovered himself, leaving her straining with curiosity at what her father had not bought.

Her mother's life was anything but a mystery. She played Frank Sinatra records, she wore bright red lipstick. John Stribling had gotten her a job at the gallery, and every now and then the three of them had pizza in the back room. Usually, though, John liked to sit in the kitchen and watch her mother do the dishes and talk. They never went anywhere, except once the dam overflowed and they went to see that.

Mr. Dover didn't come over very often, but sometimes by the way her mother looked or acted Rollin could tell she had seen him. It wasn't that Rollin didn't like him as much as it was that she didn't like her mother when he was around. She always looked like she was hoping something, and she seemed to wait to laugh at special things he said.

In spring he came over more often. Once they went mountain climbing, and when they came home, Mr. Dover took a shower, which he had never done there before. The cottage was small, and the sound of the water rushed between Rollin and her mother, who was smoking a cigarette and looking out at the field. Something had changed.

The last time John Stribling came over, he did the same kind of drawings of their living room as he had done of Rollin. Fascinated, Rollin watched over his shoulder as he glanced up at the room, down at the page, skimming it with the broad tip of the Magic Marker. (Another time he'd done a drawing of just the ashtray, filled with cigarette butts, but it was so abstract you couldn't tell right away what they were.) The big chest of drawers, the mirror, the upright piano and its skyline of clutter—everything became a shape, even the guitar and the record rack, the dog, the trunk, a lamp. The bedspread he defined as loose design—no edges—and some things he ignored completely. "Elimination, selection," he murmured. Details like the piano and flower petals were delicate scribbles, and the confusion on Sally Ann's dresser he amassed into a treasure. "Just give everything a purpose," he said. Then he stopped. He threw the pad over onto the daybed, and sighed, and stretched.

Rollin never saw him again. It occurred to her when she missed him that perhaps he had taken the place of Douglas, whom she had not seen for a long time. For her birthday a huge box had arrived. It had sat in the living room for days, until she opened it, when each box yielded a smaller one and she opened a tiny box with a topaz ring in it. Boxes and wrapping filled the small living room, and her mother had been annoyed, as if Douglas had used the occasion to point out how small her house was.

That spring there was an article on Peninghen in the *New York Times Magazine*—an article, and pictures of the buildings and grounds and Douglas; the picture Rollin recognized of him at Harvard in a top hat, although no one had ever mentioned the word "overseer" to her. (The picture referred to something going on at Harvard having to do with a poet and the war; apparently he was supposed to receive an honorary degree but he had refused an invitation to the White House because he was against the war, and Harvard thought if they awarded him a degree it would be seen as backing his position—and Douglas had gone against this.) There was also a picture of the huge sculpture which had been erected in the turnaround, and a picture of an artist's studio, a largish room with a sink at one end.

It was one day in late spring that Sally Ann took the portrait to Peninghen, alone. Rollin was at Lad's and would be furious, Sally Ann knew, but this was something she wanted to do on her own. She'd considered giving the portrait back to Lad, but she wanted to take it to Douglas and she wanted to see it hang there, almost desperately. The painting was heavy and awkward, but Ed Fisher helped her. They got it up the steps, wrapped in a mattress pad, and slid it into the back of the car, covering it like a body. The roads were smooth and it didn't move, but Sally Ann felt its presence, as though the girl lying down might sit up. Peninghen was a two-and-a-half-hour drive, and all Sally Ann had had was a Coke—she'd always relied on Hershey bars for energy, but she couldn't keep them down anymore. It had been the same with Rollin. She drove, she turned on the radio, she turned onto country roads which reminded her of that spring Lad was gone and she'd just learned to drive.

Two hours later she turned off Route 413 and the road narrowed, a hall through great trees. Her heart beat faster with each curve, and as the car tipped through the gates a thrill of sadness went through her, as if she were going home. There was the smell of lilac, a song she loved, the headiness of what she saw: Peninghen spread in front of her with a beauty and grace she'd forgotten. To her left was the Nell Dayton sculpture, turning as the car turned, metal flashing in sun for half a second of pure danger: blinded, she almost hit the car approaching the turnaround from the opposite direction. Still shaking, Sally Ann guided the car into the shade and sat for a moment. She looked back at the sculpture. The big challenge, she remembered, had been to keep as many trees as possible, as apparently trees had inspired the piece. She heard voices, and then nothing. She'd read somewhere that the poet Rosemary Walter was here.

She had started towards the main building when she heard her name.

"Mrs. Thompkins?"

Sally Ann turned to face an efficient-looking young girl, who said that Mr. Kipps was waiting for her. Sally Ann followed the girl down the shiny hall and up some stairs. Puffed white light came in through the leaded windows, and it was true—the painting would be incredible here.

"Well. Sally Ann," Douglas said, turning. He had been standing at the window like a true headmaster waiting for a tardy student. Sally Ann said something to that effect as the girl closed the door.

"And the sculpture and—everything," she said. "And I see you've planted roses. And the hedge! The tiny—"

He said, "I hope you know what the fuck you're doing."

Sally Ann blinked and looked away from him. "The painting's in the car," she said softly. "If you'll have someone—"

"There's time," Douglas said. "There's time." He sat sideways on the massive desk, one foot on the ground. There wasn't time, she wanted to tell him, but she couldn't. She fooled with her sunglasses. "That piece in the *Times* was quite something," she murmured, but he laughed it off.

"Oh, you know. Weren't even sure they were going to run it till the last minute." He was looking at her intently, as if he were trying to remember something. Then in a nervous gesture he rapped on the desktop. "So, where did you park?" he said. He said he'd send the grounds people for the painting. "What? You locked it?" he said, laughing. "This is the last place someone would steal a painting, Sally Ann, for Christ's sake!"

There had been the old Douglas, long enough to remind her. He offered her a sherry and she said no, she'd like a glass of water. He went over to a cabinet. "I thought you'd bring Rollin with you," he said. "A Saturday—I was looking forward to seeing her." He set the glass of water down in front of her. "Don't see her very often these days."

"That's not my fault," Sally Ann said.

Douglas laughed and said of course it wasn't her fault. He went back around and sat behind the desk and propped his feet up and said, "Jesus, you're trouble." He leaned back in the chair towards the open window, hands locked behind his head. "I remember when I met you," he said. "Ten years ago? No, Rollin's almost twelve now, isn't she? One of those smoky parties I made Lad go to and there you were and I knew you were trouble, I knew. But there are some kinds of good trouble. Lad said that, poor son of a bitch. Don't get angry, come on." He got up again, shaking his head. "Come on, Lad's got the brains and the what shall we say—instinct for self-preservation. And Winifred's got the money," he said, looking up at her suddenly. "And we just float around, don't we, you and me? In the middle of it all, like the sentimental part of the brain. Like memory." He laughed shortly. "Kind of float around, fuck around—"

She slapped him finally, her heart beating from years of wanting to.

He said in a level tone, "I don't think you know what the hell you're doing, that's all, and I'm trying to make you mad enough to think about it. That's all. Because no one else will. Don't you realize—" His voice had gone up an octave.

"Oh, Douglas," Sally Ann said, tears running down her cheeks. He was right. She had always had the impression that the fights she had with him were fights she wanted to have with Lad. But now it was too late, and she pulled away. "I don't have the choice," she said. "It doesn't matter if what you're doing is wrong, or bad, if you don't have the choice." She laughed softly. "I really thought we could talk today. I wanted to tell you about the gallery where I'm working—oh, it's just a little gallery in town, but somehow—" She shook her head. "Anyway that's over now too, so—" She looked down and he relaxed his grip on her arm, perhaps now realizing the gravity of her situation. "Please, now. Let me go," she whispered.

Douglas nodded. A slight breeze came in when he opened the door. Someone far down the hall waved and approached, saying something about the gallery. A black man and a young man with a ponytail met Sally Ann at the car and took the painting. "Heavy mother," he said. Then she left. A ways down the road, she saw a woman unloading a paint-spattered car with a broken taillight. She remembered when she'd come to get Lad that summer and Douglas had torn his pants helping Nell Dayton load the prototype of her piece into the car. (They had fought, according to Lad, and she had threatened to cancel it.) Furious, Douglas said she shouldn't make something so goddam big it wouldn't fit in the goddam car. Nell Dayton had answered coolly that usually she had nothing to do with that end of it—the transporting of pieces, she said, was always handled by professionals and always insured. "But of course you don't know a fuck of a thing about this business!" she said. "I have pieces at the Whitney—do you think I need this crap from you?"

"I don't give a goddam if you have pieces at the Whitney or on the moon," Douglas had said, "and when a cop stops you for your broken taillight he's not going to care either. He's not going to care whether you're making the gates of heaven!" And with that he'd grabbed one of her tools from the trunk and smashed her taillight.

And then they started to laugh. They'd been drinking buddies all summer, and Douglas slung his arm around her and said, "You've got some fuck of a vocabulary, Miss Dayton. I'd be damned pleased if you'd join me in a beer."

The car seemed lighter without the painting, and Sally Ann was hardly out of the gates when she started to cry. She stopped. What, after all, had she expected? A few times in the past he had sided with her, agreeing that Lad needed to "loosen up," as he put it. But he always knew how to play within the limits, and the point was that if Lad had done what Sally Ann had done, Douglas would have distanced her anyway. When he had offered her money for the painting and Sally Ann had refused, he had laughed. "Trying to restore your honor?" Douglas had joked on the phone, and it had been all Sally Ann could do not to hang up on him. She couldn't be humble, she was too afraid. And didn't that count for anything, being afraid? "Up north" had always meant New York to Sally Ann, and Jim had gotten a job in Massachusetts. What did she know about Massachusetts? And Rollin: what happened to children? Once in the old house Sally Ann had given one of those dinners which ended punctually before the last train into the city. The usual people were there—Pauline, Douglas and Winifred, a painter Pauline had brought, and a journalist someone knew. Pauline had just seen her daughter for the first time in years, and had told a rather touching story about Mathilde as a child. She had been mystified by the stars. She thought they didn't like her, because they came out after she'd gone to sleep. How could Pauline have let her go? How could mothers ever leave their children or let them go in the world? Sally Ann had gone up to check on Rollin and what she saw broke her heart. The door was open and the private world which greeted her away from the dinner and noise made her want to weep. Moonlight shone in on Rollin's bed on a pile of money she was counting. She had a cash register bank which wouldn't open until ten dollars had been deposited, but Rollin had found that the French francs Douglas had given her passed for quarters, so when she wanted to get her money out that was how she did it. So what Sally Ann heard as she stood in the hallway was the *ping*! of the cash register, and why did it tear at her so? Pauline Dampierre's daughter had grown up far away, following her father through foreign countries where he drew cartoons and painted handkerchiefs, did anything so that they could ski in the winters and summer on the Riviera. Mathilde had been eight, younger than Rollin, when her grandmother pulled her through the window and out across the snowy fields to escape her mother and the police on the other side of the door. And now that that girl had grown up, was she all right?

What will you become? Sally Ann had thought when she'd gazed at Rollin as a baby. "Why were you doing that? What will become of you?" she'd cried last week when she'd found Rollin smoking a cigarette. That night, half in sleep, it occurred to Sally Ann that this baby would be a girl. That the girl lying in the back of the car under the sheet would be replaced, or think she had been replaced, and it would all fall apart from there.

Chapter 11

o o o

Jim Dover climbed mountains on weekends and his work boots shook the floors at home, these were his strengths. He had replaced one household with another, but this had done nothing to alter his exuberant if limited attitude towards daily life. Every morning he rose at five-thirty and walked through the house, turning on two lights downstairs. He walked back and forth, back and forth in his khakis and big red sweater; he wore his work clothes for hours as he pushed the night into dawn. He fed the cat and the dog, and then he made his own breakfast of grapefruit and cereal and toast, eggs and coffee; and it didn't matter who was asleep upstairs. At the breakfast table he listened to his transistor radio, which he afterwards carried up to the bathroom. If it had snowed during the night, he shoveled before showering, Rollin could see him from her window, a red knit toboggan darting about in the bluish snow. At some point before daylight he made his lunch, which he carried to work in a brown paper bag.

"State-salary lunch," he always announced, holding up the bag. By six-thirty in the evening he had changed back into his work clothes, and looked forward to the time after dinner when he stood in front of the television watching hockey. Between periods he went out to the woodpile, turning out lights on his way and calling out, "Anyone in here? No? Turn out the lights for God's sake!"

1 4 8

Sally Ann's mother, when she visited, alternated between disbelief and laughter. "Anyone else would want to see where they was going," she said. "Looks to me like he'd be turning on the lights."

Rollin hated mountain climbing, which only seemed to provide another opportunity to implement a system of rules and checkpoints. She had gone once or twice to please her mother, but after the last time vowed she'd never go again. Jim's children, Danny and Hilary, had been visiting, and it was a long climb, and on the way home all Rollin could think about was her dirty hair and her homework. Her mother handed around the usual peanut-butter-cheese crackers, and then announced that there wasn't any water left.

"Good," Jim had said. "Now we won't have to stop at any rest rooms."

Jim had an album of pictures taken at view points. All the pictures looked the same: wavy gray stripes, purplish, some sky. That was why there was an introductory page for each mountain—because they all looked the same. Recorded was the location and then information about distance and gas and weather and who cared? What, Rollin wondered, would he do with it all finally—add up the elevations to see how high he'd climbed in his life? One weekend after Amy was born Danny and Hilary came up and he took them climbing. Granny T. stood with Rollin at the door, shaking her head and trying not to laugh as Jim loaded the car.

"You reckon he thinks if he goes high enough, it'll all add up to heaven?" she said.

"You can do anything you want to, Rollin, once we reach the summit," Jim said when Rollin had gone with them. "I'd be glad to see you doing some drawing." As if he owned the mountain! He talked about nature constantly, but to Rollin, walking in the woods with her father, sometimes coatless, perhaps getting lost (they didn't do it often), was much more natural than taking an Instamatic to the top of a mountain. With her father, they always walked as far as the fallen cherry tree, where he smoked a cigarette. So what if she got a sore throat? So what if her shoes were wrong and she slid on dead leaves?

Rollin remembered thinking, the night they drove to Massachusetts after the moving van left, that Jim imagined himself as a pioneer. They took two cars, and Rollin could tell that her mother was afraid. He told them where to sit, Granny T. packed in like another piece of luggage on her first trip that far north. Ropes securing the roof rack formed Xs on the windows.

"Ready? There," he said, and slammed the car doors one final time.

Granny T. burst into hysterical laughter. "Oh, law," she said. "I've got to go to the ladies' room. I don't reckon he'll let me out, though, do you?" Tears ran down her cheeks as she jabbed Rollin in the ribs.

Her mother said the house reminded her of a house Pauline had had once, by the sea.

"Wouldn't it be wonderful if it were by the sea," she said dreamily, like a new bride with hope.

It was an old farmhouse with weathered shingles about an hour from Boston. Rollin had seen pictures of it, and if it was not bad enough that they didn't own it, she was horrified to learn that they were going to share it.

The Jacquettes were Canadian, and when Mr. Jacquette wasn't working at the curling rink he was drinking. One day soon after they'd moved in Rollin was waiting for the mail and he appeared around the side of the house before she could duck inside.

"Too bad they're different, eh?" he said. All the Jacquettes talked that way, ending their sentences with "eh?" Rollin realized he was looking up at the curtains. His breath was foul. "If your mum and Mrs. Jacquette got together we could make it look like one rich happy family lived here like the Powells up the hill there."

He laughed—an awful rasping laugh. Rollin didn't, she looked up at the windows. Exactly half of them—the upstairs and half the downstairs—had white organdy curtains. Her eyes traveled to their part of the house, where the curtains varied radically in pattern and color. When Granny T. had announced that her first project would be to hem those partridge curtains in the dining room, Rollin's mother said no, what good would that do, the wrong-length curtains in the next house.

"What are you thinking of, the next house?" Granny T. had said. "You keep waiting on the next house and you'll never have anything."

The organdy curtains had come in cellophane packages. Her father was a writer who had just gotten a Guggenheim. Mr. Jacquette had a tooth missing. Her godfather was a millionaire.

Even her thoughts sounded like lies.

Mary Jacquette had looked at Rollin as if she were crazy when Rollin showed her the article in the *New York Times Magazine*, and Rollin didn't blame her. This man, sitting in a club chair in a room lined with books, a room with leaded windows and a zebra rug— this was her godfather? Mary's dresses cost $3.99 at J. M. Fields, and if Rollin lived downstairs from her what possible connection could exist with a man like that?

Every morning before school Rollin hesitated in front of her mother's door. The baby was due in March, and Sally Ann stayed in bed a good deal, in the dark. Rollin stood for a moment in the doorway as her eyes focused towards the bluish light which came in under the shade. She could see the folds in the clothes on chairs and the papers on Jim's desk; she could see the brass fittings on his bureau, on top of which were pennies and keys and a trophy. Her mother's voice came to her warm and thick with sleep, dazed with the accent Douglas said sounded as if she'd had an easy life.

"You ready for school, honey? You're not wearing too much makeup, are you, sweetie? Promise me—" she whispered like a last wish. She always wanted to know about the weather, and one morning Rollin told her a snowstorm was predicted.

"I know," she said. "That's all Jim's been talking about." Sally Ann was afraid of snow, the Southern part of her, she said. It was as though Amy, born prematurely, was born out of fear.

A baby was exhausting. Rollin hadn't realized. She was fragile, and yet she screamed. Rollin moved into the back room, where the Jacquettes were like people living inside her head, but she didn't care. Anything to get away from the screaming. Amy's skin was soft and there was a soft spot on the top of head, but her arms were rubbery. Handling her required a dexterity Rollin would not have imagined of her mother and certainly not of Granny T. These past months that Granny T. had been living with them, Rollin had gotten used to her tucked in a corner sewing, or carrying a pimiento cheese towards the television. But she held Amy with one hand and bathed her with the other, scolding and soothing in a language which had seen it all before. "Now you hush, hear? And let your mama get some rest."

Amy slept, her fists like little unopened flowers. They had to be quiet. Jim had to keep the television down and his voice low and the heat up. The house was still a mess, but things which had to do with Amy were clean and simple, like the shapes of her toys. At twelve, Rollin was acutely aware of the mole in her eye, her braces, and the chicken-pox scar on her cheek; and looking at the perfect face, waxen in sleep, she could not believe that she had ever looked like this. For the first months of Amy's life, Rollin heard crying in the middle of the night, and then her mother's voice. She was singing. That was most amazing. Her mother's patience, the strangeness of this being her mother's child.

Perhaps once a month, Rollin went down to see her father. Thompkins had moved into a small house with knotty-pine walls, windows which looked out into a wooded distance. The house belonged to an older couple, and of course Rollin knew what belonged to them—she knew that the bird decanter belonged to the Neeleys, as did the etching of a church and various pieces of furniture. The Icarus woodcarving and the Egyptian wall hanging did not. Rollin was intrigued as she watched women who found themselves in that living room examine these clues to her past, her father's past, as though they were clues to the future. Such objects lay in camouflage to these women, however; Rollin noticed a woman named Joyce Reece give the same tender attention to the bird decanter as she did to a small stone dog from the pink house. It was sad, somehow, that none of them got closer to her father than that.

The fall Stuart was born, Rollin watched her mother focusing more inward as the world moved on without her. As the household grew, weekends at her father's became more important to Rollin, but there was no easy transition between the two households. Arriving at her father's, she was tired and nervous; there was a part of her which could not forget the diapers and tiny hands and electric sockets. She could move slowly in her father's quiet world, she could sleep late and leave doors open and knives out; but a weekend was never enough. Still in her mind was the life she'd left behind, where good manners were not as important as reflexes, where what you had to say was not as important as closing the basement door.

At least to some extent her mother realized this—Rollin was surprised, after her mother's criticisms of Douglas, to be allowed to visit Peninghen in the summer.

She could hardly believe it when she stepped off the train early one evening at the end of June and saw Douglas waiting for her. Waving to him, she suddenly felt that her whole life had been sad up until this very moment.

But that night, the night of her arrival at Peninghen, Douglas had too much to drink and carried on and told stories about when she was a child. Rollin was mortified. She had felt grown up when he had met her at the train, and now she felt like a child. A child among strangers: at the table were Ben Ocko and Bunny Parks, who were painters, and a writer named Peter Haas. A composer named Max Truly, a sculptor named Ruell—Rollin didn't catch all the names, and rather than mix them up she stayed quiet. Except for Ruell, with his ponytail and lankiness, they intimidated her.

". . . pianist, a friend of PD's I think"—this was what Douglas had taken to calling Pauline, much to her annoyance—"anyway, he was going on about a piece, some concerto dedicated to a guy who'd had an arm shot off in the war—Christ, I don't know, help me here, Max, Ravel? A piece written for the left hand, that's the point, and I'll never forget it. You"—he looked at Rollin and grinned—"were listening to us talk and you got it all wrong, thought it could only be played by a guy with one arm!"

There was laughter and Douglas laughed and shook his head and said, "Oh, you were great. Now what about some croquet?" he said. "Bunny, come on. Rollin, let's go."

The following day he announced that he had arranged tennis lessons for her. She protested, but he insisted. "I fell in love with Winifred watching her play tennis, tennis is part of our social fabric," he said. They were sitting on the stone wall. (Rather Rollin was sitting on the stone wall; Douglas was standing with one foot up on the stone wall.) "What are you, thirteen?" he said. He looked at her for another moment. "You ever—ever think about going away to school?"

Rollin looked up at him. "No. Why?" she said.

"We'll have to talk about things," Douglas said, "when I get back."

"Get back from where? Where are you going?" she said.

In his office Rollin sat in a dark-green leather chair (she had thought they'd be dark-red) as he sat half on his desk, one foot on the floor. "I'll be back," he said. "Just something in town that can't wait. Okay? Your room okay? You need anything?"

"No, but where—"

He reached across the desk into a drawer and handed her a folded fifty-dollar bill. "Just a few days," he said. "Think that'll be enough?" he said, joking.

"What about my tennis lessons?" she said.

"I thought you said you didn't want tennis lessons," he said.

She never spent the money because she was too embarrassed to break a fifty-dollar bill: how could you pay for an ice cream cone with fifty dollars?

When he had been gone three days and then four, Rollin pretended she had known.

"It was so great of Douglas to trust me and let me stay here alone," she said to Lucy, the big black woman who took care of the kitchen.

Lucy shook her head energetically. "Always going, going, going," she said. "He's here, he wants to be there. Wherever you go, that's where you'll be, but that's something he just don't understand."

Rollin played croquet with Ruell and Bunny Parks, and Peter Haas taught her backgammon. One night she joined a group going to the Charlie Chaplin festival. It wasn't a bad time. Peninghen was a beautiful place, and everyone was nice to her. It was quiet. Sometimes the quiet echoed in her ears. It was summer, and as as she stood at the top of the steps on the terrace facing the Great Lawn at twilight, there was a serenity about the scene which in her words was "old-fashioned." Or there was the view from her window in early morning, when a mist enshrouded the maze and the man who walked there at that hour, a quite thin man with a hook nose whom she was told was a poet, seemed to completely disappear. His name was Mr. Brandy. She had seen him the first night at dinner, and then only twice, from a distance.

"What's *un*believable is how seriously they take themselves," Douglas had confided in her. "Their fucking egos could hold up the whole building!"

One day, she went to Ruell's studio. His sculpture mystified her, and the only question she could think to ask him as she walked around a box which leaned was how did he get to be a sculptor anyway.

Ruell Pullman leaned against the wall, arms crossed, amused. He liked to tell this story. He lit a cigarette, striking the match on his belt. "It was kind of like this," he said. "I got sick of working in this restaurant, where I carved birds out of ice and melons." He said to her through smoke, "Kind of a drag when everything you make melts or gets eaten, you know? I mean, I'm not even talking about posterity, man, I'm talking about tomorrow."

He walked around the room in long strides, nodding at the box. Then he gave it a little kick. "My first show, man, and Andy won't even be there."

He said Andy was his brother, and he was up in Canada. Immediately Rollin pictured Mr. Jacquette. Otherwise she didn't know much about Canada except that it was where all the good hockey players came from.

"What's he doing there?" she said.

Ruell pointed to a pamphlet Rollin had noticed tacked on the wall. "Escape from Freedom!" he said. "At the border, the applicant should appear neat. Conventional dress and hairstyle should be worn. The applicants who are most successful present themselves as good middle-class persons determined to work hard and be a credit to their new country." He stopped. Rollin looked from him to the pamphlet and back at him again. He shook his head and ground out his cigarette with a black boot. "Can you imagine? Can you imagine how it feels to be forced to go to another country because *your* country is ready to send you to die? Otherwise you go to jail. Go to jail, do not pass Go, get fined ten thousand bucks." He laughed shortly. "Irony of it is the money probably goes right back into it."

Into what, Rollin wondered. She sighed. People were always talking about the war. Now he was talking about a sculpture about the war.

"Land of the free and home of the brave, he calls it," Ruell said.

"And it's a coffin? You can't make a sculpture of a coffin. A coffin's a coffin."

"It's the interpretation you put on it," Ruell said. "You know, the context. And you've got to see it. It's—" He set his hands in the air. They were nice hands, full of veins. "Okay, it's black—crude—you know, because he made it. Built it. You realize that.

It's not just some coffin he picked up at the undertaker's, right? And so inside—you know those wooden dolls, you open one there's another inside and another inside that one? I think they're Russian. Well, that's it. That's his concept." He looked at Rollin for some sign of comprehension, but there was none. "One coffin inside another, don't you see? Because war is people. Not countries. Not just soldiers, but people—women and children!" His voice had risen and Rollin was embarrassed.

"And someone bought that?" she said.

"No, no. Museum stuff," he said.

"You went to *Bonnie and Clyde* with a twenty-eight-year-old man?" her mother said. "Rollin, tell me!"

"He was nice!" Rollin said. "We also went to Charlie Chaplin." What could she say—that she had asked Ruell for a cigarette and he had said no and that proved he was nice? "He was like an older brother," she said. "We talked about the war."

Sally Ann had crossed the room and was searching madly in the overflowing desk for her address book.

"Mom, please don't call. I'll die if you do that. I'll feel like such a fool," Rollin said.

"You are certainly not a fool," her mother said. The phone was on her lap and she was dialing. "I am, for having allowed you to go in the first place."

"I wish I'd stayed there and never come home," Rollin said miserably, remembering the farewell tea, the smell of turpentine in the halls, and the smiles of strangers—even Mr. Brandy had smiled at her finally—and Lucy's loud laugh.

Of course, Douglas handled her mother—"I'll handle Sally Ann," he'd said more than once—but in balancing the inferiority she felt in her father's and Douglas's world with the superiority she often felt over her mother's household, Rollin feared losing Douglas. At Mathilde Dampierre's wedding, Douglas gave the bride away, provoking a feeling of jealousy Rollin had not known before. Her father

would always be her father—letters arrived from him once a week.
But Douglas's communications were at best erratic, and when there
was nothing from him on her birthday, Rollin blamed her mother.

"Honey, you've just been so spoiled all these years," Sally Ann
said. Her voice was kind and sad and made Rollin furious.

"It isn't spoiled when it's what you've always had!" she cried.

Except for her grandmother's funeral and Mathilde's wedding,
Rollin did not see Douglas for almost a year. The wedding was
held at Peninghen, and Rollin spent most of the time with Misty
and Ann, sneaking cigarettes and watching the festivities from the
window across from Douglas's office. They watched Don Sheedy,
who played the saxophone, put his hand down a girl's dress; and
they saw people who thought no one could see them kissing in
the maze.

"Go find Douglas," Winifred kept whispering. "Douglas adores
you. Go find Douglas, he's with that pretty English girl with the
blue on her eyes." Her fingers crept on Rollin's shoulders like a bird
on the ledge of a building. "I've known you all your life," she
whispered.

She went away after Thanksgiving. No one ever really explained
why. They used the word "nervous." Rollin understood from her
father that Douglas still lived in the apartment on Park Avenue, but
he also had an apartment across town. He called it his office. Rollin
didn't see it until the following spring, when Douglas stopped to
pick up something on their way to a game. It was a mess: records
were stacked in towers of various heights, there was a keyboard
which belonged to a friend of Don Sheedy's. There were filing cabinets, and papers, and suitcases. There were two dresses in the closet
which were obviously not Winifred's dresses—bright pinks and oranges and lime green, and very short.

There was nothing to drink except beer, which Rollin drank from
a Harvard glass. That spring day, a glass of beer between them, was
the first she'd seen him in almost a year, and neither could think
of what to say.

"How's Lucy?" Rollin said.

"This first time you've seen me in a fucking year and the first thing you ask me is 'How's Lucy?'?" Douglas shouted.

"You don't care. You didn't even remember my birthday," Rollin shouted, and started to cry.

"Come on," Douglas said, and he threw a pack of cigarettes on the counter. "Don't cry."

Rollin looked up at him smoking the cigarette. She didn't think she had ever seen him smoking a cigarette, although she must have.

Another year went by and although Thompkins did not talk to her about money Rollin overheard him talking to Douglas, saying he'd gone over his deadline and the Guggenheim had run out; and since he couldn't get any more money he was negotiating to go to another publisher. She never asked questions but she wondered, as cartons filled with pages one after another. Douglas didn't seem to be sympathetic—his offer of Peninghen had gone unappreciated, he felt. "What the hell else can I do?" he asked her father in an undertone at dinner in New York one weekend at a Czechoslovakian restaurant called the Pra Ha, and that was the night the subject of boarding school came up.

"A place where social gains will be rooted," Douglas said in his snobbiest voice as they looked at catalogues.

"Well I don't see that a chapel has anything to do with that," Thompkins said, looking at the catalogue from Kent, where chapel was mandatory every morning.

"Fine, no chapel," Douglas said. "But she's not going to one of those do-it-yourself places. I remember when PD was trying to straighten Mathilde out and we looked at a school where the students cleaned outdoor toilets and milked cows."

Rollin laughed and her father laughed. "All right," Thompkins said, "no toilets, no cows, no chapel. Where does that leave us?"

They were all laughing, and Rollin looked back and forth between her father and Douglas and felt their protection. She couldn't remember a time like this.

Her mother was furious with Douglas for what she called his checkbook mentality.

"He thinks he can win you back by promising you things," she said. "He always has."

They were at a stoplight near the mall. The weather was gray. Her mother went on talking and Rollin tried to remember the last school she had seen, which had been in Pennsylvania.

"What about me, don't you think I'm old enough to know what's right for me? I think it's generous of Douglas and I don't see why you can't see it that way," Rollin said.

They got home, carrying Amy and Stuart inside, always a big production when there were groceries and packages. It was dusk, and lights were going on in the houses and her mother was saying, ". . . your father's fault because in the end he should have been the one to say something—no one would listen to me."

Amy, waving over over her mother's shoulder, called: "Listen to me! Listen to me!" like a little bird.

"They bought you dresses at Bergdorf's and then there were those French lessons for ten minutes, and for what?" They were inside now and Sally Ann turned on a light. "To go to one wedding?"

The question hung in the air. Rollin's eyes traveled over the cluttered living room. Her mother put Amy in her high chair and then she went into the kitchen, where Rollin could hear her opening cabinets. The television was on—the news, the war. Rollin was almost fifteen now, her face was broken out and she would live here forever, the rooms growing smaller as she grew older. Amy and Stuart would take over—they already had, Amy could reach doorknobs now.

Her mother's voice came from the kitchen. "I'll bet you can count the games Douglas has taken you to on one hand," she said. "And the disappointments—could you count them all?" She said she didn't care whether Douglas Kipps had gone to Harvard or had all the money in the world—he was selfish and irresponsible, and he drank too much. "And that Don Sheedy, he *is* an alcoholic." She

handed Amy her cup with the animals on it and looked at Rollin
sadly. "Oh, honey, it's just that I don't want you to expect things.
Those girls who go to those schools, well, they're like Winifred.
They have lots of money."

Rollin said nothing. Stuart's bottle was ready, and she took it out
of the boiling water. Testing it first, she gathered him up in her arms
and sat down in the rocking chair. She couldn't see the television
but she could hear it, but she wasn't listening. Douglas's generosity
didn't include her mother anymore and she was jealous, that was
all. Rollin looked down at Stuart, who had been taking his bottle
with his eyes closed, but he wasn't sleeping; and now suddenly he
opened his eyes and smiled at her. Rollin had never seen such a
smile. Today at the mall, a woman had thought he was hers.

Chapter 12

...

The island house was the same, and different. What Rollin remembered was this: her mother and father and Douglas and her grandmother, standing out in front surveying the damage. Her father smoking cigarette after cigarette as he stared at the house, shaking his head; her mother looking worried; Douglas half serious, half joking:

"Jesus Christ, like some beautiful woman with a past," he said, "she fooled us all."

Her father had flicked his cigarette butt into the bullrushes and said he hoped it started a fire.

"No," Mary Thompkins said, standing between the two men.

Years later Rollin was told that the town had tried to condemn the house, but her grandmother had prevented it as she had prevented the mayor and his men from walking through afterwards. Rollin could see her grandmother doing that: a big-busted woman with good legs and open-toed shoes, standing in the living-room doorway, saying no. For her grandmother had been strong then, and that was the way Rollin wanted to remember her.

On the other hand, it was as though neither her grandmother nor her mother had ever been there. It had taken three years (and Thompkins's Guggenheim) for the island house to be restored: for it to be jacked up and painted inside and out, for the walls to be reinforced, for the porch to be rebuilt, the back deck rebuilt and extended. Now it was sturdy, and even beautiful: the floors had been stained dark, and they gleamed. But there was no life. While they had been gone, the house had grown old, and the parts which had been redone only emphasized this. Dark massive bureaus and beds with rusted iron bedposts crowded the upstairs, and trunks like old sick guard dogs sat worn and peeling at the foot of each bed. A desk here, a table there, handles and drawer pulls missing; the cords of old lamps (one made from a butter churn, another from a jug) eaten and yellow and trapped in spiderwebs.

Their first summer back, the summer Rollin was thirteen, hardly anyone visited. Her grandmother had died, leaving Rollin and her father to share the big house. Every day for an hour, Rollin sat on the metal swing reading. The book was *Uncle Tom's Cabin*, from the school booklist, and she found it difficult to concentrate. Sometimes she read the same paragraph twice, once she counted the windows. When she tried to imagine Eliza on the ice, she found herself trying to imagine winter here: the boardwalks as bands of snow, icicles, instead of plants, hanging from porches. The Sweet Shop, its cut-out entrance sugared, no color, only white. A snowy beach and ice-splintered ocean, the lifeguard sitting in his chair under a weak sun, not buttery like summer but lemony, the sky not blue but white. Her eyes glazed and the mosaic of windows became one shining square of light suffused with gray. They were dirty. Numbers for the plumber and the electrician and the men who had rebuilt the porch, but no number for the boy who used to wash all those windows and bring her mother, then her grandmother, clams from the cove. She scratched a mosquito bite. The next time she scratched it, it would probably bleed. Moving in the swing, she sent it clanking. New, it had been black and shiny as tar, now it was old and just as heavy; her father joked that to send it over on the freight boat as junk would cost more than it had ever been worth. The same with the mirrors, which after years of sea air had started back to glass.

When the typing stopped, Rollin waited for her father to appear. If he did not, she might assume he had gone to make his tea, and she might take that opportunity to sneak into the living room and set the clock ahead. Just five minutes or so, and then she slipped back to the swing.

Thompkins worked on the other side of the porch as he always had, and when her hour was up, Rollin went over to where his steaming tea balanced on the arm of the wicker chair, and asked if she could go. Tapping his pocket for cigarettes, he looked at her over his reading glasses and asked where she was off to, even though he knew very well. Across the walk, a new house had gone up. Constantly, children poured out and down the front ramp to claim bicycles, shouts and flashes of silver in the bright sunlight. The Halls played tennis, they swam, they knew what summer was for. It was as though even their colorful processions to mass—they were Catholic—were especially conceived for the summer. Meanwhile the house itself stood as a monument to the men who had turned their backs on its monstrous proportions. With its ramps and angles, its three decks and two bicycle racks, it violated the building code seven times. To say that Thompkins hated it was an understatement. He had turned his desk to face the wall, but this did nothing to protect him from the noise.

Of course what he was most angry about was the view. His mother had bought the house for its windows, a meadow of reeds and cattails and desert roses, and beyond, the lighthouse. Black-and-white and strong, it had stood in distant perfection, as useless as a statue until night, when its light swung back and forth across the island until dawn. Now, bisected and decapitated by the Hall's upper deck, it existed as an annoying reminder of the dignified whole it had once been. Its light skittered between the deck slats, colliding for a frantic moment with the yellow spotlight on the Halls' front ramp and the milky streetlight, lights which all converged like sour daylight on the Thompkinses' low-lying, dimly lit porch.

Rollin saw none of this. Tired of the yellowing charcoals, the stained bird prints in the dining room, she felt an energy from the bright strawberry wall hanging in Susan's room, an energy and happiness from watching Mrs. Hall dart about in her tennis whites, a pink headband separating her blond hair.

"Rollin, I'm not going to eat my dinner at six o'clock," Thompkins said. "Now don't be ridiculous."

And so Rollin and her father sat down at eight o'clock, what he called a civilized dinner hour, as the Halls escaped down the ramp, their voices carrying and dying in the twilight. Her father chewed thoughtfully, looking into the middle distance, testing her patience each time he went for the serving spoon.

He seemed to prefer the house without guests. Once she was reading and the typing stopped and he appeared around the bend of the porch, and in the silence overtaken by summer sounds—a motorboat, a wagon—Rollin laughed to herself; she had half expected the typing to go on without him. He stopped mid-porch, his right arm hanging limp at his side, veins running down towards the breathing cigarette. He was wearing those old baggy khakis, those embarrassing sneakers. A faded blue shirt, the sleeves rolled up, and her mother would have said he needed a haircut. He was muttering, staring at the panorama of dirty windows without seeing them, and she might as well not have been there either. For his air was thick with characters she could neither see nor hear; he could summon them up at any moment. "Good one, Harry!" Mr. Hall might call as he rode by after playing tennis, but her father could have been blind the way he simply stood there.

Rollin had seen her mother's world through the eyes of others, but never her father's.

"Who's that?" Susan said the following summer when she saw Pauline Dampierre for the first time. "She's so pale. Is she sick or something? And who are those other people? They look weird."

"They're French," Rollin said.

Douglas arrived on the next ferry with a girl, Sandy, and the disruption that weekend occurred when he tried to write a check at the Sea Turtle restaurant.

"You see, they do that in France," Pauline said to the waiter over Douglas's own drunken explanation.

"The waiter doesn't give a damn what they do in France," Thompkins said.

The French couple, a husband and wife who were both film editors, thought it all quite amusing; thought that if paying by check in a restaurant was *très français*, then arguing about paying by check in a restaurant was *très Américain*.

"*Il aime faire du cinema, n'est-ce-pas?*" Pauline said, but the scene was so confusing with explanations that she ended up by speaking French to the waiter and English to Suzanne and Marc. Douglas was adding a few slurred words of Spanish, and Sandy had started going through her purse.

"I've never been to France," she said. "I guess I'm the kind of girl who's never been to France but can always pay the check," she said, and dumped out the contents of her purse on the table. She had understood nothing of Lettrisme or Infinitesimal painting (a little drunk, she had trouble with the word itself), which they had been discussing because Douglas wanted to present a dialogue on the idea of the "supertemporal framework."

"I guess I don't get it," she said. "I thought the artist was the creator." She was a strawberry blonde, and her freckles, a smattering across the bridge of her nose, gave her an empty look. "But you're telling me the artist would give me the paint and brushes and everything and I'd make something? But I don't know anything. About art. I mean it would be like having a stopped-up sink and the plumber coming and giving me all his tools."

"Indeed," Thompkins said. He laughed a little, but she was serious. "I mean, would you let someone else write your book?" she said. "Douglas, cut it out. But really, would you?"

She said to Thompkins, "Sure, I know the color wheel, but I mean I wouldn't know how to get *brown*. Well, I got brown icing once but that was because I didn't know what I was doing. Do you understand?" she said, looking around the table. "Or am I—"

Thompkins nodded. "Completely," he said.

"I mean, I'm not an artist and I'm not a plumber," she said.

"Certainly not," Thompkins said.

"*Plombier*," Pauline translated.

"You go to school for those type of things," she said. "I mean am I wrong?"

Douglas had behaved abominably ("*El reloj es de oro*," he said to the waiter when they didn't have enough cash, and then about the remaining clam, "Oh, stuff it up your ass, you'd like that, wouldn't you?"); but he appeared on the porch the next day showered and cheerful, his memory spared.

Later Rollin saw her father buying more scotch and Douglas putting away beer and someone taking a nap and she knew what that meant: another night of talking about old times and dead writers and wars. Pauline and the French couple had arrived the day before yesterday and even though the man had put on a tiny black bathing suit they hadn't been up to the ocean yet. It didn't matter whether it rained or not—they liked the indoors as they liked the past. Don Sheedy never went to the ocean. When he came out he and Douglas went to bars late and sometimes one or both of them didn't come home at all. Or the next day a girl they had met the night before would come to the screen door and knock, looking for one of them (usually Douglas). Always pretty girls, and Rollin felt sorry for them. Some were shy, but once a blonde yelled up at Don's window, "Who gives a shit if you played with Tony Bennett? Asshole!" Another time a girl named Renee (Rollin didn't think this was her real name) called through the screen door to Thompkins, "Are you the writer? Can I come in for a minute and talk?"

They had names like Chris and Cindy and Kim and Barbara.

Maddie (for Madeleine) was the only one whom Douglas seemed to really like, and who gave him trouble. She had red hair, and she only stayed one night. Rollin heard their raised voices and the next day Maddie was gone. When Rollin asked where she was, Douglas grinned.

"Maddie," he said, "was smart. Maddie got the hell out of here."

"She was nice," Rollin said. She was sitting on the swing.

"And smart," Douglas said. "Don't forget smart," he said, a touch of sarcasm in his voice.

"You mean she wasn't pretty enough?" Rollin said.

"Maddie's a gorgeous girl," Douglas said.

"Well then what was the matter with her?" Rollin said.

"Nothing was the matter with her," Douglas said, leaving Rollin with the impression that what was the matter with her was that there was nothing the matter with her. "She's too smart for me," Douglas said. "How do you like that?"

"How do *you* like it?" Rollin said.

"If I told you that I could be put in jail," Douglas said, and shaking the porch (even the new porch) he headed back towards the kitchen.

Rollin didn't know what these girls meant in terms of Winifred, who had been in and out of a hospital. Usually people tried to avoid answering her questions, and Rollin had to make due with what she overheard. All the arguments were the same. What Rollin overheard was the end of the argument, but they were all the same.

"You do nothing!" Pauline cried.

Rollin was in the kitchen and Pauline and Douglas were on the back deck—she saw them through shades of gray through the screen, saw Douglas sitting backwards on one of the metal chairs like a boy being scolded.

". . . know what she says? She says she can't really go crazy because then one will believe that she had good reasons! She actually said that! What the hell am I supposed to do? Jesus, I have needs too, I have—"

Pauline's voice rose as Rollin had never heard it: "And they're all that have ever mattered! Other people have needs, everyone has needs! But you can't even be discreet. Winifred's needs—"

"—don't concern you!" Douglas said.

"Well, they certainly don't concern you," Pauline said glibly, and walked away.

Beyond wondering about Douglas and Winifred, Rollin had never figured out what the relationship between Douglas and Pauline was.

Enough time had passed away from the island house that by the time the summers out there started up again Rollin was older—old enough to see things more as they were, and not as she had as a child. The interim had been taken away from her, which made certain things quite clear. Pauline regarded Douglas as a son, but she had also remained close to Winifred. So had Douglas, in a way. It was as if even though they didn't really like each other, they needed each other. Winifred needed Douglas's love, even if it wandered, and he needed her money. Pauline needed to organize other people's lives and Douglas needed what he called credibility—it was Pauline who knew many of the artists who came to Peninghen, and more important, influential money and gallery people. (It was she who had introduced Douglas to the Arte Povera group and arranged for him, when he was in Europe, to stop over in Turin, Italy, and visit the Depot, a large garage where artists and filmmakers made and presented their work. He had come back full of Italy: "They've all these pasta names, you know, pista this and that. One's even named Parmagiana. No kidding," he said, and showed around a picture of Claudio Parmiggiano's *Pellemondo*, or Leather World, a globe covered with what looked like the hide of a cow.)

But he didn't follow up on things, and more and more, this was what irritated Pauline and others who got involved.

"Hey, wait a sec—hold on," he said to Rollin the summer she was fifteen. "Come here," he said. She had brought him a beer and was walking way. He was looking her over and said, "Your knees. They're so low." He looked up at her. "I never noticed that before."

"What do you mean?" Rollin said. She could never tell when he was kidding. "They are not." Her kneecaps bobbed involuntarily. "You're just used to seeing women in high heels all the time," she said.

"Not *all* the time," he said, and she blushed.

The screen door slammed (it was broken) and Pauline came out. "What are you telling her?" she said. "Rollin," she said, "is the mistress of this house." She made her way to a chair in the shade.

"Well the mistress has got low knees," Douglas said. "So where's the fruit? Your fruity friend," he said, referring to Orrin West, who had come out with Pauline that weekend. He was a birdwatcher and he frowned all the time—he looked as if he were focusing on a bird when he talked to you.

She repeated what she had said before. "Orrin is all alone in the world." She said, "Now this about low knees." She glanced over at Rollin. "One wouldn't want high knees. I would think low knees would give the illusion of a long leg. Douglas, how can you watch that, turn that off. On such a beautiful day."

"Oh, all the days are beautiful," Douglas said, looking back at the game. He took a swig of beer and said, "Diana Hartmen Smith was fourteen when she joined the Rockettes."

"Who," Pauline said, "is that?"

"I just told you," Douglas said. "Come on, PD, prick up your ears. Sometimes I think you don't—"

"Do not call me that, I told you not to call me that." She turned her attention to Rollin again. "A woman's legs are only as beautiful as the way they carry her into a room," she said. "Do you understand that? Marilyn Monroe cut off part of one heel for her walk. There are arms and legs and bottoms and bosoms, but what matters is how one drags it all around."

"Horseshit," Douglas said.

"Posture," Pauline went on quietly. "Winifred's mother would pin her shoulders to the wall while they were waiting for the elevator, every day." She looked at Douglas. "And they would stand that way until the elevator came."

"Jesus fucking Christ."

"So don't listen to him," Pauline said.

But Rollin did listen. The summer before, she had had impetigo, and her father had had to change the bandages because she couldn't reach. She had been embarrassed at the cold wet cotton, guided by his fingers, and she had thought, I'm too old for this. It was the past compromising with the present to produce the present; she was going away to school in the fall and she was at the age where she was balancing between the safety of family and what lay beyond, expressed in her father's and Douglas's ideas of what a woman should be. Her father preferred quiet, even-tempered women—no surprises. And then there were the girls she saw around Douglas, who liked women and flirted with them (he liked sexy women— he thought there should be nude beaches like in France) but made fun of them when they left the room. He didn't take most women seriously, and those he did he didn't like. He was condescending. "Did I tell you Cindy plays the guitar?" he said about a girl who had come around after one of his wild nights at the Kismet Inn. He acted as if she were a wind-up doll. Then he complained when they weren't stable. But they were all so young! What did he expect? On his birthday that year, he said astrology was where he drew the line. "As soon as she starts asking my sign, that's it. How often have I heard that Leos are generous, love flattery, but they fuck up with their kids, only have one or none and if they do have any, quote, 'sadly this relationship often ends in estrangement,' and what do I need to hear that shit for? What's my ascendant, what's my midheaven—do you believe that? Midheaven? I told her it was in hell!"

He wanted someone like Amanda, who would sit quietly reading a fashion magazine and look pretty while he reeled off batting averages or talked about the strike zone. He wanted, as Pauline Dampierre said in one of her ornery and less elegant moments, a woman who kept her mouth shut and her legs open.

Like the others, Amanda was pretty, involved somehow in the

fashion business, and crazy about Douglas. The usual makeup bottles littered the bureau in the ocean bedroom and skimpy bathing suits hung on the line. When Rollin first saw Amanda she had been impressed with the long thick braid which hung down her back. Later she saw the braid curled on the bureau, winding through the bottles of perfume and makeup. It was like a snake, and the sprig of braids beside it like a group of baby snakes. The smaller braids were shinier than the big one, but the big one looked more like real hair. Amanda wore the smaller braids when they all went to the Kismet Inn for dinner: they sprouted everywhere, like decorations. Like the flowers on the hat she wore, she didn't even pretend that they were real.

"Such a charming, uncomplicated creature," Pauline said pleasantly, but it was clear to Rollin that she was glad to see Amanda leave on the boat on Sunday.

Douglas couldn't leave—he'd cut his foot on some glass coming back from Kismet. He yelled at her father, yelled at the town: "Jesus Christ, why don't they pave that fucking road! And if you were a member of the goddam club your guests wouldn't be out here walking in the dirt, for God's sake!" He sang: "The road to Mandalay, the road to Mandalay amanda lay—"

The cut was just bad enough to confine him to the house, where he spent his time on the back deck watching baseball (wearing sunglasses because of the glare, and a healing black eye) and annoying anyone who walked in his path towards the bike rack or the outdoor shower.

"Hey, Lad, what page are we on, huh? Making some progress?"

Thompkins cleared his throat. "Is it healing, do you think?" he said.

"I know, I know, you want me out of here and I don't blame you! Hey, did I tell you I saw Charlie Fontenals the other day? Jesus, the guy looks bad, fucking stranger in his own shorts. Oh well, poor bastard never did have what it takes . . ."

Finally Thompkins resorted to going out the front door and walking around to the side of the house to the bicycle rack. But usually Douglas heard and called out, "Hey would you pick up some beer? It's dry as a desert around here. And some gum, do you mind?"

It seemed to be a crush towards the finish line: "Come on Lad," Douglas yelled late one night in front of an audience, "recognition is like sex—a man can only do without it for so long. Finish that thing! For Christ's sake!"

Rollin thought her father was going to hit him. But it went on. Food, more wine, each weekend the house filled up with strangers and the more it filled up, the more it disintegrated. Her father tried to ignore it, he walked carefully by, carrying his tea as though he were the guest. The windows stayed dirty but he didn't seem to mind, in fact he liked them dirty, Rollin decided, like a screen protecting him from the Halls and the whole outside world. As long as he had his mornings, he didn't care how crazy things got. The later the nights went, the more likely he was to have the mornings to himself. The more chaos he saw spinning around him, the easier it was for him to slip away unnoticed.

"Rollin," Pauline Dampierre was fond of saying, "is mistress of this house."

On the contrary, there was none, and each summer was louder and more disorganized. Things broke, and broke down—the screen door, the refrigerator. All George Semard did when he visited was wash his clothes, and one weekend a new washer arrived from Macy's. It had his name on it, it was paid for, but in broken English and French he claimed to know nothing about it.

After a while the weekends didn't even exist anymore, they spilled over. Making beds, meeting ferries, the telephone ringing, and buying food. There were women in the bathroom, women making dinner, strangers staying up and wandering on the porch.

The Halls had a guest book, in which the same families wrote in the same neat handwriting every year. What would her father's friends say in a book like that? What would Don Sheedy say in a guest book? "I left my heart in San Francisco and my memory in the bar"? What would the strangers say? Someone like Orrin West who came one time, or the photographer? He had complained the whole weekend about his hay fever. He walked everywhere with his cameras around his thick neck. He had worn socks with his sandals, and when Rollin said she thought that was pretty weird Pauline had jumped to his defense.

"He has a webbed foot," she said.

"What?" Rollin couldn't believe what she heard.

"I said, *he has a webbed foot*," Pauline repeated. "A webbed toe, and that is why he wears socks. It is something he is embarrassed about, and so he covers it, and then he is called weird because he covers it."

Pauline was her own kind of crazy—what would she say in a book like that? Or David Gamble. He was British and wore an ascot to the beach. His hair had little waves in it and he said "bloody-minded" all the time. His accent seemed stronger, more clipped, every year. In fact, these people were more who they were each time Rollin saw them. The Halls' friends would probably stay the same, but Douglas's drinks got stronger and the girls got younger. Her father smoked more cigarettes. Pauline was paler. Winifred got crazier and the drugs got stronger.

Then, suddenly, the summer was over. The typing stopped—the silence was always so abrupt—and a fly buzzed in the sunny corner of a window as a spider waited in the web below. The swing clanked with Rollin's impatience, and the September sun widened its eye at her through the quaking aspens, flickering with color now at the passage of a bicyclist. It wasn't one of the Halls, it wasn't anyone she recognized. She remembered, vaguely, when the whole walk had been theirs.

Chapter 13

o o o

They had compromised on a Quaker school—Sally Ann had used the term "sheltered" and Douglas had said that being away at school would "broaden Rollin's horizons" and they were both right: on Rollin's hall were a Nigerian, a redhead from Texas who ran away with one of the groundsmen before midterm, a French girl who snuck cigarettes, an orphan, a girl with acne, a black girl from New Jersey, a blonde whose father had donated the science building, and a girl from Caracas whose father ran a textile firm which made lingerie. Hearing María on the phone in her own language, angry and rolling her Rs, Rollin could think of nothing less Quaker than lace panties and Latin tempers.

The school was coed. There were boys' dorms on either side of the main building where the girls were housed; not two hundred yards away were four floors of boys showering and telling dirty jokes. Rollin turned sixteen that fall, rewarded by one demerit for smoking and one for necking—it was almost touching the following summer when Douglas railed on about her revealing bikini. He'd been out of the country and Rollin had been wearing the bathing suit all summer by the time he arrived and she had laughed at him and told him he was taking her to the Kismet Inn.

But that summer his drinking was bad, and when, in the fall, he came to her school to take her out, Rollin wasn't allowed to go. This was doubly ironic, as he was paying for her to attend this school and he had given her a car for her sixteenth birthday. Boarders were not allowed to drive at all, and at first this was where Rollin thought the misunderstanding lay.

"No, I'm not driving, my godfather is," Rollin told the girl in the dean's office when she was signing out.

In a moment it was clear. Rules regarding boarders leaving campus in cars were determined each year by the parents. Permission cards were sent home and filled out and signed with the purpose of designating those with whom the boarder could drive. Last year it had been fine. Her mother had allowed that Rollin could drive with anyone in a school capacity, and then she had listed friends and relatives who might pass through the area and take Rollin to dinner, and this had included Douglas and a friend of her father's. But this year Douglas's name was not on the card. Even a relative Rollin had never met before who had moved to the area had been included, but not Douglas.

The girl in the dean's office, a student, moved behind the counter. The fluorescent lights above them buzzed and the card lay between them as she explained again that Rollin could sign out for dinner with this man, but she could not drive with him.

"What do you mean, 'this man'?" Rollin cried. " 'This man' just happens to be my godfather, and he pays my tuition here." She was just debating what to do when the door burst open and Douglas came striding in. Rollin was shocked. She hadn't seen him since the summer, and he'd gained weight and his face was puffy.

"Rollin!" he said, hugging her hard and grinning. He walked like a cowboy. "I've got reservations at that Powder Ridge place," he said, throwing his keys on the counter.

Rollin looked at the girl, who was flustered and avoided Douglas's eyes as she said, "Look, why don't you try the Temperance House? You can walk and it's not bad, actually—"

"The Temperance House?" Douglas said, laughing. "What the hell kind of a place is that, the Temperance House?"

The girl, whose name Rollin thought might be Martha, started to explain the situation. Douglas laughed and said, "Wait a minute, protection of the students, I'm all for that—but I'm her godfather. I'm the," he laughed, "financially responsible person here." He turned to Rollin. "I keep getting letters from this place addressed 'financially responsible person.' " He grabbed the keys. "Come on, you ready?"

"Rollin," the girl said, looking back and forth between them.

"I can't go!" Rollin said. She said to the girl, "If I had known I would've lied and said he was my father." She hated the girl suddenly: her ironed shirt, nothing to do on a Friday night except keep people from having a good time. Turning to Douglas, she told him about the card, but he completely missed the possibility that his name might have been omitted on purpose, and suggested she call her mother.

The girl behind the counter looked genuinely pained. "But how would I know it was really your mother?" she said to Rollin.

"What the hell's with you, anyway?" Douglas said to her. "You want to make up a game here like children, is that what you want to do here? You want me to tell you Sally Ann's eye color or where she was born? I've had enough of this bullshit," he said. He was quiet for a moment. "You call a taxi, okay? You got anything against taxis? What does the fucking card say about taxis—any particular driver she's not allowed to have?"

They waited on the porch of Main, Douglas pacing back and forth, his hands in his pockets. A boy she had gone to the movies with last weekend walked by and Rollin looked quickly away. His name was Tony, and when he came out of the building he looked at Rollin and then Douglas and then back at her.

"Was that your boyfriend?" Douglas said in the taxi.

"Who?"

"Who? The guy who couldn't keep his eyes off you and nearly fell on his ass going down the stairs there."

"No," she said. "I mean, we went to a movie."

They ate in a restaurant worth a taxi fare of thirty dollars. It was on the river, and it made Rollin think of men and mistresses. There seemed to be reflections everywhere—in glasses and in the water below and in his eyes. It was fall, dark early, and in the taxi street-lights had jumped between them, greasing his face, making him look older. According to her father, Douglas was going somewhere to "dry out." He wasn't well. He'd spent time with friends out in California—Santa Barbara—but there had been trouble and he had come home early. Although where "home" was these days was not exactly clear—he seemed to spend an inordinate time traveling.

They ordered dinner and when she said she was cold he offered her his jacket and she thought it was going to be all right. But then he ordered a second bottle of wine and started talking about his Harvard reunion. It had been over a year since that week in Cam-bridge, but he still had not forgiven her father for not going. Rollin tried to change the subject, but he interrupted her.

"I missed Winifred at that reunion," he said. "Cindy didn't have a good time, she was younger than all the wives there, and—" He frowned slightly, as if understanding what had gone wrong for the first time. "And it's like Lad says at those things: the ones who show up are either a success or they want a job. The jerks. The people you're curious about . . ." His voice trailed off. "Shit," he said, setting his glass down hard. "What's the matter with your father, anyway? Huh?"

Rollin moved so the waiter could clear her plate. "Douglas, you know Papa hates things like that. It has nothing to do with you, he just—"

Douglas was playing with the candle. "Yeah yeah yeah," he said. "The special writer, yeah yeah."

On and off Douglas had mentioned ideas he had for a book, a lunch with a publisher; but nothing came of it, and his references to it were seen more and more as a tool to undermine what Douglas called "Thompkins's last leg." Douglas's magazine had folded long before Thompkins had published the excerpt in *Harper's*, but that wasn't the point—Douglas was jealous of the book, critical, because Thompkins had not yet offered him the manuscript to read.

"How's Winifred?" Rollin said. "It's been a long—"

"She's fine!" Douglas said. "The women are always fine," he said. "Well, what the hell are you looking at me like that for?"

"At you?" She wasn't, she was looking at the monogram, over his heart. He asked her if she remembered when they had gone to the Met a long time ago, and she remembered; the opera had been *Tosca* with Renata Tebaldi and Rollin had clapped with hollow palms like a man, the way Jim clapped for goals. Someone, Winifred probably, had leaned over and showed her how to tap a row of fingers on her other gloved palm.

Douglas laughed. "Oh, you were great," he said, as if she had disappointed him by growing up.

Then he asked her about school. When Rollin told him she wanted to be a painter, he laughed. The candle burned sympathetically in front of her and she repeated it, with more force this time: "Well, I do, Douglas—I want to be a painter. In Drawing last year—"

But Douglas was too loud for her: "Sure!" he cried. "Be a painter!" He swallowed brandy. "And you want me to pay for art school now, is that it?"

"No, I wasn't—"

"Get all the Thompkinses out there expressing themselves, is that it? Is that what this dinner is all about?" he said, smiling. "Another round for the sucker who pays?"

Rollin stared at him and tears came to her eyes. As he was calling the waiter, she grabbed her purse and ran to the ladies' room.

"Where'd you go?" he said in the same loud voice when she came back. "Huh? I saw you leave, and I didn't worry about you with the car because we have no car." There was a new glass of brandy in front him and he picked it up and swirled it, and said,

"Sit down. And you've been crying. Your eyes are all red. What's the matter? You're not calling a man at this hour, are you? Because whatever else I'm not I'm a man and I'll tell you—" He stopped. He shook his head. "Nah, I'm not going to tell you." He looked at Rollin, narrowing his eyes. "You think I'm drunk, don't you?" he said. "You do. Hah, maybe I am. I'm drunk—I'm a drunk—I'm drunk—" He cocked his head to one side, then the other, the same piece of hair falling away each time. "I'm drunk—I'm a drunk—see the difference? Just that little *a*." He laughed to himself, a silent nod. "You want a nightcap?" he said. "Go ahead. Thanks to your friend, we're not driving, so go ahead. Hah. Nightcap, you remember? That's baseball for doubleheader." He was quiet for a moment and then he said, *"Por la noche todo está en silencio."*

"What does that mean?" Rollin said.

"At night everything is silent," he said.

She did not see him at Thanksgiving, nor at Christmas, and there was nothing about that night that she wanted to remember, until she wanted to remember it all.

In March, Pauline Dampierre gave a party for her daughter. It wasn't Mathilde's birthday, but in the French tradition, March 14 was Sainte Mathilde. "Well of course she's not *here*," Pauline said when guests asked. Neither was Douglas. Rollin had taken the train up from school. It had snowed, and the city was white and silent when she arrived and by the time she left at the end of the weekend the snow was dirty and the taxi drivers were swearing at broken traffic lights, and Douglas hadn't called.

Rollin had been back at school barely a week when her father called, and at first she thought he had a cold. Then she heard an unsteadiness in his voice, ice in glass.

"What is it?" she said. "Have you got a cold?"

"No," he said. "Rollin, get ahold of yourself now—"

"What?" she said. Hair seized her scalp. "What?" she cried, and then those in their rooms on Second North heard the screams echoing up and down the empty, shiny corridor. Her father's voice, telling her to come home, and all she could do was scream. "Douglas! No! No, no, no." A vision of Harlem sprang up from her childhood: the dark streets and fire escapes, the scattered neons of bars. She had looked out the car window and she had felt safe from that landscape which flew past in moonlight too fast to yield details, fast enough that parked cars were a stream of light broken by stripped cars or trash cans, the rest darkened except for those neons. They were coming home from her grandmother's, they had no business here and no friends. There was laughter and in summer the hollow sound of trash cans and children out playing even so late, opening fire hydrants against the heat as the car flew over potholes towards the ships lit white and grand.

"What was he doing there?" Rollin screamed senselessly. "What did they want? Why won't you tell me?"

But there was phlegm in his voice, a muscle torn raw by the warmth of whiskey, and screaming at him did no good. He had been to the morgue. "Come home," he said again, and his head ached, pounded against her questions. Was he black, Puerto Rican, was he— "Oh, Rollin, don't, you can't. No. He could've been black white Chinese Puerto Rican—" And what her father meant was, You know how many jokes Douglas had. "It gets late," Thompkins said. "In a place like that—sometimes it doesn't but when it does you'd better know it, get out, but he never knew. What was funny a moment ago suddenly isn't, you pay when you get the drink because you just don't know." His voice was low, almost secretive, a little slurred. "I used to watch him, he always thought he could bring it back around, poor bastard, start it, fight it, and bring it—"

"Stop!" she said. "It was probably like Kismet. When he said that thing in Spanish and the man thought it was obscene. There was almost a fight. It was a mistake and—" She let the phone dangle and went to be sick.

He realized that no watch had been found. He had not realized it at the morgue but now it occurred to him.

El reloj es de oro.

181

o o o

In New York an ugly man's voice droned on behind a massive desk in a dark-paneled room until Rollin couldn't stand it anymore.

"The deceased, the deceased, like he died in his sleep!" she cried. "The newspapers say tragedy. They say knifing as if it's all the same but it isn't. I don't want to hear this shit. I don't care about the stocks and shit and—"

"Rollin—"

"Stabbing, why don't they say that? They won't say that and they won't say murder. No one wants to say murder, and what are you laughing at?" she said to Winifred.

Winifred covered her mouth in an effort to stifle a laughter Thompkins never wanted to hear again. Her face was absent of makeup, her eyes were red, and there was still a wildness about her left over from the morgue, where Thompkins had found her holding the plastic bag containing the bloodied shirt. He had gotten there too late. He had hoped to spare her that and he tried to take it from her, but she had resisted. In shock, she had commented on the trip to the Turnbull & Asser counter at Bonwit's in Beverly Hills where she had bought the shirt; then, pulling it out of the bag, she had expressed relief that the blood was mostly on the front—the women in Texas would still get a few good squares. When Thompkins tried to take it from her she had snatched the bag away, stuffing the shirt back into it. "I'm fine," she said brightly. "Really I am." A few minutes later an orderly had found her in one of the examining rooms brandishing a pair of scissors. She tried to explain to him what she wanted to do, but he had thought she was dangerous and this had made Winifred laugh. Thompkins had heard her all the way down the slick corridor, laughing.

"If we could continue—" Mr. Crath said. Looking nervously at Winifred, then Rollin, he addressed Thompkins. "While the institution is closed there is the question of maintenance," he said, and his fingertips met on the desktop. "This is out of our domain, of course, but until the young lady comes of age, the property cannot be sold. However, in the interest of an eventual sale—"

"You don't want to start seeing broken windows," the junior partner interjected.

The senior Crath nodded and pulled the ashtray back. The conference was over.

They took the elevator down in silence, but once through the revolving door in the lobby Winifred turned and said to Thompkins, "He was screwing that harpist, wasn't he?"

A provision of the will had been that a certain harpist have access to Peninghen. "Wasn't he?" Winifred repeated. Rollin stared at her, and Thompkins, sensing a confrontation, put himself between them.

There was not much else he could do—they were staying with Winifred until the funeral. Rollin was uncomfortable there. She was staying in the guest bedroom, and when her mother had called she had sat on the chintz bedspread and looked around the room and wondered if she had ever slept there before. Somehow she knew her mother would not know and would answer anyway, and so she did not ask. In fact she hardly said anything. A part of her blamed her mother for the fact that she would never see Douglas again. It was that simple. But she had been given the tranquilizers when she was called to the phone and she could have been talking to anybody, even her mother, across town in a Sheraton Hotel.

"I drove right down," she said. "Rollin, honey, are you all right?"

"All right," she said, laughing shortly, her eyes filling with tears. In the background she could hear voices.

"Thank you," Sally Ann said. "We're just having room service, here," she said to Rollin. "Yes, honey, there's your BLT. Poor thing, she just told room service she was here for a funeral," Sally Ann said. "The first time she comes to New York and it's— No, sweetie, not that way; here, let me do it for you. There. Rollin? I'm sorry, we've been driving and she was starving. Are you there?"

"I'm here," Rollin said.

"I still can't believe it," Sally Ann said. "I had to pull over a couple of times, I— How's your father, is he all right? I want to talk to him. I've been remembering things, all kinds of things keep coming back and yet I don't believe it. I don't believe it."

Her voice was shaking, and it occurred to Rollin as she looked at a Louis XV ormulu-mounted clock that her mother was better at remembering her life than she was at living it.

"It was a wonderful part of my life," she was saying now.

The clock was a little over a foot high. Two white porcelain dogs painted with flowers sat at the base, and between them sprouted a freestanding arrangement of porcelain flowers which surrounded the clock face, on which was written *Festeau Le Jeune, à Paris, 1785.* The auction catalogue would say "Louis XV *style* ormulu clock," because the clock was actually twentieth-century; but as Rollin sat staring at the gold fleur de lys hands, which in five minutes did not move, the romance of an antique remained intact.

"Do you remember?" her mother said. "The jockeys holding the lanterns outside?"

"What are you talking about?" Rollin cried.

"I am talking," her mother said, "about your grandmother's apartment. We drove by it earlier. One forty-three East Nineteenth Street. *That* is what I am talking about."

Rollin had come to the apartment on Park Avenue straight from the train. The black door on the twelfth floor had opened and she had been stunned by the familiar smell of dust and brocade tinged with a cooked vegetable. Beyond, the apartment was the same— triumphantly, so it seemed. The Chinese screen in the dining room, the cut-out figures which once had been her size, at an angle towards the living room, where later she heard a man say the rug they stood on, a Mochtashem Kashan palace carpet, was worth in the area of forty thousand dollars. People turned to look at her, a sea of pale faces, some familiar, some not. Rollin had not seen Douglas in that room since she was a child, but for some reason that made his absence even stronger. She looked at the people and she thought, But Douglas had not been old.

Then she saw her father. The weak Sunday light from the window at the end of the living room set off his strong profile, and Rollin smiled. She was unable to move from the landing, and she stood there. But he had heard the door. He came towards her, the color of his suit the gray indigo of the rug he walked on, and a glance at his tie revealed a more ordered study of it, rich russets and blues which in that particular weight of silk lost its design to any light. The tears in his eyes watered down the distance she saw so often there, but she was conscious of a restraint in his embrace, not where she was concerned but within himself.

"Some people who would like to see you, I think," he uttered, and took her elbow. Poised aggressively on the landing, she had been a surprise to him. He had seen the fear in her face, the strength, and he had seen her beauty. At seventeen, she was built the way his mother had been built. He said to her, "You remember the Rileys . . ."

Rollin tried to smile. Smiles faded in sympathy around her and it all came back, Ann and Misty, the beach and those houses and learning to swim. That had been the summer Douglas had begun to drift away. Rollin turned. Once she had been a spoiled child on a loving man's shoulders. Now she was on the ground.

The funeral was at St. Mark's, a few steps away from Jack and Jill, where Rollin had gone to nursery school. Rollin borrowed a suit from Winifred, navy-blue gabardine, and since the jacket was too small across the bust she left it unbuttoned over the ivory silk blouse. It made her look, Pauline Dampierre said sadly, *très parisienne*.

But her face was red from crying and by the time the ceremony was over the suit was not right at all, as though her shape had changed under it. In the short week since Douglas's death, she had alternated between walking around in a daze and plying her father feverishly with questions. She wanted to know about Douglas's family, she nagged him about when they could go to the apartment on Second Avenue and get the records, she wanted the records and there was a pair of cufflinks she wanted and some plates with animals on them she remembered. When Thompkins pointed out that the plates could very well belong to Winifred (they did; they were a set of eighteenth-century faience from Nevers, France, which had belonged to Winifred's mother), Rollin was furious.

"And I suppose the cufflinks belong to her father!" she cried. "Or else they're eighteen-karat gold, which doesn't matter a damn to me but to her—"

"You can't just go in and start taking things," Thompkins said. "We've been over this. The will has been read. Now if there are a few small things, other things you remember—"

"I remember everything! Don't you see? Those cufflinks could be made of aluminum for all I care—I want them because I remember them!"

It was all he could do to deal with her, but there was Sally Ann, and that Rollin hardly spoke to her did not make things easier. When Thompkins had seen that she had brought the little girl he had determined to avoid them, but in the end he had found it easier to look at the five-year-old than at Sally Ann.

"It was lovely," Sally Ann said about the eulogy he had given. "But it wasn't, oh I don't know—"

He pitched a match. "Sentimental," he said. He did not go into Winifred's hysterics at what he had originally planned to read— there was no point.

She said, "But you evoked sentiment. You, his friend for so many years. When your voice cracked—oh, Lad." Her voice was full of feeling and she was trying to get him to look at her but he would not.

He was watching the little girl, who was blond and blue-eyed and chewing on a hard candy.

"Don't you recognize her coat, Lad?" Sally Ann said.

The coat was light blue with a black velvet collar, and had been a present to Rollin from her godfather around the time the portrait had been painted. Sally Ann said all she'd had to do was replace the buttons.

"They used to be brown," the child said. It was the first thing Amy had said. She was timid, pale, so unlike Rollin at that age. For a moment Thompkins had wondered why, if Sally Ann had not had to bring both children, she had brought one. But although he knew her presence here had to do with self-affirmation, he decided that the child playing the key role had less to do with driving home what life had accomplished than with her own loneliness.

"Rollin is very angry with me," she said, looking at her older daughter standing amid the clutch of furs and waiting cars.

By late afternoon, Rollin and her father had arrived in Key West. As they let themselves in the porch at the back of the house, Rollin noticed a *New York Times* dated a few weeks before Douglas's death on the glass coffee table. She stared at it, impressed in a detached way at how strange this was; how incongruous that her godfather's death had occurred at a convenient time for them to borrow a house in a sunny place, a house with a porch and no history. She had a feeling, suddenly, that this was how life was.

Thompkins had thought if he got her out of New York, if he took her to a place she didn't know, she would be better, but they had not been in Key West for more than an hour when she broke down and buried her head on the dusty card table where he had put his typewriter, and sobbed.

"Oh, Rollin," he said, a roughness and futility in his voice. "I don't know what to tell you. I don't know what to do."

Her emotion made him awkward and he laid a hand on her head. Her hair was warm and dark. He lit a cigarette, which he smoked as he tried to soothe her. The screened-in porch got little sun at this time of day; it was like a cage in the jungle. Beyond the plush tangle of green Thompkins could see the neighbor, a blonde of about twenty-five, contemplating a pile of bricks. She wore a bright green blouse which looked like silk, and as she began to arrange the bricks there was something about the unsuitability of the top which stirred him. The screen between them and the dust of the bricks formed a sort of haze in the last light of the day as she walked back and forth, laying the bricks two at a time. They made a sound as she placed them which was dry and chalky, agreeable.

Rollin was watching too—it seemed to have calmed her. "Whose house is this again?" she said.

A year and a half ago Thompkins had taken a teaching job at a college in upstate New York, and the house belonged to a professor he knew there. It was a small house, furnished with odds and ends (the bright-orange chair she sat in now); a few pieces of cheap rattan brightened by cushions made from sheets. One coat of white paint on the walls had produced a milky effect, and it was this and the red and pink plastic beads hanging in the kitchen doorway which gave the impression that the house was not sturdy.

Thompkins remembered Key West as emotion, Rollin's anger, the heat and dampness close about them as the world moved on without them for those two weeks, nights when they ate at LUMS and found themselves back at the house early with nothing to do except drink and argue. Then there were the times, such as now, when she was quiet; and he was as unprepared for these moments as he was for her outbursts and incoherence. She was a child throwing tantrums, and yet he had also seen her over the past week suddenly older, her clothes and the way she stood, holding out a cigarette for a friend of his to light.

But if he found her changed, Rollin was shocked to find her father working one day when she returned from the beach. "How can you work now?" she said. Her hair was wild and the shirt of Douglas's that she'd been wearing hung about in wrinkled stripes over her bathing suit. She was sunburned but she'd been crying and it was all mixed up in her face. She looked at the manuscript, the black print on the thick white paper her father used. She smelled like coconut and perspiration as she drew near, reading one sentence over his shoulder, then another. "You'll never see Douglas again and you're thinking about how someone walks?" she said.

"Rollin, you've to get ahold of yourself," Thompkins said.

"I don't want to get ahold of myself!" Rollin cried. She gestured and in the breeze several pages drifted to the floor. She leaned on the card table, white knuckles and sunburn. "What if I had died?" she said. "Would you still be sitting here, working away? Just pretending that—"

"Don't be ridiculous," Thompkins said. She was sunburned and hysterical and it was not even noon. Abruptly he got up from the table and walked to the far end of the porch. It was warm, damp, and he tucked his hair behind his ear. Next door a battered white truck had pulled into the driveway and he could see the neighbor talking to a man with a ponytail. Closer, a lizard disappeared without moving.

Later, he returned from getting groceries and the porch was littered with charcoal drawings. He saw leaves, and upside down, Douglas's face. On his way to the kitchen he heard her say, "I tried to draw from memory but my memory's shit." She was sitting in the corner of the porch on the floor. He hadn't even seen her.

Then she was gone. From the kitchen Thompkins heard the screen door slam lightly, and the house was quiet. He walked back out onto the porch and stood there, his mind empty. He was drained. Her anger, her energy, had usurped his own and left him with nothing. He sat for a while with students' papers—a short story which wasn't bad and the beginning of a novel, which was. The neighbor easily took his attention when she appeared in the periphery of his vision. Earlier, he had crossed by her in the street and he'd been rude to her. Part of it was desire and part of it was women. He couldn't talk to any more women. For the past ten days women had depended on him and needed him and so when an attractive woman in light clothing who wanted nothing from him smiled and said hello, he couldn't think of anything to say. He had nodded curtly and kept walking.

He went back to reading the novel. The student, a boy Thompkins hadn't seen all semester, had shown up after Christmas break and handed him a thick manila envelope. The boy had taken an incomplete with a gravity which had convinced Thompkins that he was earnest, but this did not spare the work; and when Thompkins put it aside he felt the flat characters leave him without a struggle except perhaps for the character who was obviously the author himself, a boy whose acne fought its own self-conscious description until the reader gave up. Thompkins was just stacking the pages when the phone rang. He sat there. He had never heard the phone ring in this house, it was not his house, not his phone. He moved in his chair, and when the phone stopped ringing he got up and washed out a shirt. Then it was that awkward time of day when if he had been working well he might push, a choice he made by putting on the kettle or getting out the ice. He got out the ice. He thought if the phone rang again he would answer it, even though he was sure it would be Sally Ann calling back. But the phone did not ring. Dusk settled. He took a shower and saw in the mirror that he needed a haircut. "You'll go gray and I'll go thin," he remembered Douglas saying, as though they were making a deal.

On the coffee table on the porch were the drawings Rollin had done. Thompkins began to look through them. They were done on newsprint, and the paper was flimsy. She had done a few of vegetation, no shading, just line—the charcoal seemed to turn with the curves of the leaves. There was a wildness, and he was impressed with the carelessness, the effortlessness in the quick, fluid lines. Next were the two of Douglas. Upside down he had only seen a man's face, but now he saw a face he knew. Broken lines gave the drawings an urgency and the inconsistent weights of lines worked to shift the balance of the face, disturbing it enough to describe the man himself. The porch was dark except for one light, and Thompkins wiped a hand over his face, his eyes. He poured himself another drink. He went into the bathroom to add tap water, which normally he would have done in the kitchen (those goddam beads) except he was looking in the mirror again.

Another hour went by and Rollin did not appear. He remembered the night they'd gone to Mallory Dock. Applauding a sunset was the silliest thing he'd ever heard of, but it was a tradition here and Rollin had wanted to go. Thompkins had followed her past motorcycles and street performers, artists selling bad watercolors and T-shirts. He had never seen so many beards in his life, and from his students Thompkins recognized the smell of marijuana. When a fellow with hair as long as Rollin's failed to interest her in a leather vest like the one he was wearing, he grabbed her arm with one hand and his belt buckle with the other and said, "Well, what about one of these for your old man?" The buckle had a train embossed on it and Rollin had looked at Thompkins and said, "Come on, let's go," but it was the way the fellow looked at them that made him realize that "old man" did not mean father.

He began to wonder if she had been the one to call. He had assumed it was Sally Ann, or someone calling for the owners. Standing there, he took comfort in the lights next door. He smoked another cigarette and had another drink, and feeling the drink—he felt it quickly, having had no dinner—Thompkins stepped out into the yard. It was drizzling slightly, which added to his alarm (although she had not taken the car, she had mentioned hitchhiking at school a few times), and what started out as an excuse to go next door became a reason. The yellow spotlights in the palms blurred in his vision with the rain, and halfway over there he realized he was still holding his empty glass. He also had to pee. He had just set the glass down in a clump of ferns when he heard voices. Rollin had been at the neighbor's. She was coming closer, two women's voices separating in the night air.

"Goddammit, where have you been?" Thompkins said. He could see the neighbor, a silhouette still sharp through the drizzle.

Rollin jumped. "What are you doing out here?" she said.

"Where have you been?" he said again. "Doesn't she have any children of her own?" he said loudly. He held the screen door open for her and then let it slam. Shaking his head, he tucked his hair behind his ear and walked unsteadily towards the bathroom.

Rollin stared after him. She had seen him drunk perhaps twice in her life. He closed the door. There was the muffled sound of something dropping, then she heard the toilet flush. Then the phone rang. Her father opened the bathroom door and they stood there on either side of the ringing phone, looking at each other.

She woke with a cold, which kept her in bed the whole second week. On the worst day she slept all day, and when she woke what she thought was the sheet pattern, a haze of puffy flowers, was crumpled Kleenex. Her muscles ached, there was a throbbing in her neck and a stabbing pain in one eye.

Of course, Thompkins was not glad she had a cold, but it did seem to have broken her fever. The grief which had worn her down had worn itself down. Perhaps he thought that in her weakened state she would listen to him, that something would get through. He told her he had been impressed with the drawings she had done, which was true; but he also wanted her to keep up a level of consciousness about what had happened—what it meant and did not mean in terms of her and the world. He knew she wanted to be a painter and he did not want Douglas's behavior at the end to mark her. And although he had his own problems with Sally Ann, they had agreed on the matter of Rollin's mental state.

"Rollin, are you listening?" He sat at her bedside. He tried to explain that Douglas's behavior—his wildness—had not been an interim, but the result of interims growing closer together. "Last summer he missed a party because he'd been drinking before he got there. He was driving, Rollin. Do you see that?"

She frowned and looked away.

"He stopped on the side of the highway because he was drunk, and he never made it. He slept through it." Thompkins went on, "Then there was the business in Santa Barbara. I don't know what happened in any detail, just that he started out at the Biltmore and it was fine. It was when he got over to that Alisal place—"

"That was that ranch," Rollin said, smiling. "I remember he wrote me about this town nearby which looked just like a miniature Denmark. Solvang, it was called. He'd bought all this 'Western wear.' There was a funny picture someone took of him near the pool wearing it."

She was still smiling, and Thompkins saw it was too early for her to hear these words about Douglas, it would be a long time before she understood that her childhood possession of him had nowhere to go which would benefit her growth.

After she had come home that rainy night Thompkins had gone into the bedroom and closed the door. His worry gone, his anger receding, he let the drinks bring him down and it was all just sad; the loneliness after the horror, now the phone ringing in a house where no one would answer because no one wanted to talk. Or rather Rollin did want to talk, but she had gone across the way as she had done at age twelve on the island. He sat there on the edge of the bed, staring at his empty shoes.

Rollin told him that their neighbor lived on the North Shore above Boston with her husband and his family, that they sailed, that she had no children—each miscellaneous bit of information, while describing her, put her more at a distance. Thompkins did not understand why in an odd way he was angry with both of them. He should have thanked her (her name was Margaret Booz, pronounced, Rollin informed him, to rhyme with "rose") or apologized but the first thing he said to her blamed her. She was busy with her bricks when he approached, and she turned only to say, "Oh. It's you."

"Rollin woke up with a cold," Thompkins said.

She said she knew—Rollin had sneezed a couple of times last night. "I could hear it in her voice," she said. "Even though I don't have any children, I knew that this girl was getting a cold." She was kneeling, her back to him. He said something about "the ambitious project" she had undertaken.

"Look—" he said.

She turned and shaded her eyes and said, "You're a pretty rude guy, aren't you?" She stood then, brushing dirt off knee-length pants. Then she looked at him.

Removing his sunglasses he saw that she was older than he had thought—at least thirty-five. Her eyes were gray, and though her tone had been cool she was watching him now, smiling, and there was a confidence and buoyancy about her he found unnerving. It didn't matter what he knew about her, he wanted to know more. They introduced themselves and the next thing he knew he was sent away with a handful of aspirin not quite knowing what had happened.

He walked back across the yard, the aspirin in his hand. There was a freshness in the air after the rain. Once inside the porch, he heard Rollin call from the bedroom. Of course her voice was familiar, but what struck Thompkins as he avoided the rumple in the rug was that suddenly everything was familiar. The card table, the ghastly orange chair, the coffee table, its glass surface chipped on one corner. He could not see the imperfection from where he was standing but he knew it was there. Up until now, his surroundings—this house—had been neutral, foreign, and like a chemical reaction his relation to these things had somehow changed.

He couldn't work. He tried, but he couldn't. The next day Margaret came over with a pie and Thompkins watched as the pink and orange beads parted around her and clicked behind her. During the forty minutes or so that she was in with Rollin, he scrapped the entire last section of Part II. He did it bit by bit, as a man will shave a beard. He had forgotten that he had made tea, and when she emerged he was in the kitchen pouring it down the drain. The Key lime pie she had brought sat on the counter. He had not told her that neither he nor Rollin liked meringue, but apparently Rollin had. He stood there holding the kettle and feeling like a fool, for he had thanked her rather profusely.

"It's all right," she said. "I didn't make it, I bought it." She stood in the doorway, smiling. It seemed he had forgotten what he was doing. She looked down at the kettle.

"Oh," he said, and turned towards the sink to fill it. He didn't even want any, he realized.

"They haven't done great things with it, have they?" she said. She was talking about the house.

"Houses," he said, exasperation in his voice. "Are you—" He cleared his throat. "How's your terrace coming along?" She moved from her post and was leaning on the counter.

"Oh, just fine," she said.

The next day, when they were taking a walk, she told him an orchid had been named after her.

"A hybrid my mother-in-law came up with," she said. Seeing his expression, she laughed. "I said hybrid, not mongrel." Then, softly: "Actually I've always thought Cattleya would be a pretty name for a girl." They walked slowly.

"And they'd call her Cat," Thompkins said.

"No, they'd call her Lea," Margaret said.

"No, they'd call her Cat," Thompkins said. "Children are mean. They'd call her Cat."

"If she were pretty though? Do you think?"

"Especially if she were pretty," Thompkins said. "You've heard the expression 'catcall.' "

She held his gaze. The aura of money and vague acquaintanceship with cities which floated around her was borrowed and troubling, secondary to who she was. Married young, she had been protected. Thompkins understood that it had been her husband's family who had taught Margaret an indignation at the world which kept it at a distance. The Caribbean vacations, the way her father-in-law ordered martinis (he did not even look at the waitress, but recited in a monotone, "A very dry Beefeater's martini on the rocks with a twist"). Her mother-in-law ordered her clothes from catalogues.

"It was protection," Margaret said. "Security. The family more than the man. But maybe you can't understand that."

"I understand that," he said, looking sideways at her. "As well as a Democrat can."

"Now wait a minute," Margaret said, laughing. "I'm a Democrat—I was born a Democrat! In fact," she said, "it's funny that you said that." They were walking on the beach now. Margaret said she remembered going with her father, who had been a newspaper man ("And I don't mean cigars and desks, I mean a good old-fashioned small-time reporter"), to a reception after the town elections. "It was on Pat Connelly's lawn, and as we walked around my father whispered, 'These are *Republicans,*' as if it were a dirty word." She paused and went on, "But I was only twelve, and I didn't understand why anyone would want to be a Democrat. Republicans had money. To me, Republicans lived in a certain part of town. Don't laugh," she said. "I had it backwards. A twelve-year-old girl . . ." Her voice trailed off. "Anyway, I thought it was funny that you should put it like that."

Later she told him that it was not long after that afternoon on the Connellys' lawn that her father was killed changing a tire on a highway.

She said, "You see, that's why I understand what Rollin is going through now."

Thompkins nodded.

She saw he was not going to talk about it and so she was quiet. But one day after Rollin had left, he presented her with a typed page and a book.

"But this is Eliot," she said, looking up. " 'Prufrock.' "

"Yes," Thompkins said, and he had a flash of Winifred's hysterics, pushed aside by Margaret's voice as she began to read. She read well, not faltering at "to murder and create," which was circled in orange.

"Thank you," he said when she'd finished. The long ash fell from his cigarette and he stared at the gay blue gingham curtains with tears in his eyes.

They spent parts of every day together, the nights; until one afternoon when he had been working and looked up and seen her moving through the green, and it was as if he were already remembering how it had been.

When he asked about her marriage, she said that there had just been a point where she had stayed. "You think it's the money, the comfort," she said. She shrugged easily. "I guess it is. But money isn't what people who don't have it think it is."

She started to talk about sailing—cruising. She mentioned places Thompkins had never heard of. "Little Dix, Caneel Bay—they're lovely. But I always felt like we lost something on the way. The real idea. The sailing. The people—Harry's business—it's very social," she said hopelessly, "and one year I couldn't do it. So we went camping. It was on an island. We all sailed there together and they dropped us off. We—well, I—thought it looked great. There were tents, but they weren't on the ground, they were on boardwalks—"

"Boardwalks and tents, good God," Thompkins said. He laughed, coughed.

"It was awful," she said, laughing. "There were horrible mosquitoes and we had to rent bug bombs. By the time they came to get us we were waving a white flag." It had occurred to her to try the Keys when she heard a couple talking in the hotel lobby in Miami. "I thought they were talking about the keys to their room," she said.

"And so you got this," Thompkins said.

"I got this," she said.

"Playing shepherdess," Thompkins said.

"Shepherdess?"

"When Marie Antoinette had had enough of the king and all those French, she had her own place to go to," Thompkins said. "Not a palace at all. I think she kept chickens."

"And lovers."

"I suppose. Goats and chickens and lovers," he said.

"And we know what happened to her," Margaret said, laughing. They walked for a moment, and then she stopped. "If it had only stayed simple," she said. She looked at him. "Do you know what I mean? Do you ever feel that way?"

"Every morning, and then about forty times before the end of the day," Thompkins said.

Margaret laughed. "Okay then. You see." And she described how she and her husband used to take out a sailboat, just the two of them, no racing, no cruising. "Just us and the Rhodes," she said, and then she explained. "A Rhodes 19 is a sailboat. A sail, and a boat. Simple."

In the years that eventually gathered behind them stories were repeated; seeing each other infrequently did not change that, and one Thompkins remembered, recognized as she began it again, was about the first time she had ever sailed with her husband's family.

"The race hadn't started yet—handicaps, you know—and suddenly Frances's hat blew off. So of course I called out. But Frances whispered not to tell Harry, she said the launch would pick it up, never mind. Frances is tiny, but Harry wouldn't have anyone else crew for him, and as she turned around and the hat drifted in the other direction I understood. But I understood more than that. I was so young," she said.

It was the second time she told that story that Thompkins realized no matter how many times she told it youth would bloom in her face and voice; there was no other place she could find her youth than that—a woman who had gone from childish to childless overnight—and that would be the reason she would never leave.

But he did not know that then, and when she casually told him one day that they were coming, it was a shock.

"Coming here?" Thompkins said. They were sitting outside and he looked at her little house. "Here?"

The day she had brought over the pie, he had caught himself looking in the mirror. He had done it after the morgue and in restaurants and at the airport; a quick, close look at himself, as though he would finally get used to what he suddenly saw. He was fifty years old. Douglas had been forty-eight.

"Don't tell me you've never sailed; you must have," Margaret had said, and there had been an excitement in her eyes and he had seen that she was restless, as if she had only just realized that her bare shoulders were more seductive, when she leaned on the counter that way, than the wide-spaced breasts.

"I took the tiller once," he had answered, and in a confused slide of thinking Thompkins realized that Douglas and Margaret would never meet. That this struck him hard made him know two things: that he expected this woman to be important to him, and that he would never see Douglas again.

By the time her family arrived, Thompkins was gone. After the seven-mile bridge, she began to fade, although he felt her again in Miami, where he just had time before his flight to order a great big steak. He could not remember ever eating as much as he did that night.

Chapter 14

...

Sally Ann had thought the new house would make a difference. She saw summer as open doors, the garden and children, day trips into Boston and Harvard Square and Crane's Beach. The older children would help with the younger ones, and she and Rollin would have time together. But these days Sally Ann lived more and more in another world. Going back to bed in the mornings was no longer enough to prepare her for even the easiest days, when the children played quietly or took long naps. Amy and Stuart filled her days with small battles and laundry, and by the time they were in bed and the dinner dishes were done she was so tired she knew she would not sleep. She drifted through the house, making plans and promises to herself. Meanwhile Jim stood with his arms folded and legs apart, as though frozen in an exercise position, the television screen reflected in his glasses. He might shift, he might scratch his head in a nervous gesture which had claimed him as he lost his hair. The night deepened, the television ending its exhaustive day with a last inning or match point as Sally Ann gravitated towards the rocking chair in the corner, where, away from the television and the progressive cycles of the dishwasher, between the cheers and silences, came the strains of WGBH, the classical music station.

When she had the strength, they argued. It was always the same argument, about money, and always ended the same way, with

Sally Ann going out to get cigarettes. The house was in a new section, as yet undeveloped, and the nearest place she'd found to get cigarettes was at Starlight Lanes, a bowling alley. It was a ten-minute drive through trees, and the bank of lights which greeted her from a distance was always a welcome sight after the crowded living room. The cigarette machine was at the entrance, through dirty glass doors, beyond which an interchangeable group of boys played pool under fluorescent lights. The first time she went she stayed a while. The place smelled like sweat and rubber, and the sound of the balls hitting the pins, followed by shouts, was comforting. It was the sound of people having a good time. Once a man on one of the Tuesday-night teams had smiled at Sally Ann and she had smiled back. He looked as if he would drive a truck, and she was ashamed.

There was a loneliness in her, and that was why she wanted Rollin home. She hadn't seen her since Douglas's funeral, and lately there had been a fear at the back of her mind, a haunting of the day she took the portrait to Douglas at Peninghen. Somehow, the guilt that characterized that period of her life had crystallized in the memory of that day, the last time she had seen Douglas. She had almost seen him when he came up for his reunion at Harvard but she had not. It was all tied up in a way she could not understand, except that it was part of her past and belonged to her as much as anyone who had shared it. Yet at the funeral there had been a barrier. She had stood away from the furs and dark cars in her camel coat, trying not to cry. Lad had come over, because it was the right thing to do, and they had stood there talking about Rollin, because when she had tried to talk about Douglas Lad had cut her off.

"There's where Rollin went to nursery school, when she was just your age," she had said to Amy, but Amy was not interested in that. One night, for no reason, Sally Ann had told Amy about the giraffe. It had been thrown away long ago, but perhaps the fact that it no longer existed was what had engaged the child's imagination. Her mother's exhaustion, the slight Southern accent—there was a dreamy quality to how she told it, like a fairy tale. Thompkins was

the man in the story (of course, Sally Ann left out the mugging);
that was all, he was the man who carried the giraffe everywhere in
the snowy streets of New York City the night Rollin was born. And
when they had left that morning for the funeral, Sally Ann had
mentioned the giraffe in connection not with Lad, but with Pauline.
Amy had looked up at her, realizing for the first time that the story
was true. She called the woman in the story the giraffe lady, and
now that was what interested her as they stood in the cold. Where
was the giraffe lady?

"She was here, but I don't see her anymore," Sally Ann said,
even though it wasn't true—Pauline Dampierre stood not twenty
feet away, her natural paleness set off by her dark cloth (she had
never worn furs) coat and the winter sky.

The drive home had taken six hours, she remembered, because
of an accident outside Hartford. She had arrived home exhausted.
Off and on that week she had tried to call Rollin at the number in
Florida that Lad had given her, but there was never any answer. In
an odd way, Sally Ann had felt she belonged down there with them.
Imagining the palm trees, she stared out at the snow falling and felt
far from her life. She got out old pictures, which started a round of
questions from Amy, who had seen that her mother was crying and
didn't understand.

However, Rollin wanted no part of the household that summer.
After Key West, she'd gone back to school and spent her time at
baseball practices and games, letting the sun wash over her like
someone who had been physically ill. A senior had been kicked out
midyear and she was given that single at the end of the hall, where
she stayed up nights playing jazz (Douglas's strange thick 78s she
eventually replaced) and getting stoned. Before Douglas's death she
had been one of the nine or so students content to sit on a faded
rug and pick at her jeans for three hours while a plump bearded
forty-year-old wearing peace paraphernalia talked about the as-
signed reading. No one did the reading but it didn't matter because
even if the discussion started with a passage from the reading it

disintegrated soon afterwards, straying and gathering force before exploding into current events. Rollin didn't care about the war. What did it have to do with religion, and anyway, didn't Quakerism have to do with pacifism? In the eulogy her father had given at Douglas's funeral he had talked about the war and America and the end of its innocence and what did that have to do with Douglas, lying on some cold floor she imagined? Sweat and blood and winter and loneliness—how could she read *Soul on Ice* without thinking about him, the dark streets and what she would never know? Her father ignored it (and had fallen in love, apparently) and her mother romanticized it. All four children—Amy and Stuart and the Dover kids—saw the picture of Peninghen, and when Thompkins brought Rollin home from school they didn't see anger and grief, they saw a convertible:

"Is Rollin a princess now?" Stuart asked.

Her mother and Jim had moved, and the new house was a curious mix of years and places and children: clothes outgrown and handed down, books with Rollin's name crossed out and Amy's crayoned in. Toys lay scattered around the coffee table, which overflowed with books and magazines, a box of Kleenex balancing on top of one pile and the tile ashtray Rollin had made in second grade on another. On the marble table where once Thompkins had proudly placed a photograph he had taken of Sally Ann in front of the pink house there were now a few packs of Burpee seeds, a deck of cards, a camera, a bowl of curtain hooks, a pair of broken sunglasses Sally Ann kept because she liked their shape, pens, pencils, and a vacuum-cleaner part. If the seeds were planted, a light bulb or a ball of yarn would appear. If the ashtray was emptied, the ashes would be replaced by straight pins.

There were colonies of clutter like that everywhere. Other houses had been a mess, for instance the cottage; but there had been a strength in that mess, the passion of a woman who was changing her life. Here, nothing was going to change.

Rollin's first night home she watched as Jim pushed back an

invasion of batteries, tweezers, roll of Scotch Tape, and a pacifier, quickly replacing them with a potholder so that her mother could set down the casserole. As Rollin looked from him to the cluster of things to her mother and across to Stuart, who was crying and pushing Hilary away, she had a moment of wondering who these people were and what she was doing here. Perhaps because Amy and Stuart had been babies when she had gone away to school, she had hardly thought about them. In her mind, they had remained as controllable and uncontrollable as when she had left. She hadn't paid much attention to Danny and Hilary over the years either. When they had first moved to Massachusetts and Danny and Hilary had visited, Rollin had hated seeing Hilary's bags in her room. She was kept awake by Hilary's little light breaths, and Jim felt he had the right to burst in anytime to open the windows for fresh air. She noticed that Danny wore glasses like his father now and Hilary had foot problems, but neither of them had anything interesting to say and Rollin thought they probably wouldn't have very interesting lives.

All she wanted that summer was to be left alone. Why couldn't they leave her alone? But they fluttered around her like moths drawn to light. All she wanted to do was watch the Red Sox in peace, and she had bought herself a television because Jim was so proprietary of the one in the living room. It was a color set, and had taken on exaggerated importance with the children, which made Jim angry because all the children wanted to come and watch with her.

As the years passed and her mother's marriage fell away, Rollin felt the adolescent disdain she had felt for Jim dwindle, losing its intensity to a theoretical repugnance of a limited man who had used authority without earning respect, who justified such authority by lumping himself together with the times ("You kids have no respect," he would say, citing an article in the paper about drugs or the war—in fact in a later argument about the television it actually seemed that he was saying that color television led to drugs). World

War II had been his pride in life, and so what could he do but talk about the solid American values of his generation? He sat there, picking his cuticles over a placemat littered with crumbs.

In fact the television had nothing to do with it. Rollin had inherited five times what this house had cost, and the color television represented that.

Of course he wouldn't admit this. "Come on, you kids," he said. "She can do whatever she wants, but I won't have you sitting around inside on a Saturday afternoon. Danny, come on. We'll be doing some climbing in a few weeks and I expect you to be in shape." He tousled the boy's head. "Man can't do anything unless he's in shape, huh? Huh?"

A chill went through Rollin. When she had first seen Harvard, when they'd moved up here, she had been so excited: where was the *Lampoon* building? Her father's initials were carved in a table there. And where had Douglas played baseball? She had tried to imagine her father and Douglas, drunk, stumbling in the Yard. Yesterday, her mother had ruined her thoughts, saying wasn't it a shame about Douglas. They were driving along the Charles on a beautiful day and her mother had to ruin it.

"Douglas could have had a career in baseball," she said. "That's what I admire about Jim—he takes care of his body."

"Well, Douglas never would have coached," Rollin said indignantly.

"And what does that mean?" her mother said angrily. "I'm glad Jim is out there with those kids! So he's not a pro—so what! He's out there. He's not sitting in front of the television drinking and criticizing. That's all Douglas did for twenty years. And your father—they're the same! Spectators, watching it all go by! Watching other people sweat and make mistakes and take risks!"

Watching Jim walk out of the room with his hand on Danny's shoulder, she was horrified at wondering why Douglas was dead --and Jim was alive.

Yet she hardly even hated him anymore. Since Douglas's death the loneliness Rollin felt had removed her from the world and she noticed things, as if she saw each person out of context. At some level she felt sorry for Jim as she watched him go back and forth to work, repeating the action as if he could never get it quite right. He sweated in the semitransparent shirts he wore, which were the color of lampshades and seemed to describe what he expected from life:

"Art? What about this house?" he said to Sally Ann one day after she and Rollin had been to the Museum of Fine Arts. "What about a decent-looking house as a priority?"

Sally Ann had said she wanted a museum membership. She had said, "I am saying that it is sad that art is not a priority in this house." She left the room, then came back through the shutters in the kitchen. "I need a housekeeper," she said. "How about that as a priority?"

Jim started to say something, but Sally Ann turned and said, "I am forty-six years old and you want me to be content with a library card!"

What was her mother talking about? It was as if they were arguing in code. Rollin, who was sitting on the couch, stared at them. It was the first time she had really seen them independently of herself in this household. "Where are you going?" she asked. Her mother was getting the car keys and it was eleven-thirty.

"I'm going to get cigarettes," Sally Ann said, her voice suddenly soft. "I'm going to the bowling alley for cigarettes."

Rollin quickly saw that it wouldn't have mattered if she had had cigarettes or not—it had become an excuse to get out of the house.

"I had hoped we could go through this together," Sally Ann said the next day.

"Go through what?" Rollin said. "What are you going through?"

Her mother had chosen the wrong life, and she was using Douglas's death to justify giving up.

"Not a day goes by that I don't think of Douglas, that something doesn't rem—"

"You didn't even know him in the end," Rollin said.

"That's right," Sally Ann said. "I knew him in the good times. I feel lucky I have that. No one can take that away."

"That's just what I'm saying: you didn't know him at the end. The Village fifteen years ago—what does that have to do with anything? It's the past."

"It's my life!" Sally Ann cried. "It's the past but it's *my life*, and you and Pauline and Winifred and your father all seem to think that since I'm no longer with your father I have no right to that!"

Rollin wasn't listening. She had smoked part of a joint (her mother never noticed) and she was calm now, enjoying the hammock and looking up into the trees. She closed her eyes. Her mother was talking about the island house now. Sunlight warmed Rollin's eyelids. She was floating, but it was a heavy floating. Her mother had stopped talking, then she said, "Oh, Rollin, look. Look, honey."

Rollin opened her eyes to see Danny walking towards the swing set, Amy on his shoulders.

"He used to carry you just like that," her mother said, her needless words destroying the vision, and the memory and the air.

Rollin's room—the back room—had a separate entrance, and late one night Sally Ann saw dark figures come and go, their glowing cigarettes moving jerkily towards waiting cars. Sally Ann was afraid to say anything to Rollin, and how could she? They were the kids from the bowling alley.

Rollin slept until noon most days, then stopping for coffee, she settled into the hammock. It became a familiar sight: the children at her heels as she made her way slowly through the sliding glass doors.

"They're friends," she said. "Didn't you ever have summer friends? People you knew you'd probably never see again but it was fun while it lasted?" The voice came from a swaying heap of color under the trees.

"No," Sally Ann said. "No, I guess I never did."

Night after night girls stumbled through the living room on their way to the bathroom, but the boys didn't bother; one night Sally Ann jumped at the sight of a figure near the woodpile before she realized it was only one of the boys peeing. Jim had gone to bed, and she had turned out the lights and was watching an old movie. The boy had known she was there, but Sally Ann had gotten the feeling from the way he walked—a stride—that he wouldn't have cared that she'd seen him.

She did not know anymore what she had expected of that summer, which as it wore on alienated her from all those around her, even from Amy and Stuart. She had never taken to Jim's children, perhaps because they had never taken to her. Danny was a smart aleck, and Hilary hardly spoke at all. Sally Ann remembered her as a child, whining, falling down in her chair at the dinner table, complaining that "my mother doesn't make it like that." But she also recalled how the child had clung to her father with a paleness which was almost frightening. On Saturday mornings she went to the dump with Jim and if anyone tried to join them she screamed. They'd had to divide the errands. She had been about the age Amy was now, and it had delighted her to sit in the front seat of the Rambler while her father emptied the garbage. Now she was thirteen, cold blue eyes in her mother's flat face, her mother's problems with her feet. That was why she could not go climbing, and sat quietly in the new house that summer, enjoying the breeze like an old woman. It was she who stayed with the children the night of the accident, and as Sally Ann ran out of the house, grabbing her keys and cigarettes and calling out about the children to the figure in the doorway, it seemed that this person had existed in her life, testing her patience and taking her time, solely for this moment.

The accident occurred out on Hambling Road. Sally Ann had not even known that Rollin had left the house. As usual, she had knocked on the door to ask Rollin to turn down the music, but when she peeked in on the circle of faces Rollin's was not among them. The kids were sitting around on the rug in a cloud of smoke, a blur of hair and arms.

"Excuse me," she said, trying to smile. "Where is Rollin?"

One boy laughed and a girl said something she didn't catch. She asked again and a boy wearing a shirt with ladies' faces on it said, "Gone to Nick's, but she'll be back."

Sally Ann did not know Nick's last name or where he lived. "Well, would you turn down the music down, please?"

The boy with the wild shirt saluted her. "Hey man, no problem!" he said.

Sally Ann went back out into the living room. Hilary was reading—insects hovered above her blond head in the light from the lamp. Danny had gone climbing with his father, and the children were in bed. Sally Ann heard the music stop. She went to the window. Were they leaving more hurriedly than usual? Five minutes later the phone rang, as if they'd been warned.

The balding doctor talked about the right tibia and the short doctor talked about eyes. There were words like that: tibia and fibula and short oblique; ellipse and laceration.

"But what is that?" Sally Ann cried. "Is it part of brain or a muscle or—tell me! You know I don't know! Don't take my arm —stop that! Tell me straight. I've got to call her father," she said. Then she collapsed.

Thompkins arrived late the following afternoon.

"Where the hell have you been?" Sally Ann cried when he appeared at the end of the slick hallway.

"I'm here now," Thompkins said. "What—"

"You're—" she began. But suddenly she was exhausted. He hadn't been here when it had first happened, but nothing could have changed that, she didn't want to argue with him, not now. "Oh Lad—"

"What?" He cut her off. "You said she was all right. Is there—"

"And she will be," Sally Ann said. "They tell me she will be, but you have to listen to them now. I can't anymore. They talk about it in medical terms and I don't—oh, *Lad*—"

"Who the hell were they, Sally Ann?" he said. "Kids she's running around with, you obviously didn't know who the hell they were or maybe that household you've got going Lord knows there's got to be a lot you don't even—"

"Stop!" she cried. "I'd hoped you'd—how *can* you?"

Thompkins looked at her—just looked at her. Then he went to find a doctor.

What he would remember was sitting by Rollin's bedside and knowing she thought he was looking at the bruise, when what he was looking at was what was missing. He was looking at her eye: she had hit some part of the dash, and because of a laceration to her eye, they'd had to remove the mole.

Her right leg was another story. When the car had been rear-ended, Rollin, the passenger (they had taken the boy's car), had been thrown to the floor. The doctor reconstructed it like a crime: she must have been sitting with both feet on the floor, and the impact must have been strong, resulting in a fractured right tibia. He talked about her like a car: normal alignment had to be reestablished if she was not to have a bowleg.

"Oh no," Sally Ann said, and one could hear her Southern accent when she took the doctor's arm and said, "We mustn't let that happen, doctor. Do you have any idea what that would do to a young girl? Why, she's not even eighteen."

The doctor turned to Thompkins and explained that even after the cast came off, Rollin would be on crutches, then one crutch, then a cane. He talked about physical therapy, and lowered his voice when he mentioned a limp, which would be temporary. Thompkins asked how long she would be in a cast.

"Oh, four months," the doctor said. "The rest depends on her, really." His face softened for the first time. "Is she a very athletic girl?"

Thompkins almost smiled. "Well, no. In fact I would say not at all."

"We'll see then," the doctor said. "Maybe we could get her to do some swimming. It's a while off yet."

Thompkins drove up weekends for the rest of the summer, and sometimes even further north, to Margaret.

Rollin stood in front of the mirror that fall and wondered if she had changed. Nick had never written, never called, and although the cast was to come off in mid-December she did not want to go home for Christmas because she did not want to face him not calling, and then run into one of them somewhere—it was not her town, that was all. And although her cast was crowded with signatures and jokes in bright colors, she did not feel she had many friends at school either. She felt different. All her life people's gazes had veered to the mole in her eye (or, being self-conscious, had she imagined it?), and now the mole was gone. Yet it seemed she had always looked as she did now. She couldn't remember the mole.

Or perhaps she had changed more inside. After Douglas's death she had produced drawings in a frenzy. Many charcoals had hung on the walls in various stages of completion—fixed, not fixed— Dede, the hall resident, had said if you lit a match in that room it would explode. Rollin hardly recognized those drawings now. They embarrassed her and she admired them and they had nothing to do with her. She remembered Key West and how it had been, how her father had hidden behind his grief while her own had been so visual and passionate. Was that what she needed, and had she lost it? Back at school that year she often stayed by herself.

When the thigh-high cast came off she was shocked. She had been so eager to put on a pair of pants again, as if it would be that easy. But her leg was light and weak and strange, and reminded her of when she'd gotten her braces off and expected perfection, and instead had seen her bare teeth, exposed and stained.

One day in early spring Thompkins stood with Rollin on the edge of Peninghen property, making a deal with her.

"I don't give a damn what the will says, I'm your father and I'm telling you," he said. "If you're serious about painting, if you want to come and live here and try to make it, no more trouble, Rollin." When she had walked out of her dorm with the cane he'd had to look away. In the car she had talked about the physical therapist. "Bob calls himself my trainer," she said, smiling, and even though Thompkins knew the cane was temporary he could not look at it.

Rollin stared up at the buildings. It had been a year, and the place was still empty. Her father had been living in the tower room, and Lucy and Jim had stayed. But the paintings had been put in storage (the sculptures and installations had not been removed), and whenever she had thought of it, the long halls and cold gray buildings, the bare trees, Peninghen had existed in her mind as an extension of the horror of what had happened. The lawyer's references to various debts incurred, a boiler which had to be replaced, had escaped her completely.

Now, imagining living there, Rollin was stunned by the beauty and silence, the lilacs in bloom and the faint haze around the buildings, which were a lighter gray than she remembered. It was then that she realized that Peninghen had replaced the island house for her. For Rollin, Peninghen, the late-afternoon sun on the stone buildings as she and her father stood in the shadow of the hedge, represented the future. The island house represented the past.

She returned to Peninghen after graduation, a glorious day of boys in dark suits and girls in long white dresses pinned with roses; there was something hatless about them under the hot sun, Thompkins thought; in fact during the ceremony one of the mothers had fainted.

Later Rollin stood at her window. She had changed out of her dress (and pinned the rose on Amy, who had been thrilled) and was watching the graduates—her friends—and parents below, a slow procession of cars.

"Oh look," her mother said.

Rollin turned. "Mom, I thought you were packing, not unpack-
ing."

Sally Ann had found the picture of Douglas in Rollin's suitcase.
"That was in Ponte Vedra, Florida, in 1962," she said. "Rollin,
honey, we should pack this better. You don't want it to get broken."

Rollin turned back to the window. She knew Douglas's expression
in that picture by heart. The day was ending, and there was a chill
in the air. At noon there had been a red Cadillac parked under the
trees, but now it was gone and so were most of the people. She
heard tissue paper behind her. "There," her mother said. "I wrapped
it in tissue paper and then in your white dress, so when you take
it out be careful, okay, honey?" Shadows had moved, and though
it was chilly there was still sun, and as Rollin looked out across the
great expanse of lawn past the buildings, past the tennis courts out
to where the trees bordered the earth, she finally knew Douglas was
gone. But she could still hear his voice. It was a voice which invited
them all to dinner, to better times. Tears rolled down her cheeks,
as now the shadows fell in great triangles.

PART THREE

...

PART THREE

Chapter 15

o o o

James Mount, head high, walked past the window at a distance. Mount was a sculptor, quite full of himself, and it had been Lucy who had helped Thompkins locate his sense of humor about the man. Mount wore tailored suits when he worked, but to please the cocktail circuit, hostesses and collectors, he had contrived a studio look—old pants, a shirt (torn perhaps), an out-of-date tie, but a tie just the same—all part of the extreme thought which went into it. Thompkins had heard this from someone, and when he mentioned it to Lucy she simply didn't understand: "People dress up to go out," she said fiercely, "not to stay by hisself and slam some clay around."

Mount disappeared from view. Thompkins turned back into the room. One o'clock had come and gone, and Margaret had not called.

The following day was the same. In the mail was the phone bill, something addressed to him as Kipps's executor, something—trash; alumni Harvard more trash. He went back to the typewriter. He worked until noon, when the sky clouded over, an immense sweep of shadow like a giant bird flying over the maze. Peninghen was a strange pocket of the world, weatherwise; squalls and then bright blue skies, as at sea. He wasted the next hour and when the phone did not ring he turned from the window where he was standing and looked at the stack of manuscript beside the typewriter, shaking his head. After a plate of leftover meatloaf, he found himself back at the window. He saw John Littlefield, walking briskly, then Rollin caught up with him and Thompkins could tell by her gestures that she was angry. The tower room was well located for watching what was going on, bad for his concentration and bad for getting anywhere: for example in order to get to the common room or the library, he had to pass by Littlefield's office. He rarely ate in the dining room.

He was working well when the storm began, first the little ticks of rain, then the downpour. He turned on a few lights and had made tea, and if he wanted another interruption here she was: the door ground open and Rollin stood there, wet and angry.

"Would you close the door?" Thompkins said.

Rollin would have slammed it if it hadn't been so old and heavy. "Would you just tell me one thing?" she said. She threw her leather jacket on the couch and clawed at the mass of wet curly hair. She pulled out a cigarette, which she threw away because it was wet, and then she took one of his. "I can't believe you smoke these things," she said.

"Well, would you give me one of those things?" he said.

She thrust one at him, and he caught a glimpse of dirty fingernails before she started on her habitual angry tour of the room, picking up objects and putting them down again, sometimes carelessly so that once a small sculpted dog had broken.

"An attention span to last an *en*tire sunset," the Southern playwright Bart Laws had observed about Rollin when he had spent time at Peninghen, and this did seem to be a trait passed on (although impossible) by Douglas Kipps to his goddaughter. School, men, painting, plum tomatoes in the garden one summer—each of her consuming interests burst forth with a passion too strong to last. She had been only nineteen when she came to live at Peninghen. She had been accepted at Rhode Island School of Design, but she had opted for attending the local community college, feeling that whatever it lacked in instruction or equipment would be made up

for at Peninghen. But the extremes were too great: the level at the
college was below even what she had imagined (one field trip to a
museum the first semester and one to Peninghen, where the exercise
in perspective was to draw the maze), and the atmosphere at Peninghen was alternately stimulating and stifling. How could she take
the portrait assignment seriously when the faces around her were
a hall of fame? Other students drew their grandmothers. "Sure,"
her professor said, "draw James Howell—at least I'll know if there's
a resemblance." Rollin had had the idea of asking the pale scrappy
girl who helped in the kitchen, but Jenny Crow had turned proudly
and said, "I should start charging. Dianne Yett was in here last week.
I could be hanging in the Modern Art museum next year."

The decline in Rollin's attitude was not helped by the specific
conditions imposed upon her at Peninghen. She had been there for
a year or so when she realized that her godfather had not had
confidence in her, nor in the person she would grow up to be. His
will detailed that she would be allowed a studio at Peninghen if she
so desired, but not one of her choice—that would depend on the
needs of the guests in residence at the time. If Rollin spent time
there, she was expected to behave "in a manner not contrary to
and in support of the other members of the community . . . and at
times . . . be at their disposal." In other words there was a fine line
between her presence as guest and servant, a condition newly determined with each arrival. The will went on to say that if in due
course she decided to take over as director of the place (the word
used throughout the will was "institution," which made her think
of a mental ward) she would be expected to present herself to the
board of directors, "whose judgment it will be to determine the
fitness of the candidate . . . for a trial period deemed acceptable . . ."
and so on.

Thus in three years Rollin was obliged to change studios eleven
times. No sooner would she settle into the next space when a note
would arrive from the director, John Littlefield, informing Rollin

that as of such and such a date this space would be accorded to so and so. It wasn't even the physical inconvenience which bothered her as much as the haunting presence of the imminent arrival.

That was what was angering her now. Littlefield had just notified her that in two weeks she would have to give up her studio to Leon Guttman.

"You knew that," Thompkins said.

"But this is a week early," Rollin said, waving the sheet of paper. "And not only that, I have to go out and buy some stupid ladder for him." She threw herself on the couch.

Thompkins had the tower room and Rollin had the bungalow just inside the gates, and sometimes they went for days without seeing one another. Lately he dreaded seeing her.

"What the two of you doing here anyway," Lucy had said more than once. "Don't care how big this place is, can't hold you two."

Had Rollin been a man, had she been Thompkins's son, he would have told her to get out of here, leave Peninghen and go out and see the world. But one didn't do that with a daughter. There had been no heating in the bungalow when she had come to live at Peninghen, and she had lived in the main building, alone. There was a room across from what had been Douglas's office, with a fireplace, and even now she continued to go up there as a child will go up to an attic and secretly try on clothes. Thompkins worried about her.

"I never should have let you stay up there," he had said recently, but she said that she had done some of her best work up there.

"You'll do other good work," he said.

She shook her head. What was happening was that the past was slipping away and there was nothing to replace it. The beauty of the property was alarming, but there was hardly a moment when Rollin looked up at the main building that she did not feel her tentative claim upon it. In winter when there were no residents, only the gray trees and short afternoons, the place seemed to belong to her. Otherwise, she had merely been willed the right to live there, and any thoughts of ownership were dampened by the select population in residence there, a collective talent superseded only by its tremendous ego.

At first she had rejected it completely. She drank too much at openings, and at night Thompkins would hear the ripping sound of a motorcycle belonging to some boy from town. In fact it had gotten so he couldn't sleep until he heard it and knew she was safe.

"If I'm old enough to get parking tickets I'm old enough to drink," he remembered her saying at one point, probably around the time of the accident; and it had occurred to him that to her, innocent did not mean naive, it meant the opposite of guilty, as though the very act of losing her innocence meant changing its definition.

In January he went to Florida, and when he returned he found Rollin sitting in the common room, absentmindedly striking matches. He had been gone for two months. They had argued the night he had left, and he had left her sitting in that exact spot. For all he knew, she had been sitting there, lighting matches, the whole time he'd been gone.

Then she quit school. She claimed that the only drawings she put any life into were the ones she did at Jane's. The cracked green vinyl stools, the scarred booths and sweet smell cutting the hamburger grease exclaimed over by the mechanics from Al's—that was the only real life around her.

He did not disagree, but off by herself she wasn't getting any feedback. She sat in front of the fire, nodding and twirling her hair as he talked. "Rollin, are you listening?"

"I thought you said being taken seriously didn't start with other people," she said.

"It starts with the work," he said, but he had the impression that they were talking in circles.

On the other hand, when things were good at Peninghen, at dinner when conversations or even arguments got going, it was like a big family, and Rollin had the impression of being right back under the faded fringe lamp at the island house. However, she was no longer that little girl, and the only recognition of her capabilities showed in what others expected of her as far they were concerned. She changed, chameleonlike, according to what was asked of her. She read the part of Rose for Bart Laws, she gridded up canvases for Susan Western, she was the model for J. T. Houghton. But the longer she played these roles, the less likely she was to take her own work seriously. She could tell that she was living outside of a world like theirs that she might one day create for herself. She floated, isolated from any guiding principle and from those about her, who alternated between kidding her and pretending to take her seriously, or ignoring her completely. Not in a rude way; it was just that being so taken up with themselves, with their work and their reflections of themselves in each other, they forgot she was there. Eventually, this was probably good for her, but certainly she didn't see it that way then, and since she could not take out her frustration on the residents, a triangle had formed between her and her father and Littlefield.

In the beginning, Rollin had gotten along with John Littlefield. Basically, she had felt sorry for him. He was short, and seemed to prefer neither men nor women. He had no friends—she assumed that because she distributed the mail and he never got any, and he never left even for a weekend. Peninghen was his reason for being. And yet he had no real power. He carried out the wishes of the board, and existed only between Thompkins and Pauline and Douglas. (It made Rollin furious when he called Douglas's will "our contract.") He was not allowed the key to the tower room, nor was he permitted to alter any room except for practical purposes. To his dismay, Douglas Kipps's old office had been turned into a sort of reading room (as it was above the common room a circular staircase had been put in; also this was where Peninghen's records were kept) and he had been given a modest office on the ground floor.

Rollin's dislike of him began when she saw that he actually enjoyed his middle position: he liked gossip, he liked manipulating people, even if it was just at the dinner table. (Not surprisingly, he was a friend of Pauline Dampierre's.) Then he started interfering in Rollin's life, which he defended by saying that what concerned Peninghen concerned him.

Until Bart Laws drove into Peninghen in his battered 1958 T-bird, there had been a few boys, a couple at boarding school and a few from the town near Peninghen, mainly Tom Buck, a sullen boy with a cowlick who even on a motorcycle was not very convincing. (Once after they'd had an argument he had roared up and around and around the driveway during a tea, but no one had paid any attention.) Rollin had slept with him a few times but it hadn't been anything and she had been relieved when she had found out about the waitress at Jane's. Tom Buck had quivered on top of her like an insect, and Rollin knew from merely watching Bart Laws rise from a chair that he would not be anything like that.

A Southern gentleman: later she decided that that simply meant that somehow, he had made her think she had been the one to seduce him; that he had only gone through with it to be polite, or because it was expected of him.

"Will you sit down," he said to her the first night at dinner as she ran in and out.

Bart Laws was the first man who ever gave her flowers, a sweet heavy bundle of color buzzing and crawling with insects, a wild humid study of nature he announced that she should paint.

"If I could paint I'd paint you sitting right there by them," he said the day he came to the bungalow with the bouquet. "So strong and wild—not any woman could sit in a room with those and hold her own. You know that, don't you." He set the flowers in the vase as if he were setting down a small child.

His wife's letters came on lavender stationery. She had one of those double Southern names: Taylor Lee. Taylor Lee Hilton, whom Rollin pictured as fragile and pretty, perhaps unwell. When Bart Laws gave her his work in progress to read, there was a woman she thought must be his wife. "She pronounces 'bourbon' like a favorite nephew," the stage directions read. The play was about the artificial towns started in the early 1800s in North Carolina.

"Towns were just proposals for towns," Bart Laws explained. "Lots were sold, but the towns never did come into being." He said that the idea had been that the development of waterways would give reason for the existence and growth of such towns. "Got a town that was laid out in 1815, but by 1819 nothing had been built."

"Sort of the opposite of a ghost town," Rollin said.

He nodded, but she had the feeling he had not heard what she had said. He was looking at her and smiling.

"I almost married a Northern gal," he said. "She was from the state of Vermont. And her daddy wasn't crazy about me one bit,"

"My mother's from the South," Rollin said.

"But you told me you can't cook," he said. "You mean your mama's a Southern gal and she didn't teach you how to cook?"

She sat with her bare legs crossed, and when she looked up he was looking at her in a way which described what she felt. When she was working, she had to work fast to control the mediums— ink and gouache were wet, charcoal and pencil were dry, and there was a lightness about her body as she moved. Now, sitting close to this man in the bungalow, there was a heaviness about her, about the weather and the light in the room. He had said, "You must be about twenty-five," and Rollin had not denied it, and lying there afterwards she thought this must be what the South was like, a slow afternoon near a river with a man.

It had ended almost as soon as it began (when Bart Laws found out that Rollin would be twenty-two the following December), but Littlefield wouldn't let it go. She told him it wasn't any of his business.

"My dear, of course it is, because image is my business," he said. Littlefield had a habit, during a conversation, of rubbing his right eyebrow and smoothing it over. "Will we have a problem like this again, do you think?"

She had gone to Winifred. Some wild idea of following Bart Laws had made her think of her inheritance. But as she stood in Winifred's living room she had the feeling that the older woman had been expecting this; and what followed sounded like either a speech she had prepared or the result of tranquilizers.

"There are responsibilities one is born with, and those one takes on," she said. "Those one—creates." She leaned over and fluffed a pillow, and when she looked at Rollin again she held her head high. "Because you see that was who Douglas was. He wasn't creative, so he created responsibilities towards creative people. Do you understand?"

Rollin understood that Winifred was already saying no. Briefly Rollin had seen a softness in her face, but it was gone now. "A club, a foundation," she went on. "A scholarship for a player." She turned. "Peninghen." She walked around a gilded armchair, her heels clicking on the parquet. "But I remember Douglas told me once—creative people always want more. More time, more money—but then you've seen that with your father." She was wearing a conservative blue dress the same color as the Chinese screen, and Rollin could not believe she had been Douglas's wife. "You'll get the money. The money will come. And why would you need it there anyway? You have a studio, a place to live—food," she said vaguely. "You're painting," she said, "aren't you? What—"

"I need air!" Rollin said. "I—" She tried to control herself. "You can't understand because it's—well, it's hard to understand, I guess. I just need to be alone. Or something. I need to be around people who aren't already where they want to go. Do you see? Am I explaining it? Of course I love it there—it's beautiful. But it's not real. I need a city, maybe. I need friends. Littlefield's always asking me to do things and he makes me feel like a servant."

"John says you're indispensable with the French," Winifred said.

"So what?" Rollin said. "I'm tired of reading about other people. Reading their catalogues and bios, looking at their slides. I want my own! I'm almost twenty-two. I'm tired of being Papa's daughter or

Douglas's goddaughter, and Littlefield asking me to get gesso, or a bulb for the overhead projector."

"Go away for a while, why don't you," Winifred said.

Rollin almost laughed. Wasn't it Winifred who "went away for a while"?

"I don't mean alone," she went on. "But don't you have someone, a friend—a boyfriend?"

"No!" Rollin said. "That's just what I've been telling you!"

She left Winifred standing there, and when the elevator didn't come she ran down twelve flights of stairs. She ran out into the city, taxis honking and men in suits filling the sidewalks. She went to the Whitney, and for the rest of the day she just walked. She arrived back at Peninghen exhausted.

The next day she took the station wagon and picked up the ladder, and for the next few days she sat and stared at her drawings, a series in ink, gouache, and pencil, the sunsets a warning of Guttman's invasion—his mad reds and oranges. As the sun went down the shadow of the ladder was pulled across the wall, and the ladder looked as if it were made of yellow gold. Two days before he was due to arrive, Rollin lit a joint, and looking around the familiar room, she decided it was time. As usual, she started with the trash, then she started with the scotch.

When Rollin had first come to Peninghen, she had spent a lot of time with Lucy, who had been devoted to Douglas. Sometimes one heard it in her language: "Come on, honey, you can't just say Rothschild, you got to say if it's a Mouton or Lafitte!" Then the great laugh.

"I knowed all the trouble," she was known to say. "That little fire? It was me that called. That chunk of *con*crete that fell off the wall?" She nodded. That chunk of concrete had been an early relief piece lent by Robert Lamb, and it had been generally agreed that if it hadn't been for Harold Sand's cowboy boots, his toes wouldn't have stood a chance. "I called the police and I called the fire department and when that doctor didn't come I got that nice veterinarian. And then I took him over the bottle," Lucy always added, laughing.

"I just told him," she said about Douglas. "I said you leave my kitchen out of it. You tell those ar-tists to stop coming around and stealing my eggs."

It was when Rollin heard her talk like that, tell stories, that she felt it was all over. A hospital was going up across Route 413, and more and more it seemed that Peninghen had been a time and a place, that no matter who came and stayed nothing would be created which would equal its aura and history. Mathilde Dampierrre had been married for ten years, but it seemed like yesterday that Rollin had watched from the window in Douglas's office as the wedding guests arrived. It had been like looking into the future. These were her guests. Her portrait hung in the main hall, but it was more than that, and it wasn't fair: not only was Mathilde getting married there, but Douglas was giving her away. He had rented big tents and had catered huge amounts of food, a cake with a bride and groom and Eiffel Tower on top.

"What do you mean, it's made of paper?" he'd said, referring to Mathilde's dress, which was actually a bridesmaid's dress, street-length with long sleeves and pockets, from Dior.

"Jesus Christ, I'll feel like I'm walking a nurse down the aisle," Douglas had said.

"I would like to know," Pauline said, "what she is protesting. Her own marriage, perhaps. Well, it is from Dior—just tell them it's above the knee from Dior," she said, referring to the *New York Times*.

"I don't see what's wrong with a dress made of paper," Mathilde had said. "Money's made of paper."

"I guess you'd better just hope it doesn't rain, baby," Douglas had said, and followed Pauline out into the hall, leaving the others to deal with Winifred's craziness: she hadn't thought of rain; what if it rained? She had planned for the flower girls to do a maypole around the bride, and if it rained the crepe paper would bleed all over the dress.

Rollin, too old to be a flower girl and too young to be a bridesmaid, had watched the preparations with not a small amount of jealousy. Still, the wedding had stayed in her mind like something she had dreamed, and after reading Mathilde's thank-you note in a messy dark corner of the living room, she had run upstairs and looked at the wedding picture to make sure it had really happened.

Now when she looked at the picture Rollin was struck by how dated it was, the makeup and hairstyles, and especially the maze. It had doubled in height since then. Stories about it ranged from Douglas with a girl and a bottle of champagne to the wild party for the unveiling of Franko's *Botticelli's Venus Loves Day-Glo at Dawn.* The hedge was still tended by Lucy's husband, but people did not even seem to notice it anymore. Once a child had gotten lost in it, he couldn't have been more than three or four. There were his cries (his mother had fainted in the hallway), and then someone had seen him from an upstairs window, a roving spot of color in the alleys of the maze.

When had that been? Three years ago? Rollin had been at Peninghen a year or so at the time. She found she got the years confused: last night at dinner there had been talk of a painter who had been here one fall, and although Rollin remembered which studio he had had, she could not recall who had been here at the same time.

"François Jacomet was here the year Susan Western was with us," Littlefield said.

"I don't think—" Rollin began.

"My dear, I'm sure of it," Littlefield said. "Because I remember they didn't get along." He laughed a polite little laugh, and rubbed his eyebrow. "For isn't that the way it always is. We never remember when people do get along, it's when they don't get along that we remember."

There was a peep of a laugh from Mary Fitts, but William Tepper barely managed a smile, and continued to cut his meat into trapezoids.

Jacomet was a French painter Pauline had sent over, who had left behind a trail of Gauloises and a box of Lefevre Foinet paints, held over at customs for a magnificent sum he could not afford. His name had come up because talk had turned to France, the challenge being to find Mary Fitts a "new" place to paint. The discussion had jumped between Spanish light and Italian food, the color of the water in Antigua. What was cheap, what was expensive, who had been where last. Ted Yerkes, the poet, had been to Greece, an island called Spetsai. Then talk was back in Europe again: a village outside Paris called Vetheuil, the colors of Rome.

"And the Tuscany Hills—now there, there's the place to go," someone said.

"Where are the Tuscany Hills?" Rollin asked.

"My dear!" Littlefield said.

"Rollin, they're in Italy," Mary Fitts said. She was a quiet woman, whose husband was a banker and might as well have been on the board. She had just started painting last year. Before that, she had done painfully detailed pencil drawings of paper bags which showed every crease. To Rollin, they were too contrived. Technically incredible, but static. She spoke of elevating the everyday object by isolating it in space. "I wanted to make boring objects interesting," she had said, but in rendering them exactly she accomplished just the opposite.

At first Rollin had not understood why her father had extricated himself from the judging of applicants, but having watched how the system worked for a few years she didn't blame him. Mary Fitts's work was all right—more a skill than a talent, certainly no risk or gift involved; and Rollin knew that she would not have been admitted against another painter, much younger, who had applied, if Bill Fitts had not been in the background moving money around. Didn't she know it?

From her window, Rollin watched William Tepper emerge for his afternoon walk. She owed it to him that she had this studio: he had requested the studio at the back, which usually no one wanted because the light was bad and it faced the road. But Tepper worked with artificial light. He actually liked facing the road, he said; it reminded him of the city.

"You know what he likes?" Jenny Crow said later. It was as though she were about to reveal William Tepper's sexual preferences. "He likes those processed cheese slices."

Rollin laughed, thinking about the article about his last show in *Artforum*. Cheese slices could definitely have fit into the molecular landscapes he called "Structure of Fantasy."

Just then Littlefield poked his head in the door. He just wanted to remind Rollin to pick up Mr. Horcher at the train?

"And what's his specialty?" Lucy asked, meaning what didn't he eat.

"I'm sure we'll do fine by Mr. Horcher, Lucy," Littlefield said, and bowed out of the room (out of the doorway—he never entered the kitchen).

Rollin arrived just as the train was pulling out, leaving the man she recognized as Frank Horcher (she had seen the jacket cover) standing on the platform, people deserting him right and left. It was a role Jimmy Stewart might have played when men still wore hats.

"I've never read your father," he said in the car after they'd introduced themselves. He said it quickly, looking sideways at her. "Started it ten times, you know. It's dog-eared to page thirty." Then: "And you're his daughter? You type his manuscripts?"

It was meant to be a joke, a throwback to another century, and Rollin stared at the road. "Anything you need in town, Mr. Horcher?" she said.

"Uh—yeah. I could use a ribbon, actually," Frank said. "That's what I'm here for, isn't it?" He laughed. He was looking out the window now, and Rollin decided there was a distinct city quality to Frank Horcher; crickets probably set his teeth on edge while honking relaxed him. Not that he was sophisticated—he had the air of the Midwest about him, someone born in a city one defended. As if confirming her suspicions, he sneezed. "Hay fever," he said.

Rollin never asked painters about their work, and when she spoke to writers her father's estimation was never far from her mind. "Not a bad book," he had said about *The Corner Booth*, which when it came out had not only been a best-seller, but had also been the focus of articles dealing with the fine line between literature and something to read. ". . . just as the character Rich Westerly, the proverbial boy from the wrong side of the tracks, sought to overcome his rash beginnings . . . succeeded in endearing himself to those on both sides of the tracks."

That evening after dinner they took a walk.

"Sure, he was me," Frank said when Rollin asked. "But they made him into something different. Made him a hero." Without making a choice, they were headed towards the bungalow. "But of course I'm not supposed to say anything. I can hear him like I'm the ventriloquist and he's the doll. 'Take your humble beginnings and stuff them,' he says."

"It sounds like you're jealous of your own character," Rollin said. They had come to the tower room, where the window burned yellow with the sunset.

"The flip side of your father, I imagine," Horcher said. He walked with his hands in his pockets. "With him they'll never dig deep enough and with me they keep digging even when there's nothing there." He flashed her a smile. "Gives them something to do."

"But come on, it must be great to see your name on the best-seller list," Rollin said, pushing open the door to the bungalow. "I remember when your book came out people knew who Rich Westerly was when they didn't know who the vice president was," she said.

"Just because I made some money on it doesn't mean I can't be cynical," Horcher said. "Your father doesn't have the market on that, you know." He looked around. "Nice," he said.

"When my father's book came out we couldn't even find it," Rollin said. "My grandmother took me into bookstores and ordered five copies just so there'd be some in the store."

She asked him what he was working on now, but he had abandoned the conversation. He didn't even ask about her work. When he came the following night, they sat outside until the mosquitoes got bad. A spotlight lit giant leaves, and Frank drew back, then kissed her. He kissed her again, looking at her quizzically, the same curious expression on his face as when Jenny Crow had served him beets. He drank a few more scotches and gave her a few more kisses like that; but then the first time she moved towards him, he backed away.

"Got to get up tomorrow," he said. "Get the juices flowing." He set the glass down on the table. "Not that anyone's interested in anything but the sequel," he said. "You wouldn't believe the money they offered me! And wouldn't she just love that—oh, yes!" He brought up the empty glass. "Got another of these?" he said, pacing the room in long strides. He went on, and Rollin realized he was talking about his ex-wife. "A sequel: what would I call it, anyway—*The End Booth*?" He stopped short, whiskey spilling over the back of the couch.

". . . of fiction are strange fish," he said. "They come into your mind. They grow. They acquire suitable characteristics. An environment surrounds them. You think of them now and again. Sometimes they become an obsession so that you can think of nothing else. Then you write of them and for you they cease to be. Maugham," he said. "And they do not cease to be, because these are modern times!" he announced. "These are times of alimony and sequels!" he said as he stumbled out the door.

Two days later Rollin got a postcard from him in the local mail. It was a picture of a Ramada Inn. He said he had started to work, and maybe it was better this way. For whom? Yesterday she had drunk too much coffee and fiddled with a piece she'd been happy with, ruining it.

Back in her studio she stood at the window for twenty minutes, fanning herself with the postcard. The air was heavy, and she pulled back a mass of hair, annoyed.

A rustle in the hallway signaled that it was four-thirty, but what was the point in going down? What was the point in staying if she couldn't work, though? How did the others do it? Because what did it mean? What did it mean right now when the air was close and she heard laughter? Sitting here? Rollin had never been disciplined but she knew enough to know that it was more than the ability to sit in a room with the door closed.

William Tepper was disciplined. The way he timed his walks, even the way he ate. Her father was disciplined, although through the years Rollin had seen him stop in exasperation a thousand times as some evasive character asked a question he couldn't answer, and forced him to pace and argue out loud.

The next day another postcard arrived (Frank must have had a stock of Ramada Inns, she decided) telling her he was thinking of leaving. She'd heard he'd been out late at the Red Baron. Later she ran into him outside the gallery. "How's the work going?" she said.

"Work, what work?" Frank said, and he smiled and did a little dance and reached into his pocket. "You want to know? Here! Catch!" He tossed her the stationer's bag containing the ribbon he'd bought the day he arrived.

He depressed her. He came to her one night drunk, full of assurances that that was not the reason he couldn't make love to her. "No, just makes it easier to swallow," he said. "Sorry," he said. Then: "When's your father coming back? Huh? I'd like to meet your father. He ever tie one on? You know, really get talking, drinking?"

"No," Rollin said.

"Too bad," Frank said.

"No, that was my godfather," she said.

"Oh, right," Frank said. "Someone told me about him. Real *bon vivant*, huh? And what, you grew up between them sort of? That it?"

Rollin moved behind the counter, looking at him, watching him pour himself another drink. She had had a couple herself, but she still saw clearly that she was bored. Once she would have liked to go into all of it, she would have cried as she had with Bart Laws, sitting at his knee and waiting for his slow deep voice to comfort her. But the vision of a drunk splayed out on her couch disgusted her and bored her.

The next day he apologized, except that he didn't know how. He started out by saying again that he was thinking of leaving.

"Really?" Rollin said.

He shrugged. He walked around her studio, hands in his pockets as though the room were full of delicate sculptures. "Might pick up a bus," he said. "Ever seen the country?"

Rollin shook her head. She put down her coffee and lit a cigarette.

"None of it?" he said.

She wanted him to leave. That morning she had come up to the studio and she had seen that her work bored her. The blind contours she'd done four years ago were better than the charcoal-and-ink washes she'd been working on, for at least with the blind contours there was a spontaneity in their wrongness, whereas the washes were boring. At least Mary Fitts delivered what she promised, and even though the washes promised more they didn't deliver. Rollin had thought she had ruined them by pushing, but early compromises had doomed them from the beginning. Out of five, there was only one she thought was worth keeping.

". . . thing is I'd rather work two jobs and write when I want to," Frank was saying. "I used to do that until I got married and fucked up my life. Well, I did it after I got married and fucked up my life too, except then I was doing it because I had to. And she's screwing some other guy, can you imagine? All that time."

After he left, Rollin went to the window. There was thunder far off and a strange sour light on the maze. She watched as William Tepper completed the second round of his walk before the downpour.

In the end Frank Horcher did leave, which surprised her. There was his reputation as a writer, but as a man he had seemed insubstantial, incapable of making even the smallest decision. But what shocked her more than his leaving was that according to Littlefield it was her fault.

"Mr. Horcher left because he wasn't getting any work done," he said.

"I know," Rollin said, and she put out her cigarette and looked up and realized he was blaming her.

"He couldn't work here!" she said to her father when he returned a few days later. "It's happened here before. It's not so unusual. And anyway, what about my work?" she said, approaching him. "I was working and he was bothering me but no one even thinks about that."

Thompkins turned and shook his head. "What's going to happen to you?" he said, and looked out the window as though the answer might be out there somewhere.

"What's going to happen to me?" Rollin said, and suddenly it mattered. "What's going to happen to me, what do you mean? Don't you believe me?"

The question hung in the air.

Then Rollin did something she hadn't done in a long time. She went upstairs, where Douglas's office had been. The light in the long hallway bleached the bare floors all the way down to the end, where her portrait hung in the alcove, and that was where she sat. Servant, woman, painter, daughter—who was she? When Susan Western had been here and asked Rollin to grid up a canvas, she had been in awe. Susan Western had houses in New York and London, she had a staff and assistants, and here she was, treating Rollin like one of them. She was a hard drinker and smoker, and they spent long hours together. Rollin had even done correspondence for her. But Susan Western hadn't cared whether Rollin had seen or liked her show at Mary Boone or not. She had hardly looked up from the letter she was reading to say, "Good for you."

By the time her entourage came for her—her husband was in London but there was the New York assistant and the nanny and the golden-haired child—Rollin knew everything about Susan Western. She didn't like the woman but loved her work. And although the painter had confided in Rollin with a desperation, Rollin was not surprised when she never heard from her again. Susan Western was used to calling people late at night when she drank, and it had infuriated her that there was no long distance out of Peninghen. So she had turned to Rollin.

They all had, in one way or another, and she couldn't do it anymore. She read a note from Littlefield about vacating her studio for Daphne Ainsley and she felt nothing. She glanced through the catalogue of the woman's work. Her last show, "Precipices," showed roads ending suddenly, curves which made the eye jump; the medium was some combination of pastel and paint which achieved what the text termed "a hard softness of dreams."

A memo the next day asked her to buy mousetraps.

"Mousetraps," Rollin said aloud in the mailroom.

The only part of Peninghen which continued to interest Rollin was that now and then there was an application from abroad, accompanied by a recommendation from Pauline Dampierre.

But she had retreated so far that when she brought over a set of slides Thompkins thought had no merit, he could not tell her. It was as if, having abandoned her own work, it took all the self-confidence she had left to present the work of someone else. He had not paid particular attention to what had happened that day in the tower room—there had been so many others like it in the past. It would all go on, he had thought, and had turned his attention to the assorted letters on his desk, his notes for Chapter Thirty-eight.

He was still on Chapter Thirty-eight. The bar. He needed that joke of Harry Booz's. Jesus Christ, would he ever get this book out of his life?

"What do you mean, the first half's better than the second half?" Kipps had said about the first book. "One half's gotta be better and you'd better hope it's the first half because if it isn't they ain't gonna stick around for the second, are they?"

Then, as always, he thought about the boy; a conversation with his mother about a violinist who had been in Vietnam. She said that each time the cannon had gone off in Tchaikovsky's *1812 Overture*, he had ducked. She said she had finally had to quit, the baby had kicked so hard.

Chapter 16

∘ ∘ ∘

The memory came from long ago: New York City, a girl walking towards him, pale with dark hair and red lipstick. She was carrying a letter, looking for a mailbox. Later on that day Thompkins had pictured the girl as Douglas had gone on about another girl:

". . . used to take baths together, for Christ's sake!" Kipps had said, leaning over the simulated wood table in the booth. "I'd never done that before. Well, have you?" Shaking his head, laughing. "There was something so fucking innocent—aw hell, you know how great it is when it's good." Smoothing back his hair, still smiling. "What they call 'free love,' right? And it's great, great, great. But then everything has its way of going sour, right? Yeah. So each time she's getting out of the tub a little earlier until she's getting out when I'm getting in! A good lay now and then, but basically I'm getting nothing but her dirty bathwater, for Christ's sake!"

It was a conversation they'd had so near to the end that when, eight or so years later, he saw a girl walk up through the parting in the trees, saw the top of her skirt marking the boy's height, he knew. He knew because of the description (she still had that long hair) but he also knew from his reflex at trying to recall that dark-haired girl's face.

Ah, Kipps, what have you done to us? Carelessness in a child's world comes from not paying attention, those math problems I used to help Rollin with where she didn't use her common sense, does it make sense, I used to ask her . . . but carelessness in an adult world comes from knowing better, and what the devil happened? Stranger in his own shorts, you always used to say. That fool son of a Polish count we knew, father rich as God but there he was, charging shirts at Chipp and selling them off, twenty-five bucks apiece, for a night at the Copley, and why were we surprised when he put his head in an oven? Stranger in his own shorts was always your line, as if you knew better. If anyone's been careful in his life I have, but that's the thing about carelessness, when it's near to you it's on you. You used to say it took more strength to pitch a ball than father a child, you bastard. You goddam fool.

Chapter 17

∘ ∘ ∘

One fall afternoon after Rollin left the tower room Thompkins had stood at the window for a moment watching her walk towards the main building, remembering when she had first come here. He had hated watching her walk, traces of a limp which reminded him of a boy he'd known in college who had had polio; the same tendency to press on the thigh while walking up an incline. Thompkins had had to remind himself that of course that was not Rollin's case, she'd been in an accident, the limp was temporary.

He had driven up almost every weekend that summer to see her. Separate in his memory was the weekend of the accident, when, reassured that Rollin was "out of danger," Thompkins had driven on past the exit Sally Ann had given him and followed a sign for "Points North." He still did not understand the panic which had seized him in that moment, why hearing that his daughter would recover from a near-fatal accident had thrown his own life into peril.

"Lad!" Margaret had cried, slamming the car door behind her in the parking lot where she probably did her marketing. Brown's Market, Allen's Pharmacy, a restaurant called the Seven Central where later she told him they often went after sailing. "Lad Thompkins," she whispered; in a fleeting intimate distance where they just looked at each other. People greeted her—a woman with two children piling into a station wagon, a man in plaid shorts—but she didn't answer them. She just looked at him.

"I want you to come back with me," he said.

He told her what had happened and that Rollin was all right and then he repeated what he had said. He held her, bright sun shut out, telling her he had done two impulsive things in his life. "I bought a convertible once, and this is the second," he said.

Margaret pulled away slowly, propelling the curious people into motion again. "We'll leave your car here," she said. She took his arm firmly and steered him. "How is the work?" she asked.

"Of course you'll come to the house," she said, adding in a low voice that it was the Newcomb's Ledge race this weekend.

They drove up, up through gates and a hill of gear changes (she drove a sports car), until the air was cool and his vision was flooded with rhododendrons, which hid a low house the color of bark.

"Well isn't *this*—" he said, extravagance in his voice as he stood in the living room and looked out to the sea. The room stretched in an expanse of gold and pale green, orchids craning here and there like strange listening devices. A huge television was not intrusive.

Margaret had laughed easily and thrown her keys on the glass table. He had looked for her at that end of the room, but she was so well camouflaged—the pale colors changing in the light thrown back off the sea, light wood and her bare arms—that had she not moved Thompkins might not have picked her out right away.

Margaret, in the tower room? She took his arm and showed him the rooms of her life, and it was with her help that he was able to recover from whatever rashness had overtaken him in the last few hours. He saw his life from here: pages and pages, the horizon in front of him like a deadline; that was all there ever was. How could he ask someone to share in that? Instead, he shared others' lives.

Harry Booz and the young boy Kevin, appendages and extremes of his life:

"Lad? What kind of a name is that?" the boy had said. Aside

from one or two other things, that was all he had said, something rude that any eight-year-old would say, and Thompkins had watched him pick his nose with fascination. He was so ordinary, so real before the idea of him was real at all. Yet the three of them had stood in this room; Thompkins had seen Douglas's eyes look away from him with an unfamiliar shyness. He was clearly his mother's son, though, as if Catherine Byrd had named him Kevin so that he would never carry his father's name.

However, Catherine Byrd did not look as if she would think this way ("We took baths together, for Christ's sake"). She was tall, quiet, bending to the boy once in a while, a curtain of straight blond hair not so blond when close to his. Margaret might sit on a sofa holding a cushion, she would wear a sweater which was tight for the way it felt against her skin. But Catherine Byrd was what men used to call "a tall glass of water."

"What can I do for you?" Thompkins had said, vaguely aware of the weight the words carried, the grayness of Crath's office.

"Do for us?" Catherine said.

How old was she? Thompkins had wondered. Older than Rollin, but not by much. What had they talked about? The beauty of the property, the cost of insuring a harp. She had told him if he really wanted to quit smoking, he should try lettuce-leaf cigarettes.

"Someday I could give a concert here, maybe," she said.

The boy had wandered around the room, picking things up and putting them down as Thompkins was used to seeing Rollin do.

"Could I have this?" he said, holding up the dog, but he already assumed the answer was no, and put it down before his mother answered. "It's broken anyway," he said, shrugging a shoulder.

They had stayed perhaps an hour, and the only trace of their presence was the window Catherine had opened.

Thompkins had heard nothing from them in the year which had passed. Catherine had mentioned the Seattle Symphony and he kept that in his head; but he knew when he thought of the boy that what he had convinced himself was a sense of responsibility had more to do with selfishness and the idea of a son.

And it was at times like this that he thought of them, when he turned from the window and faced into the smoky room and thought about lunch, his imagination stretching from his own choice between Lucy's meatloaf and going into town, out into the wider world, the world where people ate lunch in foreign countries every day. Lately this seemed impossible to him, and when he read at night he worried in the back of his mind about the day that craft would no longer matter to him; writers read in the evenings, but so did old men.

Late one afternoon, Thompkins felt a rush of cold air at his back and turned away from his tea to see Rollin standing in the doorway. She was wild and pale and feverish, as though something had exploded within her and left her standing.

"All these years I've watched you," she said breathlessly. "The island house—my whole childhood! You taught me control. Discipline. But I couldn't learn that. I'm not that way. It's passion that matters," she said, a sloppy sleeve trailing and then sailing out over the table. The dog flew into a corner and she turned, her hair spinning fanlike. "Oh, no," she said, reaching for the figurine in a dusty corner. There was a new chip where its ear had been. She frowned, pushing the hair out of her face. In a coarse voice she went on, slower now. "The limits—the boundaries. They're what you learn. I had to find out my own way and it was the hard way." She said quietly, "It was the only way."

The display embarrassed him, but he had seen the light of discovery in her eyes that youth brought just once, if at all—a belief in oneself. She said she'd been up painting all night. Longer.

"I mean—is today Thursday?" she said.

Thompkins looked at her and said yes, it was Thursday, and Rollin looked at him but her focus fell short. She saw that he only half understood and she was shocked to realize that this didn't matter to her. It was as though she could see over everything. He wouldn't—couldn't—understand; after all he hadn't understood Jean Bessac's work at all.

No one did. Except for Pauline, of course, who said in her letter of recommendation that in this case especially one had to see the original work. Rollin hadn't understood right away. Bessac had studied anthropology and basically his forms paid homage to primitive cultures. Also he had traveled extensively: Borneo, Martinique, Africa, Australia, New Zealand, as well as in Europe, where he was based in Paris. His objects—vases, bowls, animals, tools—were alternately described as pure design and three-dimensional. In terms of composition, there was a search for balance which was purposefully left unresolved in an exploration of tension and penetration of space; objects leaned forward and back, and one which constantly drew her attention seemed to tip farther and farther towards the point of smashing. The text in the brochure noted that the reproductions could not bring across the parchment quality of the paper used, nor the material. He used blood. Rollin realized this when she looked at the slides, and read the packet Pauline had sent. Blood. Ox blood, apparently. Rollin studied the irregular shapes, solid or outlined, and the negative shapes they made. There was one composition in particular which intrigued her. A clawlike tool, an unidentifiable object, and off center a rough-edged oval. In black and white, the oval appeared as a sort of stone, the value coming off as simply black, whereas in the slide one could see the variations in color depending upon the thickness of the blood. It was in the slides that one could appreciate the relation of Bessac's works to old prints, as the blood, when dried, was a dark brownish red on a mottled ground. But the point was that the tension Bessac had created in the pieces was just as unsettling. The artist did not rely on the shock value to carry his work. He was confident with his exploration of pictoral elements, space, his description of two- and three-dimensional objects. On the one hand he was saying why should blood be any different, but on the other hand he was using it as a claim that the ground he was exploring merited such a radical material. And while at first she had seen reproducing the blood pieces in black and white as pointless, she realized that that would underscore Bessac's thesis, and would be the basis for arguing in favor of his admission.

Rollin had been to four board meetings at Peninghen. She knew that Mr. Jarre was half French and full of himself, that Mr. Fellows was an alcoholic, that Mrs. Smithfield's husband was a bank president. Joan Townsend had money and dressed as if she had none, and seemed to have a cold every time Rollin saw her. Mr. Connelly was a retired consultant and still sat on boards here and there where more was at stake, at least in the world's view, than promoting artists and writers. Portly in a dark suit, he was the most intimidating; his ties, pigs or horns or feathers sprinkled on a dark ground, attested to a warmth and lightheartedness he knew nothing about.

Rollin said little at meetings, adding something or agreeing mostly, but she saw this would have to be different—if she didn't support Bessac no one would. When she entered the room, Mr. Jarre was alone. He was going over the French text with supreme concentration, and frowning. Works from abroad were accompanied by texts such as this. In France it was a custom to have a writer—the more famous the better—write a blurb reflecting the painter's vision by whatever aspect—materials employed, the painter's war experience, a childhood by a river—the writer felt was relevant to the work. At first Rollin had attempted to translate the texts, but the poetic license taken in the other language was awkward and even embarrassing in English.

This one was no different, and served to get the meeting off to a bad start. "Mr. Bessac—" Mr. Jarre cleared his throat and corrected himself. "Excuse me. The impression we are to be under here is apparently that the material"—he again cleared this throat (it was perhaps his French side which promoted ascots at his throat)—"that it's the great coursing of life through our veins—"

"This is morbid," Joan Townsend said in her nasal voice. "How is smeared blood life?"

Mrs. Smithfield was in her sixties. "Is he going to work with the blood here?" she said.

"Oh, it's a gimmick," Mr. Fellows said. "Anyone can see that." He laughed. "And obviously sexual."

"Wait a minute," Rollin said.

The room was quiet.

"Rollin," Littlefield said.

"Well—" Mrs. Smithfield was looking at her and Rollin looked away as she said, "Blood eats paper, and Jean Bessac had to find a way to treat it. His process takes months. That's not a gimmick."

"It's still blood," Fellows said.

Rollin disagreed. "It's just another material. He's changed the context. It's just another material, it has its own properties, and if anything he's given himself a challenge. He has to measure up to the shock value."

Mr. Connelly had taken off his glasses and was looking at her, but as usual said nothing. Joan Townsend coughed, and it seemed all Mrs. Smithfield could do to stay at the table. She said, "Maybe he does other things we could see?"

"Maybe it would help to just look at the work in black and white," Rollin said. "The composition, the—" She looked up and met the black stare on Mr. Connelly's meaty face. She tried a last time to defend Bessac on technical grounds, comparing him in his use of a new material to Alan Gates, who in his last show had had a few paintings where gold had been used, except apparently there wasn't enough glue in the gold paint and it was peeling off. There was a polite silence except for Joan Townsend blowing her nose. Rollin tried to tie the work to cave paintings, blood used on animal hides.

Mr. Fellows laughed and said, "Next thing you know she'll be talking about using cat guts to make tennis rackets." He began to gather up his things. "Better luck next time," he said, whiskey on his breath, as he filed out after Mrs. Smithfield.

"And you bought one of these?" Mrs. Smithfield said to Rollin. She looked quite worried.

It was the first piece Rollin had bought. "Yes," she said. She had exchanged a few letters with Bessac and now she had to tell him he'd been rejected.

Mrs. Smithfield paused another moment in the doorway. "We might be interested in seeing it, all the same," she said.

Littlefield came up behind her. "You did a good job, my dear," he said. "Really, I was impressed."

They walked down the hall together. Littlefield babbled on as usual; maybe she shouldn't have the piece sent, he said; customs could be such a problem and someone was always coming over, Pauline or in the spring George Semard was coming, perhaps he could bring the piece over—

"What studios are free?" Rollin said.

"Hmm?" Littlefield said. "Oh." He rubbed an eyebrow, concentrating. "Well, until Sarah Yard arrives on the nineteenth the center left is free. Why?" he said. He looked at her. Rollin had not had any interest in a studio for months.

She had gone there and it was as if it had been waiting. Light streamed in, all space and air now feeding an explosiveness within her, her brain and a heartbeat, a speed frozen by a constant moment of being so alive. She started, she moved, the air got stronger, the paint and her energy and the color, the color a smell of its own, the smell of living in it, the canvas her insides vermilion and white, ivory black and thicker, she wanted to lie in it, be in it, be what it was, her insides in front of her, breathing and intoxicated by the smell of the paint, and the music working on her memory scratched thin and built up under her skin and deep in her heart thrown up, breathed in and fed by light and juice of tasteless food, dull color and textures which made her thirsty. She talked to herself and laughed to herself and scattered into pieces when she thought of lying down, she was sick and afraid and fragile and powerless, all her strength going into coming out, being used, her work was new to her and angry with the world.

She started another piece then, back and forth, an obsession towards each precluding any need to articulate; she was a boat tossed around in an angry sea, lines and weights all hurtling in different directions around her. Distance and darkness took over as she watched abstraction take over, and while this had not been the intent behind the original conception, she had given up control as the pieces had started to work on their own. And they did work: she recognized that especially the second one could stand on its own precisely because it had once been such a part of her. The fusion of what she had heard other painters call vision had now matured to form the cleave between herself and her creation. The only thing Susan Western had told her concerning her work was that because it was of a high emotional caliber it would require a distance on Rollin's part, in her execution and judgment, in order to force the viewer to confront the same experience. She had not understood this until now.

She slept, and woke some sixteen hours later to a light rain; she heard it far away like distant clapping. Around her was ordinary life; the gray light, dirty hair, the sight of a man whose car had broken down on the main road. Rain had dulled the scene to a gray-brown; she couldn't tell the age of the man or the color of the car. She had been on the edge.

In winter with Littlefield in the Caribbean and her father in Key West, the whole place was hers, and that winter she used it. Heated it; with those high ceilings, it seemed possible that she would spend her whole inheritance. During a particularly cold week in January she stayed in the bungalow nights, but otherwise she slept in the studio, waking to a weak sun and frost on the windows and out across the Great Lawn. And if she stayed up all night there was a moment at dawn when the sun on Franko's piece made it move and bloom like a mirage. The piece, *Botticelli's Venus Loves Day-Glo at Dawn*, was a statue which had originally been intended for the center of the maze, but the whole point of it was that it should be seen at dawn and the maze, as it grew, had blocked the sun coming up on the horizon. So they'd moved it. Rollin couldn't remember when—whether it had been moved before Mathilde's wedding or not. Pictures told her nothing: Douglas talked to the workers, Douglas and the workers posed, laughing; the workers posed with their beers beside the statue as the sculptor stood looking on like an anguished movie director gone over budget.

The pictures told her nothing because as time passed even the ones she liked lost their power. When she had arrived at Peninghen she had looked at them all the time, and now she never looked at them. She might glance at the series hanging in the common room, or in Douglas's old office, but it was as if they'd lost their dimension. This wasn't possible, because they were photographs, but this was how it seemed. There were dozens of them spanning the fifties and sixties, and when she had first come to Peninghen she had pored over them in tears. Then there had been the vague idea of organizing them, Winifred's idea, or no, probably Littlefield's ("My dear, putting them in order might help you put yourself in order"). But the pictures themselves had resisted organization. There were so many, first of all, and although the rubber stamps on the backs identified the photographers, there were no clues to the events, dates, no clue to the identity of a man on Nell Dayton's right or to a woman with big dark eyes, laughing at something Lad Thompkins had said. Instead of organizing them, she had taken from the collection a few she liked, and put the rest away.

Now it was the anonymous elements in the pictures which intrigued her, the strangers who preserved a certain mystery and thereby a spontaneity, an edge symbolic of the times. Because over time, the photographers had unwittingly become photojournalists. They had tried to freeze a time which had defined itself as not wanting to be frozen; and as Rollin grew away from her past and

Peninghen's history it was the anonymous faces with their vivid expressions, the gestures—in the wreath series a woman's bare arm cropped at the shoulder floated in midair—which kept these pictures alive. Not Douglas's head thrown back in laughter. Not her father's head bent listening.

Stretching, she turned away from the window one day in late March and looked at the canvases leaning against the wall. Chaos surrounded them—an opened jar of peanut butter, a knife licked clean beside it, was hardly discernible from the brushes and palette knives and scattered paint tubes, the hardened crusts of color and labels on other dirty jars. Her eyes traveled up for freedom and air, up the wall where her favorite picture was tacked beside a Diebenkorn she'd ripped from an art magazine. The photograph showed the back of her father's head and two strangers. There was a man and the same woman with the big dark eyes, who was describing something which obviously couldn't be described, her eyes towards the ceiling, eyebrows raised and her mouth open, a raised hand cupping air. The mantelpiece was not easily identifiable as the one in the common room, but Thompkins had been sure the picture had been taken at the opening of Peninghen because in profile to his left was the sculptor George Semard laughing.

Chapter 18

o o o

"And what's his specialty? 'Cause I'll tell you, sculptors, they's the worst. Person can't eat a food 'cause they's sick with it that's fine by me. Almost cried watching that little poet watch everybody eat them strawberries. Then here comes Mr. Mount, says he don't eat chicken cause he don't like the contact of feathers with skin! I says well no one eats a chicken with the feathers Mr. Mount but he says it's the idea of it. He can't take the idea of it. Comes right down to aesetics, Lucy, he says, and I says well it just comes down to me in the kitchen Mr. Mount so I hope you like vegetables."

Littlefield nodded, rubbing his temples, and said he was sure they would do fine by Mr. Hull, whose only specialty seemed to be that he was missing two fingers on his left hand. Richard Hull reminded Rollin of that painter who had been so crazy about her mother that year they lived in the cottage. Sandy hair, gentle eyes, and tennis shoes. Rollin hadn't thought of John Stribling in all these years; and how odd that a stranger would bring it back—not only the man but that living room, that time in her life—so intensely.

He was certainly in direct contrast to George Semard, whom Rollin remembered vaguely (she remembered he was funny) from those last crazy days at the island house.

"There was something with a washer," she said to her mother on the phone.

Her mother burst out laughing. It seemed that she had not laughed in years. It was as though she were suddenly awake. "Once he put all these bright shirts—he loved red, I remember—in with Bill Dowling's—oh!" She laughed. "Pink, everything was pink! And poor Bill had an interview at one of those fancy Madison Avenue advertising agencies—" Sally Ann was laughing so hard she had to stop talking. "Oh, dear," she said. "They had to go to one of the awful stores in Bay Shore I remember, before Bill got the train. 'A white shirt,' he kept saying, and George didn't understand that, you could see that—"

A few days before he arrived, a letter came from Pauline assuring Rollin that George Semard was bringing Bessac's piece.

"And you called me in for that?" Rollin said. "I mean, it's nice, but—"

Littlefield tugged at an eyebrow. "But it isn't my style," he said. He looked at her for a moment as if trying to make up his mind about something, then he asked her what she would think about a show in the gallery.

All Rollin had ever wanted was for her work to hang in the gallery. Now he was handing it to her.

"Well?" He gave his pencil a final tap. "I must say you don't seem very excited, my dear."

"But you haven't seen my work," Rollin said.

"Well." He explained that a painter had canceled. "Then I got to thinking we should have done this a long time ago. You and me. It would have gotten us off to a better start."

Rollin laughed. "I wasn't ready a long time ago," she said. "You mean you'd give me the space without even seeing my work?"

Littlefield had started going through papers. "If you want me to come up and look at your work, I will," he said. "Of course."

What was he saying? That the system would have offered her a place whether her work had evolved or not? That it didn't matter, that all that mattered was that the time and politics were right?

"Well, Rollin, that's often how these things come about," her father said. "Look at me, my work. That director. Took an option, fooled around—" He shrugged. "Nothing came of it. Don't think that because in the beginning it seems too easy—"

"I just want to know I've passed a standard," Rollin said.

"Your standard," Thompkins said. "That's all anyone's work should ever be."

"I know that," Rollin said. "And that's why I don't need Littlefield coming back from his vacation and offering me a favor. It isn't even a favor—he'll look ridiculous if that space isn't filled."

She looked at her father helplessly. She was glad to see him but sorry he was back, sorry for the fact, each year, that he wasn't happy to be back. He never said much about Margaret, and beyond polite questions she didn't ask. Once she had sent a charcoal down with him for her, and over the years there had been a few phone conversations, strained but friendly; a warmth left over from the winter Douglas had died.

Rollin picked up the dog and put it down again, and said quietly, "Don't you see? It's not the kind of show I need. I need exposure, not prestige. People coming in off the street, not gallery people up for a Sunday in the country."

Thompkins was listening, but his mind had wandered. A letter forwarded to Key West from a graduate student doing a thesis on his work had been dry and to the point, but the voice on the phone that morning had been timid, respectful to the point where he now dreaded the meeting. Sitting on the terrace and reading the letter to Margaret in the warm January sun, April had seemed impossibly far away, and now it was here—George Semard was due any day. He said, "Have you talked with this fellow Hull at all yet?"

"A few times," Rollin said. "He's okay. His work's not so great." She paused and then said, "So you think I should do it."

Rollin was right about the system, and it was for this reason that Thompkins thought she should take advantage of it. He didn't understand her work; he might even say (he had said it, to Margaret) that he doubted it. He knew she had talent, but the vein she had chosen—abstract—did not define it. He took comfort in the fact that much in modern art was beyond him. He chose his words carefully. (Lad Thompkins always chose his words carefully, but with Rollin there was a degree beyond even that.)

"All I'm saying is that you're not being singled out, and you won't be; not for the breaks or the hard luck. The decision of whether to show, when to show, will always be there until you make it. And as for rejection—" He shook his head. "I knew if I stopped sending things out it would only be harder when I started again. That was a long time ago, but some things don't change."

She said it didn't feel right and he said it might never feel right. "Nolan Perry, I remember he had canvases stacked, rolled—dust everywhere, Lord. But he wasn't ready. It was always too soon. We all say that."

"But you don't—" She looked at him and knew she'd get nowhere. It wasn't too soon, it was too late.

She was standing in the common room when an old white van drove up, and she watched as a man about her height got out and walked around and slid open the door. As she wondered who this might be, he dusted off his hands and glanced up at the building and then out over the grounds, as though he knew someone was watching or as though he'd been here before. Then he turned and walked towards her, with the blind look on his face of someone who has not seen you, and it was when she saw that he was older than she had thought at first that Rollin realized that this must be George Semard. Suddenly, she felt the closeness of the sculpture beside her. Often, as she had read a book, she had looked up and stared at the piece for minutes at a time. In mahogany, a rhombus leaned back into space, twisted slightly. Just over a foot high, it stood beautifully in sun through leaded windows, the leather chair beside it the same warm color. In Peninghen's collection the piece had always stood apart somehow, because of what it was but also because she had never made any association between it and its creator. So it seemed strange now that not only was the man walking towards her, he was coming to take the piece away.

As he approached, she remembered things: His mother had been Mexican—or was it Spanish; his brother Johnny was actually his half-brother. There were her mother's memories of him, and on the phone, her father had laughed and nodded vigorously and said, "Well it certainly has, George, it certainly has. Good Lord." And he'd settled back into a friendship which had subsisted on notes now and then and news through mutual friends, Pauline Dampierre mostly, for ten years. And although her own memory of him was blurred by Douglas's death and the years since, Rollin did remember laughter.

That was why his manner surprised her.

"You're Rollin I suppose," he said when they met in the driveway. He stood with his hands in his pockets. His eyes were brown, and in the fading light Rollin saw that his hair was a strange dark gray, enough to comb but not enough to be disheveled. Nodding, he smiled at her, but even then there was an intensity to his face, a frown almost. It was when they started to walk that she sensed a warmth about him, perhaps having to do with the fact that they were the same height. She felt as if they were children, except he was strong. She glanced at him. He wore what looked like a garage mechanic's shirt, pants of some indeterminate darker color. She thought of his work. Apparently he was headed out to California to do a commission which was concerned with movement, like his other pieces in wood, which extended and retracted and changed form completely, their magnificence founded in their conception from just one mass.

As they reached the tower room he returned her glance. One day, he would tell her he expected to win the Nobel Prize, not for sculpture; he knew they didn't give Nobel Prizes for sculpture, but for geometry.

"Lad Thompkins!"

"Well George good God," Thompkins said, and then the two men were laughing, embracing, a short formal embrace they echoed by gripping each other's arms and elbows.

"Lad Thompkins," George said again, and cackled, and then they were talking about a girl they'd known a long time ago. "Well, who could not remember her—she was such a silly girl!" George said.

"Oh, what a rascal," Thompkins said.

Actually George had already proved this; even before his arrival a woman had left her name and number. And then there was Jenny Crow: no one had ever made Jenny Crow blush, not Jacomet with his accent or Bart Laws with his. But as she went about making up George's bed in the common room he said, "And I suppose I will have to sleep here alone," and Jenny blushed beet-red with his laughter. Thompkins shook his head; George had always been one of those men women didn't notice until the most stunning woman in the room walked off with him, and here he was, torturing poor Jenny Crow, who had dusted his sculpture every week for the past six years.

"You're sure you'll be all right here, George?" Thompkins said. "There are rooms here, you know," he laughed. But George reminded him that often he spent the night in his van, that this would be fine. Thompkins nodded. From the moment he had opened the door he had felt a warmth towards George which had surprised him. They had never been particularly close, George ("Georges," his father's name and the French spelling) being younger at younger ages, when it mattered. But it had been the same world, and the gap had closed as those around them had begun to drop away.

Rollin, of course, saw them differently. George was seven years younger than her father, a gap she felt widen with each conversation. George said anything for a laugh, or an argument, when if challenged he would burst out laughing and bury his head in his hands, swearing by the truth. His heritage and marriages—the second, to a Brazilian, had lasted just a year—and the fact of his living abroad had molded his English. When he spoke about his work, he was quite formal; this was when he was serious; but at other times he mixed words into a chemistry which seemed to confuse even himself. His speech was a sweeping flow of words and unexpected intonations, questions which swam downwards into gentle persuasions.

"Can you believe that," he would say to Rollin, having said something outlandish. "I can see that you do not."

But who could make up such stories?

"She had such a temper!" he said about his second wife. "You could not believe *that*. I do not know why she married me, really. We fought all the time." He was smiling, grinning. (He liked wine, and when he had seen there was only scotch he had gone out and bought a few bottles.) Pouring himself another glass, he said, "She used to hang up on me. For no reason! I would call her back and she would hang up again. I could not believe *that*. Once she unplugged the phone, and what could I do?" he said, laughing and nearly spilling his wine with his gesture. "I went over and plugged it back in!"

"You—"

George was still laughing. "What else could I do?" he said. "She lived on the first floor. Luckily for me."

Was he crazy? "But why didn't you just talk to her when you were in the apartment?" Rollin said.

George looked mystified. "But I did not climb in for *that*," he said. "I wanted to call her back, simply that. For me it was very clear." No one ever believed him, and George laughed, covering his eyes and shaking his head—he had told this story many times in many living rooms and it always made him laugh.

Rollin had not asked him about Bessac's piece right away, but when she did, the way he put her off made her wonder if he'd forgotten it or if it had been lost. "I will get it later," he kept saying. He seemed injured, the second time she asked about it, that she would even be thinking about something else while he was recounting one of his adventures. Finally Rollin asked if he had really brought it. He said no, actually, the *douane* had kept it, and he lowered his head and it was quiet in the room until he laughed. He then told a story about when he was crossing the border between France and Switzerland and the *gendarmes*, convinced that the sculpture in the back of his van was machinery, wouldn't let him pass without paying a fine.

"It was a lot of money," he said. "And I could not explain to them—they would not believe the truth! I even tried to make them laugh. Can you imagine that? I wanted them to tell me what kind of machinery it would be." He laughed. "Finally I remembered I had a catalogue of my works with me."

The evening had gone, it was too late for dinner, and when Rollin announced that she was tired, she was going to bed, George got up and said he would get the piece for her.

Outside he became quiet again. He walked beside her, his hands in his pockets, and tracing his warmth was the unfamiliarity of his odd worldliness.

Rollin said, "You said you know Jean Bessac?"

"Well I know him," George said, adding that Jean was a very strange person. "He has a collie rug in his living room," he said. Rollin looked horrified and George touched her shoulder, laughing. "You think I invent things," he said. "This is true, but they are better than that, I can assure you."

Rollin left him, the parcel under her arm and his laughter echoing in her ears. She could not have explained why, but she was annoyed with him. He had not spoiled the picture, but when she got it down to the bungalow ar.d opened it and propped it on the mantelpiece, she could not see it sharply enough to feel it. There might have been a thin layer of gauze over it. She left the room and came back, but there was simply no tension left in her body to respond. The laughter had gone but in its place were names (Who was Nancy DeWitt?) and information and images and countries. In the bathroom, she broke a glass. She wasn't nervous; she had no control. She was limp. She wasn't drunk, she was exhausted. He had exhausted her.

In the end, Lucy concluded that he didn't have a specialty, he was one. The first thing he asked her was where he could wash his clothes, and that afternoon a row of shirts and mud-colored pants appeared on the line in the spring sun. He offered to cook one night (Lucy kept muttering about a "stew full of bones") and he didn't care where he slept.

At first Rollin thought he might have been different had he been here to work, but as they talked over the next few days she realized this was how he lived. George had never exhibited in a gallery in his life. He had refused to comply with the gallery system, and so while one found his sculptures in public spaces and private collections here and there in the world, in two museums, he had never achieved a success which was financially remunerative. Although he appeared as the direct opposite of her father, she saw that they were alike in a fundamental way. Both men had made their work the center of their lives, and each had paid the cost of a life of extremes. Thompkins hardly left Peninghen, while George, owing to the nature and scale of his work, his low bank balance, moved about constantly. He had no home. Last year was not the same as this year, nor would next year resemble this year. For instance, last year he had had the use of a woman's courtyard until he had lost both when a symposium in Austria came through and he was gone for a while. There were the constants in his life—a house his older son owned in Limours, outside Paris, and the apartment on the rue de Lille which Françoise had kept and where he sometimes stayed. Or there were the apartments of various friends, Pauline Dampierre among them; her apartment was probably his favorite he said; there was something of the sea about it, catching the high corner of a building which looked down on the Invalides.

"Invalides," Rollins repeated.

"Where they have buried Napoleon," George said.

In the background of the pictures he showed her of his recent work, she saw a château. She could only see part of it, but it was obviously quite grand.

George laughed. "I can see you are not looking at my sculpture."

Actually Rollin was looking at the sculpture, which was in mahogany, partially shadowed and camouflaged in the surrounding colors of fall. George explained that the château, which was in the Loire valley, belonged to a friend who had not lived in it since he had left his wife ten years before. Now the wife lived in Versailles with the son, who went to school there (Rollin didn't understand; she had thought Versailles was a palace), and from time to time they came on the weekends. Otherwise George lived there.

"Of course it is very nice of Arnaud," he said. "But I think he thinks with me there he will get it back, you see. And his wife, she never wants that the mistress of Arnaud lives there."

Rollin looked at him the same way she had looked at him when he said he stayed with Françoise sometimes. He had tried to explain that they were old friends.

"She is the mother of my sons," he said. "I was going to stay with Pauline, but there was no place. Simply that."

"But—" Rollin said.

George covered his eyes, laughing. She was so American! He'd been abroad so long that he'd forgotten what a real American girl was, looked like, even smelled like. When he had first arrived, she had been shy; he'd watched her as she walked around the room, head bent, picking things up and putting them down again with a rhythm which seemed to relieve an urgency he sensed in her every minute he looked at her. As a sculptor, he appreciated her tactile sense as she turned objects over in her hands as though she'd never seen them before or as though she could not trust, by merely looking at them, what they were about. He had hardly remembered her: she was obviously older than the American girls he saw greedily eating pastries and looking in shop windows on the boulevard Saint-Germain; yet she had to be older than Isabelle's daughter, which he found incredible. (Isabelle was the owner of the courtyard and had passed sophistication on to Sophie as if it were a gene.)

But what Rollin Thompkins missed in sophistication, she made up for in a passion which showed in her face and in the way she moved—there was an impatience about her he found extravagant and attractive. "Going through a bad time," Pauline had said around the time of Douglas Kipps's death, and he had tried to picture the young girl he had met once or twice. Looking at her now, he supposed it was that experience of death which had left the raw edge, a femininity which had less to do with women than growing up between two men.

She mentioned Douglas just once. "I guess it was your brother who really knew Douglas, wasn't it?" she said.

It had been Johnny who had known Douglas—Johnny had been a pallbearer at the funeral. But they had all kept up with each other, even when Johnny and George stopped speaking, and George had the good memory, which he shared with Thompkins, of Peninghen's first year. But when Douglas had come down to Mexico for the '68 Olympics, he was already on his way down, picking fights, drinking, throwing out his few words of Spanish, and money when he thought it would help; and George hadn't been surprised at the news of his death. George hadn't minded his comments about Johnny (it was common knowledge that the brothers hadn't spoken since Johnny had gambled away one of George's sculptures) but he'd treated the girl miserably and that had been sickening to watch.

"Fragile? Christ, you get her playing that harp and listen to her breathe, then you tell me how fragile you think she is. Jesus, you'd think she was having a fucking orgasm or something." He'd treated her as though she weren't even in the room. The only time he talked to her was when he was really talking to George: "You can't imagine how fucking easy this guy's got it," he said. "All he's got to do is give a woman some pendant he made and she signs on for life. Doesn't cost him a cent. Didn't you say, George? They go out and get the chains themselves! Poor suckers like me go out and buy harps."

George and the girl had stood at opposite ends of the room, embarrassed. Then it passed—Douglas came and put an arm around

George and said, "But hey, I'm impressed, George, Jesus; I thought it would be dancing in the streets and here we're off to another private reception. They've even got the tanks out! A poor country's prodigal son. Shit, I think it's great." Slapping his shoulder, gathering up the girl on the way out.

George never saw him again. They were staying at the Camino Real—of course—and the following night when George had gone to the hotel he had found the girl in tears. Douglas had simply disappeared.

"Oh, you know, he does this sometimes," she said, the curtain of blond hair half hiding her face. She had turned away and said, "He does love me, though."

"He loves you and he treats you like that or he doesn't love you and he treats you like that," George had said. He shrugged. "He treats you like that." For him it was very clear.

He assumed Douglas came back—an actress had been choreographed to dance around his sculpture at the inauguration and he didn't think Douglas would have missed that ("Come on, George —who is she? Stop holding out on me, who is it?" he'd kept asking)—but there was no message from either of them.

What George remembered was that they somehow balanced one another. It was uncanny: there was Douglas's stockiness and her height and long hair, the same dirty blond as his.

"She was beautiful really," he said to Thompkins. "I wanted her for myself," he said, laughing, for this was not true; he had never favored blondes. "What is it you say?" he said. "*Gentlemen* prefer blondes." This brought on a new explosion of laughter, which Rollin echoed.

At the mention of Catherine, Thompkins had lit a cigarette, and now he looked through smoke into the muffled distance of the round room, which pressed in on him with George's and Rollin's laughter. It was strange: George had brought Douglas alive, while Catherine, it seemed, had only once existed. Thompkins moved on the sofa, disturbed. He had never told Rollin about the boy because of her rages and depressions, and now there was her laughter, which seemed an even better reason, but also described the secret in a different way—as a symptom of his own isolation.

"Lad Thompkins, you are not listening. I am trying to convince Rollin to drive to California with me and Nancy DeWitt."

Thompkins looked up. "Oh?" he said. He coughed. "Imagine," he said. "California."

"Well this is not what I am imagining," George said, laughing.

Thompkins cleared his throat. "Who is Nancy DeWitt?"

"A blonde," Rollin laughed.

"She is a natural blonde," George said, quite seriously, and Rollin was laughing again.

Thompkins appeared not to hear: he spoke through a smoke screen which seemed to protect him from the joy and laughter in the room. "I've never understood about California," he said. "Never been there, never wanted to go." He shrugged, as if willing to admit this could be a shortcoming. "They say people go out there to find themselves, but it seems like a place where people get lost. Lose their—well, what we used to call values." There was a slight pause, and his voice had relaxed when he went on, "Of course, I guess what are you going to get when everyone's thinking the floor's going to slide out from underneath them any minute, you can't blame them for thinking about the fast buck if it's going to be their last."

He had given a small speech, and the exasperation and intolerance which had crept into his voice seemed to have surprised even him—he shrugged deeper into the corner of the couch.

George was laughing. "Lad Thompkins," he said. "You are so cynical! I think you are more cynical than I am."

"Well, George," Thompkins said.

"He thinks California's all Hollywood," Rollin said.

George missed the sad way she looked at her father, the disappearance of laughter from her voice; he was too busy talking, swept away in the fever of wine and the moment and his imagination.

"Hollywood?" he said. "But this would be much better. This would be real. I can see myself driving into that city with two heiresses." He laughed, and buried his head in his hands. "This is the problem in America. The American dream—you do not know what is that," he said, laughing.

Rollin couldn't stop laughing. He had pronounced "heiress" *hairess*, he was shameless and shameful; impish and devilish. He took life lightly on one level—"Sometimes I must stop at the side of the road, I am laughing so hard," he said—and bravely and seriously on another. He told her he had climbed Mont Blanc not once but twice; he told her he'd had not two Guggenheims but three.

"I can tell you do not believe me," he said. "I asked them for another one a few years ago, but they told me most people never got more than two. Probably they made a mistake," he said, laughing.

Rollin knew he did not mean this—she had never seen an ego quite like his.

"I am aware, that is, when I see these works they do not seem like I have done them," he said one day in the common room as they looked at his sculpture. "It seems that someone else has done them—God perhaps," he said.

She laughed, but part of it was embarrassment. "You're so egocentric," she said.

George said of course he was not; he was a sculptor and what did a sculptor do but have dialogues with himself?

"Still," she said, "it's obvious you feel pretty superior."

"I do not feel superior," George said. "I know I am *that*. Well, this is one of things," he said, and clarified himself, explaining that knowing he was superior did not make him feel superior. "You can understand that," he said. "Or perhaps you cannot." He had been washing his clothes, and walked back to where they were soaking. "And how do you want me to feel superior when you are watching me wash my clothes?" he called across the room, laughing.

She was headed to the studio the next day when George hailed her.

"You are not going to work now!" he said. "In the country I am always running with the dogs at this time. Let's go for a walk."

Each day Rollin tried to get to her studio and couldn't. She thought of the painting she was working on, the days which remained before she was to vacate the studio. Leaning against the van, she felt the sun warm her cheeks. Sometimes, when she was blocked, all she had to do was walk into the studio having had a glass or two of wine, and she knew exactly what a picture needed. This one was different. "Okay," she said.

"I am talking about the anguish of something that does not exist," he said to her at the Red Baron that night. "Can you understand that? Perhaps you cannot. That is—" He paused over his glass of wine. "A painter creates," he said. "A sculptor only shows what is inherent."

"Only shows what's inherent?" Rollin said, smiling. "Only? Why do I feel like even though you said 'only' you think it's more important?"

"There is baseball," George said, looking at the television above her head. "You said you liked that."

"I'm talking to you," she said.

"What?" he said, like a child.

"You act like painting's some sort of hobby," Rollin said. " 'Create'—I hate that word." He asked her what "hobby" was, and when she explained he laughed and said what was wrong with that?

"Hobbies could make many people happy," he said. "Come to California," he said, laughing. "I will teach you better hobbies."

Rollin wondered how many women had slapped him, and George raised his eyebrows, laughing, as if he could read her thoughts.

It seemed like months had gone by when Rollin finally opened the door to her studio, a space which had become so familiar, and now was just as foreign. The early spring light had taken the color from the room, except for the canvases, leaving behind an air of neglect as tangible as dust. Her eyes traveled over the clutter, over months of late nights and cold dawns, an energy she felt had disappeared forever. As the light had taken the color, so he had drained her of her energy. But she became aware that it was a different kind of energy, like using a muscle she hadn't known she had.

"Do you have a refrigerator in here?" she said one morning. George was washing the van and the windows were clean, streaming water and soap. Inside was a dense gray world of chaos: a beanbag chair, a box of something, the sharp edges of a sculpture wedged between. "This looks like you drove it all the way from Paris," she said.

"What you mean is that you do not think I will get to California," George laughed.

"Is it one of those drive-away things?" she said, but of course George did not understand.

"Drive away? What is that?" he said.

Rollin said, "Anyway, what makes you think I'd get in anyone's van I didn't know and drive three thousand miles?"

"But I am very well known," George said, laughing.

He was tireless. Exhausting. Being with him was like chasing a child and losing him, only to have him jump out at you around a corner.

"God, you're exasperating," Rollin said at the Red Baron one night. "How does anyone put up with you? Is Nancy DeWitt crazy?"

"No she is not," George said.

"Well, she must be," Rollin said. "What are you doing?" She had paid with a twenty-dollar bill, which George was in the process of tearing and folding. For a moment she allowed that perhaps he wasn't used to seeing dollars. He was like a child who did something quietly under everyone's nose until the grown-ups stopped talking and suddenly realized that the child was carefully, painstakingly constructing a house out of matches.

He crowded her mind: at night, strangers moved through the room in her head, sometimes talking to her in French. Johnny, George's brother, was there, wearing a tie tack which blinded her, and Nancy DeWitt was there, a California blonde with eyes the color of swimming pools and a diamond-and-emerald necklace Rollin admired, which at closer scrutiny turned out to be the map of a country. It was a party, it was the darkened terrace of Peninghen (the fountain worked) but it wasn't; the shadowy voice of Pauline spoke of the Riviera.

"The funny thing is, I used to dream of her when I was a child," Rollin told George. "I used to dream she was a witch."

George laughed. "She is that, I suppose," he said. "She is very old now. This makes her funnier really. She forgets things, or this is what she says. But once I remember she put Jean Bessac beside a woman who was working against extinction of animals," he said, laughing. *"Et ça, ça n'etait pas un hasard quand même."*

She had dreamed of Johnny because they had talked about him, and she had found the conversation disturbing.

"All the people thought it was that," George had said when she asked why they hadn't spoken. "But really we had never spoken. This was when people noticed. You know the people, they must always have something to talk about. Johnny is a very silly person really. Why should I care if my sculpture is in a gambling sort of situation? I would like to see a sculpture of mine in the house of a gangster—really!" He gripped Rollin's arm. "Can you imagine *that*?" Sun lit up his brown eyes, creased in the corners, ready to laugh. "And Johnny, you know he is not my real brother. You knew that. There are other friends of mine I consider more as my family."

"And your sons?" she said.

George shrugged. "They are my friends," he said.

"And your friends are your family," she said softly. She was confused. His attachments seemed so many and slight, deep but expendable.

He ruffled her hair. "Rollin Thompkins," he said, smiling. "You seem to be thinking very hard."

"I've just *got* to get up to my studio," she said.

The next day they went on a picnic. "Is it that you think paintings are superficial?" Rollin asked him as they walked.

"Well, they are that," he said, passing it by her in the literal sense.

"You know what I mean," Rollin said. "Inferior." She stopped. "How can you think that? You act like—I don't know," she said, and walked on ahead of him.

"What?" he said, catching up.

Out of frustration Rollin thrust the plastic bag with their lunch in it at him. "Here. Carry this," she said. Then she turned on him, an adult angry with a child. "You think painting's no more important than wrapping paper," she said. "Something pretty, like a woman getting dressed or something."

"Precisely that," George said. All the humor had gone from his face and voice. They had stopped by the stone wall. "And a sculpture is like a woman being born."

Rollin stared at him, unable to speak.

He laughed nervously. "Come with me to California. I will teach you not to be a painter." They had started walking again, and he looked at her quickly and looked away. "You are afraid, I suppose."

"Afraid of what?" Rollin said.

George sniffed, shrugged. "All the things," he said.

Rollin smiled. "But you know, it's funny. I think if you were going to France I'd go in a minute."

"Americans," George said, shaking his head. "You have not even seen your own country. One girl I knew, she did not know that Ohio touches Pennsylvania."

"You never think of being curious about your own country," Rollin said. "I don't know why. I guess because it's yours. And other countries, they're on the news. They're on maps."

At that moment Rollin did not know that El Salvador was under Mexico. She was under the vague impression that Belgium was somewhere south of France, and she certainly had no idea where countries like Portugal or Poland fit in, Hungary or Austria. To her,

Luxembourg was a delicate doll with bright blue eyes, Germany was lederhosen, Switzerland was a cuckoo clock—the spoils of Douglas's trips and her father's, that awful summer he was in Germany, abroad. Even guests she remembered from the island house had never been defined beyond their stereotypical superficialities; a British friend of Pauline's had never removed his ascot, a Frenchman had drawn stares in his black bikini on the Saltaire beach.

But that had been a long time ago. She had never questioned the stories she'd heard about foreign countries; it had made sense that the farther away you got from home, the stranger the possibilities were, anything could happen, someone could even have a collie rug in his living room. Foreign. The word sounded like what it might describe. Jacomet's stories had come across as cold and foreign, nothing to do with the stories and complaints about ice in hotels familiar to her from Douglas and Pauline. And somehow, George bridged these worlds. He knew Jean Bessac; he had stayed at Pauline's apartment, at that address on the rue de Grenelle that Rollin knew by heart.

"Paris just seems so alive when you talk about it," she said to him. "Even though it scares me, it thrills me. But California—" She shook her head. "If I went to France I'd have a right to feel out of place. I'd be a foreigner. In California I'd be just—lost. As my father said."

As usual George had his point of view. "There are lots of French in California," he said. "You could find them everywhere. I met a French in a laundromat in California once. He wanted to share my dryer. Can you believe *that*?"

The first meeting between the two sculptors had been a disaster: Richard Hull had seen George doing his washing, and taking him to be some sort of houseboy, he had presented George with his own dirty laundry. Hasty introductions had only made matters worse. The dynamics might not have been so exaggerated had the other residents arrived, but there it was, Hull's early arrival and George's guest status, the luncheon table set for a small audience to two sculptors of opposite ideals and life-styles and a silly misunderstanding to underscore it all. At each meal they strained within the limits of politeness; George tried not to show that he thought Hull's work was worthless, and Hull, who now thought George owned the château in the photographs, tried to mask his disgust at what he took for a false disdain for the gallery system on George's part.

"Well, this is something I know nothing about," George said without hesitation, in fact with pride in his voice, when Hull asked him about galleries in Paris.

"You show over here then?" Hull said.

George laughed and said why would he show over here? "I am sure the things are the same all over the world," he said.

"We're coming at it from different points of view," Hull said. "To you there's a choice."

"There is always a choice," George said.

"Talking financially, I mean," Hull said. His tone was pleasant but his meaning clear, and he began to question George's preference for Europe, intimating that it wasn't a preference at all—George had just never made it in New York. (When Hull had said he was "uptown," George had not understood the significance.)

"I suppose some people need that," George said.

"Need it?" Hull said, watching George pour coffee. "Who needs it? Chopped to bits by the critics, who needs it? It's part of the job." He reached for his glass and in a blur Rollin saw the missing fingers, the result, he had told her, of carelessness around a snowblower when he was seventeen. It was a misleading defect when one saw it before one saw his work, which was installation pieces—his last show had been tools in confined spaces. He set his glass down. "Like coming here. Sending the slides—the whole bit."

George disagreed. Rollin looked over at him, at the way he held a coffee cup, not by the handle but by the bottom like a baby's head.

"That is, the difference for me is clear," he said. "It is only a question of morals. The galleries, they want only money. Here you come to work."

"See your point," Hull said. "But it's still a question of putting yourself on the line."

Rollin waited for George to mention his Guggenheims, but he didn't. He let the subject drop. He started teasing her father about his sunglasses, saying that sunglasses were bad for you.

"When I was a child, my sight was very bad," he said. "It was not until I started making sculpture that it improved. I started working with marble and the light which reflected off the marble was good for my eyes."

"Oh come on," Rollin said.

"This is true, really," George said, shaking his head as though he were as amazed as everyone else. "It was a miracle, I suppose."

Rollin was laughing. She said to her father, "Well, you could take them off, Papa, the sun isn't even that bright. They make you look like you're blind or something."

The conversation was interrupted by a car in the driveway. As Littlefield hurried over, Thompkins realized that this was the day he had agreed to meet with the grad student. He had totally forgotten. "Oh Lord," he muttered. At the approach of Littlefield with a boy in his early twenties, Thompkins rose slowly, removing his sunglasses. Of course he had also forgotten the boy's name. But by the time he had disposed of the cigarette and walked around the table and reached for the young man's hand, his memory was refreshed as John Wheeler introduced himself to the others. As Littlefield hurried to get another chair, Thompkins asked the boy if he had had lunch. "Could we offer you some—"

"Oh no sir I'm—" John Wheeler was tall and thin and pale, obviously nervous in the presence of a man he greatly admired. In one hand he held Thompkins's book and a file of papers.

Rollin watched all this with an emotion she did not quite understand. John Wheeler had put her father's book on the table, and Rollin stared at it. It was dog-eared, the cover creased. She had never read it. She looked at her father, who wore his usual preoccupied expression, and then at the student. This had happened once before, but it had been a former student of her father's. He had been a few years older than Rollin, unlike John Wheeler, who was a few years younger. It was perhaps this fact which made his awe of her father more noticeable. The grad student wasn't bad-looking, but he wasn't memorable either, as though his admiration for her father canceled him out. Her father's presence, on the other hand, grew stronger. The student who had stopped in a few years ago had studied with her father, but this boy was a stranger. And yet the situation was oddly intimate, and uncomfortable.

Later, watching them from her studio, Rollin had the first glimpse of her father in history. She knew there was a reader's guide to his book; he had mentioned a market value of his letters and that the University of Texas at Austin had inquired about his papers. She imagined the future suddenly, saw a John Wheeler thirty years younger than herself fired up about her father's work. Once, he had gotten a letter from a professor, an "academic," who was willing to pay the price of a plane ticket across the country to see him. Rollin would be fifty, sixty, seventy, her insignificant past behind her; and his work would still be there, strong as ever. A John Wheeler would appear, charm her, eager to hear about her father. But she would indulge herself; she would chatter on, her memory half gone, as she served tea to a man who would have preferred a beer. Then she would ask him if he would like to see her work, her portrait, she would tell him all about the portrait, about a little girl with braids who was now an old lady.

"Rollin," George said.

"So it's the state then," Hull said. "Do they pay—"

"Some people do not even know that a sequoia and a redwood are the same," George said. "Rollin, are you listening? Rollin," he said, smiling, "where are *you*?"

"Yes, where have you been?" Littlefield said to Rollin, who had avoided him since their discussion about the gallery. Richard Hull turned and looked at her, and then they were all looking at her. "You never gave me your answer, my dear," Littlefield said. He addressed Richard Hull. "I have asked this young lady to expose in our gallery, and I just can't get a yes."

Rollin had lit a cigarette, and she pulled the ashtray at her father's elbow towards her. She finished the cigarette and put it out and all five men watched as she walked away before resuming their separate conversations, Richard Hull asking Littlefield about a junkyard, Thompkins asking John Wheeler if he'd found the place easily.

George, involved in neither conversation, had watched her the longest, watched until she walked out past Franko's piece and disappeared. He didn't like painting, but if she wanted to be a painter, she could not stay here, protected, in her father's shadow. For there would come a day when she would scrape bottom and find nothing. As for talent, he didn't know if she was any good; he couldn't get past the flatness and color, or the fact that a frame went around paintings. There was an emotion about them, like women. A decorativeness. Nothing was more annoying, more irritating, than hearing a painter talk about having had a dream which led him or her to do a painting, except hearing a woman sculptor talk about a piece she wanted to do when it was obvious she would never do it because she couldn't handle the materials. The only exception—the one woman who had impressed him—was Nell Dayton, and that had been a long time ago.

As if measuring the years, George stared out at the maze. (At his level of vision, it appeared as just a hedge, which was why he could look at it at all.) Once he had actually been in love with a painter, and watching the sun set over the Côte d'Azur one summer evening, he had felt as he did now: he didn't like paintings and she was a painter, he didn't like sunsets (for obvious reasons, he preferred the planets) and she was a woman.

One day Rollin would look back at that spring day when she had turned her back on a table of men who didn't believe in her, and she would see what she had had against her. But for the moment, she could only know what was changing inside of her, which was more powerful than anything anyone might think. When she left the table, she went down to the river, where she sat listening to the water rush and her heart beat, and she knew she would leave here.

Could she? She had watched people come and go here for six years. For a quarter of her life, she had watched taillights blink a final time before they disappeared, beyond the gates and out into the world. Yet she had always been free—it wasn't like boarding school, where she'd had to have permission to leave. And of course, over the years, she had left: she'd gone into the city, up to her mother's. But it had always been with the idea of returning. This was home. The thought of leaving and building a life—how did one do that? Rollin had never paid an electric bill, or had a job; she had never even really had any friends. At least if you went to college, grad school or law school or medical school, you had friends scattered over the country with whom you kept in touch. Adults had always been her world. Now she was an adult, and what had happened? She felt as though someone had suddenly pulled her hair up off her neck, chilling her.

The day before the residents arrived, three days before the traditional tea, George left to visit friends in Pennsylvania. Rollin missed his company: after she'd cleaned her studio she had run into him in the hall before dinner and he had laughed and said, "Your eyes are very shiny, Rollin. Are you sure you have only been cleaning?"

She missed him, but not as she would have had she still been on the inside. That was how she saw it: she had been on the inside and now she was on the outside. Peninghen had come into focus. Its grandness seemed small and precious, and she took long walks and looked at it from a distance as though to justify the distance from it that she felt within herself. A week later Rollin walked around the tower room, picking things up—the dog, made of a curious kind of stone, was always, always cold no matter how long you held it—and listening to her father and George talk. She was impatient: she wanted them to talk about it—about her leaving—

but they only talked around it. She wasn't a child—they didn't have to arrange this all as if she were a child. But on the other hand she felt protected. Looking at them in the rounded distance of the familiar room, she felt as she had that summer, talking about boarding schools with her father and Douglas.

"I'm twenty-five—you can't *not* let me go," Rollin had said to her father, and she saw that she had hurt him. But she refused to see the fine point of her age, that a girl of twenty-five driving cross-country with a man twice her age was perhaps a delicate proposition. "And anyway it's not just me, there's this girl Nancy," she said. She talked on and on as her father stood at the window. "You've got to let me go," she said, and he turned to her, nodding at the double meaning of her words.

"I've always known that," he said.

Had she won? Tears came to her eyes.

"Rollin!" George called when he saw her the next day. "Rollin Thompkins!"

Rollin went over to where he stood with a blonde in her early thirties. She was elegant. One had the impression that once she had been spoiled, rounder, but that a strain (or too much high living) had reduced her to another kind of beauty. George introduced them, and in a moment the three of them were laughing—a story one could only appreciate if one knew Pauline Dampierre. At dinner, Nancy DeWitt had changed her pale blue turtleneck for a pale pink sweater, and with her blond hair she was a sharp contrast to Rollin. All they had in common was George, sitting between them and making them laugh. It was a charming picture. It was a picture of the future.

Chapter 19

∘ ∘ ∘

In two years, Rollin heard from her father not more than a dozen times. One letter, written after he had been out to the island house, made a particular impression on her. He said he'd seen a girl who had reminded him of her when she'd been about seven and he'd taught her to ride a two-wheeler. Rollin remembered. They'd taken the training wheels off, and gripping the back of the seat, he would run with her for a moment, steadying her until he felt that she was ready. Then he would let her go. They repeated this over and over, and each time she felt the confusion of a sudden lightness which was at once wonderful and difficult. The front wheel zigzagged back and forth, out of her control; until one time when she kept going, when the wheel straightened out and she disappeared out of her father's sight.

But when she had left Peninghen and gone out into the world, she had had no practice. Eventually, men pulled Rollin back and forth across the country, the world; but first it was a thin jagged path of anticipation which ended one day at dusk in Venice, California, where upon her arrival, she had stood at the window and cried. Blurred in her vision was one in the row of scrubby pastel houses across the street, which without the palm trees could have been Long Island. The house belonged to a friend of George's, and was certainly not the California equivalent of a château. She couldn't believe that the ocean was nearby, or a marina that George and Nancy talked about; all she had seen was the beauty and excitement of their trip narrowing to the asphalt ugliness of Venice Boulevard, which at that time of day was at its prettiest, its wide grassy median scattered with oil derricks against the sunset. They turned left onto Ocean Avenue, and George pointed to the house, to which Rollin had paid less attention than to what was going on in front of it: a black girl was walking a Doberman and the large dog was pulling, forcing an extra swivel in her hips, which was greatly appreciated by the bikers next door.

Once inside, Rollin had stood at the window and stared out at the palm trees (she could only see their bases, which were large and reptilian) with tears in her eyes. Behind her, laughing, George and Nancy were suddenly strangers. What the three of them had shared was over, and Rollin had had the impression that what she'd learned about them was as useless now as the routine and jokes which had made the trip so wonderful.

"Do you like showers at night, or—?" Nancy had asked the first night, which they had spent in a Holiday Inn; and they had rejoiced to find that Rollin liked baths at night and Nancy liked showers in the morning.

"Now we can't let George go too far," she said about the fast-food. Her voice had vigor and laughter in it, and she said, "I mean, sometimes I've just got to have a steak."

It had occurred to Rollin that only a woman who had seen the world would say something like that, and when they arrived in California she realized she really didn't know Nancy DeWitt any better than that. Even though through George they were aware of each other's situations, and one night in Texas Nancy had had enough to drink to look at Rollin and say life was funny, wasn't it—"You're leaving home and I'm going back." She was going back to sign divorce papers, and then she was planning to return to Paris. Already she wore a large square aquamarine on her left hand.

"Oh, George, you break my *heart*!" she said when George tried to get sympathy, like the first night when he said he liked to sleep in his van really. After he had gone away Nancy and Rollin had stood on the terrace looking down at the van, which was parked under the streetlights in the motel parking lot. At the same moment they had turned and looked at each other and Nancy had said, "It looks so lonely." They started laughing, and after that George had slept on a cot at the foot of their beds.

Nancy didn't smoke, didn't suntan; her ring and small Italian handbag fit exactly with the privileged California childhood she referred to now and then, the white gloves she'd worn every Sunday to visit her grandmother.

"My grandmother always had one of those," she said about a white Cadillac they saw, and Rollin couldn't tell if it was sadness or disdain in her voice.

"She is a kind of poet," George had said, but if Rollin had expected to gain any clearer a picture of Nancy through the slim volume of poetry she had published herself (the paper was as thick as the cover), she was wrong; the words and images were as warm as her laughter and as cold as the aquamarine.

"Look!" she said the night they arrived in Venice, and Rollin had turned and looked out the window to the house next door, where a pit bull was poised on the windowsill. White organdy curtains billowed out around his stunted body as he stared back at them, a Dinty Moore's Beef Stew can in his ragged-looking mouth. Meanwhile, the bikers stood around drinking their beers, a motorcycle on the ground between them like something they had hunted down. Rollin felt a sort of desperation. What was she doing here? Nancy had her family and George had his work—already there was mail waiting for him here. It didn't seem possible that they had left Peninghen two weeks ago, and it occurred to her that the trip itself had become her new life, she hadn't thought of actually arriving anywhere. Nancy and George were laughing, and with the coming darkness, the walls and noise seemed to close in around them, and Rollin was frightened, as if she knew that the house on the other side of them had been broken into recently, or that the last time George had stayed here, he was working on a sculpture in the garage and he had killed a black widow.

For a fleeting instant that night, she had realized that one day they would leave her here—George planned to stay about three months—and she would start her life. It wasn't until later that she put into perspective the exaggerated emotions and anxieties which described that period of her life, and saw that any behavior would have been normal. It was reactionary. It had to do with not only embracing the larger world, but dealing with an alienation from her father as well.

"Just go in a new direction a little farther each day," her mother had said on the phone one night. "That's what I did, and not only did I get to know New York, but each time I came home that little apartment was more like a home."

Finally the day came when Nancy left for good, and George went up to Sacramento. Nancy had taken Rollin places—to Beverly Hills and Westwood and Malibu; but the places made no sense to her from here, they were all connected somehow in a circuit Nancy had known and shown her in a series of spontaneous afternoons. And L.A. was not like New York. It was not dirty or mean or fast; it was new and bright and wild, like the Iceland poppies growing in the medians. It was flashy, like its cars. As in any city, there were the rude, the strange, and the poor, but L.A. supplied its own brand of the rich; fortresses behind gates and hedges in Bel Air which belonged in England or Italy or France; the dark fancy cars one saw in Beverly Hills, where women dressed in cool clashes of silver and gold.

But basically, this was real life, where people went to work and spent money and sat in traffic jams. This was a city, where people fell in love and committed murder. Rollin had never had to lock a door, and pulling the door behind her she locked herself out four times in two weeks. Yet there was a particularly pleasing aspect to life, which was anonymity: Rollin realized if she embarrassed herself, it didn't matter. If she saw the person again, she could pretend she didn't. In fact, she didn't have to be nice to anyone. But mostly people disappeared back into the world, as she could choose to do or not.

Still, it took time. Without being aware of it, she did what her mother had told her; she drove to the marina for the third and fourth and fifth time, she went to Westwood, and then there was her first experience on the freeway, when she went to see them work on the sculpture. (Once, coming back to Venice on Overland, she had turned onto Venice Boulevard and she had seen snow-capped mountains receding in the rearview mirror. She had not even known of their existence until that day, when there was no smog and they simply appeared, as clear as in a calendar photograph.) And her mother had been right; finally there had come a day when Rollin felt that she was coming home. It seemed like the only thing her mother had taught her, something which could not be learned because it had to be felt. All she knew was that one sunny day she pulled the car into the alley, and maybe it was just that she'd been there long enough, or that Pete, the man who cruised the alley on his bicycle collecting junk, tipped his hat to her. It was like a dog which usually barked, and didn't this time.

George's inevitable departure was delayed several times. At first the steps he had outlined had gone quickly. He had spent time in Sacramento, where the Forestry Department was, and in Eureka, where he had chosen the logs. (He claimed that although he had been allowed to choose the logs, the ones which had been delivered were not the ones he had selected. "They have sold them, I am sure of that," he had said.) Then there was the problem of the availability of trucks.

"That's ridiculous," Rollin said.

"I agree with you," George said, laughing. "I am not a high priority, for me this is clear."

When the work had actually commenced, Rollin had driven out to the park to watch as the cranes pulled and dragged the logs to their final position of grace. But physical strength was also required, and George had laughed at Rollin watching the men.

"Are you impressed?" he said. "Well, this is something I have never understood with women. All over my life, I have seen this. I can say that the one time Isabelle had any love for me was when I carried a piano across the room." He burst out laughing and tousled Rollin's hair.

Rollin looked at him and smiled. It was the first time she had known she would miss him in a way which had nothing to do with needing him. They shared a house, they did their laundry together; they had agreed, early on, that she would do the shopping and he would do the cooking. She had set up a studio in the back room where there was a cross breeze, and she worked well during those months: her paintings were made from days which were never bright enough, nights which weren't long enough, and the work showed that, a gestural energy which represented a freedom she had never known.

Like the trip across country, their life became a routine tinged already with a nostalgia of its ending, but this also provided an edge to their life together. Nancy had introduced them to people, and George took her to openings—a sculptor who had done earthworks all over Los Angeles County, and provided a map, like a scavenger hunt; a gallery which was in darkness, and people looked at the work with flashlights.

"I have met many women in these washing machine kinds of places," he had laughed when they had gone to the laundromat the first time, and Rollin had rolled her eyes and laughed, and had continued sorting clothes. She had reacted similarly when he mentioned a woman at the Forestry Department, a woman who from his description was twice as big as he was and wore lots of gold jewelry. George said he was sure she wanted to go to bed with him.

"I do not think there would be anything left of me," he said, laughing.

Women confided in George—Rollin remembered seeing that with

Nancy. There had been nothing sexual between them, that too was clear—although not right away; the first time Rollin had heard them laughing together there was a hint of the kind of intimacy one associated with physical privacy. Rollin had never known what jealousy was, at least not beyond her fierce attachment to Douglas; and certainly then she had not thought levels upon which a woman wouldn't trust George would ever matter to her. He had gotten her out into the world, and that was as far as she could see.

He mentioned the woman a few more times—"We had some drinks and we laughed a lot really"—and Rollin had known, one night when he didn't come home, where he had been.

"You know sometimes I sleep in my car," he said in the alley the next day, and he tousled her hair and laughed. When Rollin didn't say anything, he laughed, rubbing her arm. "But I thought about you, Rollin," he said. "I wondered what you ate for dinner," and he laughed again.

The following day Rollin accepted when an engineer she had met, a man named Mike, called and asked her to dinner. He had called once before, and she had made some excuse. She didn't want to go now, either, and she didn't know what it was about George's presence in the room which made her say yes.

George thought it was funny. They had met the man together, through friends of his, and he had seen the way the man looked at her. "Well, you will have a boring time," he said when she got off the phone. He started to laugh and said, "But you will have a better dinner than you had last night."

Mike was a nice man with a clean, expensive car, the only thing, he told Rollin, that he had gotten out of the divorce.

Rollin looked at his profile, his good haircut.

He turned to her and smiled a salesman's smile, and asked her where she'd like to go.

"We go to El Coyote sometimes," Rollin said. "They have good margaritas."

"Oh, come on," Mike said. "What about a French restaurant?

That's what the women I know like," he said. "Where they light a fire at your table."

When she got home, George was watching television. It reminded her of once when she and Nancy had come back to the motel room one night and the door had flown open and like a child he had said, "I wasn't watching television!"

Now he appeared to be concentrating on something. Sirens were going and there were shots, but he didn't look up. "Rollin," he said. He looked up then and broke off thread in his teeth. He had been sewing on a button. He watched as she took off her high heels. He didn't say anything, but the question hung in the air.

"It was nice," she said. "We went to a French place."

"Well, you should come with me to France," George said. "If you come to France with me, you can have French food *every* night. There is French salt and pepper there, and French potatoes and French corn, and you can wash the dishes with French dish soap. You can drink French milk and water, and you can breathe French air."

She had gotten up and turned away, and she could hear him cackle to himself.

"And oh," he said. "How could I forget the wine?" There was another cackle, and then he asked her if she had any sewing she wanted done. He said, "I enjoy doing this really. When I was a child, I was the best in embroidery." He laughed at her surprise and went on, "And it is funny, but my son too, he was the best."

They had never talked about his sons in any depth. Nor had they talked about Douglas, except once. "Well, I suppose you wanted to go to bed with him," George had said. Even Nancy had been shocked. "But this is normal," George had said. "It is the other women who went to bed with him who were not normal." He laughed and went on, "But I have seen this all over my life. These men who pretend to be interested in art because they know women like that."

The conversation had taken place in the car. "But that's such a generalization," Nancy said, turning down the radio, and George had nodded and said, "Well, I can say that knowing how to generalize could be one of the most intelligent things."

They had gone on, Nancy getting more frustrated by the minute, but Rollin was quiet. After Douglas had died, she had had sexual dreams about him, about which she had told no one, and George's casual pondering of the subject had made her freeze.

Rollin found herself thinking about the trip often, especially after George had left. In a way, although she had started out with a curiosity about the people she was with, she had learned more about herself. As George said years later, geography had had nothing to do with it.

"For you, California was on the way to France. It was a process, simply that."

George left two days after the dedication ceremony of his sculpture, a triumphant day of solemn words punctuated by laughter and good weather and champagne.

At the airport, he said he had left something for her, and when she got back to the house she saw the prototype for the sculpture, balanced on the counter like a toy. She had handled it before. It was made of aluminum and it was cold.

"Why is it made of aluminum?" she had asked. "How do you know that what you've done in aluminum will work in wood?"

"Well, I could have done this in wood," he had answered, as if had he chosen, he could have used water.

He had talked about the importance of sense of touch ("I can say that if I were blind, I would be happy really"), but when Rollin had closed her eyes and run her fingers along the planes and edges, it had meant nothing to her, because there was never the impression of knowing the piece as a whole.

"When you see it, you confront all of it right away," she had said to him. "I see it that way probably because I'm a painter. It's more visual with me."

But that moment was different: George was gone, and seeing it she had to touch it. How, she wondered, could it be so impersonal, so perfect and cold in its conception, and still evoke emotion? She reached for it, and turned it over in her hands. It was cold, smooth; a tunnel in a wave as sleek as a highway, angles and a slope more subtle than a cheekbone; she thought of his face; it was even and hard and hidden and obvious; how could she feel his touch?

It was a warm day in early September, and it occurred to Rollin as she sat there that this was the first time in her life that she had been alone. She felt the distance now. It would be fall in the East soon—the prettiest time at Peninghen. It was strange. The landscapes she had seen across the country had been strong enough to erase Peninghen and her emotions were violent enough for her to get what she had seen on canvas; but now memory returned, strong and confident and merciless with her father's silence, his absence from her life.

The arrangement about the house had been that when George left, it would be put on the market. Once or twice in the four months she had spent there, Rollin's mind had wandered and she had imagined what she would do with it if she owned it. There was only one real possibility, for the house was quite small—which was to tear down the two walls which, at perpendicular angles, separated the space into three rooms. Then she would have one large studio space, the kitchen walled off. Skylights in the roof would let in even more light. Someone had made the unfortunate decision to put wall-to-wall carpeting in the kitchen—that would certainly have to go. There was also the garage—perhaps she could use that as the studio and keep the house as it was.

It never occurred to her that she couldn't afford the house. The spirit of freedom had overextended itself; she had automatically thought of her money in direct proportion to her sudden, boundless freedom. Of course, you didn't have to worry about money if what you wanted was in the realm of how much you had, and this house did not seem too much to want, not after Peninghen. She felt like a child doing a math problem: if Rollin has three hundred and fifty thousand dollars and she wants to buy a house which costs two hundred and seventy-five thousand dollars, how much can she spend monthly if she wants her money to last ten years? Douglas had not left her enough money to buy a house she did not even really like.

It was Mike, the engineer, who saved her. She had put him off when he had called her again, and she was surprised and not displeased to hear from him now. And it was that day, walking along the canals, that she saw the house for rent.

The first thing that struck her was that he looked funny in that living room after George. With his height, the house became something out of Alice in Wonderland.

"Your friend do this?" he said, looking at the sculpture.

"Why, doesn't it hold up under engineering standards?" Rollin said, smiling.

"Well, it would have to," Mike said, his tie hanging as he leaned to look at it. He seemed to be doing calculations as he turned the piece around.

Rollin looked at the piece, remembering the night she'd come back and found George sewing. She hadn't realized it, but at dinner she had talked about him constantly—everything seemed to remind her of him, or of something he had said.

"Were you with this guy or what?" Mike said. "Or I guess I should say are you."

"It's a long story really," Rollin said. "I mean, no, not in that way, not at all."

"He's a lot older than you," Mike said. She was looking around at the restaurant, thinking Nancy surely would have approved. "Like it?" Mike said.

Rollin smiled and nodded. If he wasn't exciting, if he didn't make her laugh, she was comfortable with him. There was something about a man who dealt in the real world. She didn't understand exactly what he did; when he told her he worked at an aircraft company as an engineer she pictured him out on the runway with tools.

"No," he said, laughing. "I'll take you over there sometime. It has nothing to do with the airport."

One night they went to his apartment, where shelves were lined with books with titles like *Mechanics of Fluids*.

"You impressed?" Mike said, throwing his keys on the table inside the door.

Rollin looked around the apartment, which was furnished in blue and gold and shades of brown, the brushed silver of an elaborate stereo system. She wanted to take off her heels, which were hurting her, but she knew he would take it the wrong way. She said, "I think I'm a little tired. Would you mind if you took me home?"

He came towards her and put his arms around her, but his cool suit against her cheek provoked nothing except the desire to cry.

The bikers were in the alley when he brought her home, and he insisted on walking her inside.

"And watch the glass," he said, noticing she had taken off her shoes.

She put George's sculpture away. In his first letter, he had asked if she had seen Mike again. ("One thing I must tell you is that if you want to get married you must wear those high heels.") She had answered that letter, sending him her new address (describing the house, asking him if he remembered it), but when he wrote again, she didn't answer. She wasn't even sure why, except that it was all tied in with her father's silence and Mike's kindness; the distance George had put between them so easily. He wrote again ("Rollin Thompkins, have you joined a convent . . ."), but she didn't answer that either. "Come with me to California," he had said. "Well, you should come with me to France." He ran his life dependent on a support from others he felt he was owed; she saw that now. The sculpture had insisted his presence; first it had troubled, then irritated her, and she had wrapped it up and put it in a closet. But when she moved, she could not bear to throw away the cardboard models George had made, a group of beautiful, playful geometric forms she had rescued from a shelf in his closet. He had used anything: empty film boxes, calling cards, a toilet-paper roll.

"I admire what you do," Mike said. "I can't say I understand it, but maybe it's sort of a release for me. The color and freedom you've got in your work—it's—well, it's like coming here."

The house she was renting which was on one of the canals, was smaller on the inside than she had thought, but the space was divided well for a studio, the bigger of the two rooms facing the canal in a block of small windows. The other house had had furniture, but this had none, and although Rollin had meant to buy at least a couch and a few chairs, she had never gotten beyond a mattress on the floor.

She didn't mind if Mike watched her paint, in fact she loved it when he appeared during his lunch hour in a suit and she met him at the door, threatening him with whatever color was on the brush. She supposed he represented security: it was a comfort to think of him working in that windowless building near the airport, dealing with numbers and stress, wearing a tie and a badge and talking about helices and torques. The first time she had seen the badge she couldn't believe it.

"Clearance, you know," he said. They were at dinner, and he had forgotten to take it off.

"You mean I couldn't go in there?" Rollin said.

"Some areas," Mike said. "I'll take you around sometime," he promised again.

One day he did. A guard gave her a visitor's badge, and she followed Mike down a long slick hallway as clean as a hospital. He stopped at a door with four numbers on it, and they walked into a room with machines on high strong tables, lit by fluorescent lights which buzzed. The room was airless. He was so proud, but all Rollin could think of was getting out. Where were the windows? Twice a week she took a class, and she had just come from drawing the model; and the cold hard metal, so heavy and complicated, so powerful and impersonal and efficient, was too much for her. She wanted to see food or a flower or even the bones they had drawn last week. As a child, she had stroked the satin binding of her blanket constantly (so she had been told), and that was what she wanted now, to touch that satin binding.

Instead, she had driven home and gotten George's piece out of the closet. Then there was the sculpture in the park: one day she found herself in a part of town she recognized, and in a moment she knew why. But that surprise was nothing compared to the day she was wandering around Westwood and chanced to look in a bookstore window, and saw her father's name.

Chapter 20

∘ ∘ ∘

In California, storms took vegetation and palm fronds like ripe fruit ready to be peeled; bamboo grew in a week and Iceland poppies sprang up in the medians overnight. Forests burned, and with torrential rains grew back. Rollin stood in the common room and stared out at the maze, which like the giant trees seemed not to have grown at all in three years. As California had frantically replaced itself each season, the maze had merely stayed alive. And the trees: so old, sad, giants so big they couldn't take care of themselves. Their limbs broke off in storms, they were attacked by caterpillars and diseases, they had grown to such height growth no longer made a difference. Rollin had been taught to measure with a pencil, but you couldn't measure the distance to the sky.

"Rollin."

Her father's voice.

Thompkins was standing in the dark corner of the large room, the heavy door ajar behind him. He was wearing a pale sweater, and he looked older.

"Papa!" she cried.

Thompkins had won the National Book Award, and a few days later Rollin sat in the darkened auditorium of the Academy of Arts and Letters and watched as he accepted an envelope. There was a moment of levity as Thompkins stepped up to the podium and held the envelope up to the light to make sure the check was in it. The audience laughed, but Rollin's eyes filled with tears. Nineteen years for that laugh and a thousand dollars. He gave a short speech, but she was overcome by how alone he looked up there, as if his suit were too big and he were trying to hold his own. He had worked on the book for two decades. It had sat in closets in cartons under coats, it had been rescued and protected; and yet this audience only saw the glory of the day, the ease and elegance with which Lad Thompkins stepped up to the microphone.

At ages too young to know more than she saw, Rollin had thought Douglas would be the one to be remembered, but that day she saw she was wrong. Thompkins had "followers," he had critics and professors and scholars who were ready to meet with him in his corner whenever he was ready. Still there was not the joy she had felt at George's dedication in California.

Back at Peninghen, she hardly knew what to say to him.

"Of course it's sold the usual thirty-three copies," he said about the book, and Rollin realized that it had never occurred to her what would happen when the book was published—she had held it in her hands and that was enough. Whether or not it would sell seemed unrelated to its existence.

"That's the spirit," he said, between a laugh and cough. "I brought you up right, didn't I?"

The tower room seemed stuffy and small to Rollin now, especially at this hour, when the dew fell and the light went.

She said, "You said something about going to St. Louis? Is that true? Are you going?"

They shared an ashtray and the sun was going down and Thompkins looked out the window. "It looks like it," he said, as if he were saying it looked like rain.

"Well, don't you want to?" Rollin said.

"Oh." He shrugged. "They want me to read. I told them I'd talk. Not read."

Rollin asked him about a next book, and he shook his head and muttered something about an outline. Looking around the room, she couldn't imagine his days—she hardly remembered living there. "And Margaret? She's—"

"Still in the picture," Thompkins said, nodding. After the book had been turned in, he had come to Margaret with a heaviness even though the burden had been lifted. He'd never known her without the book between them, abstracting his thoughts, protecting him. He had taken her to the island house, where he had smoked and stared at the ceiling and wondered why he had done such a thing. His eyes had traveled over the old flower prints, the charcoal drawings from the pink house (he still thought of them as the charcoal drawings from the pink house even though they had hung in the island house three times as many years). Why had he come back? When his mother had bought the place she had been presented with a foot-long gold nail in red velvet. The town didn't do that anymore; new owners (and all residents) were now furnished with information about where to buy regulation-size metal numbers to be screwed into the boardwalks in front of their houses. A digit had been added to the telephone exchange.

The couple who had run the store when his mother was alive had vanished back to their dairy farm long ago, and now even the men who had taken over had sold out. The store had been taken over by an ambitious young couple who skied in the winters, and it was obvious what paid for that—the prices were appalling. And so after buying what they needed for the first night, he and Margaret had taken the ferry back over to the mainland, where they had shopped angrily at the Grand Union (Thompkins had shopped angrily; and he had been unnerved that to Margaret it was all just new and strange and funny). One thing that had not changed in twenty-five years was that boxes were prohibited on the ferries, and only cans and "containers" of food were permitted on the freight boat—the town's way of discouraging families from stocking up on food instead of patronizing the island store.

"Lad, what are you doing?" Margaret said when she saw the suitcases.

They were in the parking lot, and Thompkins began taking the food out of the bags and transferring it into a suitcase and a nylon duffel bag, which when they arrived on the island leaked blood on the dock, leaving a trail all the way from the ferry to the cluster of wagons and women talking. It was Margaret who noticed.

"Lad, the steaks," she said. She gripped his arm and glanced in the direction of the women. "The steaks, they're leaking," she said in a tight voice.

"We don't care," Thompkins said, patting her arm. He had never cared about this town.

"But they'll think—"

"Let me tell you a story about what happened with the dog once," Thompkins said, and told her about the time Sacha had stopped short on the dock to do her business. "Right in the middle, no warning," he said.

Margaret looked away from the women and tried not to laugh.

"And so of course I tripped over her," Thompkins went on. "Got it all over my shoes—"

"Lad, *stop*—" Laughing, she hid her face against his shoulder.

"There. You see?" he said. "It's a nasty little town. You come over from Kismet and a big sign greets you, a sign probably put up by these women's husbands. NO, it says in giant letters. Then it lists everything you can't do. Can't picnic, can't barbecue, can't drink on the beach, can't ride after dusk—right? Right. There they are," he said as they passed the women. "Don't they look happy?"

"Lad, stop," she said again, laughing.

"Here we go," he said, and the wagon wheels squeaked louder as they turned from the boardwalk onto cement, where the blood showed up bright red. They walked the familiar stretch along the bay and then turned again, back onto the boardwalk. Margaret looked this way and that, the curious newcomer; Thompkins had seen her expression on dozens of guests' faces, and he waited for the usual questions. What do you do here at night? Are there *any* cars? What do you mean, the police ride bicycles?

He had described the house to her and she had seen early pictures of it, but when the wagon wheels stopped, she looked at him uncertainly. In front of them was a house which through neglect had become a kingdom of its own. Behind the wild growth of vegetation, the only traces of a house were bits of window here and there catching the sun, and a pale gray, almost white roof.

"Is this—" she said, and he nodded. "It looks like something from the bottom of the sea," she said.

There was pride in his voice when he said, "It hasn't been painted in a while."

He had come back, he supposed, to reclaim it. The house had always been a symbol to him that on one level he had held things together on the world's terms. That the decision of whether to rent it or sell it still existed confirmed each year that the house belonged to him, although, having sold the corner lot to buy the place in Key West, he'd come close to letting the house go several times. But even selling it would require investing in it—each year it was easier to count the glasses and towels and hope the smell from the septic tank would hold back until mid-August.

"Is it what you'd expected?" he asked Margaret.

Of course not, she had said, but wasn't that always how it was?

"If anything's what you expect, aren't you disappointed?" she said. "If something is as exactly as someone has described . . ."

Later, he had looked down at the ocean and the sand and then into Margaret's light eyes, somehow amazed that she did not see what he did.

"Oh, dear," he said; for there was Kipps breaking out a beer; Dowling, black hair glistening from a quick dip; Pauline in one of those bedouin-like robes she was so fond of, motioning for him to come down and telling the others, "We must enjoy him, we only get fifteen minutes—" And Rollin, running, running—couldn't she see? A room full of people drinking and laughing, someone just out of the shower, the screen door slamming; or down from a nap and Can I get you another one of those? Shake you something, Sally Ann? Bare feet, tan legs, the odd guest who had arrived pale and left sunburned—

Thompkins stared down at the sand, where a man about his own age was sitting beside the empty lifeguard stand, reading the Sunday *Times*.

"They used to wear pearls with their bathing suits," he said. It was all he could think of to put it all where it belonged.

"Now they jog," Margaret said.

"Isn't that silly," Thompkins said.

Margaret had smiled at him and he had smiled back. She was so faintly in his life. Like this place off-season, that was her place with him. They were the kind of couple people listened in on in restaurants, her dark glasses or his spurring the comment "Who's she?" or "Isn't he somebody?" Usually, though, they walked into Jack's in the Keys and attracted no attention. They walked slightly apart from each other, which only confirmed that there was more between them. They knew the odd things about each other, facts and impressions normally collected quickly in a shared daily life, details of money and habits and health; childhood and houses and friends. But still, without the book he felt his footing was uncertain with her, as it was with the world.

This was not what Rollin saw now, though—an avoidance and preoccupation which at first she had thought had to do with her and her leaving. He had assured her she was wrong, but when she told him she'd been accepted for a group show he had hardly reacted.

"And that's, that's how it starts, I suppose?" he had said without much interest.

Rollin had been prepared to be modest and instead she was hurt. She stared at a pile of books on the table. "You know, someone

told me once I should at least be glad I wasn't trying to be a writer,"
she said.

"I agree with *that*," he said.

Rollin smiled. "Well, even if I were there wouldn't be any basis
for comparison," she said. "I mean, you're a statistic," she said
quietly. "I think that would take the pressure off somehow." He
said nothing, and she went on, "The worst would be if you were a
painter and I was trying to write, because it's—you can get by with
more in painting. I'd have a harder time."

He said he thought you could tell a bad writer easier. "But just
think if we were both painters," he said. "Think of that. I'd be
selling for seventy thousand and you'd be selling for three, and you'd
know it was only because I was older than you." He smiled elfishly.

He was trying to make light of it, and Rollin saw that and smiled.
"It's so strange to be here," she said, looking around again at the
room. "I don't—I just remember I was always afraid of embarrassing
you. I don't mean by my behavior, that was awful all the time. But
failing. Not being any good. I think if I hadn't been able to come
home and tell you about something, a show, *something*—I wouldn't
have come at all." She thought she might cry. "It's funny," she said.
"Most kids want their parents to be proud of them, but I couldn't
even get that far, I—" She stopped.

Thompkins shook his head and looked up at the ceiling, and his
voice was rough and sad. "Oh, Rollin," he said. "That's not all there
is. Work." He leaned forward and awkwardly squeezed her elbow
across the table. "Don't think that. Don't think I think that."

But the next day he fell silent again. It was exhausting: she tried
to make conversation, but her father had never been one for small
talk; as a child she had always felt she talked too much.

"How long—" he said at lunch. He cleared his throat. "How long
did you plan to stay?"

"I don't know," Rollin said. "I thought a couple of weeks. The
show, you know." She stared at the dog.

He nodded. They had talked about going into the city, but he didn't mention it and when she did he shrugged and said no, he didn't think he wanted to do that.

"Before long *this* will be a city," she said. "It's gotten crazy here. That awful new mall—"

Thompkins rose. He tucked his hair behind his ear and walked slowly over and poured himself a scotch, and then he went over to the sideboard. Rollin watched as he pulled at a drawer, stubborn from dampness, shook it, and for a moment with his hair falling in front of his face he looked quite mad. He stood in front of her, holding a sheaf of papers, abstracted as if perhaps he'd changed his mind; but then it all came at her, letterheads, typed pages and letters all at once, documents and papers falling on the floor, the flourish of signatures of men in authority.

"What—"

"Something you've got to know," Thompkins said.

Mostly the letters were from the State Department of Transportation, although there were two from the governor's office, trying to reach a settlement with Lad Thompkins, executor of the estate of Douglas G. Kipps. The highway was called the Blue Route.

"There you are," Thompkins said. He had picked up the papers off the floor and put them on the table. "That's the award they're giving me," he said. "That's the award they think I deserve."

Then he told her about Catherine and the boy.

Rollin stared at the pile of papers. Had they been there, she would have focused on details: the boy's pale eyelashes, a scar on Catherine Byrd's elbow Douglas must have seen a hundred times.

But as it was, her first reaction was to turn inward. She felt changed. It seemed to her that she had been told something about herself, for she felt changed. She wondered if children who had been adopted felt like this. It was quiet in the room except for the ticking of the clock. Yesterday, she had seen a harp in one of the reception rooms. She had never seen one close up before, and she had always imagined that harp strings were gold. But these had been gold and copper and red and purple and silver, and not delicate but cordlike.

She had examined the inlaid wood and precise construction with awe—there was something so mathematical and strong about its grace.

"Winifred has known for a while," her father was saying. "There was the thought early on—oh, Lord. The hope that a legal heir would change something. Make a difference."

"And will it?" Rollin said.

When they had gone to the book awards, the taxi had flown and bounced in the sun, through green lights and over potholes until Rollin realized they were in Harlem, which on a Sunday afternoon was slow and kind, too still for a murder. They had stopped for a red light and Rollin had swallowed hard and stared at the buildings and garbage cans in the four-o'clock sun and she had even seen the beauty of it; a street Hopper might paint. How she hated New York, and how it insisted on being a part of her she loved. She had not known that they would come this way, but in a way it had made all the sense in the world. Suddenly Douglas's death had become a part of her adolescence, inseparable from the hysteria of hormones and bad grades.

And now? She saw that he had been a different person from the man she had loved. The golden light around him was gone, and she was forced to remember when her godfather, whom she had adored, had finally allowed her to accompany him to the in-famous Kismet Inn, where he had alternately hovered over her and ignored her until he was too drunk to stand. Steadying him in the moonlight on the sandy road, Rollin saw she had been cheated, although she had not been sure how. He had stopped to pee in the reeds, a wet sound which made her look away. Perhaps she had imagined him defending her, but there had been no need for that; baseball had been on and no man had even noticed her. Such a spoiled child, she had been faced with the notion that neither of them was a superior person, she was not beautiful, he was not brave.

She said, "I can't—" and shook her head.

"I know," her father said, but his sigh was also one of relief, and he got up and went for another drink.

"Well, does he look like Douglas?" she blurted out. A part of her wanted to cry out, What gives you the right? What gives you the right to keep these secrets? If it hadn't been for this horrible road, would you ever have told me?

He was running tap water, feeling for it to be cold enough to add to his scotch. He shrugged. "Thinner. His mother's thin." He turned the water off.

Rollin's gaze fell on the clock. It was three hours earlier in California, where the sun was shining and Pete was making his rounds in the alley on his bicycle, and the Sparkletts man was leaving bottles of water on porches. How frivolous it all seemed from here, where even the trees were serious. And yet it was her life. And over the next few days, thinking about what her father had told her, she was glad to have a life to think about. The questions came, slowly, and sometimes she forgot the answers.

"What did you say about where she was from?"

"Seattle."

Once or twice she just said his name. "Kevin."

"He's just this boy," her father said, emphasizing his innocence.

It almost seemed that he had told her both things at once, each to take her mind off the other.

"We'll support the legal system for a while and then we'll lose," he said about the road. "It's the government. We'll lose."

"But there'll be a settlement," Rollin said. "We won't *lose*, there'll be some kind of—"

"Just money to go out and buy another goddam piece of the world," Thompkins said. "Another house and walls and septic system. Jesus Christ," he said under his breath.

o o o

Fighting the Department of Transportation became the cause of the rest of Lad Thompkins's life. Over time, Rollin saw that his anger about the case represented his anger at the world. It had become a vehicle. His health was going, but he wouldn't stop smoking; "If there was ever a time in my life I needed cigarettes, it's now," he said.

The legal battles lasted two years in all, although with the fairs and picnics and the auction held on the grounds to raise money for the appeal, Peninghen had stopped functioning as an institution long before the last appeal was lost.

"Give it up, let it go," Rollin pleaded. After attending a few meetings with her father she saw it was useless; she saw, too, that it could be one of the best things which could happen to them. But her father refused. He didn't come to California for the show, even though he said "We'll see" up until the last minute.

It was amazing that Rollin even got it together to do the show, for it wasn't until she got back out to California that everything her father had told her hit her. Her whole life seemed uncertain. Out of five canvases, only three were finished, and the show was a month away, and she hadn't even thought about framing.

Then her mother came. Rollin hadn't wanted to think about that: her mother, divorced from Jim Dover, living with Amy while Stuart lived with his father. During the whole two weeks that her mother and Amy were there, the three of them stood at distances from one another, triangles with longer and shorter sides. Rollin did not know what it was, but her mother's presence in the studio seemed to influence the pictures. It wasn't what she said about them, it was her presence. It was her clothes hanging on the backs of doors, reminding Rollin of her childhood and clothes on the back of doors in other houses, houses which she had hated and which had formed her as much as anyone's love.

"Rollin, I hope you'll pay attention to Amy," she said. "She thinks you're so great."

"Does she," Rollin said.

When they had arrived, Amy had wandered into the studio and she had stood for a moment, her arms crossed in front of her, looking at *Rightside Up*. Then she had moved away. She had not realized that Rollin was watching her, and when she turned there was that moment when Rollin caught her eye. It took that split second for Rollin to see that Amy thought of her sister as a wild girl with lots of money who painted once in a while, but preferred to drink and smoke pot. An acrylic Rollin had done a few months ago looked at her from a corner. Amy moved slightly, her delicate perfection against the white wall on one side, and her fair complexion in direct contrast to the strong dark colors of the painting on the other.

Amy wasn't a child anymore. How old was she—fifteen? Pretty —blond and blue-eyed—sixteen. Rollin figured this out by subtracting the age she had been when Amy was born from the age she was now, implying a closeness they did not share. Rollin was seeing a jazz saxophonist at the time, and one night they went to see Larry play. "That was great, Rollin," Amy said afterwards. She had put on eyeshadow and lipstick, and the way she would think Larry was great had nothing to do with being a child. There was a shyness about her, but the woman shone through, and Rollin experienced an uneasiness she'd never known before. These children—her mother carried a picture of Stuart, a tall lanky kid who played basketball—were growing up; Amy was growing up in a corner of her life Rollin had thought she had sealed with her own adolescence. And it wasn't that she was jealous. Rollin wasn't sure whether it was being caught unaware which bothered her, or the past—the fact that she had given up her own adolescence in order that this young girl could stand so calmly in front of her. It was the jealousy or resentment a mother might feel; but Amy was not her daughter, Rollin would receive none of the rewards a daughter returned. As confrontations and emotions had crisscrossed so wildly in front of Rollin, she had been charged with the mundane task of changing a diaper. Then she had gone away and left these children to grow up, and they had. They were growing up at a rate which seemed to be gaining on her, they made her want to run.

Still, she did finish, her mother helping with the framing. The show was at a fair-sized space on Rose Avenue, and Rollin was pleased with the way it was hung. She sold two paintings and one of the paper pieces at the opening, and two more red dots appeared before the show was over. She had sold more than half.

But it was as though she'd put her life on hold, and all the emotions she'd kept in check to make the show happen couldn't wait any longer. Like anyone else in those smoky, crowded clubs, she felt her thoughts were more profound with each set, and armed with another scotch, she felt Douglas come closer. She closed her eyes and listened, and she saw him with a blind person's memory, and it was a high; if she could just get out of here with the dark and the music and the fever of memory still around her, the smoke and the burn in her throat, she knew she could work.

She painted if someone drove her home, and the work was strong. But what usually happened was that she drank too much and didn't want to leave, they'd break and Larry would want her there, and if she wasn't there she knew there were other girls. Rollin had never known jealousy before—she had never known it could be something physical and crazy. He brought it out in her.

"Hey, blondes are blondes," he said the first time. "They act like that, man, I don't know why. Now come here. Where'd you go, anyway?"

She'd gone out into the parking lot and smashed bottles and it had scared her.

"Come here, hey," he whispered. He was like a bear, and Rollin leaned into his neck, his hair, which was curly and tickled. "Hey," he said, "what did you do that for, I thought only redheads got like that."

Night after night she gave in to an intensity she mistook for participation when what it was about was dissipation. The nights

drained the color out of her face as she stood in the bland cool
dawns leaning on Larry's shoulder, yawning in the parking lots of
those windowless clubs he played; Tuesdays, Thursdays; she mixed
up the days and the clubs, one had square tables and round ashtrays
and one had square ashtrays and round tables, and in the end it
was all the same, it ended the same, with a gravelly voice and hair
that smelled like smoke, and a renewed resolution to paint.

Meanwhile, the news about Peninghen wasn't good; a pessimistic
article in the *Times* with a picture of Douglas and a hideous one of
her father.

"Your father needs protection from the outside world," her
mother had said when they'd talked about Peninghen, and Douglas.
"Whereas with Douglas it was the opposite."

Rollin had thought she meant that the world needed protection
from Douglas.

"No, no, honey. Douglas needed protection from himself, and
that was harder because no one could help him."

And now no one could help her father, either.

In fact the first overly polite conversation Rollin had with Catherine Byrd was about her father's health and state of mind. She had
flown back for the series of events which had been organized to
raise funds for Peninghen. The first time she saw Catherine and her
son was from the window opposite the alcove where, so many years
ago, she'd watched the beginning of its first season. Now, the scene
below, the people and color and activity, much resembled what she
remembered. Then, though, the crowd had been more reserved.
Rollin had been amazed to arrive at the familiar gates and see activity
spill over into the road. There had been much publicity about what
the state was trying to do; and apparently the case had become a
forum. Artists across the country had raised money, and for the
auction, painters and sculptors both well known and less known,
those who had spent time at Peninghen and many who had been
rejected, had donated their work.

". . . if not we'll just go higher," she had heard a raspy voice say, and she had turned and seen the nametag NELL DAYTON. The man she was talking to was a gallery owner Rollin recognized. The work which was being auctioned was under a tarp in an area which had been cordoned off. It was heartbreaking. It also made her angry: she had agreed to auction the painting Douglas had given her, but why should she give her portrait away? She had run upstairs, as if she thought it might be gone. And it was from there—that window—that she saw Catherine and Kevin for the first time. What struck her, to begin with, was that there was something incredibly light about them both: their blond hair, the way her skirt moved about below her knees. Approaching the crowd from down by the river, they were unhurried, which gave them a certain air of wisdom; they knew this was useless. They were like explorers, roaming the earth, skirting the crowd. Watching them, Rollin realized she had depersonalized them; she had made them into what Douglas had "done," and she had been ready to avoid them.

The funny thing was that she could have. Neither of them had any interest in forcing anything on her. But it was perhaps the circumstances which broke down the barrier, which made what could have been difficult only awkward. They were introduced before dinner in the common room. Rollin stared at Kevin, who wore a typical boy's expression; slight interest in what was going on, the suspicion that perhaps he should be more curious than he was.

But it was Thompkins who was the most ill at ease and out of sorts. "Rollin, this is Catherine Byrd and Kevin," he said. "My daughter," he said to Catherine.

Rollin looked at Catherine, then at Kevin. It was interesting how he looked like Douglas: certain angles of his mother's thinner face. But what was incredible was that once in a while a gesture flew by belonging to the father he had never known. The way he spread his arms and said "I don't know" was uncanny. When Rollin mentioned this, Catherine looked skeptical for a moment, and then said proudly, "But Kevin plays tennis."

They had just come from Detroit, she said, where she had auditioned with the symphony there.

"Did you like it?" Rollin said to Kevin.

He replied with nonchalance. "Pretty polluted. All those auto plants, you know."

"Pretty environment-conscious for a kid your age, aren't you?" Rollin said, smiling.

"He's heard me talk so much about it," Catherine said. "But it's amazing really. My harp—I don't know how much you know, but it's the quality of the wood in a harp that determines the sound."

"Of course I thought it was the strings," Rollin said. "What kind of wood?" She remembered from George that cedar was expensive, but mahogany was the most expensive, but she had no idea about a harp. Catherine said most were made of maple.

"But the sounding board is spruce. Anyway, with the acid rain, none of it's the same as it was even sixty years ago. Strings can be replaced, but—" She shrugged, and pulled her hair back on her shoulders.

There was an awkward silence, and then Kevin broke it by saying, "Mom's auctioning her harp away."

"You are?" Rollin said.

"After the concert," Catherine said. "It's the Salvi Douglas gave me, I think it's the right thing to do. I think he'd want that." She said quietly, "I have my Healey."

People had begun to come inside, and Catherine and Rollin moved towards the edge of the room. Rollin saw her father a distance away, talking to Nell Dayton.

"So much energy," Catherine said. "So much energy for something which isn't going to work."

"I wish someone could convince my father of that," Rollin said.

"I've talked with him a few times, but he just lights another cigarette," Catherine said. She shook her head. "It's just such negative energy, smoking."

The next day, they took a long walk, and as Catherine talked about Douglas, Rollin found herself recognizing him again.

"His favorite story, well it wasn't a story it really happened," Catherine said, "was about a sixteen-year-old boy who— Do you want to hear this, are you okay with this?"

"Please," Rollin said. Catherine walked easily, gracefully, and Rollin had to walk quickly to keep pace.

"His name was Robin. He was sixteen, and in the summer of 1965 he sailed out of L.A. alone in a twenty-four-foot sailboat named *Dove*." Catherine smiled. "He was gone for five years, and when he sailed back in, it was in a thirty-three-foot sailboat with a pregnant wife." Catherine said, "The boat was called *The Return of the Dove*. Douglas loved that story. He saw something of himself in it, I think." She went on, "I guess I think of him every day, Kevin, or I'll see something which reminds me of him but also shows me how different the world is. Baseball, even. Have you seen these gloves they use now? Some outfielder I read about. They're from Japan. Of course. Black and blue and orange—they're not even leather! They're made from fabric, synthetic they use for bulletproof vests. Can you imagine Douglas with that?"

"No," Rollin said, smiling. "No, I can't."

They walked in silence for a moment and Catherine said, "I want Kevin to do what he wants to do."

Rollin nodded. "I understand," she said, but it was hearing her play the harp which explained everything. Rollin had expected a delicate magic, and instead she heard passion. It was then, when she realized how much Douglas had been given, that she understood how much he had needed.

There was the settlement, and the ruling, which gave Thompkins a year to "relocate."

"They've given me a year to live," Thompkins joked. He acted as if he didn't care. He made no move to find a house. He had a year, but all he did was joke about the places he went to speak: "Maybe I'll live in Rumson, New Jersey," he said to Margaret. "Would you come to visit me there? Or what about Media, Pennsylvania?"

As the months dwindled, he started talking about the island house. He could live there, he said; why not? It was ironic, wasn't it, he said, that he had sold the house in Florida and held on to the one which was uninhabitable most of the year. "But I could put in heating," he said.

Then he announced he was going to Europe.

"How can you?" Rollin said. "You can't do that when you don't even know where you'll live after February. And what about your papers? You can't just leave everything. What about your books?"

He said he was seeing to that. She saw there was no point in arguing with him. He did go to Rome; the American Academy had invited him for two months, apparently, and he left in November.

Being there seemed to renew his spirit. Rollin visited him in December, and he was positive about things. They took walks, down the hill from the academy on Via Garibaldi, lined with busts of historic figures under huge bare trees. The buildings were that deep orange one saw in Rome, their shutters and ironwork a pale green, such a contrast in the December light with the blackish-green cypress trees. Thompkins's quarters consisted of two large rooms with ash-colored walls, the larger of the two with a big fireplace, a kitchen, and a bathroom. The atmosphere was one of a summer house, unimportant furniture, articles left behind by previous tenants—an umbrella, books, pens and pencils, a raincoat. Thompkins had chosen a table near the window in the living room to work, although beside the typewriter Rollin saw just one slim folder—she didn't know how his work was going. He joked about his next book being shorter, and when she asked how it was going he shrugged and said, "Oh, they get me up in the morning," meaning his characters.

A book tracing sources for his first book had come out, and passing it to Rollin he shook his head and said, "Now here's a man bent on having at least as small an audience as I do."

"And you," he said, "what about you, any prospects for another show?"

An ironic note of the auction had been that one of the gallery owners had bid for Rollin's work. It wasn't anything decisive, but she had been encouraged. She told him about a good reaction she'd had when she'd taken her slides to a gallery in Santa Monica.

"But it's unbelievable," she said, remembering another gallery she had gone to. "I always take slides and then a couple of canvases, you know, I roll them up. Anyway I went to one gallery and the woman liked my work except she asked me if I could 'take out these lines'! Can you imagine? I said no, I couldn't take out those lines."

Thompkins laughed. "Well, you're seeing it, aren't you," he said. "The world." He kept nodding, reassured, and then he found something else. "And what do you think of all this?" he said one day, looking out over Rome from the Via Garibaldi. "Maybe you'll live in a foreign country someday."

Later, remembering that time with him, she cried. Then, she only said, "It's funny, but I always thought I'd see France first."

"Oh," he said, "there's time. There's time for all that," he said. He laughed. "The French."

"You always made fun of the French," Rollin said.

"Well no, the French do that fine by themselves," he said, a laugh escaping.

"See?" Rollin said. "I remember you always liked Spain."

The next time Rollin saw him was when he came out to Berkeley to speak, when he said, "No, I think I would not like to stand up, there are only twelve people here and I think we can call it an intimate gathering."

Laughter was uncertain until the expression on his face let his audience know he expected it. Rollin had never heard him speak. His theme was "America, Failure as the Absence of Success," and out of the eighteen or twenty people in the room, she counted three women. She stood at the back of the room, waiting, nervous in a way she hadn't expected.

Thompkins walked into the room as though headed towards something broken which he meant to fix; there was a sense of purpose and yet a sense of doubt, even annoyance, as he settled behind the desk, spreading out papers. He tapped his pocket for cigarettes and asked if anyone minded, then quickly lit one. Two other older men had come in with him and there were introductions and then he stepped up on a raised platform where there was a table and ashtray and pitcher of water.

"Just making sure about my carfare," he said without waiting to be introduced. There was chuckling here and there and he was lighting a cigarette and this left the professor who was supposed to introduce him standing there for a moment smiling. The momentary contact Thompkins had established with his joke disappeared as the professor talked about his work. Rollin caught his eye once, but there was a distance between them.

". . . want to thank you," Thompkins said, and then he began to talk. (He specified, as he did each time, that he did not do readings.) And as he talked and then answered questions and talked some more, the smoke grew thicker around him until it separated him from his audience completely.

". . . maybe you'd like me to go through that again?" he said once or twice when his talk wandered. Or someone asked a question and after talking for five minutes or more, Thompkins paused and frowned and said, "What was the question again?" The small audience laughed. The administrators relaxed, fanning their papers. Each time he answered a question or made a point, Thompkins settled back into the smoke until the next one came around.

"Do you consider your writing experimental?"

"Experimental? Well, I've always considered 'experimental' a term for failure. No."

There was laughter, and there were a few more questions, but

Thompkins looked ready to leave as soon as anyone would let him, as if he were just earning that carfare home. He talked about the contract between the writer and reader, the work he expected a reader to do in exchange for his own ("Entertainment is at the movies," he said), and when he had finished Rollin watched as the admirers gathered up their papers, nodding thanks but not approaching him. It was hot in the room, and the white lights lit his silver hair. For a man who had stayed aloof so long, he was finally being left alone.

Berkeley was the last time Rollin saw her father. He wrote to tell her he thought the talk had gone well, sending her a tape of it, and he wrote her a few letters after that and that was all. It was a heart attack. The typing stopped.

Rollin walked with her mother in a cemetery mottled with dark patches, but there were no trees big enough to cast such shadows; clouds made these. The minister's voice came at her in waves with her dizziness as she thought of everything and nothing, of that cold windy day on the hill behind gates at Douglas's funeral, where she'd had to keep moving to keep warm.

What these men had given her! Again and again, she played the tape of Berkeley. She remembered the day she had seen her father's book in Westwood, she had stood over the brightly lit display table in a daze. The book was so new and foreign, so glossy and sharp; it had had nothing to do with her bursting into the tower room and seeing him looking so used. The cover was elegant, done in the same red and gold as the first book, and like it, this one had no picture, no dedication of its eight hundred and some pages. She had bought five because one was somehow too much, and then she had sat in the car and absorbed the richness of the black print, intoxicating as scattered familiarities leaped up at her from random pages. Names and places he had taken from life, these stared back at her and then distanced themselves as they announced their importance in his fictional world, a world far removed from that in which they'd originated. In that world, there had been the letters, written on the back of page 329 or 648 or 712, which she had always turned over, curious to read the one or two lines of dialogue, so incomplete taken out of context; private bits of anger or conversation which were at once significant and random and gave no clue really to the part of him she didn't know. And while her father had been shaking his head alone in a room, Douglas had been out in the world shaking his fist at it, and which way was she to go? Without meaning to, they had left her in the middle, stranded. Literally, figuratively, however you chose to look at it; it was like that day in Westwood when she couldn't even make up her mind whether to turn right or left, and so she had just sat there watching the light change from green to yellow to red, green to yellow to red, over and over again. These men had been her strength, but developing such strength would not have been necessary had they not encouraged her weakness. As a child, being led out onto the Great Lawn by Douglas had been like being led onto a dance floor, but that had been as far as he could take it. When she had gone to Peninghen the summer she was twelve and he talked about the island house as if they would never see it again, it was true from his point of view. Of course they could go back, but it would never be the same as when she was five, when all anyone had had to do was pull her in the wagon and she beamed.

Among the papers found at her father's death, Rollin was filed under Rollin and Margaret Booz was under pending; and there was something about that, about her father's orderliness and loneliness, that finally reached out to her to break her heart.

Epilogue

o o o

"I knew George in the old days," Alan Gates said. "Tompkins Square? We used to drink wine out of these ceramic bottles. George would come over and I remember he always used to ask for this one glass. It was one of those wineglasses in those cheap sets you buy, and George loved this one glass because it had come out of the factory crooked. The glass part was attached to the stem wrong and old George loved it."

"A sculptural wrongness," Rollin said, laughing. "And I'll bet the more he drank the more he appreciated it," she said.

"Absolutely," Alan Gates said. "And it was funny—you'd set it down on a completely flat surface and the level of the wine would always be uneven."

They had come around to the Nell Dayton sculpture, which was going to Atlanta of all places. There was also the Franko piece, which was going to L.A., and two other sculptures which had already been claimed.

Rollin looked up at the sculpture, a violation of steel in the air which made the trees, crowding around the steel shoots like spectators, seem almost human.

"How the hell are they going to get this out of here?" Gates said, shaking his head. "They really ought to find a way to leave it. The trees and everything."

"How?" Rollin said. "Build a rest area around it?"

"Shit," Alan Gates said. He wasn't here to pick up any art, but one of the marble fireplaces. "What about the library?" he said.

"Schools, other libraries," Rollin said. When she had been in the library earlier she had looked up Alan Gates's work. Even though of course she knew a period of it quite well—a catalogue from an exhibition of his had traveled with her to and from California.

"There you are, proof that we should have had a dark cover," he said when he saw it in her studio. He had knocked because he had heard the music, he said. "You're just painting up here all by your-self?" he said. "*Fan*-tastic." He wore the usual corduroy jacket, and she saw a square face, big grin, dark thinning hair. The description Rollin had read of his work referred to his "wide-open handling of the canvas," and it occurred to her that this was a good description of the man.

She walked him out to his truck, where the mantelpiece was tied with ropes.

"And you can visit your fireplace when you come up," he was saying. "I'll give you— What the *hell*?"

He was looking behind her, and Rollin turned to see a group of workmen standing around Franko's piece. They were drinking beer, and trying to figure out how they were going to load it. From their laughter and banter, it was obvious that they were embarrassed by the piece; they kept posing and flirting with the object of their affection. Having no idea of the name or significance of the statue, they had dubbed her Eve.

"Hey, Eve, baby, give me a sign!" one of the men said. Another of the men dropped to his knees, pleading to be forgiven for some imaginary wrong. But no matter how they crowded around her, in on her, her gaze was averted to a point in the distance. It was strangely touching.

Later, at dusk, Rollin sat in the tower room alone. Next week, she planned to go to the island house, and from there she would decide what to do next. She would sit on the metal swing, and it would be so quiet, not like the summers in her memory. It made sense: although she was a painter, the sound of typing had a stronger association for her than anything visual from her childhood. It was a mechanical sound, to her the most individual sound in the world.

Walking back up to her studio, Rollin stopped for a moment and looked out over the Great Lawn. It was Catherine who had talked about land, and tried to tell Thompkins. She had said if anyone should understand what lasted he should—work lasted. Houses were bought and sold and torn down, and even if they remained, the people changed and changed them. Work was what mattered. Work was the only thing that lasted, remained unchanged no matter who bought it or sold it.

She looked over at the maze, which had taken so long to grow. But so had she. And yet it was the thought of them coming with their bulldozers to dig that up that was a thousand times worse than the buildings.

Her dream was one she was used to: she was having a show, and it was the day before the opening and she wasn't ready. The paintings in front of her were as yet unframed, and they were unfamiliar. They were not hers. They were smallish, strange, serious, dung-colored portraits of bearded men with a foreign air about them. Rollin was standing in a group, and she looked away from the pictures to the huge space where they were to hang. It was not a gallery, but a barn, the barn where they had brought her after she was born. And seeing the abstract designs made by the beams and architecture, she saw what she wanted to paint.

She woke to sun streaming in the windows. How long ago it seemed that she had moved from studio to studio, sleeping in each the last night in order to seal whatever experience it had been.

Her mother and Amy arrived in the afternoon, and they took a picnic down by the river. But first they walked together down the long hall and stood in the alcove, looking at Rollin's portrait. (They speculate about the painting now; it is the only portrait Nolan Perry ever painted, and one critic has offered that the left-hand hole was a purposeful abstract element, nothing to do with a quarrel on a rainy afternoon.)

"It's so lovely," Sally Ann said, tears in her eyes.

The portrait showed none of Rollin's anger or impatience. It had been painted before everything had happened; as one critic said, ". . . the fire has yet to bloom in those pale cheeks." Indeed, it was as though the thick creamy colors did not allow her to move, an unsmiling little girl in a sailor dress, not Rollin but any little girl, and yet Rollin, only Rollin; and it is in the lower left-hand corner that it is unfinished. "Although less disturbing than had it been a foot," one account reads, "the missing floor nevertheless manages the special disturbing affect of suspension in time, as though the little girl will remain so."

"You were so impossible," her mother said, remembering the sittings. She shook her head and bit her lip. Then, "Do you remember the wax museum?"

"Wax museum?" Rollin said.

"Her favorite exhibit was 'My Fair Lady,' " Sally Ann said to Amy. She looked at Rollin. "You don't remember? Where you pushed the button and watched Liza Doolittle change from rags to riches." She paused. She smiled and said, "And your father, he tried to tell you it was all done with mirrors, but you wouldn't listen. You just kept on, pressing that button again and again."

Rollin smiled. They had come to the terrace. The fountain had not worked for ten years.

"You were stubborn—so stubborn!" her mother went on, and Rollin nodded. Years ago she had clawed at the ocean floor in the crashing surf and come up with nothing, sand through her fingers; the prized shell she had seen had vanished with the undertow. Not that she had seen anything since that she had wanted as much as she had wanted that conch, and she had gone back down for it and almost drowned, and made a man a hero.